Chantelle Shaw lives on th
her stories while walking on
married for over thirty years and has six children. Her love affair with reading and writing Mills & Boon stories began when she was a teenager, and her first book was published in 2006. She likes strong-willed, slightly unusual characters. Chantelle also loves gardening, walking and wine!

Lucy King spent her adolescence lost in the glamorous and exciting world of Mills & Boon when she really ought to have been paying attention to her teachers. As she couldn't live in a dream world for ever, she eventually acquired a degree in languages and an eclectic collection of jobs. After a decade in southwest Spain, Lucy now lives with her young family in Wiltshire, England. When not writing, or trying to think up new and innovative things to do with mince, she spends her time reading, failing to finish cryptic crosswords and dreaming of the golden beaches of Andalusia.

Also by Chantelle Shaw

Housekeeper in the Headlines
The Italian's Bargain for His Bride

Innocent Summer Brides miniseries

The Greek Wedding She Never Had
Nine Months to Tame the Tycoon

Passionately Ever After… collection

Her Secret Royal Dilemma

Also by Lucy King

Lost Sons of Argentina miniseries

The Secrets She Must Tell
Invitation from the Venetian Billionaire
The Billionaire without Rules

Passion in Paradise collection

Undone by Her Ultra-Rich Boss

A BABY SCANDAL IN ITALY

CHANTELLE SHAW

STRANDED WITH MY FORBIDDEN BILLIONAIRE

LUCY KING

MILLS & BOON

First published in Great Britain 2022
by Mills & Boon, an imprint of HarperCollins*Publishers* Ltd,
1 London Bridge Street, London, SE1 9GF

www.harpercollins.co.uk

HarperCollins*Publishers*
1st Floor, Watermarque Building,
Ringsend Road, Dublin 4, Ireland

ISBN: 978-0-263-30112-0

12/22

MIX
Paper | Supporting responsible forestry
FSC™ C007454
FSC
www.fsc.org

This book is produced from independently certified FSC™ paper to ensure responsible forest management.
For more information visit: www.harpercollins.co.uk/green.

Printed and Bound in Spain using 100% Renewable Electricity at CPI Black Print, Barcelona

A BABY SCANDAL IN ITALY

CHANTELLE SHAW

MILLS & BOON

CHAPTER ONE

THIS WAS THE big one. The contract that was guaranteed to show his detractors he was a worthy successor to his father. Rafa Vieri permitted himself a brief smile of satisfaction as he contemplated the business deal he was about to finalise that would cement Vieri Azioni's position as the largest financial holding company in Europe.

He looked around at VA's board members seated at the polished mahogany table. There was a palpable air of excitement and expectation in the boardroom. The white-haired man sitting opposite Rafa was Carlo Landini, who was the head of Italy's most prestigious private bank, Banca Landini. Rafa had used his considerable charm and persuasive powers to convince Carlo to sell a controlling stake in his bank to Vieri Azioni. Banca Landini would continue to operate under its own executive management team, while its assets were protected, and Vieri Azioni would profit hugely from the sound investment.

A few of VA's directors had been doubtful about Rafa's suitability for the joint roles of chairman and CEO following the unexpected death of his father two months ago, pointing to his playboy reputation and the messy divorce from his ex-wife which had been played out in the public eye. Rafa had been a paragon of virtue lately in an effort to impress the board.

Just as importantly he had needed to show Carlo Landini that he'd given up the celebrity lifestyle he had led when he'd been a professional basketball player in America before returning to Italy eighteen months ago to utilise his MBA and work alongside his father at Vieri Azioni.

Rafa knew that Carlo had hoped to pass Banco Landini down to his only son—but Patrizio's body had been found on his yacht in the Bahamas amid rumours that he'd died from an overdose of cocaine. The scandal had been hushed up, but Patrizio's death had left Carlo Landini without a successor. Perhaps unsurprisingly, after the problems with his son, Carlo did not want a whiff of scandal to be associated with his family's centuries-old bank.

Rafa called the meeting to order. 'Are you ready to proceed?' he asked Carlo.

The older man nodded. 'I am ready to sign the deal. You have convinced me, Rafa, that Banca Landini will be safely and successfully managed by Vieri Azioni under your leadership.'

Carlo picked up a pen, but he paused with his hand poised above the document on the table in front of him when the boardroom door flew open.

What the hell? Rafa jerked his head towards the source of the disturbance and stared at the young woman who had burst into the room. His confusion quickly turned to anger. He had instructed his PA that the only reason for the meeting to be interrupted would be if the building were burning down.

The woman froze like a rabbit caught in car headlights when every pair of eyes in the boardroom focused on her. The most noticeable thing about her was her bright pink hair, which clashed violently with her orange tee shirt. Her jeans were ripped at the knees and, to complete the bizarre spectacle, she had a baby in a carrier strapped to her front. All that was visible of the child was a tuft of dark hair and two chubby legs poking out of the bottom of the carrier.

Memories of Lola as a baby flashed into Rafa's mind and his gut twisted. He had been captivated from the moment he had held her in his arms. His princess, his little girl—or so he had believed until his lying, cheating ex-wife had blown his world apart. With a ruthlessness that had made him a champion on the basketball court, and more recently had earned him a reputation as a take-no-prisoners business tycoon, Rafa shoved his past back into a box marked 'do not open'.

He stood up. 'My apologies for the interruption,' he said smoothly to Carlo Landini, disguising his frustration when the deal had been so close to completion.

Rafa's usually unflappable personal assistant hurried into the room. 'Miss Bennett, this is a private meeting. You must leave immediately.' The PA spoke in English to the woman whose garish hair and clothes jarred in the room full of grey-suited businessmen.

'Giulia, *cosa sta succedendo*?' *What is going on?* Rafa demanded furiously.

'I'm sorry.' The PA sounded rattled. 'I explained to

Miss Bennett that you were unavailable to see her. Shall I call security?'

'*No*. You can't throw me out.' The woman with the baby ran across the room and halted in front of Rafa. 'Rafael Vieri, I'd like you to meet your son.'

Ivy heard a collective gasp of shock from around the room. She had hoped to speak to Bertie's father in private, but she'd panicked at the prospect of being bundled out of the boardroom by a security guard and blurted out her announcement.

'Is this some sort of joke?' Rafael Vieri's cold voice sent an ice cube slithering down Ivy's spine. She had discovered, when she'd researched him on the Internet, that he was sometimes known as Rafa, and he was a former international basketball superstar and a notorious playboy.

'It's certainly not a joke.' She was angry that he was acting as though he was shocked. After all, her sister had written and informed him that he was the father of her child, but he had not responded. Gemma hadn't told Ivy much about the man she'd had a brief affair with, which had been odd, because they had always confided in each other. All Gemma had said was that Rafael Vieri was the CEO of a financial company in Rome called Vieri Azioni.

Ivy had felt apprehensive about how Rafa would react to her bringing Bertie to Italy. But what else could she have done, now that Gemma was dead? Grief clutched at her heart when she thought of her sister. Technically, they had been half-sisters, and shared the same father, but despite a ten-year age gap they'd always been close.

Gemma had been a confidante and best friend to Ivy after her parents had split up and her mum's complicated love-life had meant she'd had little time for her daughter. Now Ivy was Bertie's legal guardian and her final words to her sister had been a promise to take the baby to meet his father.

The receptionist behind the front desk had been dealing with someone else and hadn't glanced at Ivy when she'd arrived at Vieri Azioni's headquarters. But Rafa Vieri hadn't been in the CEO's office, and she'd been about to return to the lift when she'd heard voices from behind a door further along the corridor.

An elegant woman had emerged from the room and told her that Signor Vieri was busy. Ivy had recognised her voice as the woman she'd spoken to on the phone when she had called to try to make an appointment with Rafa. 'I remember I spoke to you a few days ago, Miss Bennett,' his PA had said. 'But you refused to say why you wanted to see Signor Vieri.'

At that moment, the PA's phone had rung, and while she'd been distracted Ivy had seized her chance and darted into the boardroom.

Now she felt uncomfortable that she was the focus of curiosity from everyone in the room, although only one man held her attention. Rafa Vieri was looking at her as though he could not quite believe what he was seeing. It was her pink hair, Ivy supposed. On a dismal, wet day in England, she'd impulsively dyed her hair bubblegum-pink to cheer herself up.

She flushed when she saw him glance at her old jeans and trainers. Three months ago her life had changed irredeemably when she'd become responsible for her baby half-nephew, and since then she hadn't had the time or energy to think about herself. Every morning she pulled on her jeans and got on with the job of caring for Bertie, and most nights she cried herself to sleep grieving for Gemma.

Rafa's online profile stated that he was six-foot-four. His height hadn't been exceptional when he'd played in the American professional basketball league, where some of the players were seven feet tall, but he towered over Ivy, and she had to tilt her head to look at his face. Photos of him on social media did not do justice to his stunningly handsome features. In those pictures, his mouth had invariably been curved in a wickedly sexy smile, and the gleam of sensual promise in his grey eyes had made Ivy understand why Gemma had been swept off her feet by him.

In the flesh, Rafa was even more gorgeous, more compelling, more *everything,* despite the fact that he was not smiling and his eyes were as hard and uncompromising as steel. Ivy's body responded to the irresistible pull of his magnetism. Her skin felt too tight, and heat radiated from her central core in a surge of sexual awareness that confused and horrified her. How could she be attracted to the father of her dead sister's baby? It was *wrong*!

She exhaled slowly when Rafa released her from his penetrating stare. He looked across the room as an older man, who had been sitting at the table, stood up.

'Rafa, what is the meaning of this interruption? The boardroom is hardly the place to conduct your private affairs. I may have to reconsider our deal.'

'Once again, please accept my apologies for the disturbance, Carlo,' Rafa said smoothly. 'We will take a short break for refreshments.'

He put his hand on Ivy's arm and she felt a zing of electricity shoot through her. 'Come with me,' he ordered curtly, steering her towards the door. He paused next to his PA and said in a low voice, 'Giulia, tell the caterers to serve the champagne and canapés while I deal with this situation.'

Ivy's nerves jangled as she walked beside Rafa along the corridor. His initial reaction to his baby son had not been promising, but she needed his help. The eviction notice she'd received from her landlord, giving her two weeks to move out of her flat, had prompted her to set aside her shock and grief over Gemma and take Bertie to his father. She had used the last of her savings to pay for a budget flight to Rome and had booked to stay for two nights at the cheapest hotel she could find.

'In here,' Rafa growled as he ushered her into his office. It was a masculine room, all marble and chrome with a black, glass-topped desk set at an angle in front of the floor-to-ceiling windows that gave a panoramic view across Rome. Despite the air-conditioning in the building, sweat trickled down Ivy's spine and her tee shirt was sticking to her. It had been a twenty-minute walk from her hotel to Vieri Azioni's headquarters and Bertie was heavy. The straps of the baby carrier were digging into her shoulders. Bertie was stirring and soon he would want another feed. Ivy had packed formula milk, nappies, wipes and all the other paraphernalia necessary for a four-month-old infant in her backpack.

Tenderness swamped her when she looked down at Bertie. She loved her half-sister's baby with all her heart and was determined to do her best for him, but she had struggled without any family to help her. Gemma's mother had died many years ago. Their father was divorced from Ivy's mum and had a new family. He had only seen Bertie once and wasn't interested in his grandson. The same was true of Ivy's mother, who had not been close to her stepdaughter and was not involved with Gemma's baby.

Rafa Vieri followed Ivy into his office and slammed the door shut. He looked grimly forbidding, and her heart sank, knowing that she must try to persuade him to acknowledge Bertie as his son. She lifted her hand to push her hair off her face and caught sight of the tiny butterfly tattoo on the inside of her wrist.

Gemma had been fascinated by butterflies and their symbolism of hope when they emerged from a cocoon and were free to fly away. When Ivy had been diagnosed with cancer as a teenager, Gemma had hung a butterfly mobile above her bed in the hospital and had told her to imagine the future when she was free from the illness that ravaged her body. The butterfly tattoo was in memory of her sister. Ivy took a deep breath, and a sense of calm came over her.

Rafa scowled at the woman with crazy hair whose untimely interruption threatened one of the most important deals of his life. She was making crooning noises to the baby as she lifted him out of the carrier. If it hadn't been for the child, Rafa would have instructed a member of his staff to escort Miss Bennett out of the building.

The baby let out a wail and the sound evoked more

poignant memories for Rafa. He remembered the nights he'd spent walking up and down the nursery, rocking Lola in his arms to try to soothe her to sleep. Once he'd believed he had everything he could wish for, but his happiness had been an illusion built on Tiffany's deception. After the divorce, he had vowed never to trust any woman. And he was adamant that he did not want a child. When he'd discovered that Lola was not his daughter, he'd felt as though his heart had been ripped out, and he could not bear to experience that intensity of pain again.

Rafa strode round his desk and threw himself down onto the chair. He was desperate to find a semblance of normality in a situation that felt increasingly like the implausible plot line of one of the very bad films his ex-wife had starred in.

'Are you an actress? Is this a stunt?' Maybe it was someone's idea of a joke. Or could a business rival have paid Miss Bennett to sabotage the deal-signing meeting with Carlo Landini?

Her eyes widened. Despite himself, Rafa noticed that her eyes were startlingly beautiful, huge and dark brown, fringed by impossibly long lashes.

'I'm not an actress. I used to be a show dancer on a cruise ship, but I can't do that job now I have Bertie.'

She shrugged off her backpack and dumped it on Rafa's desk. 'I need to prepare his milk,' she explained as she rummaged in the bag and took out a feeding bottle and a carton of ready-mixed infant formula. Holding the grizzling baby against her shoulder, she deftly unscrewed the lid on the carton with her free hand and tipped the formula milk into the bottle.

'I'm Ivy Bennett. Gemma's sister.' She looked expectantly at Rafa. 'You must remember her. She wrote to you four months ago.'

'I don't know anyone called Gemma. More to the point, I have never met you before,' he drawled as he moved his gaze over her. He had intended to sound dismissive, but his voice was annoyingly husky. Ivy had taken off the baby carrier, and he could not help noticing how her tee shirt clung to her high, firm breasts.

He leaned back in his chair and studied her. She was petite and slim, and her tight-fitting jeans moulded her narrow hips. Her hair had been cut into short, wispy layers framing a heart-shaped face. She was nothing like the glamorous supermodel types Rafa went for, but there was something about her elfin beauty that captured his attention. He wondered what her natural hair colour was. Probably mid-brown, the same as her eyelashes, he mused. His gaze lingered on the sensual fullness of her lips, and he felt an unexpected tug of desire.

Celibacy did not suit him, Rafa decided self-derisively. He assumed that going without sex the past couple of months was the reason for his unwarranted reaction to a fragile-looking girl with atrocious dress sense. He had ended an affair that had been going nowhere shortly before his father had suffered a fatal heart attack. Shock, grief and the responsibilities that went with his new role as the head of Vieri Azioni meant that he hadn't had the time or inclination to dive back into the dating pool, and one-night stands no longer held the appeal they once had.

Ivy Bennett had said that she'd worked as a dancer and her toned figure was an indication that that, at least, was true. An image flashed into Rafa's mind of her slender body beneath him, her small breasts pressed against his chest. He watched the rosy flush that appeared on her cheeks spread lower over her throat and décolletage, and silently cursed his libido which had inconveniently sprung to life.

His gaze meshed with Ivy's, and he recognised her awareness of him in her big brown eyes before her lashes swept down. Rafa always knew. It had happened to him since he'd been a teenager, but these days he was less likely to be tempted by an invitation in a woman's eyes. Especially this woman, who had disrupted a vital business meeting and falsely accused him. He was impatient to return to the boardroom and try to salvage the deal with Carlo Landini. His jaw tightened when Ivy walked over to the sofa and sat down with the baby on her lap.

'Do you mind if I feed Bertie while we talk?'

As he watched the baby greedily suck on the teat of the bottle, Rafa's mind flew back to the past. When Lola had been born, he'd tried to spend as much time as possible with her, and during pre-season he had rushed home from training sessions to give her a bath and her evening feed. The professional basketball season ran for six months of the year and teams travelled to every state in North America. The punishing schedule of playing home and away games had been detrimental to his family life. Tiffany had complained that she was bored and lonely while he was away, but she had not stayed lonely for long, Rafa thought grimly. It had been Tiffany's decision to end their marriage and the divorce had exposed her devastating lies.

His gaze narrowed on Ivy, who was undeniably pretty, but demonstrably a liar. 'We have nothing to talk about, Miss Bennett. You know damn well that I am not the father of your baby and I demand you retract your false allegation. You can consider yourself lucky if I decide not to sue you for slander.'

Her Bambi eyes grew as round as saucers. 'I'm not Bertie's mother. But you are most definitely his father. He is my sister's baby. Gemma met you thirteen months ago while she was working on a cruise ship, and you were one of the passengers. She fell pregnant by you, but when she wrote and told you about your child she never heard from you. It's the old story,' she said, bitterness creeping into her voice. 'Men have the fun and women have the babies.'

'Enough,' Rafa snapped. 'I have never been on a cruise ship. Frankly, it's my idea of hell to be trapped on a boat at sea with hundreds of other people.'

Ivy's nose wrinkled when she frowned and for some reason it made her look even cuter. When had he ever found *cute* a turn on? Rafa thought grimly. He was furious that he could not control his unbidden reaction to Ivy.

'Gemma told me she had met Rafael Vieri aboard the *Ocean Star* on a cruise around the Caribbean islands. Usually we worked on the same ship, but I had been promoted to lead dancer on the company's sister ship, *Ocean Princess*. Gem was a social hostess.' Ivy grimaced. 'To be honest, I was surprised that she'd had a relationship with you, because it is a sackable offence for a crew member to become involved with a passenger. I guess she must have really liked you to have risked her career.'

He swore. 'I repeat, I did not meet your sister on a cruise ship.' His exasperation increased when Ivy looked unconvinced. 'It is feasible, I suppose, that Gemma met a passenger on the ship who had the same name as me. Rafael and Vieri are fairly common names in Italy.'

Rafa had been named after his father. But the possibility that his workaholic father could have spent weeks away from the office to go on a cruise was laughable and Rafa instantly dismissed the idea from his mind.

'Gemma said you had told her that you owned a successful business in Italy called Vieri Azioni. That's how I knew where to find you.' Ivy sat the baby upright and rubbed his back until he gave a little burp. 'His proper name is Roberto,' she explained when she noticed that Rafa was staring at the child. 'Gemma gave him an Italian name, because he is half-Italian, but somehow Bertie stuck.'

'He did not inherit his Italian heritage from me. Roberto, Bertie, or whatever you choose to call him, is not my child,' Rafa said savagely. When he had sex, he was obsessively careful to use protection so there was no risk of an unplanned pregnancy.

Ivy's jaw was set in a stubborn line. 'Pass me my phone and I'll show you a picture of Gemma that might jog your memory.'

Dio! He'd wasted enough time on Ivy Bennett. Rafa was ninety-nine percent sure he had not slept with her sister, but it would do no harm to look at the photo, he conceded. There was a tiny chance that he'd met Gemma, although not in the Caribbean.

Thirteen months ago he had moved into a penthouse apartment close to the iconic Colosseum. He'd worked long hours at Vieri Azioni to prove to his father his commitment to the company and win the approval of the board, some of whom had believed that the vice-chairman would be a better chairman and CEO. But Rafa acknowledged that his life had not been all work and no play. He'd met women in bars and clubs and had occasionally spent the night with them. The nearby port town of Civitavecchia was where the cruise ships docked, and it was a short train ride for passengers and crew members into the city. Could Ivy's sister's ship have been in Italy shortly before or after it had sailed to the Caribbean? If so, it was just possible that he'd met Gemma in a bar in Rome.

Rafa looked away from the baby who was lying, milk-drunk and contented, in Ivy's arms. Undeniably, Bertie was a beautiful child, but not his child. Rejection burned inside him. Never again would he be fooled into believing he was a father. The bottom had dropped out of his world when he'd discovered that the daughter he had adored was not his. In the unlikely event that he recognised Ivy's sister as someone he'd slept with, he would demand proof that Bertie was his son.

He picked up Ivy's phone from where she'd left it on his desk and strode across the room to hand it to her. Seconds later, he studied the picture of an attractive redhead she showed him on the screen.

'I have never seen this woman before.' Rafa's relief quickly turned to anger. Something was going on here and he was in no mood for games. 'I don't know what you are playing at, Miss Bennett. If the baby belongs to your sister, why did *you* bring him to Italy?'

'Gemma's dead.' Ivy's brown eyes were luminous with tears. 'She died when Bertie was five weeks old. My last words to her were a promise that I would find her baby's father.'

'Why?' Rafa ignored a flicker of remorse when Ivy blinked at his abrupt tone. Everything she had told him so far sounded improbable.

'I thought you should know that you have a son.' She hesitated, 'And I hoped you would offer to support Bertie…financially.'

'You want money?' It was what Rafa had expected, and he could not understand why he felt a fleeting disappointment that the English rose with her understated sensuality was so predictable. 'Finally, we are getting to the truth,' he said cynically.

'I don't want money for me.' Twin spots of colour flared on Ivy's cheeks. She had perfected her air of guilelessness, Rafa thought cynically.

'Bringing up a baby is expensive,' she said. 'I told you I had a job as a dancer on a cruise ship, but I haven't been able to work since my sister died and I became responsible for Bertie. When he is a bit older, I hope to open my own dance school, but I've been living off my savings and the money has nearly run out.'

She caught her bottom lip between her teeth and the action drew Rafa's gaze to her lush mouth. A deliberate ploy? he wondered.

'If you don't want to be involved with your son, I will take him back to England and be the best mother

I can to him as I promised my sister. But I did some research about you, and I know you are wealthy. You have a responsibility to provide for Bertie and you can afford to set up a trust fund for him.'

'As his legal guardian, you would no doubt have control of the money in the trust fund!' Rafa laughed. 'You must think I am an idiot, Miss Bennett. What I am curious to know is, did you sister falsely tell you that I had fathered her baby? Or was it your idea to accuse me of being the child's father in a bid to get money from me?'

He ignored Ivy's gasp. 'You admitted that you had looked up information about me. Perhaps you do not know who fathered your sister's baby and you thought you could somehow fool me into believing I had slept with Gemma. You are not the first woman to try to pin a paternity claim on a wealthy man.'

When Tiffany had told him she was pregnant, he'd had no reason to doubt that the baby was his, Rafa brooded. She'd later admitted that, after having been rejected by her child's biological father, she'd allowed Rafa to think that Lola was his daughter because he could provide the affluent lifestyle she craved.

'It wasn't like that at all.' Ivy stood up. The baby was dozing and she carefully placed him on the sofa and wedged cushions around him to prevent him from rolling over. 'Everything I have told you is the truth.'

She tilted her head and glared at Rafa. He noticed that her brown eyes were flecked with amber. 'My sister told me that you are Bertie's father and I believe her. It's more likely that you were lying when you denied receiving Gemma's letter.'

'There was no letter.' Rafa growled, exasperated by

her stubbornness. 'Admit defeat, Miss Bennett. The child is not mine and if you ever repeat the allegation you will face serious legal consequences.'

His gaze swivelled towards the door when it opened and his PA appeared. 'What now, Giulia?'

'Landini and his team are about to leave.'

Rafa swore. 'Try and stall them for a couple more minutes. I'm almost done here.' He sent Ivy a simmering glance. 'I will talk to Carlo and explain that there was a misunderstanding.'

The PA nodded. 'I had hoped that Sandro Florenzi might help to smooth things over while you were busy, but he left the boardroom immediately after you, saying he had a migraine.'

Rafa frowned. He knew the deputy CEO occasionally suffered from migraines, but the timing was inconvenient to say the least. Giulia left the room and he looked at Ivy, infuriated by the heat that flared inside him.

Dio, how could he be attracted to a pink-haired pixie who had come to him with a frankly unbelievable story? It would have been laughable if he hadn't been uncomfortably aware of his arousal pressing against his trouser zip. Because of his height, he preferred women who were taller than average. If he kissed Ivy, he would probably crick his neck unless he picked her up and plastered her body against his.

What the hell was the matter with him? He swung away from her to avoid the temptation of her lush mouth that right now was set in a sulky pout. Once he'd secured the deal with Carlo Landini, he would take some time off, Rafa decided. He'd been working flat out since his father had died and he needed a break. He would spend a few days at his castle in the mountains. It was the place he retreated to when he needed some head space and wanted to be alone.

And, when he returned to Rome, he'd start dating again. He always made it clear to women that he could offer expensive dinners and nights of pleasure in his bed, but definitely not commitment.

'Are you staying in Rome?' When Ivy gave him the name of her hotel, he said curtly, 'I'll arrange for you and the child to be driven to your lodgings. Wait here in my office until my personal assistant comes to escort you down to my car. I suggest you return to England immediately, and I strongly advise you not to try to contact me again. Stalking is a criminal offence for which there are serious penalties.'

Rafa studied Ivy's crestfallen face. He was certain she was a liar and he did not trust her. There was no reason why he should feel bad about dismissing her claim that he'd fathered her sister's child. But he sensed that her story about her sister dying was genuine, and he felt a reluctant tug of compassion.

'I'm sorry about Gemma,' he said brusquely. 'My father recently passed away and I understand the pain of grief.'

The amber flecks in Ivy's eyes glowed as fiercely as flames. 'Keep your pseudo-sympathy, Mr Vieri,' she snapped 'I *know* Gemma told me the truth, which makes *you* a liar.'

CHAPTER TWO

IVY HATED RAFAEL VIERI. *Hated* him for planting a seed of doubt in her mind about her sister's claim that he was Bertie's father. Gemma had always told the truth. Even when Ivy had been diagnosed with a type of blood cancer, Gemma had researched information about the illness and had honestly answered her questions about what chemotherapy would be like and her chances of survival. Gem had been a rock when Ivy had needed support and now, through tragic circumstances, she could repay Gemma by bringing up her son.

Rafael was Bertie's father, Ivy was certain. But he had refused to accept responsibility for his child. 'We'll be fine on our own,' she muttered, more to reassure herself than the baby, who was dozing in the carrier as Ivy walked back to the hotel. She had declined to get into the car when the driver had held open the door, partly through stubborn pride—she did not want to accept anything from Rafa after the humiliating scene in his office—but also because the car had not been fitted with a baby seat so she'd had no option than to trudge through the crowded city streets.

'Signorina Bennett.'

Ivy turned her head when she heard someone call her name. A sleek, black saloon had pulled up next to the pavement and a man of about fifty or so emerged. He was smiling as he walked towards her, but there was concern in his voice when he spoke.

'Do you have far to go, Signorina Bennett? You must be tired, carrying the child in the midday heat.'

'Who…?' Ivy began.

'Forgive me.' The man smiled again. 'I was in the boardroom of Vieri Azioni when you introduced Rafael Vieri to his baby son. Everyone was surprised by your revelation that the chairman and CEO has a secret child. But I was even more shocked that Rafa dismissed your claim as a joke.'

'As if I would joke about something so serious.' Her temper simmered when she remembered that Rafa had accused her of staging a stunt. She was barely aware that the stranger—had he told her his name?—had led her over to a café where there were tables outside beneath an awning that provided welcome shade from the sun.

'Please, sit down.' The man pulled out a chair. 'May I call you Ivy? I'm sure you could do with a cold drink. Would you like something to eat?'

A waiter walked past carrying an exotic ice-cream sundae. Ivy eyed the dessert wistfully. She was still feeling tense after meeting Rafa Vieri and craved a sugar hit. Her companion—she was too embarrassed to admit that she hadn't been concentrating when the man had introduced himself—laughed. 'Ah, who can resist *gelato*?' he said. 'Allow me to order for you the chocolate flavour with whipped cream and hazelnuts.'

The dessert sounded heavenly. Ivy sat down and gave a deep sigh. Her shoulders ached from the weight of Bertie in the carrier, particularly her left shoulder that she'd injured a few months ago while she had been rehearsing a dance routine.

It felt like a lifetime ago that she had been a dancer on a cruise ship. She felt a pang, thinking of her friends in the dance troupe. She missed her old life, even though it had been hard work, performing in shows twice a night, seven nights a week. But she had Bertie now, and she couldn't spend long periods of time away at sea. She loved him as much as if he were her own baby, and when he was old enough she would tell him about the wonderful woman who had given birth to him.

Bertie stirred and opened his eyes. They had been blue at birth, but now they were grey, the same colour as Rafael Vieri's eyes. Ivy did not want to think about how Rafa's eyes had gleamed with cold contempt when he'd raked them over her. She did not understand why he affected her. Sure, he was handsome, but she'd met other good-looking guys and hadn't felt the intense awareness that had hit her like a tidal wave when she'd met Rafa. She did not like him, and she was angry that he'd refused to accept Bertie as his child. She was confused that, despite his obvious flaws, she was attracted to him.

The waiter set a decadent ice-cream sundae in front of her and Ivy forgot her worries for a few minutes while she tucked in. Thankfully, Bertie had fallen back to sleep. Her companion murmured, 'Rafa denied that he is the baby's father.'

'He told me not to contact him again.' She put her

spoon down, feeling slightly sick from the rich ice-cream.

'It seems unfair that you must bear the responsibility and financial burden of bringing up the child alone.'

'I don't know what I'm going to do,' Ivy admitted dismally. She had been prepared for Rafa to be shocked at first, but she'd hoped he would come round to the idea that Bertie was his son. 'I need to find a job, but childcare is expensive, and then there's rent and all the other living costs.'

'There is a solution to your money worries. Newspapers would be prepared to pay you well for your story.' When Ivy looked puzzled, her companion leaned across the table and said in a low voice, 'I can put you in touch with a journalist who works for a leading news agency. All you would need to do is explain that Rafa Vieri has rejected his son and abandoned you. No one could blame you for accepting an opportunity to earn money that you desperately need for the baby.'

Ivy shook her head. 'If I did that, the circumstances of Bertie's birth would be made public. I won't take the risk that when he is older he might find out from an old news story that his father did not want anything to do with him.'

Even though it was the truth. She hoped that in the future, if Bertie was curious about his father, she would be able to think of an explanation for Rafa's lack of interest in his son.

The man got to his feet and handed Ivy a business card. 'Think about it and, if you change your mind, call this number and talk to the journalist. *Arrivederci*, Signorina Bennett.'

'Wait…who are you?' She looked up from the card that bore the name of a well-known Italian newspaper and a contact number for the senior reporter, Luigi Capello.

Ivy watched the man walk back to his car and wondered why his face seemed vaguely familiar, and why he was keen for her to go to the newspapers with a story that did not show Rafa Vieri in a good light. But, by the time she arrived back at her hotel, Bertie was crying, her shoulder was throbbing and she did not give the matter another thought.

Maybe it was the heat. The hotel room did not have air-conditioning. Or perhaps Bertie sensed that Ivy was stressed. Whatever the reason, the baby was unsettled all night and by morning they were both exhausted. Every time Ivy moved, she felt a sensation like a red-hot poker jabbing into her shoulder.

Bertie finally fell asleep after his nine a.m. feed. Ivy held her breath when she carefully placed him in the cot, praying he would not stir. She winced as her injured shoulder protested, and then cursed beneath her breath when there was a loud knock on the door. Concerned that it was the hotel manager to complain about the baby crying in the night, she shot across the room to open the door before whoever was on the other side knocked again.

Her apology died on her lips, and her heart missed a beat as her eyes collided with Rafa Vieri's hard-as-steel gaze. The previous day he had looked suave, wearing a designer suit. This morning he was drop-dead sexy in faded denim that clung to his muscular thighs and a black polo shirt that looked casual but expensive. He had pushed his sunglasses onto his head and his midnight-dark hair brushed his collar.

Rafa Vieri exuded an air of arrogance and power that was exclusive to the super-rich. An expression of haughty disdain crossed his face when he looked past Ivy into her functional but uninspiring hotel room.

He snapped his gaze back to her and frowned. Ivy had spent the morning giving Bertie a bath and she hadn't had time to get herself dressed. She felt self-conscious that her skimpy shorts and vest top left little to the imagination. During the night, when it had been so hot in her room, she had been glad that her pyjamas were made of thin cotton but now she wished she was wearing something that covered her from head to toe, preferably made of thick winceyette.

She was mortified when she glanced down and discovered that her nipples were standing to attention beneath her top. But, while she was intensely aware of Rafa's potent masculinity, he evidently did not feel an answering spark of attraction for her.

'I warned you of the consequences if you repeated your lies about me.' He delivered each word with the deadly force of a bullet fired from a gun.

'I haven't lied.' She kept her voice quiet, desperate not to wake Bertie. Rafa thrust a newspaper towards her and she saw a picture of him on the front page beneath the headline *Il bambino segreto del magnate!*

Although Ivy did not understand the other words, the meaning of *bambino* was obvious.

'The tycoon's secret baby.' Rafa translated the headline between gritted teeth. '*Dio*, it sounds like the ridiculous title of a novel, and the story is a complete fantasy.' He braced his hands on the door frame and Ivy had the impression that it was to stop himself from putting them around her neck. 'By the time my lawyers have finished, you will wish that you had never heard of me, let alone accused me of being the father of *your* baby.'

Before Ivy could query his surprising statement, the door of the room next to hers opened and a young couple emerged. They looked curiously at Rafa. When they had walked past, he said tersely, 'We can't have a conversation while I'm standing in the corridor.' Without waiting for her to invite him in, he pushed himself off the door frame and stepped past her into the room.

'We can't talk in here,' Ivy told him in a fierce whisper. 'Bertie has gone to sleep at long last and I won't promise not to kill anyone who wakes him up.'

Rafa glanced over at the cot wedged between the bed and the wall and his scowl deepened. 'The room is the size of a rabbit hutch.' At Ivy's glare, he lowered his voice. 'What is in here?' He opened the door to the miniscule bathroom. 'This will have to do. I'm not planning on staying long. I want to know why you did it—although, I can guess. How much did you get paid?' he asked in a cynical voice.

'You're not making any sense.' Ivy's thought process was severely hampered by a lack of sleep. Somehow Rafa had manoeuvred her into the bathroom. He was right behind her and he closed the door, standing with his back against it, and folded his arms across his chest.

He dominated the small space. It was not just his height and athletic build, it was *him*. He was truly the most gorgeous man she'd ever met. She was mesmerised by his sculpted features, the sharp cheekbones, strong nose and uncompromising brows above his heavy-lidded eyes. The dark stubble on his jaw was thicker than it had been yesterday, and she had the impression that he had come straight from his bed to find her.

An image leapt into her mind of him naked in a bed with her beside him and the sheets tangled after a night of passion. She wondered if the rest of his body was as tanned as his muscular arms beneath his short-sleeve shirt. He had a tattoo of a fearsome-looking black horse on his right forearm. Ivy remembered from her research about him that a horse was the logo of the California Colts basketball team.

Her eyes were drawn back to Rafa's face. His mouth was full-lipped and promised untold delights. Something urgent and unfamiliar coiled deep in her pelvis. She had been a teenager when she'd first started to explore her sensuality, but she had never gone further than a few kisses with her boyfriend at the time. Her cancer diagnosis when she'd been seventeen had been terrifying and the treatment—a brutal regime of chemotherapy over two years—had pushed her body to its limits. She had lost her hair and sometimes her hope. Her boyfriend Luke had ditched her, and for a long time her sole focus had been to get well and regain her strength.

Nine months ago she had celebrated being cancer-free for five years but, although she'd dated guys occasionally, she hadn't wanted a serious relationship. Partly her wariness stemmed from witnessing her mum's chaotic love life and the opinion she'd formed as a pre-teen that men were unreliable. That had proved to be true when her heart had been broken by Luke. The end of her first romance had been doubly painful because she'd been ill and vulnerable. Since then, she had been reluctant to risk being hurt again.

But as time had gone on, and she hadn't been wildly attracted to any man, Ivy had wondered if cancer had robbed her not only of her fertility, but all aspects of her femininity. The sweet ache between her thighs and her overwhelming awareness of Rafa were signs that her sexuality was alive and kicking. Why did it have to be he who had revived her desire that had been dormant until now? Rafa was off-limits, Ivy told herself firmly. She could not respect him after he had rejected his baby son.

Her dad had been an unreliable parent, but at least he'd mostly stuck around for the first ten years of her life. After her parents had split up, her mum had married twice more, but neither of those relationships had lasted. Ivy had felt unimportant when her mum had poured her energy and emotions into her new romances. Now she had Bertie to consider, and she was determined that he would never feel second-best, as she had when she'd been growing up.

Ivy saw Rafa's gaze flick to the shower screen where she'd hung Bertie's sleep suits to dry after she'd washed them in the sink. For the trip to Italy, she had only brought what she could fit into a backpack, because the airline charged extra for luggage to go in the hold. Draped next to the sleep suits was a pair of her knickers that she'd rinsed out. Of course, they had to be the black lace panties with the slogan *Hands Off!* printed on the front, which Gemma had given her as a joke last Christmas.

Flushing hotly, Ivy reached up to retrieve her underwear and couldn't restrain a yelp of agony as her shoulder muscles spasmed. The pain was so intense that she felt sick and swayed on her feet. Above the buzzing noise in her ears, she heard Rafa swear. He clamped his strong hands on either side of her waist and sat her down on the edge of the bath.

'Lower your head towards your knees to allow the blood to flow to your brain,' he ordered. She complied, and after a few seconds the light-headed feeling eased, but the knot of tension in her stomach tightened when he remained close beside her and she breathed in the spicy scent of his cologne.

'What happened?' His tone was still curt but held a faint huskiness that sent another coil of heat down to Ivy's pelvis.

'Just an old shoulder injury that plays up sometimes,' she mumbled, cringing when she sounded breathless and gauche. 'It's fine now.' Her shoulder was throbbing, but she needed Rafa to move from where he was crouched next to her. He was so close that he was bound to notice the frantic thud of her pulse at the base of her throat and hear her uneven breaths.

He straightened up but could not put much space between them in the cramped bathroom. His laugh was harsh and humourless. 'A lightning recovery or another lie? Did you pretend to be in pain to win my sympathy? The same reason that you made up a tragic story about your sister dying?' Rafa ignored Ivy's gasp. 'You said you're not an actress, but you have a talent for make-believe.'

'I told you the truth. Gemma is dead.' Shock at Rafa's callous attitude brought tears to Ivy's eyes. She stood up and was conscious of how much taller than her he was, but she refused to be intimidated by him. 'Why would I make up something so awful?'

'You tell me!' he snapped. 'If Bertie is your sister's baby, why is there no mention of her anywhere? Does Gemma even exist? The story is all over social media, as well as the newspapers, stating that *you* are the baby's mother. It is reported that, when you told me I was the father of your child, I sent you away and warned you never to contact me again.'

Rafa's eyes were icy cold as he raked them over Ivy, starting at her bright pink hair and slowly moving down her body to her bare feet and the chipped varnish on her toenails. 'You are not my type,' he drawled. 'I did not make a child with you.'

Shameful images flashed into her head of just what that would entail, followed by humiliation at his scornful rejection. Obviously she wasn't his type. There had been no need for him to remind her that she was nothing like the glamorous and statuesque women he was often photographed with.

Rafa's comment that he had not made a child with her had delivered another wounding blow to Ivy's bruised heart. It was a painful reminder that she would never hold her own baby in her arms. She would have liked a family of her own and, although she was deeply grateful to have recovered from cancer, there had been a lingering sadness in her heart that she almost certainly couldn't have a baby. Becoming responsible for Bertie had given her a chance to be a mother, but at the terrible cost of her sister's life.

Doubt slid into Ivy's mind. Rafa was adamant that he had never met Gemma. She could not believe her sister had lied, but Gemma had been in Accident and Emergency and being prepared for surgery when Ivy had rushed to the hospital after she'd heard about the accident. Their conversation had been hurried and emotional, but Gemma had clearly said that Rafael Vieri was Bertie's father. It had been the last time that Ivy had seen her sister alive, and she could not hold back her tears at the memory of watching Gemma being wheeled away to Theatre.

Rafa muttered something in Italian that, from his tone, Ivy guessed was not complimentary. 'I might have guessed you would cry when your lies were exposed. It's a clever act, but I am not affected by tears.'

'I'm not acting. I can't help crying when you say such vile things,' she said in a choked voice. As a child, she had rarely showed her feelings. There had always been a drama at home, and she'd learned to be stoical about her parents' volatile relationship and her father's absences when he'd become bored of family life. Even when he had left for good, she'd kept her feelings of disappointment and abandonment to herself.

Cancer had changed Ivy. She had recovered from a life-threatening illness, but she felt like an onion that had had its layers peeled away one by one, leaving her raw and exposing her deepest emotions. She found joy in simple things, but tears came easily when she was upset.

'You treated my sister badly,' she accused Rafa thickly. 'You ignored her when she wrote to tell you that she'd given birth to your baby.'

He threw his hands up in the air. 'I did not sleep with your sister. And why did you tell the newspapers that I am the father of *your* child?'

'I didn't.' Ivy swallowed and tried to regain her composure. It was difficult when Rafa loomed over her like a beautiful, dark angel. 'I told him I wouldn't talk to the press.'

She bit her lip when Rafa glowered at her. 'There was a man,' she muttered. 'He came up to me in the street after I'd left Vieri Azioni's office building and said he'd heard that I had introduced you to your son.'

Rafa looked disbelieving. 'What was his name?'

'I don't know.' She couldn't admit that she'd been unable to think straight after the shock of finding herself attracted to Rafa. 'He…the man…was concerned that I'd had to walk back to my hotel carrying Bertie. There wasn't a baby seat fitted in your car,' she said in response to Rafa's frown. 'He took me to a café…and bought me *gelato*.'

Rafa's brows lifted, and Ivy flushed at the sardonic look he gave her. 'He suggested that I could sell my story to the press for a lot of money,' she continued. 'I told him I wouldn't do that because I didn't want Gemma's and Bertie's private lives published in the newspapers.' She frowned. 'Although, come to think of it, I don't remember that I mentioned Gemma.'

'So you allowed a random stranger to believe that I'd got you pregnant and refused to accept responsibility for my illegitimate child,' Rafa said in a dangerous voice. 'Did it occur to you that Gelato Man could have been a journalist?'

She flushed again at his mocking tone. 'I'm sure he wasn't. I have no idea how the story is in the newspapers or why some of the facts are wrong.'

'The entire story is a complete fabrication that has cost me an important business deal and led the board members of my company to question my suitability to be the CEO.' Rafa's teeth were gritted. His withering tone stirred Ivy's temper.

'My sister was not a liar, and neither am I.'

He snorted. 'Frankly, I don't give a damn whether you or your sister are the baby's mother. I am not his father, and I will prove it by taking a paternity test. When I have the irrefutable truth from the lab report, the newspapers will have to retract the story, and I will sue you for making false allegations to the press, Miss Bennett.'

'I have no objection to a DNA test being carried out. In fact, I was going to suggest it,' Ivy said calmly. 'The test will prove that you are Bertie's father. What will you do then?' she asked Rafa. 'Will you be prepared to make room in your life for your son? And will you love him as he needs and deserves to be loved?'

Ivy was calling his bluff, Rafa assured himself. The baby was not his. Everything inside him rejected the possibility. He had made room in his life and indeed welcomed the birth of a child once before. He'd loved Lola unreservedly, but the revelation that she was not his daughter had almost broken him and made him bitter and untrusting.

He had no recollection of meeting Ivy's sister. It was true he'd enjoyed numerous sexual liaisons with women who understood that he did not want a long-term relationship, but he had always been sober when he'd taken his lovers to bed. He would swear he'd never slept with the woman in the photo who Ivy had told him was the baby's mother. Why then was it reported in the media that Bertie was Ivy's baby? The whole thing smacked of a scam that Ivy was trying to pull. Yet it was odd that she had agreed to his demand for a paternity test without argument.

The bathroom was hot and airless, and sweat beaded on Rafa's brow. He had every reason to mistrust Ivy, but his libido did not seem to care that she was a liar. He roamed his eyes over her grey vest top and matching tiny shorts that clung to her narrow hips and stopped high up on her thighs. Moving his gaze lower, he noted that her legs were shapely, with the defined calf muscles of a dancer. When he'd followed her into the bathroom, his eyes had been drawn to the rounded curves of her pert bottom.

Now she stood facing him and he could see the enticing outline of her nipples pressing against her thin top. If he'd had sex with Ivy, he would not have forgotten her, he brooded. His wayward imagination indulged in an erotic fantasy in which he undressed her and kissed his way down her body. He was intrigued to discover if the body hair covering her femininity was dyed bright pink too.

Dio! Rafa jerked his mind back from going down a path he was definitely not going to follow. At best Ivy had made a genuine mistake in believing he was the father of her sister's baby. At worst—and, to Rafa's mind, more likely—Ivy was a deceitful gold-digger from the same mould as his ex-wife. Why then was his body reacting as if he were a hormone-fuelled teenager on a first date?

Lust for Tiffany had resulted in their marriage, which in truth had been rocky almost from the start. Rafa had been willing to work at the relationship for the sake of their daughter until Tiffany had admitted that another man was Lola's father and that she'd married Rafa for his money. Since the divorce, he had made decisions based on cold logic rather than unreliable emotions.

Proof that Ivy was a liar would be revealed in the result of the paternity test and he would have no qualms about throwing her to the wolves, or in this case the paparazzi, Rafa thought grimly. He'd see how she liked being fodder for the gutter press. He had been woken early in the morning by the constant pinging of his phone as new messages arrived from friends congratulating him on becoming a father. Immediately, he'd flicked to a news stream and blistering hot rage had surged through him when he'd discovered that Ivy had gone to the press with her scandalous story.

It had to have been her. Rafa remembered Ivy's startled reaction when he'd showed her the front page of the newspaper. She'd admitted that she had been approached by a stranger. Surely she could not be so naïve that she hadn't realised the guy was a journalist? She must have arranged to talk to the press after he had refused to believe her story or give her money. Ivy looked as though butter wouldn't melt in her mouth, but he wasn't fooled by a pretty little liar.

When she stepped closer to him, Rafa's muscles tensed, as if he was preparing to defend himself from an attack by an enemy—which she was, he reminded himself. It was entirely Ivy's fault that Carlo Landini had called him an hour ago and cancelled the deal for Vieri Azioni to buy into Banca Landini. Now he was facing the threat of a vote of no confidence by the board, and some of the directors had suggested that the deputy, Sandro Florenzi, should replace Rafa as chairman and CEO.

'I understand that finding out about Bertie has been a shock for you,' Ivy said softly. 'Especially if you did not receive Gemma's letter. I really don't know how the media got hold of the story.'

It was crazy that he wanted to believe her. His failed marriage and Tiffany's betrayal had made Rafa deeply cynical, but he could not look away from Ivy's melting, chocolate-brown eyes. His body tightened as he watched her pupils dilate. The strap of her top had slipped off one shoulder and his fingers itched to slide it back into place, or better still tug the other strap down until he'd bared her breasts with their pebble-hard nipples. His mouth watered at the prospect of curling his tongue around each taut peak.

The atmosphere in the tiny bathroom simmered with sexual tension that made the hairs on Rafa's neck stand on end and his pulse thud hard and fast. His gaze dropped to Ivy's mouth as her tongue darted across her lips to moisten them. He did not know if it was an unconscious action or a deliberate invitation, and frankly he did not care. He wanted to kiss her. It infuriated him to admit that he desired her, but he was confident that he was in control, and kissing her would simply satisfy his curiosity.

A high-pitched cry from the bedroom shattered whatever had or hadn't been about to happen between them. Rafa told himself he should feel relieved when Ivy gasped as if she had been jolted back to reality and spun away from him.

'I can't believe Bertie is awake already. I hoped he would sleep while I had a shower. I have to check out of the hotel by ten o'clock and my flight back to England is at two this afternoon.'

'You will have to reschedule your flight.' Rafa followed her into the bedroom. 'I have arranged for samples to be taken from me and the baby today. The DNA testing company guarantees that the results will be ready in twenty-four hours.'

'The airline doesn't allow changes to bookings at short notice, and I can't afford to pay for another flight or stay at a hotel tonight. It will be better if I go home today. When you receive the test results, you can let me know what, if any, involvement you want with your son.'

'*Dio*, you don't give up, do you?' Rafa said tersely. He wasn't going to admit he was rattled by Ivy's certainty that he was the baby's father.

'Poor little mite. He's wet through.' She scooped Bertie out of the cot and, from the way her breath hissed between her teeth, Rafa guessed the movement had hurt her shoulder. Whatever else she might have lied about, her shoulder injury was genuine, and she'd almost passed out in the bathroom. 'I should have changed his nappy before I put him down, but I didn't want to risk waking him. Will you pass me one of his sleep suits from the backpack? Tip everything out if it's easier.'

Rafa spotted the backpack on the floor. He opened it and dumped a pile of baby clothes onto the bed. Caught up among the clothes was a business card. He picked it up and gave a harsh laugh.

'*Di Oggie!* The most popular daily newspaper in Italy. I hope they paid you a lot of money. You will need a good lawyer when I sue you for defamation of my character. The fine is likely to be thousands of pounds, or you could be sent to prison.'

He refused to be taken in by Ivy's stricken expression. The reporter's business card was proof that he was right not to believe a word Ivy uttered.

'The man I met in the street gave me the card, but I didn't call the number and speak to the reporter. I've done nothing wrong.'

She was good at playing the innocent victim, but Rafa wasn't fooled by her denial. He was exasperated that he could not control his body's response to Ivy's elfin beauty. 'I suppose you told the journalist the name of your hotel,' he accused when he moved away from her and looked out of the window. 'There is a crowd of reporters outside. Did you tip them off that I was here?'

'No. How could I have done? I haven't been out of your sight since you arrived, and my phone is over there.' She glanced towards her phone on the bedside table.

Anger had brought colour to her pale cheeks and there were sparks of fire in her eyes. Rafa preferred her temper to her earlier sadness. He had an intense horror of tears—a throwback to his childhood when his mother had suffered deeply from depression and Rafa would often hear her crying desperately when she'd thought he was out of earshot.

When Ivy had spoken about her sister, Rafa had seen that her grief was raw and, despite his mistrust of her, he'd felt an urge to comfort her. He understood the gut-wrenching sense of loss. His father had died not long after Ivy's sister. Rafa hadn't realised how much he'd loved his *papà* until it had been too late to tell him. Why did this woman stir his emotions that, like a hornets' nest, were better left alone? he wondered.

'Get dressed,' he told Ivy curtly. 'You and the baby will spend tonight at my apartment. Tomorrow, when the paternity test result exonerates me from any responsibility for the child, I will personally drive you to the airport and put you on the first plane to England on the understanding that I never hear from you or see you again.'

CHAPTER THREE

IVY EMERGED FROM the bathroom, where she had gone to get dressed, and found Rafa's driver in her hotel room. The two men were talking quietly in Italian and there was an infant car seat on the bed. The driver gave her a curious look before he left.

'Aldo says it's a scrum downstairs,' Rafa told her grimly. 'When we leave the hotel, stick close to me and do not say anything to the reporters.'

'It's not my fault that they're outside.'

The scathing look he gave her said he did not believe her. His eyes narrowed as he studied her canary-yellow sundress with a shirred bodice that supported her small breasts. Any movement of her shoulder was agony and she'd given up trying to reach behind her back to do up her bra.

She was conscious that her nipples had tightened and hoped Rafa did not notice her body's response to him as his gaze lingered on her breasts before moving up to her pink hair.

'Very colourful,' he drawled.

'I like bright colours,' Ivy said defensively, wishing she was taller and more elegant and could afford to wear designer clothes like the women she'd seen with Rafa on social media. She was angry with herself for wanting his approval and wishing that he found her attractive.

Her heart sank as she wondered if she had inherited her mother's poor judgement in men. Her mum had always fallen for bad boys, convinced that she would be able to make them love her. As a child, Ivy had felt that her mum had cared more about her pursuit of romantic relationships than her. Seeing how her mum had been badly treated by her husbands and lovers had been a warning that falling in love was a risk that too often resulted in disappointment and heartbreak. When Ivy's first romance as a teenager had ended with Luke heartlessly dumping her because he couldn't cope with her illness, it had reinforced her belief that men were unreliable and likely to let her down.

'You are certainly noticeable,' Rafa told her. 'Is that the point, to grab the paparazzi's attention and sell them another fantasy story? Your plan will backfire when I can prove that I am not Bertie's father.'

Frustration at Rafa's refusal to believe her made Ivy halt on her way over to the cot. She was tired of trying to defend herself. 'We could just stop this now,' she said tautly. 'It's obvious that you don't want Bertie. I'll take him back to England and care for him on my own, and I won't ask you to contribute a penny for him.'

Rafa gave a cynical laugh. 'I've been waiting for you to try to back out of the paternity test, but your luck's out, little lady. Your publicity stunt when you involved the press has damaged my personal reputation and my business credibility, and I have lost the support of many of my board members and shareholders. If you refuse permission for the test, I will seek a court order for it to go ahead.'

'Fine.' She leaned over the cot, but as she lifted Bertie out she felt a tearing pain in her shoulder and could not restrain a sharp cry.

'You had better let me hold him.' Rafa crossed the room in a couple of strides and took the baby from her. A curious expression flickered on his face as he looked down at Bertie lying in his arms. Ivy supposed she was biased, but anyone would have to admit that Bertie was an adorable baby, with his olive-toned complexion and mass of almost black hair. Like father, like son, she thought ruefully. But Rafa did not want his little boy and he believed that she had an ulterior motive for bringing Bertie to Italy.

'Have you seen a doctor about the pain in your shoulder?' he asked her while he strapped Bertie into the car seat. His confident handling of the baby was a surprise, as he'd given the impression that he'd never been within a million miles of a small child before.

Ivy stuffed the baby's clothes into the backpack. 'I had it checked out by a medic on the cruise ship. He thought I'd pulled a muscle from a fall while I was dancing. But that was a few months ago and my shoulder still hurts.'

'It might be a rotator cuff tear, although it's more likely to be a strain where the muscles and tendons that keep your shoulder in its socket are damaged. It's a common injury for basketball players,' Rafa explained when she stared at him. 'At one time I considered training to be a sports physiotherapist when my playing career was over.'

'Why didn't you?' Ivy couldn't hide her curiosity. This was the first conversation she'd had with Rafa without tension bristling between them. His deep voice with the hint of an Italian accent was *so* sexy.

He shrugged. 'I always knew that I was destined to succeed my father as the head of Vieri Azioni. After ten years of playing sport at a professional level, I was ready for a new challenge.' His tone hardened and Ivy wondered if there was more to his decision to return to Italy than he'd let on. She had read that he'd been through an acrimonious divorce while he'd lived in America.

'The company was established by my great-grandfather,' Rafa continued. 'I was my father's only son and there was pressure on me to take his place and continue the family's association with Vieri Azioni.'

'Now you have a son to carry on that association.' Ivy spoke unthinkingly. She wished she could take her words back when Rafa's brows lowered.

'Did you find out from your research that Vieri Azioni's revenue for the last fiscal year was one hundred billion euros? Perhaps you discovered that, aside from my family's wealth, I was one of the highest-paid players in the American professional basketball league.'

'That's not why I brought Bertie to you,' she said quickly, stung by Rafa's scornful tone.

'Paternity fraud is an occupational hazard for rich men,' he carried on as if she hadn't spoken. 'There have been numerous cases where a woman has accused a man, usually a well-known figure or celebrity, of being the father of her child. It can have a devastating impact on an innocent man's life and relationships, especially if he has a wife or long-term partner. Fortunately, I don't, but I will stop at nothing to clear my name. The reason for a false paternity claim is always money.'

Ivy felt incinerated by the scorching contempt in Rafa's eyes. She looked at Bertie sleeping peacefully in the car seat and her heart ached with love for him. He was so perfect and innocently unaware of the furore resulting from his birth.

'I hoped you would want to do the right thing for Bertie,' she muttered. 'Although, I don't know why I thought you might be a good father to him. I'm not even sure that good fathers exist. Mine cleared off when I was ten, and neither of my stepfathers were any more reliable. My dad left because he had been having an affair with another woman. Mum continued to chase a romantic dream and she married and divorced twice more.' She glared at Rafa. 'Bertie will be better off without a father than with a reluctant father who takes no interest in him.'

Rafa's expression was unreadable, and Ivy decided that he had been carved from granite. He slung her backpack over his shoulder, picked up the car seat by the handle and carried Bertie over to the door. 'Let's get this over with,' he said tersely.

The driver had parked the car outside the front of the hotel. When Ivy followed Rafa through the door, she tensed as reporters and photographers surrounded them. Flashlights popped and the clamour of voices asking questions about their relationship grew more insistent. Rafa clamped his arm around Ivy's waist and pushed a path through the crowd to where the driver was holding the car door open for them. She climbed into the back and scrambled across the seat to make room for Rafa.

He handed the baby seat to the driver, who fitted it to the anchor point in the car. With Bertie safely stowed, Rafa slammed the door shut. The driver slid behind the steering wheel and, as the car sped away from the hotel, a few die-hard photographers ran behind, still snapping pictures.

'They're like a pack of wolves,' Ivy said shakily. 'Is Bertie all right?' Rafa was sitting between the baby seat and her.

'He's still asleep.'

'I can't imagine how. I was worried he would be scared by the cameras and the shouting.'

'It's a pity you did not consider how he would be affected before you opened your mouth and told the press a pack of lies.'

Ivy did not reply. Nothing she said would make Rafa believe that she hadn't gone public with her allegation that Bertie was his child. The paternity test would show the truth, and if she'd been a vindictive person she'd have enjoyed hearing him apologise. But the sad fact was that there would be no winners. Rafa did not want his son and Bertie was destined to grow up without ever knowing his father.

She leaned her head against the back rest and her eyelashes drifted down. Her disturbed night with Bertie caught up with her as the car crawled along in a traffic jam.

'Ivy, wake up.'

The gravelly voice next to her ear jolted Ivy awake. She opened her eyes and found Rafa's handsome face so close to hers that she could count his thick eyelashes.

Her awareness of him was instant as her senses responded to the sensual musk of his aftershave.

She was embarrassed by the unsettling effect he had on her and prayed he could not tell that she was fiercely aware of him. *Get a grip,* she told herself. Bertie was her priority, and she hoped that when Rafa had proof he was the baby's father his attitude would change. She flushed when she realised that she must have fallen asleep with her head resting on Rafa's shoulder.

'Sorry,' she muttered as she hastily moved across to the other side of the car. 'I was up with Bertie several times last night.'

'Is he often restless during the night?'

She took it as a good sign that Rafa was showing an interest in Bertie. 'He usually wakes around midnight and nothing I do seems to comfort him.' Ivy turned her head towards the window so that Rafa would not see the tears in her eyes. 'Maybe he misses Gem.' Her voice thickened. 'I do my best, but I'm not his mum.'

She gave a start when Rafa put his hand over hers where it was lying on her knee and gently squeezed her fingers. 'What happened to your sister? Was she ill?'

'There was a road traffic accident. Gemma was knocked down as she crossed the road.' Ivy swallowed the lump that had formed in her throat. 'She had only popped out to buy nappies. I'd said I would go, but she'd wanted to get out of the flat for a while. We lived on a busy main road and the pedestrian crossing was a few metres away. We had got into the habit of nipping across the road instead of walking to the crossing where it was safe.'

Ivy looked down at Rafa's strong, tanned fingers

covering her paler ones. It was a long time since anyone had offered her a physical gesture of comfort. Her dad had given her an awkward hug at Gemma's funeral, but he'd rushed back to Scotland, where he lived with his current girlfriend and their two children. Ivy had never been invited to meet her half-siblings.

Kindness from Rafa was unexpected and tugged on her fragile emotions. 'When I saw the emergency services outside the flat, I didn't realise at first that Gemma had been involved in an accident. But she was ages at the shop, and she didn't answer her phone. The police arrived and said that a van had driven around the corner fast and hit Gem, and she'd been taken to hospital.'

Ivy recalled the PC's sympathetic expression. He must have known that her sister's injuries were life threatening. 'A neighbour looked after Bertie and I rushed to the hospital. Gemma was conscious and I was allowed to see her briefly. She told me the name of Bertie's father and made me promise to find you before she was taken to the operating theatre. But her life couldn't be saved.'

'Is it possible that your sister was confused? She was about to undergo surgery and no doubt she had been given medication before a general anaesthetic.' Rafa frowned. 'Perhaps I'd been mentioned in a newspaper article that Gemma had read. Vieri Azioni is a multinational conglomerate, and its dealings are reported in financial publications around the word. Your sister might have muddled my name with the man she'd met on the cruise ship.'

'Gemma didn't read financial newspapers.' But her sister had been fascinated by the glamorous lives of celebrities and had followed many of them on social media. When Ivy had researched Rafa Vieri online, she had found plenty of pictures and gossip about him.

What if she had made a terrible mistake by bringing Bertie to Italy? She had no idea how the newspapers had got hold of the story that Rafa was the baby's father. If the paternity test came back negative, would he carry out his threat to sue her for slander, and could she really be sent to prison?

Ivy turned her head and met Rafa's enigmatic gaze. She wondered what he would do if she leaned closer and pressed her lips against his stubbled jaw. Would he angle his mouth over hers and kiss her? She wanted him to, she admitted to herself. But she resented her intense awareness of him. He had a reputation as a womaniser, and he was the last man she would ever get involved with.

'We're here.' Rafa released Ivy's hand and she felt oddly bereft.

'I thought we were going to your apartment.' The car had slowed outside one of Rome's most famous hotels, the Palazzo Degli Dei. Opposite was the city's iconic historical landmark, the Colosseum.

'I live in the hotel's penthouse suite.'

'Why do you live in a hotel?'

He shrugged. 'I own the hotel, although my interest is purely as an investment, and I am not involved in running it. I like the convenience of living in a serviced apartment.'

There was a crowd of paparazzi near the hotel's grand entrance, although they were kept away from the door by security guards. Ivy tensed, thinking that they would be mobbed by the photographers, but the car drove past the entrance and turned down a ramp that led to an underground car park. Rafa carried Bertie in the baby seat and ushered Ivy into a private lift that took them directly up to his apartment.

She preceded him inside and her tension increased when she took in her surroundings. The penthouse was ultra-modern and sophisticated with black marble floors, and white velvet sofas were arranged in groups in the vast, open-plan living space. From every window there was a view of the ancient Colosseum.

Everything about the apartment screamed serious money, but it felt like a high-end hotel suite rather than a private home, and there was nothing on show that gave a clue to the personality of the man who lived there.

She turned to find Rafa watching her, and her heart skipped a beat as her gaze locked with his. She wished she knew what he was thinking, but his chiselled features revealed nothing.

'I'll show you where you and the baby will sleep tonight,' he said coolly.

Ivy followed him down the corridor and into a room where there was a cot and a baby-change unit. There was also an impressive looking pushchair with a carrycot attachment suitable for young babies.

'Do you have another child—or children?' It suddenly occurred to her that Rafa might already be a father. Why else would there be nursery furniture in his swanky apartment?

'No.' Beneath his curt reply, there was something in his voice that stirred Ivy's curiosity. 'The hotel provided the nursery equipment, and I ordered the push chair from a supplier.'

'I'll pay for the push chair,' she said at once, not wanting him to think she was after freebies.

He ignored her and opened a door into a connecting bedroom. 'I assumed you would want to sleep near the baby so that you can attend to him if he wakes in the night.'

The room was at least three times bigger than Ivy's bedroom at the flat in Southampton where she had lived with her sister. She would have to move out of the flat in a matter of days, and finding somewhere affordable for Bertie and her to live was another worry to add to her already long list.

Rafa set the car seat down on the floor and lifted a now awake Bertie out. The baby gave a winsome smile that never failed to melt Ivy's heart, but there was not a flicker of response on Rafa's face as he handed Bertie to her.

'The doctor will be here in a few minutes to take samples for the DNA test. I have been assured that the procedure is a simple cheek swab and Bertie won't feel a thing.' He dropped Ivy's backpack onto the bed. 'I will need yours and the baby's passports so that I can book your return flight to England.'

In twenty-four hours they would know the truth, although Ivy did not doubt her sister. Pride made her want to tell Rafa that she would pay for her own plane ticket, but the reality was she did not have enough money in her account for the flight.

She searched in the backpack for the passports. When she pulled them out, a card fell onto the bed.

She had intended to throw the reporter's business card into the bin before she left her hotel, but somehow it had ended up in the backpack, and it silently condemned her. Rafa said nothing, but the icy fury in his eyes sent a shiver through Ivy when he plucked the passports from her fingers and strode out of the room.

Rafa woke the next morning with a pounding headache. His hangover was not surprising, after the train wreck his life had become in the past forty-eight hours. He was in dire need of strong black coffee and he pulled on a pair of sweatpants before he padded barefoot down the hall to the kitchen.

His stomach tightened when he saw Ivy perched on a stool at the breakfast bar, drinking orange juice out of the carton. It had been a mistake to bring her to his apartment, he brooded. He did not want any involvement with her, or Bertie, who he was certain was not his son. He wished he'd arranged for them to stay in a hotel room, but it had seemed sensible to keep Ivy close to stop her talking to the press and making up more lies about him.

'I couldn't find a glass,' she said when Rafa glowered at her. 'I hope Bertie's crying didn't disturb you during the night.'

The inroads he'd made on a bottle of single malt hadn't blocked out the baby's cries, which had evoked poignant memories of when he'd believed he was the father of an adorable little daughter. Nor had getting drunk banished Ivy from his erotic dreams. The sight of her first thing, looking perkily pretty and as sexy as hell in an over-sized tee shirt that kept slipping off one shoulder, did nothing to improve Rafa's mood.

He took two glasses from a cupboard, filled both with juice and pushed one towards Ivy before he downed his drink in a couple of gulps. On the counter was a selection of the daily newspapers that the maid had delivered to the apartment. The front page of many of the papers had a photo of Rafa carrying Bertie in the baby seat, seemingly hustling Ivy out of a run-down hotel and into a car. She looked young and appallingly innocent with her pink hair and Bambi eyes, beneath the headline.

Il magnate, il suo amante e il loro bambino!

'What does it say?'

'It says, *"the tycoon, his lover and their baby"*.' Rafa translated the headline.

'Oh, no!' Ivy had perfected the 'wide-eyed ingénue' act. But, even knowing that she was a liar and that she had obviously been in contact with the journalist whose business card had been in her bag, Rafa felt an intense desire to crush her soft mouth beneath his and taste the orange juice on her lips. Once again, she wasn't wearing a bra, and he wondered if she even possessed one. Every time she moved, her tee shirt brushed against her breasts, and he glimpsed the tantalising outline of her pointed nipples.

'I don't understand why the papers are saying that you and I are…involved.' Unbelievably, she blushed.

'Don't you?' He had every right to be cynical and suspicious, Rafa told himself.

Ivy lifted her hands in a helpless gesture. 'What can we do?'

The neck of her shirt had slipped off her shoulder, exposing the pale, upper swell of one breast. Heat stirred in Rafa's groin, and he could not control the surge of sexual hunger that swept through him. Resting his elbow on the breakfast counter, he leaned closer to Ivy. She tensed but did not pull away. He was fascinated by the frantic thud of the pulse at the base of her throat.

'The media and half the goddamned world believe we are lovers,' he drawled. He did not add, *thanks to you*, but his unspoken accusation intensified the simmering tension in the kitchen. 'I think I'm owed some sort of compensation for the trouble you have caused.'

Ivy's face was a picture as her lips parted to form a perfect *O!* when his meaning became clear. Rosy colour stained her cheeks and throat, and Rafa's fingers itched to grab the hem of her shirt and pull it over her head so that he could see if the flush of heat had spread across her breasts.

'Are you propositioning me?' The amber flecks in her eyes sparked with temper, but her voice was oddly breathless. 'You said I'm not your type,' she reminded him.

'The pink hair is growing on me.' Compelled by the drumbeat of desire pounding in his veins, Rafa traced his finger down her cheek and neck, stopping at the edge of her shirt, where her breasts were rising and falling jerkily. Her skin was as soft and delicate as rose petals and he was intrigued by how easily she blushed.

He should stop this now before he did something he would later regret, such as kiss the sulky pout from her mouth until her lips were soft and pliant beneath his. His common sense told him that he should switch on the coffee machine and get his kick from a hit of caffeine instead of hitting on Little Miss Liar. But he couldn't move away from her.

'We could be lovers,' he murmured. 'At least then, part of the news story would be true.'

He'd meant it to be a joke, a taunt to annoy her. He wanted to provoke a reaction from her, in the same way that she provoked one from him, but his voice thickened as the heat inside him flared into an inferno.

'I've never had a lover.' The lie—for surely it must be a lie?—slipped so easily from her pretty mouth. 'What makes you think I'd want you?'

Rafa would have been more convinced that she was not interested in him if her voice hadn't become husky and seductive. Her eyes had darkened, the enlarged pupils almost swallowing up the brown irises, drawing him in. He resented the effect she had on him even as he lowered his face towards her.

What makes you think I'd want you? Ivy had challenged him and Rafa could never resist a challenge.

'This,' he murmured before he brought his mouth down on hers.

She gasped and he swallowed the soft sound, easing her lips apart with his. The effect on him was instant. He felt as though an electrical current had zapped through his body. Somehow he stopped himself from ravaging her lips with hungry passion. He had felt her slight hesitation and he kept the kiss light, flicking his tongue over the contours of her mouth and taking little sips from her lips.

He felt her mouth quiver beneath the coaxing pressure of his and a nerve jumped in his cheek as it became harder to restrain himself from devouring her. His patience paid off as, with a low moan, she parted her lips to allow his tongue to probe between them.

Dio, she tasted of orange juice and nectar, and he wanted more. He speared his fingers into her pink hair. The feathery strands felt like silk against his skin as he slid one hand round to her nape and angled her head so that he could fit his mouth even closer to hers. He pushed his tongue between her lips and Ivy copied his actions, tentatively at first, but she grew bolder as the kiss became increasingly erotic.

She placed her hands on his bare chest, and Rafa knew she must feel the erratic thud of his heart. His skin felt too hot, too tight. He wanted her naked against his bare skin. Her breasts would be soft and her nipples as hard as pebbles pressing into his chest.

This was madness. She should not be kissing Rafa. Alarm bells rang in Ivy's brain, but her body wasn't listening. The instant he had covered her mouth with his, a fire had ignited inside her, and she was burning in his fiery passion. She was intoxicated by the scent of his body, a subtle blend of the spicy cologne he'd worn the previous day, the faint peatiness of whisky and something uniquely male that triggered a purely feminine response low in her pelvis.

Her bones had turned to jelly the moment he'd strolled into the kitchen, looking like a fallen god, with his almost black hair spilling across his brow and thick stubble shadowing his jaw. His bare chest was tanned a deep olive-gold and covered with whorls of black hairs that arrowed down to the edge of his sweatpants sitting low on his hips.

While she was sitting on the bar stool, her face was almost level with Rafa's. He tightened his arms around her, and she was powerless to stop herself from melting against his whipcord body. Her breasts felt heavy and warmth pooled between her thighs. She ran her hands over his chest, fascinated by the feel of satin overlaid with wiry hairs. Her fingertips explored the ridges of his powerful abs as she strained closer to him and parted her lips beneath his, kissing him with a wild passion she'd never felt for any other man.

In truth, there hadn't been many other men, Ivy acknowledged. Her first romance when she'd been seventeen had ended with her cancer diagnosis. In hindsight, she supposed that Luke had been too young to cope, but when he'd broken up with her it had reinforced her belief that all men were like her father and disappeared when things got tough. One day she hoped she would meet a guy she could rely on. But that guy was not Rafa Vieri. He was a playboy who had slept with her sister and pretended that he did not remember.

What was she doing? Ivy tore her lips from Rafa's. Recrimination tasted like sawdust in her mouth. Her wanton behaviour was completely out of character. She felt guilty that she had betrayed Gemma, even though things with Rafa hadn't gone further than a kiss. But for a few moments she had been utterly carried away by their blazing passion and she'd longed for him to lie her down on the breakfast counter and lower his body onto hers.

'*No.*' She pushed against Rafa's chest, and he backed off immediately.

'Easy,' he murmured.

Ivy slid down from the bar stool and wrapped her arms around her body as if she could hold herself together. She ran her tongue over her swollen lips. 'I'm not easy,' she told Rafa tremulously. 'I realise I must have given you a different impression. That shouldn't have happened.'

He shrugged. 'It was just a kiss. Nothing to get worked up about.'

Evidently he hadn't been affected by the kiss the way she had, and she wanted to die of shame. *Who would look after Bertie?* demanded a scornful voice in her head. Ivy shuddered with remorse and anger at herself. For those few minutes, while Rafa had been expertly kissing her, she had forgotten about Bertie.

Ivy remembered when she'd been a child and her mum had been so wrapped up in her latest romance that she hadn't paid her much attention. Luckily, she'd had Gemma to turn to, but Bertie had no one else. *How could she have forgotten her sister's baby for even one second*?

She stared at Rafa and despised herself for the way her body responded to his potent masculinity. 'I should not have kissed *you*.'

He strolled down the kitchen and dropped a coffee pod into the machine. 'Forget it,' he drawled in a bored voice. 'I already have.'

'Good, that makes two of us.' Pride came to Ivy's rescue and insisted on her having the last word before she walked out of the room with as much dignity as she could muster. The heart-rending sound of Bertie crying piled on more guilt, and when she hurried down the hallway and into his room the sight of his red face and tears on his cheeks made her feel that she was the worst person in the world.

She scooped him out of the cot and hugged his little body. 'I'm sorry, Bobo,' she choked, using her sister's pet name for him. *I'm sorry, Gemma,* she apologised silently. Bertie was all that mattered to her, and she would never forget him again. She wished she'd never brought the baby to Italy or met Rafa Vieri. But when Bertie was older he would have the right to know the identity of his father. Much as Ivy wanted to take him back to England, she had to remain in Rome until the result of the paternity test confirmed her belief that Bertie was Rafa's son.

CHAPTER FOUR

THE AUTOMATIC GATES opened to allow Rafa to turn his car onto the driveway of his parents' villa in an affluent suburb of the city. A crowd of photographers had gathered outside the estate, and they surged towards the car. The same thing had happened when he had driven away from the Palazzo Degli Dei hotel. A few of the paparazzi had even jumped onto motorbikes and chased after his car, hoping to snap a picture that would make it onto tomorrow's front page.

Instead of driving up to the house, Rafa stopped halfway along the gravel driveway and switched off the engine. Before he had left the penthouse, he'd had a difficult conversation with his mother, when she'd tearfully asked why he had kept her grandson a secret. She was upset that she'd found out about the baby from reading the newspapers. Rafa had come to reassure his mother that Bertie was not his child, and Ivy wasn't his lover.

But he had wanted to make love to Ivy. He grimaced as he remembered how she had threatened his self-control with her understated sensuality. He shouldn't have kissed her, and he was furious with himself for coming on to her like a teenager with a surfeit of testosterone. It wasn't his style, and he did not understand why she got under his skin. But she wouldn't bother him for much longer. He was expecting the result of the paternity test, which would prove that Ivy was a liar who had caused him public embarrassment and possibly cost him his position as the CEO of Vieri Azioni.

Thankfully his father was not around to witness his humiliation. Emotion tightened Rafa's throat. It felt strange, coming back to the family home where he had spent his childhood and teenage years, now his *papà* was no longer here. Guilt augmented his grief. His father hadn't wanted him to move to America to play basketball, but Rafa had been driven by determination—and a fair-sized ego, he acknowledged ruefully—to make his own mark on the world.

As a young man, there had been a weight of expectation on him to dedicate his life to the family business in the same way that his father had done. When he had chosen a different path, he'd sensed he was a disappointment to his father, despite his successful career as a professional sportsman. The unspoken accusation that he was not committed to Vieri Azioni had added to Rafa's feeling that he was not a good enough son.

It was for that reason he had decided not to pursue his interest in training to be a sports physiotherapist when his basketball playing days had been coming to an end. Instead he had returned to the fold and discovered that he'd inherited his father's business acumen. The past eighteen months, when he had worked with his father, had been genuinely enjoyable, and Rafa had felt that they had become closer than they'd ever been.

But the sudden loss of his father meant that he'd

faced the new challenge of proving to the board and himself that he was a worthy successor to run Vieri Azioni. Progress had been good and after an initial wobble, that had reflected investors' shock at his father's death, the value of the company's stock had recovered as confidence in the new CEO had increased.

That had been until the story that Rafa had refused to recognise his illegitimate baby son had hit the headlines. It was still the most trended topic on social media. But he was about to receive proof that he had done nothing to bring shame on himself.

The ping of his phone alerted him to the arrival of an email. Relieved that he would be able to get his life back on track, he opened the report from the DNA testing clinic and read it several times. His mouth dried and he was conscious of his heart banging against his ribs. The report did not make any sense.

Ninety-nine point five percent probability. Rafael Vieri is not excluded as the biological father of Roberto Bennett.

He had fallen into a nightmare. That was the only logical explanation. The notes accompanying the report explained that the paternity test could prove with one hundred percent accuracy that a man was *excluded* as the father of a child. That was the result Rafa had been banking on. But the high percentage of probability on the results sheet indicated that the possible father, i.e. himself, was most likely the biological father of the child, since all data gathered from the test supported a relationship of paternity.

Hell!

He pinched the bridge of his nose. Only once before in his life had he experienced such a gut-wrenching shock—when Tiffany had admitted that she'd lied, and the daughter he'd adored was not his child. But this was insane. He could not have fathered a child by Ivy's sister. Rafa was sure he'd never met Gemma, yet the evidence that Bertie was his son was in front of him.

His phone rang, and he cursed softly before he answered it. *'Ciao, Mamma.'*

'Why are you sitting in your car? Are you too ashamed to face me?'

'I had to deal with something important…for work.' It was a white lie, but he did not know what he was going to say to his mother. The email had left him reeling. Once again, the result of a paternity test had blown his life apart, Rafa thought grimly as he drove up to the house.

The maid escorted him into the drawing room where Fabiana Vieri was lying on the sofa. She did not get up, but languidly held out her hand to him.

'Mamma.' Rafa stooped to kiss her fingers. His earliest memories of his mother were of her lying in bed or resting on a sofa with her pills and tonics close to hand.

'I have suffered greatly,' she had once told him when she'd explained that her longed-for hope of another child had been dashed by several miscarriages.

'You still have me, *Mamma*,' the boy Rafa had tried to comfort his mother, but her sadness had permeated the house. He had been convinced that he wasn't good enough and that was the reason she yearned for another child, a better child than him. When his mother had cried—often—and he'd been unable to console her, he had felt that he'd failed her and therefore perhaps he did not deserve for her to love him.

Now he was an adult, but the sight of a woman's tears still made him feel as inadequate as he had when he'd been a boy because he did not know how to help. Deep down, he was wary of feeling rejected, as he'd felt when his mother had locked herself in her bedroom and he'd heard her crying.

These days, instead of taking herbal remedies for mostly imagined health complaints, his mother relied on oxygen cylinders to alleviate the effects of the incurable lung disease she had been diagnosed with six months ago. Rafa had assumed that he would lose his mother first and he was still trying to come to terms with his father's unexpected death.

'Why did you not tell me about my grandson?' Fabiana reproached him. 'You know how much I have longed for a grandchild. My heart was broken when you discovered that *l'angioletta* Lola was not your daughter.'

Rafa grimaced. Tiffany had taken Lola to live with her real father, and the abrupt separation from the little girl he had believed was his child had been as painful as a bereavement. It had given him an insight into how his mother must have felt when her pregnancies had ended in disappointment.

He wondered if his father had been as deeply affected every time his mother had lost a baby. Rafael senior had rarely showed his emotions, and when Rafa had been growing up he had tried to emulate his father. Even now he never opened up to anyone about his feelings. Big boys did not cry. The mind-blowing result of the paternity test made him want to punch the wall in frustration, but he answered his mother calmly.

'I have only just found out about the child.' He could not bring himself to refer to Bertie as *his* child. He needed time to process the frankly bizarre situation. He had been utterly convinced that Ivy Bennett was a liar, but it seemed that she was what she'd said she was—a grieving sister seeking the father of her motherless nephew. Except Rafa's gut instinct was that he had not slept with Gemma and then since forgotten her.

'Of course, you will have to marry the boy's mother. You cannot have an illegitimate heir. I have seen the girl's picture in the newspaper.' For some reason, the disapproval in Fabiana's voice irked Rafa. 'She is not one of us.'

He did not attempt to explain that Ivy was not Bertie's mother. The news story had damaged his reputation, but it would not improve matters if he made a public statement that he did not remember having sex with Ivy's sister. His mother had meant that Ivy was not part of Italy's, and more specifically Rome's, social elite. The Vieri family had been rich and powerful since the fifteenth century and Rafa had never been allowed to forget his heritage.

'Ivy is devoted to the baby,' he said curtly. He did not know what to make of Ivy Bennett and her motives for talking to the press, but Rafa had seen the love and care she showed Bertie.

'I am glad your father is not here to witness the shame you have brought on the family.'

Dio! His mother did not pull any punches. Guilt added to his confusion and anger. Fabiana sagged back against the cushions. It was only two months since she had been widowed and the raw emotion in the room was too much for Rafa to take. 'I need to look for some paperwork in *papà's* study,' he muttered before he strode from the room.

It was the first time he had entered the study since his father had died. The room looked as it always had—immaculately tidy, the few items on the desk neatly arranged. Rafael Vieri senior had been a precise, controlled man who had worked hard and rarely taken time off to relax, apart from to play golf occasionally.

Rafa had respected his father hugely, and he missed the friendship that had developed between them when he had returned to Italy. He threw himself onto the chair behind the desk and dropped his head into his hands as his mother's words echoed in his ears. After a few minutes, while he fought to regain his self-control, he opened the drawer in the desk, although he had no idea what he was looking for. He was about to close it again when something at the back of the drawer caught his attention.

Why had his father kept a model ship hidden in his desk? Rafa lifted the model out. It was evidently a scale reproduction of a cruise liner, and his heart gave a jolt when he read the name on the hull. *Ocean Star.*

Gemma told me she had met Rafael Vieri aboard the Ocean Star *on a cruise around the Caribbean islands.*

It was surely a coincidence that Ivy's sister had been a hostess on a cruise ship with the same name as the model ship on his father's desk. Rafa dismissed the preposterous idea that came into his head. His workaholic father was as likely to have taken a trip to the moon as to have gone on a cruise. The model ship had probably been a gift from someone. He wondered why his father had shoved it in the drawer.

'I found this in *papà's* study. Do you know why he had it?' Rafa asked his mother when he returned to the drawing room with the model ship.

'Oh, that thing. Rafael kept it as a memento of the cruise he took last year.'

Rafa's heart crashed against his ribs. 'When exactly last year?' He tried to keep his voice calm. 'I don't remember that *papà* went on a cruise.'

Fabiana shrugged. 'You had gone on a business trip. Somewhere in Asia, I think.'

'That would have been last April. I went to Hong Kong and Singapore before I flew to Perth, and I was away for nearly a month. My trip coincided with when *papà* had been advised by his doctor to take a complete break from work. He left Sandro Florenzi in charge at the office and went to Florida to meet up with his cousin for a golfing holiday.'

'Cousin Enrico broke his ankle on the day your father arrived. Rafael did not want to go to the golf resort on his own and was about to return home. But then he called to say that he had secured a last-minute booking on a cruise ship leaving Miami for the Caribbean islands. It wasn't like Rafael to be spontaneous. I believe the stroke he'd had a few months earlier had affected him more than he'd admitted.' Fabiana glanced at the model ship. 'Your father brought that back with him. It's a cheap trinket, and I thought he had got rid of it.'

'Can I keep the model ship, if it meant a lot to *papà*?' Maybe he was crazy, but Rafa was certain that the mystery of Bertie's paternity was connected to the model of the cruise ship *Ocean Star.*

His mother nodded. 'In return you must promise to bring your son to visit me.'

Rafa avoided his mother's gaze. 'Give me a little time. There are things I need to sort out.'

'I miss Rafael so much.' Fabiana held a tissue to her eyes. 'He was my one true love. My only consolation is that, when this wretched illness takes me, I will go to him.'

Dio! Rafa couldn't reveal that Bertie was not his son, but that there was a chance the baby was his half-brother. His mother would be utterly heartbroken if he told her of his suspicion that his father had been unfaithful with a hostess on the cruise ship. She had already suffered so much sadness in her life. He needed time to find out the truth, but the situation was already spiralling out of his control. The story in the media that he was convinced Ivy had been responsible for had made everyone believe they were lovers and that she was the mother of his illegitimate son.

Of course, you will have to marry the boy's mother.

Rafa frowned as he recalled his mother's words. There was not a chance in hell he would ever get married again. But his involvement in a baby scandal meant that he was in danger of losing the support of the majority of Vieri Azioni's board members.

And then there was his mother, who he was desperate to protect. The idea that had come into Rafa's head was crazy, but the whole thing was crazy. He felt disloyal to suspect his father of having had an affair, but he had to discover the truth, for his sanity and for baby Bertie's sake. He had emailed the DNA testing clinic and learned that a more in-depth test could solve the mystery, but it would take time, which Rafa did not have. All he could hope was for the press to lose interest in the story that he had fathered an illegitimate child. And perhaps he could make that happen.

The best way to flatten the story would be to announce his engagement to the baby's mother. Suddenly there would be no scandal and no more paparazzi camped on his doorstep. Vieri Azioni's board would have no reason to vote him out and, most importantly, he would prevent his mother from finding out the awful truth.

Rafa raked his hand through his hair. Could he pull off a fake engagement to Ivy? The chemistry between them was real, and he did not doubt that in public they would be able to put on a convincing act as a couple in love, but in private he must ignore his inconvenient desire for her. She might have been telling the truth when she'd said that Rafael Vieri was the father of her sister's baby after all, but Rafa still had reasons to mistrust her, and frankly he did not know who or what to believe any more.

Where *was* Rafa? It was late afternoon and Ivy had spent much of the day wheeling Bertie in the pushchair around the penthouse. Rafa's disappearance and lack of contact were proof that he did not want his son. She knew he must have received the result of the paternity test and his absence was damning.

Neither of Ivy's parents had taken much interest in her when she'd been a child and nor had her two stepfathers. A year ago, her mum had moved to Cyprus with her latest lover, and had vaguely mentioned that Ivy should visit some time soon when building work on the villa was finished, but a date had never been set.

Ivy had given up hoping for a close mother-daughter bond and accepted that her mum loved her, but she wasn't a priority. Her feeling of being unimportant to both her parents had made her determined that Bertie would grow up knowing that he was loved unconditionally, just as Gemma had loved her. Ivy's flight back to England was in a few hours' time, but Rafa hadn't returned Bertie's and her passports.

Ivy had explored the penthouse and found a room that Rafa must use as his office. Bertie was asleep and, conscious that she should have left for the airport by now, she did something she would never normally do and searched the drawers in the desk for the passports.

'What are you doing?'

She flushed guiltily when she looked up and met Rafa's lethal gaze across the room. She quickly shut the drawer, feeling like a child who had been caught with her hand in the sweet tin. Her chin came up as she reminded herself that she was not the one at fault. 'I'm looking for the passports. You didn't return them.'

He strolled towards her, his deceptively lazy strides at odds with his razor-sharp eyes that pinned her to the spot like a butterfly in a display case. 'I admit, I forgot about them with everything else going on. The passports are locked in the safe, and that's where they will stay for now. I need you and Bertie to remain in Italy for a while longer.'

Ivy hated him for being suave, and confident that

she would obey what sounded like an order. She hated herself even more for finding him so devastatingly attractive. The black jeans he was wearing teamed with a black silk shirt emphasised how much taller than her he was. His tan belt and loafers were no doubt hand-crafted from the finest Italian butter-soft leather. He dropped his designer shades onto the desk, and the gleaming gold watch on his wrist sent a message that the wearer was wealthy and powerful, and he could do what the hell he liked.

'How much longer do you want us to stay? A week? A month? You can't try out fatherhood in the way you would test-drive a new car.'

'I am not Bertie's father.'

'Don't you dare lie,' Ivy said furiously. 'I've seen the paternity test report which states that Bertie is your child. Yesterday, when you left the room, I asked the doctor who took the samples for DNA testing to email me the result at the same time as you. I am Bertie's legal guardian and I have a right to know who his father is.'

She spun away from Rafa, feeling unaccountably disappointed that he was as shallow and irresponsible as she'd thought. She was disappointed with herself for being attracted to him even though he was a smarmy liar who used his good looks and charisma to fool people—women, *her*—into hoping he was a better man than her common sense told her he was.

'Ivy, listen to me.' Rafa caught hold of her shoulder and frowned when she gave a yelp of pain. 'You should get that looked at by a physio.'

'I'll make an appointment with my GP when I go home. Please give me the passports.' She stared at Rafa, noticing for the first time the lines of strain around his eyes. His hair looked as though he'd been raking his fingers through it.

'I need you to hear me out. Bertie is not my son.' He held up his hand when she opened her mouth to tell him what she thought of him. 'It is possible…likely…' he said heavily, 'That he is my father's child.'

Ivy decided that she must have misunderstood him. 'But…you told me that your father is dead. How could *he* be Bertie's father?' Disbelief turned to anger. 'Have you spent the whole day thinking up such a ridiculous excuse?'

'I know it sounds crazy. When the idea first came to me, I felt disloyal to my father.' His jaw clenched. 'I still do. But I think I'm right, and the facts back me up. Your sister was a hostess on the cruise ship *Ocean Star* that set sail from Southampton at the beginning of April last year.'

When Ivy nodded, he carried on, 'The ship crossed the Atlantic and docked in Miami to collect more passengers, including Rafael Vieri. If you remember, I suggested that there could have been another passenger on the ship who had the same name as me, but it did not occur to me that he could have been my father. However, my mother told me today that my father had gone on a Caribbean cruise after his holiday plans in Miami fell through.'

He looked intently at Ivy. 'Did Gemma say anything at all about the Rafael Vieri she'd had an affair with on the ship?'

Ivy shook her head. 'When Gem announced that she was pregnant, she'd said that she couldn't be with the father. I had an idea he might have been married, but I didn't ask, and she never spoke about him. She only told me his name just before she died.'

'The confusion stems from the fact that my full name is Rafael, the same as my father.' Rafa exhaled heavily. 'I can prove that I was in Asia for business when Rafael Vieri was on the cruise ship. I'd already asked my PA to look back at my diary for last April. When my mother revealed that my father had been away on a cruise at the same time that I was on the other side of the world, I could only draw one conclusion.'

'But the paternity test proves you are Bertie's father.' Ivy's mind was spinning. Initially, she'd assumed that Rafa had made up the elaborate story, but the fact that he and his father shared the same name made the whole thing plausible—except for the paternity test.

'If a father and a son are both the possible father of a child, a basic paternity test could give a false positive result. That's what I believe happened in this case.'

If it was true, and Rafa was not Bertie's father, then there was no reason for her to feel guilty that she'd kissed him. The distracting thought slipped into Ivy's head. If Rafa and Gemma hadn't been lovers, it meant that she had not been disloyal to her sister. But she had still been a fool to have responded to Rafa when she knew he had a reputation as a playboy, Ivy told herself firmly.

'What did your mother say when you told her what you have just told me?'

'My mother is unaware of what I suspect,' Rafa said harshly. 'Only you and I and the DNA testing company, who have signed a watertight confidentiality clause, know that I have requested an extended paternity test where more genetic markers are studied. A child inherits fifty percent of their DNA from their mother and fifty percent from their father. The extended test can exonerate me as Bertie's father and prove with a high percentage of reliability that he is in fact my half-brother.

'Together with what else we know, it will be safe to assume that my father and your sister were lovers on the cruise ship and Bertie is the result of their affair. It will take a couple of weeks for the paternity test company to produce a result, which is why I want you and the baby to stay in Italy.'

Ivy did not know what to believe, and tears filled her eyes as the strain of the past few months overwhelmed her. Losing Gemma in such a shocking way and becoming responsible for a tiny baby had been life-changing events. The uncertainty of the identity of Bertie's father was too much to take in.

'Is the prospect of staying in a luxurious apartment in Rome really so bad that it makes you cry?' Rafa asked in a cynical voice.

'It's not that. If what you have said turns out to be true, it means that Bertie is an orphan, and it's just so tragic.' She rubbed her hand across her eyes. 'I hoped he would have a family in Italy who would want to be involved with him.'

'It was falsely reported by the media that you and I are Bertie's parents. That is the story my mother believes.'

Ivy stared at him. 'Didn't you explain that Bertie is my sister's baby and I had thought that you were his father?'

'No,' Rafa said bluntly. 'My mother can never find out that her husband of thirty-seven years of happy marriage had a casual fling that resulted in a child. It would destroy her.' His frustration was apparent in the dark scowl he sent Ivy. 'If you hadn't sold out to the newspapers, I would have been able to manage the situation differently. But, as it stands, my mother thinks she has a grandson who she is desperate to meet, and some members of Vieri Azioni's board are citing moral turpitude as a reason to try to kick me out of the company.'

Ivy glared back at him, infuriated by his unfairness. 'You refuse to believe that I didn't talk to a journalist, but I am supposed to accept your crazy theory that Bertie is your father's child?'

'It had to have been you who spoke to the press. I'm confident my theory will be proved right by the extended test.'

'I don't care about the test. You say you have proof that you were on a business trip and couldn't have been on the cruise ship, so I accept that Bertie is not your son. Why can't we just leave it at that? Give me the passports, I'll take Bertie and you will never hear from either of us again.'

Rafa shook his head. 'Unfortunately it is not as easy as that. For a start, I don't trust you.' He ignored her gasp of outrage. 'Vieri Azioni was entrusted to me by my father, and I will do whatever it takes to save my position as joint chairman and CEO of my family's company.' His grey eyes held her gaze. 'I have had an idea. I think we should announce that we are engaged.'

Once again, Ivy assumed that she had misheard or misunderstood him. 'Engaged…to who?'

His brows lifted. 'To each other, obviously.'

'You've got to be kidding! I don't want to get engaged to anyone, least of all you.'

'It will not be a real engagement.' Rafa roved his gaze over Ivy, and she was conscious that the stretchy material of her top moulded her breasts. She wished she had persevered through the pain in her shoulder and worn a bra.

Rafa's eyes had narrowed to glittering slits. Perhaps he was thinking that he would have expected his fiancée to be a lot more glamorous and sophisticated than her. Ivy did not understand why a tiny part of her was excited at the idea of being engaged to him. But it would be a fake engagement, she reminded herself.

She shook her head. 'What will be achieved by us pretending to be engaged?'

'If I am seen to have accepted responsibility for Bertie, and am prepared to marry the mother of the child who everyone believes is mine, it will make my mother happy and appease the board members and shareholders.' Rafa shrugged. 'Everyone loves a happy ending. We will pose for photos for the newspapers looking suitably enamoured with one another. Without a scandal to fuel the story, it will quickly fade from public interest, and in a month or two we will quietly break up.'

'What will you tell your mother when we end our engagement?'

'I'll make the excuse that you want to bring the baby up in England to be near your family.' He frowned. 'Do you have family who can help you care for your sister's child?'

She shook her head. 'My dad has many children from

his various relationships and my mum is living in Cyprus with her latest Mr Right. At least she has stopped marrying men who promise to love her but always let her down. Gemma was not her daughter, and Mum isn't interested in Bertie.'

Ivy wondered how Rafa had moved closer without her realising. She was standing behind the desk, and he was blocking her escape route to the door. 'I'm going to take Bertie back to England,' she said with more confidence than she felt. 'I think you should tell your mother the truth. Lies always get found out in the end.'

'You don't have to tell me.' His harsh and oddly humourless laugh stirred her curiosity. 'I have explained why I can't be honest with my mother and must allow her to believe that you and I are Bertie's parents. Mentioning your sister will only complicate things further. I won't risk her discovering a possible link between my father and Gemma. We must protect my mother's feelings.'

'With a fake engagement.' Ivy backed away when he took a step towards her. But, while her mind was trying to focus on the surreal conversation with Rafa, her body was communicating with him on a different level. Her heart was racing and her breathing was uneven. She folded her arms across her chest to hide the betraying thrust of her nipples through her clingy top, but the gleam in his eyes told her that he was aware of the effect he was having on her. 'Why should I care about your mother's feelings?' she muttered.

'She's dying. Eighteen months to two years at most, the specialist has advised.'

Ivy bit her lip. Rafa had recently lost his father and

his mother was terminally ill. She wasn't close to either of her parents, but she had adored her big sister, and she missed Gemma every day. 'I'm sorry.'

He looked at her intently. 'I think you are. Beneath your belligerence lies a soft heart, Ivy Bennett.' His voice had deepened and it felt like rough velvet caressing her skin. The atmosphere between them had altered subtly and prickled with mutual awareness. Ivy's heart gave a jolt as her eyes crashed into Rafa's searing gaze.

'I want to go home.' It was imperative to her self-preservation that she distanced herself from this man who had such a powerful impact on her. 'You can't make me stay.'

'I have been honest with you about the reasons I'd like you to remain in Italy.' Rafa moved closer. He wasn't touching her, but Ivy was aware of him with every cell in her body. With a jolt, she recognised the gleam of desire in his eyes when he lowered his face towards hers. Memories of the passion that had blazed between them when he had kissed her in the kitchen made her blood pound in her veins, and her lips parted in anticipation for him to claim them. Her brain said *no*, but her body said *yes* to the question in his eyes.

CHAPTER FIVE

RAFA SLID HIS hand round to Ivy's nape and angled his mouth over hers. She hesitated while her common sense battled the confusing feelings that only this man aroused in her. She wanted to dislike him, but he had surprised her with his determination to protect his mother from being hurt, if it was true that Rafa's father had been the man Gemma had had an affair with. Rafa had made his astounding suggestion of a fake engagement to spare his mother's feelings. It showed that he was honourable and had integrity, and Ivy felt a begrudging respect for him.

She placed her hands on his chest, still torn between wanting to push him away or succumb to her attraction to him. The heat of his body through his shirt transferred to her palms, ran like quicksilver up her arms and flooded her breasts. Perhaps if he had pulled her towards him she would have panicked but, other than his hand behind her head, he wasn't touching her, and she felt reassured that she was in control and could end the kiss whenever she wanted.

Except that she did not want it to end. Rafa brushed his mouth over hers and, with a soft sigh, Ivy parted her lips. He kept the kiss light at first, teasing the tip of his tongue between her lips and tantalising her with the promise of sweeter delights. With a low moan, Ivy curled her fingers into his shirt and sank into him, intensely aware of how hard his body felt against her softness, and how big and powerful he was.

He filled her senses. The taste of him was on her lips and she breathed in his sensual male scent. She heard the frantic thud of her heartbeat in her ears, and beneath her fingertips she felt the thunder of his heart. His free hand settled on her waist and, when he drew her towards him so that his thigh brushed against hers, she felt a jolt of purely feminine response to the unmistakeable hardness of his arousal.

When at last Rafa lifted his mouth to allow them to snatch a breath, Ivy stared into his eyes that gleamed like molten silver. He sat on the edge of the desk so that his face was almost level with hers and pulled her unresisting body between his thighs. 'That's better,' he murmured, making her wonder if his neck ached given he was so much taller than she was. But her thoughts scattered as he claimed her lips again and kissed her with a mastery that made her shake.

She believed that he wasn't Bertie's father, and without that barrier she could not stop herself from falling deeper under his spell. He used his mouth to enchant and entice her, and she held her breath when he slid his hands up her body to rest just beneath her breasts. Her nipples felt tight and hot, and when he brushed his thumb pads across the swollen peaks the pleasure was so intense that she shuddered.

It was too much, yet not enough. Her eyelashes swept down as she focused on the new sensations Rafa was arousing in her. No other man had made her feel so needy. Privately, she'd been scathing when friends, or her mum, had confessed that they had been carried away and unable to stop themselves from having sex with a guy they'd just met.

Surely it was a matter of self-control? Ivy had thought to herself. But now for the first time in her life she exalted in her femininity, and she felt empowered, but at the same time helpless to control her tumultuous desire for Rafa.

When he abruptly released her and stood up, she blinked at him, struggling to comprehend that the kiss was over and the passion that had blazed for her had not burned as fiercely for him. His expression was unreadable and that made things worse. She felt used and discarded, not good enough. Her old insecurities surfaced. From way back when her father had abandoned her for his girlfriend at the time who'd had a cuter kid, Ivy had never met a man who was genuinely interested in her.

'I will prepare a press release to announce our engagement first thing tomorrow.' Rafa's voice was huskier than usual, and his Italian accent was more pronounced. He strode across the room and Ivy wondered if she imagined that he was avoiding making eye contact with her.

She ran her tongue over lips that were still tingling from his kiss, and was intrigued when she saw his jaw clench. It occurred to her that perhaps he had enjoyed the kiss as much as she had but, like her, he was fighting the attraction they both felt.

'Tomorrow evening we will host an engagement party,' he continued. 'You will need some clothes, so

I have arranged for you to meet a personal stylist who can advise you on a suitable wardrobe. People will be curious about my new fiancée, and doubtless we'll receive a flurry of invitations to dinner.'

'I can't afford to buy new clothes.'

'I'll give you my credit card.'

Her pride objected. 'I won't use it.'

'I thought it was every woman's dream for a billionaire to provide unlimited access to his bank account,' he drawled.

'It's not my dream. You are not paying for my clothes. I haven't even agreed to your crazy idea of a pretend engagement.'

'If you are thinking of running to the newspapers and revealing the likely true identity of Bertie's father, I strongly advise you against it.'

'That sounds like a threat.'

He exhaled heavily. 'Do you want to break my mother's heart and make her miserable for the time she has left?'

Ivy remembered how devastated her mum had been when she'd discovered that her dad was having an affair. Ivy did not want to cause Rafa's mother the distress of finding out that her husband had cheated.

Rafa was pretending that Bertie was his son to protect his mother's feelings. But now he faced the loss of support from his board of directors because of the news story that he had abandoned his illegitimate child. It still rankled that he believed she had spoken to a journalist. If she hadn't brought Bertie to Italy, none of this would have happened, Ivy thought dismally.

'All right,' she said grudgingly, turning to face him.

'I'll be your fake fiancée. But I don't want money or clothes or anything from you.'

'*Dio*, are you always so argumentative?'

'Are you always so bossy? Anyway, taking Bertie on a shopping trip would be a nightmare.'

'While you are with the personal stylist, the baby will remain at the apartment with the nanny I have hired.'

She saw red. 'Well, you can damn well un-hire her. I am perfectly capable of caring for Bertie on my own.' Her voice thickened with emotion. 'He is all I have of Gemma, and I refuse to hand him over to a stranger. Bertie needs me…and… I need him.'

Rafa ran his hand through his hair, his frustration palpable. 'Anna is from a highly reputable agency and has excellent references. I met her earlier today and she is charming. She will help out when you cannot be with the baby—for instance, when we are at the party.'

There was sense in his words, Ivy conceded reluctantly. But Rafa was so forceful, and he was clearly used to getting his own way. 'You have no idea how it feels to be responsible for a defenceless little baby.' She was puzzled by an odd expression that flickered across his chiselled features.

'If my suspicion is proved correct, and Bertie is my half-brother, he will not be solely your responsibility,' he said quietly. 'You will have my support in whatever way we decide is best to care for him.'

Ivy watched Rafa stride out of the room. She was startled by his stated intention to share responsibility for Bertie. He had sounded genuine, but she cautioned herself against believing him too readily. Having witnessed her mother's disastrous relationships, Ivy had learned to be wary of handsome and persuasive men—and she would be a fool to trust Rafa.

Rafa fixed the cufflinks on his shirt and slipped his arms into his jacket. The party was an informal event and he decided against wearing a tie with his casual but nevertheless impeccably tailored linen suit from an Italian couture house. He ran his hand over the trimmed stubble on his jaw—he disliked being clean-shaven. A visit to the barbers had resulted in a shorter hairstyle and a sharper look in preparation for the damage limitation exercise he was hoping to pull off.

Many of Vieri Azioni's board members had accepted invitations to his engagement party, although the deputy CEO, Sandro Florenzi, had apologised in advance for his absence due to his wife's poor health. Rafa walked into the lounge and poured himself a generous Scotch before he stepped outside onto the balcony.

It was early evening, and the Colosseum looked even more spectacular with the fiery rays of the setting sun sinking behind the ancient structure. Once, gladiators had stepped into the arena to fight to the death. Fast forward a few thousand years, and Rafa was facing the fight of his life to retain control of his company. But, instead of a sword or spear, the secret weapon he was banking on to secure his victory was a mock engagement to a young woman who constantly confounded him.

He glanced at his watch. Ivy should make an appearance soon, and he acknowledged that he was curious to see what she was wearing. Hopefully the stylist had persuaded her out of her hip-hugging jeans and into an evening dress that was elegant and demure, suitable for his fiancée.

Rafa frowned as he remembered Ivy's agonised expression when she'd placed Bertie in the nanny's arms before going shopping.

'I've never left him before,' she'd said in a choked voice.

'I will take good care of the baby,' Anna had reassured her. 'If I have any concerns about Bertie, I'll call you.' The nanny spoke fluent English, and Ivy had relaxed a little, although she had slunk out of the penthouse like a lamb being led to the slaughter, instead of looking excited at the prospect of choosing new clothes that she didn't have to pay for.

Most women, in Rafa's experience, did not have a problem spending his money. He could not figure Ivy out, and he was perplexed that she had the ability to turn him on so hard and so fast that his control was threatened. It had never happened to him before, not even with his ex-wife. The truth was, he'd convinced himself that the hot lust he'd felt for Tiffany was love, and he had married her without suspecting that the baby she'd been expecting was not his.

There was no danger that his attraction to Ivy was anything more than a physical response to her fragile beauty, which coincided with a dry spell in his sex life, Rafa assured himself. When he had kissed her in his study the previous day, her ardent response had blown him away, and he'd had to force himself to pull back before the situation had got out of hand. Ivy's initial shyness had given way to a fierce, yet touchingly clumsy passion, reminding him that she'd said she had never had a lover.

It seemed highly unlikely for a woman in her mid-twenties still to be a virgin. But he'd been disturbed by the effect that Ivy had on him, and he'd needed to put some distance between them. He'd spent the evening propping up a bar and had accepted an offer from Matteo, an old school friend, to sleep in his guest room for the night.

That morning, when Rafa had returned to the penthouse, he had wondered if Ivy had taken baby Bertie and fled back to England. He had half expected her to, and if he was honest he'd half-hoped she would have disappeared. He did not know where in England she lived, and it would have given him an excuse not to look for her.

Admittedly, he would have had to think of an explanation about the son he had allegedly fathered for the press and the board members who wanted to replace him. But he would have forgotten Ivy in a week or two. He'd never allowed a woman to have any kind of hold over him. However, the baby was another matter. Rafa was still struggling to comprehend that Bertie could be his half-brother, with the implication that his father, whom he had put on a pedestal, had betrayed his mother.

A faint sound from behind him pulled Rafa from his troubled thoughts. He took a long sip of whisky before he slowly turned around. He was in control, right?

Wrong! He swept his gaze over Ivy and his body tensed as desire ripped through him. Why had he thought she would choose an elegant and demure gown? Some hope!

She was wearing the ubiquitous little black dress, with emphasis on *little.* The sequin-covered dress moulded her slim figure and drew attention to her tiny waist and the gentle curve of her hips, while the low-cut neckline pushed her small breasts high. The creamy mounds would fit into his palms perfectly, and Rafa ached to explore the sweet valley of her cleavage with his lips. *Dio,* how he ached.

He forced his gaze away from temptation and felt a flicker of surprise when Ivy moved into the pool of light cast by the balcony lamps and he saw that her hair was no longer bright pink but a subtle shade of pale blonde. 'Why did you change your hair?'

'This is my natural colour.' She self-consciously ran her fingers through the feathery blonde layers. 'The stylist at the salon stripped out the pink dye.'

Rafa did not know if it was her blonde hair or the fact that Ivy was wearing make-up, making her eyes seem even bigger and her lips even more lush, with a coating of scarlet gloss, that was responsible for turning her into a sex-bomb. All he knew was that he wanted to forget the damned party, sweep her up into his arms and carry her to the nearest flat surface so that he could slake his hunger for her in the most basic way that a man and a woman could communicate. Ivy made him feel like a teenager on a first date, and he resented that she was tying him in knots.

Perhaps she was unnerved by his brooding silence or by the prickling tension that was almost tangible. 'The personal stylist suggested I should wear a full-length gown to the party. But I didn't feel comfortable in a long dress, so I decided on…um…a short one.'

'So I see,' he said drily. The hem of the sparkly dress stopped above her mid-thighs, revealing her slender legs in sheer black stockings and sexy, strappy, high-heeled shoes. He would like to have had her long legs wrapped around his hips. Rafa's jaw tensed as he tried to dismiss the erotic images that had stormed uninvited into his head. 'The dress is fine,' he said brusquely. 'You look charming.'

He immediately regretted his offhand compliment when Ivy's face fell. There was a curious naivety about her, and she was ridiculously easy to read. He realised that she had wanted his approval, and perhaps his admiration, but he'd been so intent on hiding his reaction to how amazing she looked that he had hurt her feelings. Why that should bother him, Rafa had no idea. He wanted to believe that she had her own agenda for bringing her sister's baby to him. She'd said that she wanted him to set up a trust fund for Bertie that she would control. It was impossible that she was as innocent and unworldly as she seemed.

Ivy returned to the lounge and Rafa followed her inside. He put his hand on her arm and led her over to the table, where there was a leather case. 'I arranged for a jewellery company to deliver a selection of engagement rings so that you can choose one,' he explained as he unlocked the case to reveal its dazzling contents.

'Is it really necessary for me to wear a ring?'

'Of course. Our engagement needs to be convincing. It will be best if you choose the flashiest, most noticeable ring so that no one is in any doubt of my devotion to you.' Rafa realised how cynical he had sounded when Ivy's brown eyes widened.

'It's incredible how realistic imitation jewellery looks,' she said as she picked up a huge sapphire surrounded by diamonds.

'They are not imitation. The gemstones are real.' Rafa caught the sapphire ring when Ivy dropped it as if it had burned her. He captured her hand and felt a tremor run through her as he slid the ring onto her finger.

'It must be worth a fortune.' She sounded horrified. 'What if I lose the ring? It would take me a million years to pay for it.'

'The size of the band can be altered.' The ring was much too big on Ivy's finger and the large stone did not suit her small hand. 'Try a different one.' Rafa wondered if her reluctance to choose a ring was an act intended to convince him that she wasn't a gold-digger. 'I hope you will look happier when we are at the party. You are supposed to be madly in love with me.'

'That will never happen,' she told him seriously.

Rafa decided it was good that Ivy was not spinning any romantic dreams their fake engagement might become real. In fact, she seemed to dislike him, and he felt oddly hurt. He was not a monster, but she had accused him of fathering her sister's baby, and he was determined to discover the truth.

He looked down at the precious gems glittering against the black velvet cushion. He'd asked the jeweller to send a mix of contemporary and traditional designs, and the rings were set with stunning emeralds, exquisite sapphires and blood-red rubies, but none of them suited Ivy.

'What about this one?' He hadn't planned to get involved. A ring was only to make their engagement realistic. But a square, yellow diamond with two smaller white diamonds on either side of the centre stone caught his attention. The yellow diamond emitted sparks of fire when it caught the light, reminding him of the golden flecks in Ivy's eyes.

Rafa took her hand and slid the ring onto her finger. As he'd guessed, the delicate design was perfect for her.

'It's not flashy, but it is very beautiful.' Ivy smiled as she studied the ring.

For some unfathomable reason, Rafa felt reluctant to release her fingers from his grasp. He turned her hand over and saw that she had a small tattoo of an orange butterfly on the inside of her wrist. 'Why a butterfly?'

'My sister loved butterflies. She believed they are a sign of hope.' Ivy gave a soft sigh. 'After she died, I often saw an orange butterfly on the bush outside our flat and I felt it was a sign that Gemma would always be nearby.' Her voice faltered. 'You probably think I'm silly.'

'You must have loved your sister very much to have taken on her baby without any help from the rest of your family.'

Just when he'd thought he had worked Ivy out, she confounded him again. He was taken aback by the selflessness that was in stark contrast to Tiffany's self-serving behaviour throughout their marriage.

'Gem was the best sister anyone could have. She took care of me when my mum was too wrapped up in her own life. Gemma's mother died when she was very young, and our father wasn't the best parent, to be honest. Gemma was drawn to older men. I think she'd wished she could meet someone who would look after her.' Ivy bit her lip. 'If she did meet your father on the cruise ship, I'm sure Gemma would not have known that he was married.'

'I find it hard to believe that my father betrayed my mother and perhaps was not honest with your sister,' Rafa admitted. He had admired his father more than anyone in the world but, as had happened with Tiffany, his faith and trust had been shattered by the realisation that Bertie must be his father's child. There was no other logical explanation.

There would be long-term consequences, he brooded. Ivy was the baby's legal guardian, but it was only fair for him to become involved in his half-brother's upbringing. He intended to end his fake engagement to Ivy once the media lost interest in the baby scandal, but Bertie would be a permanent link between them. Rafa was not sure how he felt about that. He had started by despising Ivy, but he could not deny that he desired her and, now he knew a little more about her, he found he admired her devotion to her sister's baby.

He called the courier to collect the case of rings and arranged for the jeweller to resize the yellow diamond ring to fit Ivy's slim finger and return it later that evening. The maid brought in a tray with a bottle of champagne and two flutes. 'Would you like some champagne?' Rafa asked Ivy when they were alone again.

'Just fruit juice, please. I never drink alcohol.'

'It's as well I found that out before our engagement party. We had better run through a few facts about each other and concoct a story of where we met and fell in love,' he said drily. 'People are bound to ask. Whereabouts in England are you from?'

'Southampton, on the south coast.'

'I am aware of where it is, but I have not been there. I know London fairly well and have visited many of the best clubs in Mayfair. We could pretend that we were introduced at a club.'

Ivy's laughter was sweetly melodious. It was the first time Rafa had heard her laugh and it could easily be addictive. 'I've been to London a few times, but never to the upmarket nightspots where billionaires hang out. The chances that we could have met in a swanky club are zero. Besides, for it to be believable that Bertie is our child, we will need to pretend that we were together thirteen months ago. I was working as a dancer aboard the *Ocean Princess* on a cruise from Bali to Singapore.'

'It so happens that I was in Singapore around the same time. From my hotel balcony, I could see the ships that were docked in the cruise terminal.'

'Did you stay at the Excelsior Hotel?' When Rafa nodded, Ivy said, 'I remember it was a friend's birthday and we went ashore and had afternoon tea at the Excelsior. Do you realise that we could have actually met in Singapore? I believe in fate. Do you?'

'I believe in coincidence. I also believe in meeting problems head on and taking decisive action to deal with them, which is what we are about to do now.' Rafa picked up Ivy's pashmina from the chair and handed it to her. 'Well, that makes a perfectly plausible back story, then. Now, it's show time, *mia cara fidanzata.*'

The hotel's grand ballroom thronged with guests, all of whom Ivy had never met before. 'How do you know these people?' she asked Rafa. 'You must be very popular with your friends for so many of them to have come to a party that was arranged at short notice.'

He lifted his brows in that way of his that made her feel she did not belong in his rarefied world of the super-rich. 'Some of the guests are my friends, but most are business associates. Deals that are signed off in the boardroom are often the result of networking and bargaining over the buffet table at social events. Besides, everyone is curious to see my future wife, who they have been led to believe by the media is the mother of my son,' he said sardonically.

Rafa's hint that he still believed Ivy had been responsible for the news story was hurtful, but it also stirred her temper, so that she forgot her nervousness when he introduced her to a blur of people whose names and faces she doubted she would remember. Many of the guests spoke English, but they were too polite to be openly curious about her, and Rafa smoothly answered any questions about their relationship without actually revealing very much.

Ivy was intensely aware of his presence by her side and the weight of his arm around her waist burned through her dress. She reminded herself that his charm offensive and the attention he was paying her were part of the show they were putting on of a couple who were madly in love.

He had said they would have to continue the pretence of their engagement for a couple of months. It suddenly seemed a terrifyingly long time until she would be free to return to her old life. A life that had changed beyond recognition when she'd become a single parent to her sister's baby.

Rafa had an unsettling effect on her. She was nearly twenty-five and still a virgin, for heaven's sake. It had never bothered Ivy before. But now she had a sense that the life she had nearly lost when she'd been a teenager and had fought so hard for was passing her by. She'd never wanted sex for the sake of it, but she had decided long ago that she did not want to get married. She was not going to chase the impossible dream of happy ever after, which was what her mum had spent her life doing. But it meant that she was in a curious limbo and, to further complicate things, her response to Rafa's kisses had revealed her sensuality that she longed to explore with him.

Rafa was chatting to an elderly man called Carlo, who apparently owned a bank. Ivy glanced around the ballroom at the well-heeled guests sipping champagne and nibbling on exquisite canapés served by white-jacketed waiters. It felt a million miles away from her rented flat in Southampton that was damp in the winter and cost a fortune to heat.

At least she wouldn't have to worry about finding a new place to live while she and Bertie were in Italy. If the extended paternity test proved that Bertie was indeed Rafa's father's child, Ivy was determined to seek financial support for the baby. She was realistic enough to know that, however much she loved her half-nephew, she couldn't give him the privileges of wealth such as a private education and a comfortable home that, as a member of the affluent Vieri family, should be Bertie's birth right.

She hoped Bertie would be happy with the nanny. She had liked Anna immediately, and felt reassured by how warm and caring she'd been with Bertie. Anna had been given a private suite of rooms next to the penthouse and had arranged for the baby's cot to be moved into her bedroom for the night. It was the first time since Gemma had died that Ivy had spent more than an hour apart from Bertie, and she felt guilty that she hadn't rocked him to sleep, but Anna had sent her a couple of texts to reassure her that he had settled happily.

She came out of her thoughts when she realised that Rafa's companion was looking at her. 'I almost did not recognise you tonight, Miss Bennett,' the man called Carlo told her. 'I was in the boardroom of Vieri Azioni when you arrived a few days ago and caused quite a stir.'

Ivy had not noticed him among the grey-suited businessmen who had stared at her when she'd burst into the boardroom. 'I only had eyes for Rafa,' she said truthfully, blushing when she realised how gauche she sounded.

The older man laughed and patted Rafa's arm. 'I am glad that you and your delightful fiancée were able to resolve your problems. When do you plan to marry?'

'Soon,' Rafa replied smoothly, tightening his arm around Ivy's waist when she gave a start of surprise. 'I am impatient to make Ivy my wife. But there is something I must do first.'

'What's happening?' she muttered as he steered her away from Carlo and moved towards the dais at one end of the room. As they mounted the steps, the band stopped playing and the bright overhead lights came on. Ivy was a professional dancer, and was used to being on a stage in front of an audience, but when she saw the mass of curious faces staring at her she wished she could disappear.

Rafa kept her clamped to his side while he spoke to the guests. 'Recently there have been false reports and rumours in the media regarding my relationship with Ivy. Tonight, I want to put the record straight.'

To Ivy's astonishment, he dropped down onto one knee in front of her and withdrew a small velvet box from his jacket pocket. When he opened it, the yellow diamond ring sparkled with fiery brilliance.

'Ivy Bennett, will you do me the greatest honour by agreeing to be my wife?'

She stared into eyes that gleamed like molten silver, and for a few seconds she imagined that his proposal was real and he was the fairy-tale prince she had dreamed of as a little girl. She had outgrown fairy tales long ago, Ivy reminded herself firmly. But she was seduced by the wicked smile that played on Rafa's lips.

Her common sense told her to run as far and as fast as she could from this man, who had 'heart breaker' written all over his arrogantly handsome face, but common sense had never seemed so unappealing. Besides, it was only make-believe, so why not play along? A fake proposal was the only kind she would ever accept.

CHAPTER SIX

'YES.' IVY'S VOICE was huskier than she'd intended, and her hand trembled when Rafa slid the ring onto her finger. The yellow diamond made her think of golden sunshine and a warm feeling curled around her heart. He kept hold of her hand as he led her off the dais and onto the dance floor.

As the band started to play, he drew her into his arms, and they danced a slow dance while the guests looked on. At first she felt self-conscious, but the lights dimmed, and the music—an instrumental version of a popular romantic ballad—was evocative.

The spicy scent of Rafa's aftershave ignited the flame of desire low in her pelvis. Through the fine white silk of his shirt, she could make out the dark shadow of his chest hairs. She remembered those moments in the kitchen when he had been bare-chested and she'd run her hands over his naked torso.

Rafa lowered his head towards her and murmured in her ear, 'For our engagement to appear authentic, I am going to have to kiss you.'

'I hope you won't find it too much of an ordeal,' she said stiffly, stung by how indifferent he sounded.

His chest shook with silent laughter. 'I assure you it will not be an ordeal, *cara mia*. I am simply warning you in advance of what I am about to do because our romance would not be believable if you stormed off the dance floor.'

Ivy stared at him and registered his sexy smile, which made him even more attractive. 'I didn't storm off the first two times you kissed me.'

'No, you didn't, did you?' His smile disappeared and he gazed intently at her mouth.

The ballroom, the party guests and the music faded and there was only Rafa. He pulled her closer to him and dipped her backwards over his arm. Ivy's lips parted beneath his and she gave a little sigh of pleasure when he claimed her mouth with a possessiveness that should not have thrilled her as much as it did.

He was skilled at the art of seduction, and she did not stand a chance of resisting him when her traitorous body succumbed to his potency. This was where she wanted to be, in Rafa's strong arms, and she gave herself up to the intoxication of his kiss. He created magic with his lips and with his wickedly inventive tongue as he explored the moist interior of her mouth. Ivy curled her fingers into his shoulders and kissed him back with increasing urgency, guided by feminine instinct and an untapped sensuality she had not known she possessed.

The sound of applause was an unwelcome intrusion. Rafa lifted his mouth from hers and Ivy wished that a hole would appear in the ground and swallow her up when she realised the exhibition they had made in front of the guests. That had been the point, of course, she reminded herself when she darted a look at Rafa.

'We need to get out of here now,' he said curtly. They were still going through the motions of dancing together while all around them the party guests were filling the dance floor.

'What's up?' Ivy demanded. Rafa looked furious but she did not understand what she had or had not done. Hadn't he wanted her to put on a convincing act that she was bowled over by him? She ignored the voice in her head that taunted her she hadn't been acting.

'This is what is *up*,' he ground out, jerking her close so that her pelvis was flush to his. She gasped when she felt the unmistakeable hardness of his arousal. There had been self-derision in his voice and something else that sent a shiver of excitement through Ivy.

'I don't understand what you are doing to me.' He sounded as furious as he looked. 'Three days ago I'd never even heard of you, and now you are all I can think about.'

'It's the same for me,' Ivy admitted. 'I came to Italy thinking I would hate you, but I don't know how I feel.'

'Let's get out of here.' Rafa kept an arm around her waist as he strode purposefully across the ballroom.

'We can't leave in the middle of what is supposed to be our engagement party. What will the guests think?' She stumbled in her high heels as she struggled to keep up with him and felt the muscles in his arm flex as he supported her.

'People will think that we can't wait to get our hands on each other, and they would be right.' He grinned at her stunned expression, but behind his smile there was an intentness in him, and the hard glitter in his eyes caused Ivy's heart to miss a beat.

They had reached the private lift that went directly up to the penthouse. As soon as the doors closed, Rafa pulled her into his arms and claimed her mouth with barely concealed impatience. He was heat and flame and she was burning up. He pushed her up against the wall of the lift and held her there with his hip while he plundered her lips, making demands that she found impossible to deny him when it would mean denying herself the heady pleasure of his kiss.

Ivy was barely aware of the lift doors opening and gave a low moan of protest when Rafa took his mouth from hers. He caught hold of her hand and led her into the penthouse. Crossing the open-plan living area, he continued down the hallway to his bedroom.

She had looked into his room once before when she'd explored the apartment. The décor, like the rest of the penthouse, was sleek and sophisticated with dark walls and gold accents. An enormous bed dominated the room and was draped with a velvet throw in rich burgundy. The room had been designed for seduction, and a voice of caution inside Ivy's head questioned how her relationship with Rafa had moved so fast that they had got as far as his bedroom.

She watched him shrug off his jacket and throw it onto a chair. He stood in front of her, and she wondered if he could see the pulse that was thudding erratically at the base of her throat, echoing the frantic thud of her heart.

'You are so beautiful, you take my breath away.' His voice was as soft as smoke, and his Italian accent was so sexy that she shivered.

'There is no need for you to give me false compliments now we are not in public,' she mumbled, remembering how he had looked unimpressed by her before the party.

'I should have told you how stunning you look. The truth is, I wanted to keep you to myself instead of attending the party. Don't you believe me?' Rafa must have sensed that Ivy doubted him. He put his hands lightly on her shoulders and turned her to face the mirror. 'Feel how much you turn me on,' he murmured as he pulled her against him so that her back rested on his chest. She caught her breath when she felt the hard ridge of his arousal nudge her bottom.

Ivy stared at their twin images in the mirror and hardly recognised herself. She had been so busy caring for Bertie for the past three months that she'd only ever worn jeans and baggy sweatshirts. Her party dress was more revealing than anything she'd worn before, and subconsciously she had chosen it because she had wanted to make Rafa notice her. She'd been disappointed by his lukewarm reaction before the party, but now his burning gaze sent a lick of fire through her veins.

She wasn't aware of him undoing her zip until he tugged the top of her dress down to expose her breasts. The air felt cool on her heated skin, and her nipples sprang to attention.

His breath hissed between his teeth. 'I had a bet with myself that you were not wearing a bra.'

'My shoulder hurts when I reach behind my back to do my bra up. Anyway, I don't need to wear one, because I haven't got much up top,' she said ruefully.

'Your breasts are perfect.' Rafa was still standing behind her and nuzzled his lips against her neck while he cupped her small breasts in his hands. His darkly tanned fingers made an erotic contrast to her pale breasts as he rubbed his thumb pads across her nipples, sending a sharp tug of pleasure down to Ivy's molten core.

'Every part of you is perfect,' he said thickly, tugging the clingy dress over her hips so that it fell to the floor. Rafa muttered something in Italian as he slid his hands down to the bare skin of her thighs above the lacy bands of her stocking tops.

Ivy trembled as he explored her inner thighs and discovered the damp panel of her silk panties. She had never gone this far with a man before. She'd never wanted to. But Rafa was a magician, and his touch cast a spell on her so that, when he slipped his fingers into her knickers and lightly brushed them over her moist opening, she parted for him, and it felt natural for him to slide one finger inside her. It was new, wonderful and faintly shocking as she watched him caressing her in the mirror. She wanted more, and made a choked sound of disappointment when he took his hand away.

He laughed. 'Bed,' he said thickly, scooping her up in his arms and carrying her across the room. 'I am as impatient as you are, *mia belleza*.'

The satisfaction in his voice pushed through the sexual haze surrounding Ivy's brain and sent a ripple of unease through her. Rafa pulled back the bed cover and laid her down on the black satin sheets. His fingers circled her ankles as he unfastened the straps on her shoes and slid them off.

She watched him tug open the buttons on his shirt and shrug it off his shoulders. In the subtle light from the bedside lamps, he was a work of art, bronzed and beautiful, with his tight abs and the arrow of dark hairs over his flat stomach. Ivy wanted to stay in the moment, to lose herself once more in his smouldering sensuality, but it was too much, too soon, and Rafa was too *everything.* He put his hands on his belt buckle and reality hit her like a ton of bricks.

She levered herself so that she was sitting upright. 'Rafa… I'm not…' Before she could say *sure about this* he interrupted.

'Don't worry if you are not using contraceptives. I am always prepared.' He pulled open the bedside drawer and took out a handful of condoms.

Of course he was prepared for sex. Ivy's heart dipped as he dropped the foil packets onto the bed. She imagined all the women he must have brought to the penthouse and made love to in his huge bed.

'That's not what I meant.'

She forgot what she had been about to say when he knelt on the mattress and bent his head to her breast to take her nipple into his mouth. The pleasure of him sucking on the tender peak was so intense that she was tempted to succumb to the throb of desire and allow him to appease the ache between her legs.

But what would Rafa think of her, and more importantly what would she think of herself? She wasn't a prude, and had not expected to be in love with a guy when she had sex for the first time, but she'd hoped she would be in a relationship where there was friendship and respect. Her fake engagement to Rafa would end in a couple of months. He wanted to have sex with her because she was convenient.

'You are so responsive. I want to be inside you, now.' Rafa stood up and quickly dispensed with his trousers. The sight of his powerfully masculine body in a pair of boxers that did not hide the bulge of his erection filled Ivy with panic. She tensed when he lay down on the bed beside her and drew her into his arms.

'Do you trust me?'

'What?' He pushed his hair off his brow and his eyes narrowed on her tense face. *'Cara.'* His voice was strained, his frustration evident in his clenched jaw. 'That's not important right now.'

'Of course it's important. I don't want my first time of making love to be with a man who doesn't trust me. And I don't think you do.'

'Your first time? *Seriously?*' He blew out his breath when she nodded. Rafa rolled away from her, breathing heavily. 'It would have been a good idea to mention your virginity before now.'

'I told you that I'd never had a lover. It's not my fault if you didn't believe me.' Ivy felt vulnerable and confused. Her body still ached for Rafa's caresses, but she knew she was right to be wary, and tears filled her eyes.

'Why are you crying?' he asked curtly. 'I would never try to force you to make love if that is what is worrying you. I respect your decision.'

Ivy had not doubted that he was honourable, and his shuttered expression made her feel worse. 'I can't help it. I cry when I'm upset, and I wear my heart on my sleeve.' She couldn't bear Rafa to see how he had broken through her defences, and she gave a muffled sob as she scrambled off the bed and flew towards the door.

'Ivy, wait.'

Ivy hesitated and turned her head to look at Rafa. His gut twisted when he saw tears running down Ivy's face, and he knew he was to blame. The boy he had once been had blamed himself when his mother had cried and he had not known how to console her. Deep down, he'd believed that his mother had not loved him, and he was a disappointment to her. Why else would she have been desperate to have another child?

His ex-wife had not loved him. Tiffany had fooled him into believing he had a daughter and that they were a happy family until her lies had been exposed. In his darkest hours, Rafa wondered if he was flawed in some way that meant he was unlovable.

Why was he thinking about love of all things? He desired Ivy and had wanted to have sex with her. He had not intended to upset her. She'd responded to him with a fiery passion that had made his body ache, and he'd been sure she'd wanted him to make love to her. Her revelation that she was as innocent as she sometimes seemed blew his mind. He couldn't blame her for rejecting him. When she chose her first lover, he hoped she would choose a better man than him.

Rafa stood up and pulled his trousers on before he picked up his shirt. He walked over to Ivy and slipped the shirt around her shoulders. 'Here, wear this.'

Black tracks of mascara were running down her face. She looked a heartbreakingly beautiful mess, and he felt guilty that he had made her cry. 'Stay and talk to me. Please,' he said gruffly.

She scrubbed her hand over her eyes. 'You don't want to talk.'

'Yes, I do.' He realised it was true. Admittedly, it was not how he had envisaged the night would unfold. When they had escaped from the party, he had been so turned on by her that he'd almost made love to her in the lift.

To his relief, Ivy did not resist when he took her hand and led her over to the sofa. 'You are a gorgeous, sexy, independent woman, so how come you are still a virgin?'

She sat down and tucked her feet under her. His shirt swamped her tiny frame, and he was struck anew by her fragile beauty. She waited until he joined her on the sofa and said in a low voice, 'I had cancer when I was a teenager and for a while it was touch and go if I would survive.'

Whatever Rafa might have expected her to say, it hadn't been that. He felt a cold sensation on the back of his neck. Ivy was so full of life, and it was shocking to hear that she had come close to death.

'It was a type of blood cancer. To begin with my symptoms were vague. I felt lethargic and bruised easily, but I didn't think anything was seriously wrong. I'd left home at seventeen because I hated my new stepfather. Gemma had been working for a cruise company based in Turkey and I went to stay with her.'

Ivy smiled. 'It was a perfect summer. I got a job as a waitress in a café, and I met my first boyfriend. Luke was also English. He was a couple of years older than me and a builder on a new hotel development. Every day after work we used to hang out at the beach. He was my first love, and I thought he loved me and we would be together for ever. But then I became ill.'

'What happened?' Rafa prompted when she fell silent.

'By the time I was diagnosed with a form of leukaemia, I was really sick, and I was given huge doses of chemotherapy, which made my hair fall out. I'd had waist-length, dark blonde hair and I was distraught to lose it, especially when Luke decided that he couldn't cope with the way I looked.'

'He sounds like a jerk,' Rafa muttered. How crazy was it that he wished he could track down Ivy's heartless boyfriend and rearrange the guy's face?

She shrugged. 'I was as bald as an egg, and even my eyelashes fell out. But, yeah, it wasn't the best time to suffer a broken heart. I should have expected it, really. My mum had always been let down by the men she'd fallen in love with, including my dad. I was worried that I'd inherited her poor judgement with Luke.'

After a moment, she continued. 'My sister and I moved back to England so that I could complete my treatment. Gem was amazing,' Ivy said softly. 'She looked after me and kept me upbeat when I had bad days. For the next few years, I put all my energy into getting better, and I wasn't interested in dating. I trained as a dancer and performed at holiday camps. Gemma was working on a cruise ship and when a position as a show dancer became available I successfully auditioned for it. I loved travelling, but the lifestyle is not good for relationships.'

Ivy sighed. 'The truth is, I'm wary of being hurt

again. I've dated a few guys, but I never know whether to blurt out straight away that I am very likely to be infertile from the chemotherapy. The doctors who treated me in Turkey were brilliant, but because I was so ill there was no time to discuss the possibility of freezing my eggs so that I might have a chance of a family in the future. If I mention children on a first or second date with a guy, it makes me look like I'm hoping for a long-term relationship.'

'Are you holding on to your virginity until you marry?'

She gave him a startled look. 'No. I never want to get married. My parents' disastrous attempts at marriage put me off,' she said wryly. Soft colour stained her cheeks. 'I didn't deliberately lead you on tonight. I don't know why I respond to you the way I do when you kiss me. You make me feel things I've never felt before.'

Rafa gave her a wry look. 'It's called sexual chemistry, *cara*, and I agree that it is inconvenient.'

It was more than that, he brooded. The developments of the past few days were potentially damaging to his position at Vieri Azioni, and more importantly to his mother's emotional state if, as he suspected, Bertie was his father's child. He still believed that Ivy was responsible for the story that had been reported in the media, and he was determined to keep her close so that she could not cause any more harm. But he did not get involved with virgins who had Bambi eyes and a tendency to cry easily. He was going to have to ignore his desire for Ivy. Surely he would not find it too difficult to think with his brain instead of being ruled by his libido? Rafa mocked himself.

He turned to her and saw that her head was resting on the cushions and that she was half asleep. 'I'll take you to your bedroom,' he murmured as he lifted her into his arms.

'I can walk.' But she did not insist that he set her on her feet when he carried her down the hall and into her room. She weighed next to nothing. Once again, he felt an odd pang at the idea that she'd battled a life-threatening illness.

'Are you fully recovered now?'

'I've been cancer-free for more than five years. But none of us can know what the future holds. I certainly never imagined that Gemma would go out to buy nappies and never come back.' Ivy's brown eyes shimmered with tears. 'The reason I wanted to find Bertie's father was in case anything happens to me and I can't look after him.'

Rafa frowned. 'Nothing is going to happen to you.' Her vulnerability tugged on his insides. 'We have to wait for the result of the paternity test before anything can be decided about Bertie's future.' He pulled back the bed covers and lowered her onto the mattress. '*Buona notte*, Ivy.'

'Rafa.' Her sleepy voice made him halt on his way out of the door. 'If I had been more experienced, I would have had sex with you.'

He swore softly. 'You are going to kill me, *cara*.'

Ivy pulled the duvet over her head and prayed that her memories of the previous night were a bad dream. Had she really told Rafa that if she hadn't been a virgin she would have slept with him? Images flooded her mind of how she had been practically naked in his arms, and how she'd kissed him so enthusiastically that it was little wonder he had assumed they would become lovers.

She couldn't even blame her mislaid inhibitions on being drunk. Having beaten cancer, she felt that she'd been given a second chance at life, and she tried to eat healthily and never drank alcohol. It was even more important that she looked after herself now she was responsible for her sister's baby.

Bertie! She jerked upright and saw on the bedside clock that it was past nine o'clock. She had missed Bertie's seven a.m. feed. The nanny would have given him his milk, but that wasn't the point. Guilt churned in Ivy's stomach as she leapt out of bed and hurried into the *en suite* bathroom. She resembled a panda, with her make-up smudged beneath her eyes, and she quickly scrubbed her face clean. She'd slept in Rafa's shirt, but when she heard the baby's cries she did not waste time getting changed.

The nanny was in the living room talking to Rafa while she pushed the baby in the carry cot, evidently hoping that the motion would send Bertie to sleep. But his yells reached a crescendo. Ivy's heart contracted when she lifted him into her arms and he buried his face in her neck.

'It's all right Bobo, I'm here,' she crooned. Gradually his cries turned to little snuffles and she kissed his flushed cheeks.

'I feel terrible for sleeping in so late,' she told the nanny.

'Bertie was fine until a few minutes ago,' Anna reassured her. 'Signor Vieri explained that you were tired after all the excitement of last night.'

Ivy's startled gaze flew across the room and met Rafa's sardonic expression. 'I told Anna that we became officially engaged at the party,' he said drily.

'May I see your ring? It's beautiful,' the nanny murmured when Ivy held out her left hand. 'Congratulations. I hope you will both be very happy.'

Bertie had fallen asleep. He'd probably worn himself out with crying, Ivy thought guiltily as she placed him in the carry cot. 'Shall I take him to the nursery?' Anna offered. She looked over at Rafa. 'I'll go and pack.'

'Why is Anna leaving?' Ivy asked when she and Rafa were alone. Although she had argued against having a nanny, she had to admit that it was a relief to share her worries about caring for Bertie with Anna, who was experienced in childcare and a mother herself to a nineteen-year-old son.

'We need to get out of the city, and I have decided that we will spend some time at my home in Abruzzo. Anna has a few things to do first and she will join us at the castle tomorrow.'

'You own a castle?' Ivy wondered if Rafa's coldness was because she had refused to sleep with him. At their engagement party she had felt a rapport with him, but now she sensed there was a chasm a mile wide between them.

'The castle was originally built as a fortress in the Apennine mountains. The remote location means we won't be bothered there.'

'Bothered by who?'

'The media. I was contacted this morning by Luigi Capello.' Rafa's voice was even grimmer than his forbidding expression. 'The journalist from the newspaper *Di Oggie*—as I'm sure you know,' he said when

Ivy looked blank. 'Capello mentioned Gemma. He said he wanted to clarify who exactly is Bertie's mother.'

'I'd forgotten the journalist's name.' She bit her lip. 'How and what does he know about my sister?'

'You tell me.' Rafa's eyes gleamed like tensile steel. 'You must have spoken to Capello. Only you and I know that Gemma was Bertie's mother, and I sure as hell haven't spoken to the press.'

'Neither have I.' Tears pricked her eyes when Rafa sent her a scathing look. 'I swear I threw the journalist's business card in the bin. Oh, it's hopeless for us to pretend to be engaged when you refuse to believe me!' she snapped, her temper bubbling to the surface. 'I only agreed to your crazy plan because I feel sorry for your mother. We will have to call off our fake engagement.'

She tugged the yellow diamond ring, but the re-sized band was a snug fit on her finger, and she struggled to pull the ring over her knuckle.

'Leave it on,' Rafa commanded. He strode over to her and captured her chin between his fingers, tilting her face up to his. 'My mother is in hospital with a lung infection. The doctor has reported that her condition is stable, but every time something like this happens it leaves her weaker,' he said gruffly. 'She wants to meet you—and her grandson.'

Ivy stared at him. 'How can we introduce Bertie to your mother when he might be the result of your father's infidelity? It feels wrong to lie to her.'

Rafa's jaw clenched. 'I agree, but the likely truth will break her heart. We must continue with the pretence that we are engaged, at least until we have the result of the paternity test. I've arranged for us to pay her a brief visit at the hospital before we drive to the mountains. We'll leave in an hour.'

He skimmed his gaze over his shirt that came to Ivy's mid-thighs, and she felt her breasts tauten when his eyes narrowed to glittering slits.

'You had better go and get dressed.' His voice had thickened and sent a shiver of response through her. Without her high heels that she'd worn to the party, Rafa towered over her, and her bare feet seemed to be welded to the floor.

'Damn you, Ivy,' he said harshly. 'My instincts warn me that I can't trust you, yet I still want to do this.'

Ivy watched as he lowered his face and angled his mouth over hers. The sensible part of her said she should move away from him, but she did not listen, and parted her lips beneath his. The kiss was slow and sensual, an unhurried tasting of her lips as Rafa coaxed a response from her that she was willing to give. He was impossible to resist, and he tempted her like no other man ever had. She tried to remember all the reasons why kissing him was a bad idea, but her body did not care if it was right or wrong, and the drumbeat of desire in her veins thudded in a powerful rhythm.

When Rafa finally broke the kiss, they were both breathing hard. 'Go,' he growled, 'Before I am tempted to take this further and do something that one of us regrets.'

The dangerous glint in his eyes made Ivy's heart miss a beat. She was no longer sure she would regret taking her relationship with Rafa to the next level. But perhaps he was less keen to make love to her now that he knew how inexperienced she was. Sleeping with him would only make the situation even more complicated.

CHAPTER SEVEN

RAFA'S MOTHER LOOKED fragile lying in the hospital bed with her hair a silver cloud on the pillows. Her breathing was laboured, and every few minutes she pulled an oxygen mask over her face to help her breathe.

'Is there anything I can do for you, *Mamma*?' Rafa asked in a gentle voice that Ivy had never heard him use before. His affection and concern for his mother was obvious. He leaned forward on his chair next to the bed and stretched out his hand to clasp her fingers.

Fabiana opened her eyes. 'You cannot help me, Rafa. I am not sad that I am dying, for I will go to my dearest Rafael, and my children who I did not meet in this life, but I know are waiting for me in the next.'

Ivy noticed a curious expression flicker on Rafa's face, almost as if he was hurt by his mother's words. When they had driven to the hospital he had explained that his mother had suffered with depression for much of her life, a result of losing several babies during her pregnancies. They must have been the children she had referred to, Ivy supposed. Rafa was a devoted son, but his mother seemed to think more of the children she had lost than her son who was so caring about her.

Rafa glanced at Ivy. 'I think my mother is tired and we should let her rest. Also, Bertie needs his nappy changed.'

Ivy nodded. She had felt awkward, pretending to be engaged to Rafa in front of his mother. Even worse had been having to lie and introduce Bertie as their son. But Rafa was determined to protect his mother from finding out that her husband was possibly Bertie's father. Earlier, Fabiana had admired the baby, but she'd been too weak to hold him.

'The child looks like you,' she had told Rafa. 'You should have called him Rafael. It is a family tradition to give the firstborn son his father's name.'

'Two Rafaels were confusing enough,' Rafa had muttered.

Ivy moved towards the door of the private room and paused when Fabiana spoke. 'Rafa, I would like to talk to your fiancée for a little longer. I'm sure you can change the baby's nappy.'

Ivy looked doubtful as she handed Rafa the baby's bag. 'Can you manage a nappy change?'

'Of course he can,' his mother said. 'My son has had plenty of practice at caring for a baby.'

While Ivy was trying to digest that surprising statement, Rafa carried Bertie out of the room. She gave his mother a faint smile, wondering what Fabiana wanted to talk to her about.

'So, you are going to marry my son. It is strange that he had never mentioned you until the newspaper reported that you are the mother of his child. Where did you and Rafa meet?'

'Um… Singapore.' Ivy tried to remember the story

they had concocted. 'Rafa was there on business at the same time that the cruise ship I worked on had docked. We bumped into each other in a hotel near the marina.' She blushed, sure that she sounded unconvincing, and wishing she had not mentioned a cruise ship. She hated lying, but she simply could not tell Rafa's mother the truth about their relationship.

Fabiana was watching her closely. 'The baby is four months old, I believe. Did you have an easy pregnancy?'

'Um, it was normal. I had some morning sickness.' Ivy was floundering. She had been working on a cruise ship for the first few months of her sister's pregnancy, but she remembered Gemma had said that she had been sick a few times.

'Tell me about your family in England.'

'My mum and dad divorced when I was a child, and both went on to have new partners. I'm not close to either of my parents,' Ivy admitted. She felt sad that there was no one in her family she could turn to for support. 'My sister…' She swallowed. 'My sister died in an accident three months ago.'

'Life can be very cruel. You were close to her?'

'Yes.'

Fabiana was silent for a moment. 'Do you love my son?'

'Er…yes, of course.' Ivy fiddled with the yellow diamond ring that Rafa had insisted she should wear to make their engagement appear real.

'Why do you love Rafa?' Fabiana persisted.

Ivy tried to think if Rafa had any loveable traits. He was arrogant, forceful and he liked his own way. But he cared about his mother, and he cared about the company he had inherited from his father. So much so that he'd given up his successful career as a professional basketball player and abandoned his ambition of training as a sports physiotherapist to take charge of Vieri Azioni. He had also promised her that, if the DNA test proved Bertie was his half-brother, he would share responsibility for the little boy's upbringing.

'Rafa is loyal and protective, and honourable.' It was a strangely old-fashioned term, but instinctively Ivy believed it was true. Even though their first meetings had been explosive, when Rafa had angrily accused her of speaking to the press, she realised that she trusted him.

'He is a good son.' Fabiana sighed. 'I know that Rafa misses Rafael as much as I do. He was close to his father and there were no secrets between them.'

Oh, Lord! Ivy could not meet the other woman's gaze.

'The one thing Rafa will not tolerate is deceit. His insistence on honesty is not surprising after his ex-wife deceived him. I suppose he has told you why his first marriage ended? He tried to keep the story out of the media to protect Lola because he still loved her.

'I never thought I would see my son with a broken heart,' Fabiana said. 'Since his divorce, I sense that Rafa has built a wall around his emotions.' She gave Ivy a shrewd look. 'Perhaps he will fall in love with you, as you hope he will.'

Rafa returned with Bertie then, and Ivy was spared trying to think of a response to his mother's astonishing statement while she strapped the baby into the portable car seat. Of course she did not secretly hope that

Rafa would develop feelings for her, and she certainly wouldn't fall in love with him, she assured herself.

They stayed for a few more minutes while Rafa chatted to his mother, but it was obvious that Fabiana had found the visit tiring. 'Get some rest now, *Mamma*,' he murmured as he kissed her cheek. He carried Bertie in his car seat, and he looked sombre when they walked out of the hospital. Ivy instinctively reached out and touched his arm.

'I'm sorry your mother is ill,' she said sympathetically. 'It must be hard for you when you recently lost your father.'

He shrugged. 'You heard her. She would rather be with the ghosts of my father and the children she lost than in this world with me.'

Beneath Rafa's unemotional voice, Ivy heard something that tugged on her heart. She wondered what his childhood had been like when his mother had been grieving for her failed pregnancies and perhaps hadn't had much time for him. It would explain why he was so self-contained and enigmatic.

When they walked across the car park, the breeze lifted the hem of Ivy's silk dress and briefly revealed her thighs and the lace bands of her hold-up stockings.

'You look beautiful,' Rafa said tautly. 'That colour suits you.'

The cinnamon-coloured dress teamed with nude heels and a matching handbag was one of several outfits the personal stylist had picked out for Ivy's new wardrobe and had deemed suitable for the fiancée of one of Italy's richest men. The dress was the most elegant item of clothing Ivy had ever worn. When she'd glanced in the mirror before they'd had left the penthouse, she had been surprised at how nice she looked. Now the gleam in Rafa's eyes made her blush. It was just sexual chemistry, she reminded herself.

He put Bertie into the car and opened Ivy's door before he walked round to the driver's side and folded his tall frame behind the steering wheel. The hospital was in a suburb of Rome, and soon they had left the city and joined the *autostrada,* where the car picked up speed. Rafa had said the drive to L'Aquila, the town close to his castle, would take a little over an hour. Ivy stared out of the window at the lush green scenery. In the distance she could see the jagged peaks of the mountains.

'Are you going to give me the silent treatment for the whole journey?' he drawled. 'Or are you going to tell me what is bothering you?'

She sighed. 'Your mother said that you won't tolerate dishonesty, but you…we…are deceiving her by pretending that Bertie is our child. It feels wrong.'

'The irony isn't lost on me,' he bit out. 'It tears me apart to think that my father was not as perfect as I'd believed. He made a mistake, and the ramifications of his infidelity would be devastating to my mother. You saw how weak she is, and you heard her say how much she loved my father and how happy they were in their long marriage. How *can* I tell her the truth?'

'It's all a mess,' Ivy said dismally. 'I wish I hadn't brought Bertie to Italy. I imagine you wish that too.'

Rafa glanced at her. 'I have a gut feeling that the test will prove he is my half-brother. Bertie is an innocent baby and none of this mess, as you call it, is his fault.

You and I are all he has. For his sake we need to be a team and do our best for him.'

A team with Rafa! Ivy was startled by how much she liked the idea. Her heart warmed to know that he was prepared to help her take care of Bertie and be involved in his upbringing. She had felt so alone since Gemma had died, and sometimes she'd felt overwhelmed by the responsibility of looking after her baby nephew.

She wondered about the logistics of how she and Rafa would be parents to Bertie. Perhaps he would suggest she move to Italy so that they could share custody more easily than if she and the baby lived in England. She would be willing to relocate, but she'd have to learn to speak Italian. Maybe Rafa would teach her. Heat coiled inside Ivy as she thought of other, more intimate things that she would like him to teach her. No doubt he would be an expert tutor in the bedroom.

She turned her head towards him and her heart missed a beat when her gaze collided with his before he looked at the road again. 'What are you thinking?' he murmured.

Too much, she thought ruefully. They did not even know yet if Bertie was Rafa's half-brother. They also hadn't discussed at what point they would end their fake engagement. She looked down at the yellow diamond on her finger and gave a faint sigh. When she had been a little girl, she'd believed in fairy tales, and had hoped she would meet a handsome prince some day. But she had grown up and realised that happy ever after only happened in books and films.

Her mum had spent years chasing a romantic dream, only to have her heart broken countless times. Ivy had decided that instead of unrealistic daydreams she would settle for achievable goals. A billionaire playboy who had the looks and charisma of a sex god was definitely not achievable, she reminded herself.

Her mind turned to her conversation with Rafa's mother.

'Your mother told me about Lola,' she murmured. 'She seemed to think that you still love her.'

Rafa tightened his fingers on the steering wheel. 'It's not easy to simply switch love off,' he said gruffly.

The sharp sensation like a knife thrust between her ribs was *not* jealousy. Ivy was simply surprised to hear Rafa, the master of self-control, talk openly about love.

'You loved your wife even though Lola deceived you?'

He frowned. 'Lola wasn't my wife. I was married to her mother, Tiffany. For two years I believed that Lola was my daughter.'

Daughter! Shock ran through Ivy. 'When I asked, you told me that you didn't have a child. She stared at his chiselled profile. 'What do you mean, you believed? Are you saying that Lola *wasn't* your child?'

'I suppose you had better know the whole story,' he muttered. 'I had been dating Tiffany for a few months before we got married. When she told me she was pregnant, I had no reason to think the baby wasn't mine, and I immediately proposed.'

He frowned. 'I was under a fair amount of pressure from my father to marry and settle down. With hindsight, I can see that one reason why I married Tiffany was to please my father. I knew he had been disappointed by my decision to move to America. He made no secret that he hoped that I would bring my family to Italy and prepare to take over running Vieri Azioni, but I wasn't ready to give up my basketball career.'

A nerve flickered in Rafa's cheek. 'Cracks started to appear in the marriage early on, partly due to the amount of time I spent away from home during the professional basketball season. Lola was born six weeks early. At least, that's the excuse Tiffany gave. I missed the next match and rushed home to meet my baby girl, and I fell in love with Lola Rose.'

He fell silent and Ivy sensed it pained him to revisit his past. 'I tried to make my marriage work,' he said finally, 'But maybe I didn't try hard enough. I was unwilling to give up my basketball career,' he admitted with raw honesty. 'A month or so after Lola's second birthday, Tiffany told me she wanted a divorce. Even then I hoped the break-up could be amicable and we would share custody of our daughter.

'That was when Tiffany dropped her bombshell and told me that Lola was not my child. Her real father was a well-known film director, Brad Curran, who Tiffany had been sleeping with at the same time as with me. She had known that she was pregnant with Curran's child, but he hadn't been interested, so she'd let me think I was the baby's father. The dates didn't tie up, which was why she made out that Lola was born earlier than the due date.'

Rafa did not try to hide his bitterness at his ex-wife's betrayal and Ivy didn't know what to say that would not sound trite. She sensed he did not want her sympathy and that his pride had been hurt as well as his feelings.

'While I'd been away on tour with the basketball

team, Tiffany had met up with her old flame. Following a positive paternity test, Curran accepted that he was Lola's father and offered to marry Tiffany as soon as she'd divorced me. I had no legal right to see Lola and Tiffany decided that a clean break would be best.

'I was gutted,' Rafa said rawly. 'I stood in the empty nursery. It felt as though Lola had died, but I did not have any right to grieve for her, because she was not my child. If that wasn't bad enough, Tiffany tried to sell the story of our so-called love triangle to the tabloids. I didn't want details of my private life in the media, and more importantly I was anxious to protect Lola's privacy. I had to pay my ex-wife a fortune on top of the divorce settlement I'd given her so that she wouldn't speak to the press.'

It was little wonder Rafa was convinced that *she* had told the journalist he was Bertie's father, Ivy thought. But it hurt that he did not trust her and believed she was as deceitful as his ex-wife.

The rest of the journey passed in silence. Rafa's brooding tension did not invite further conversation, and Ivy retreated to her own thoughts. They left the *autostrada* and the narrow road twisted as it climbed higher into the mountains. The town of L'Aquila was a few miles behind them and the dense forest all around added to the sense of remoteness where even the sun did not venture. The mountain peaks were hidden by clouds and the fine drizzle had turned into a heavy downpour. The car turned a sharp bend and in front of them was an imposing, grey fortress.

'Welcome to the Castello Dei Sogni,' Rafa said, and Ivy's heart sank. The building looked like a prison. 'The name means Castle of Dreams,' he told her. 'The story goes that it was built by a man who dreamed of winning the woman he loved by building her a grand castle. But she turned him down because she loved someone else. The man had the castle's walls reinforced and he spent the rest of his life living alone in his fortress so that love could not find him and make a fool of him again.'

'What a sad story,' Ivy muttered as the car splashed through the puddles in the courtyard. 'What made you buy the castle?'

'When I was a boy, my father sometimes took me trekking in the mountains around here. The castle had been abandoned many years ago and we used to explore the grounds. After my divorce, I needed a project, and a bolthole,' he admitted.

'Everyone, including the agent who had been trying to sell the place for years, warned me that it would be a money pit. Much of the restoration work has been completed. There are about forty bedrooms, but apart from a couple of live-in staff I'm the only person who comes here. The remote location ensures that I have privacy from nosy reporters.'

Ivy climbed out of the car. At least it had stopped raining, but the castle still looked like a forbidding fortress. Rafa carried Bertie up the front steps and Ivy walked slowly behind. Hearing about Rafa's failed marriage and how his wife had betrayed his trust had given her an insight into why he had built a fortress around his emotions. Her heart thumped painfully. Was she doing the right thing by bringing Bertie to a castle that looked as grim as its owner?

Standing next to the front door was an olive tree in

a terracotta pot. A sudden movement caught Ivy's attention, and her heart fluttered when she saw an orange butterfly land on the silvery green leaves. It hovered there, opening and closing its delicate wings, before it flew up into the sky towards the patch of blue where the storm clouds had parted.

Ivy took a deep breath and a sense of peace filled her. *Goodbye, Gemma,* she said silently. The butterfly had flown away, but she was sure it was somewhere nearby. She followed Rafa into the castle and was pleasantly surprised to find that the interior was much more welcoming than her first impression of the craggy walls of the fortress. They were greeted by the butler, who led the way through a vast entrance hall and into a sitting room where a fire was blazing in the hearth.

'Arturo lights a fire if there is one grey cloud in the sky,' Rafa said drily. 'It tends to be cooler here in the mountains than in Rome.'

'I thought the rooms would be dark and gloomy, but the pale walls and colourful rugs on the floor give a homely feel to the castle.' Ivy felt happier when Rafa showed her around. All the rooms had been decorated in muted shades and the furniture was a tasteful mix of antiques and contemporary pieces. 'I love that it's quirky and unique. The castle is special to you, isn't it?' she said perceptively. She'd noticed that Rafa had relaxed the moment they had arrived.

He gave one of his rare grins that made him seem carefree, as he must have been before his ex-wife's terrible betrayal had left him bitter and mistrusting. 'Everyone said that I was mad to buy a half-ruined castle, but I like a challenge. Although, restoration of the castle is still an ongoing project.' He hesitated. 'I could show you my plans for the unfinished rooms, if you are interested.'

Ivy could not look away from Rafa's searing gaze. When she had met him for the first time—unbelievably, it was only a few days ago when she had burst into the boardroom and confronted him—his eyes had been as hard as steel. But right now his grey eyes were as soft as wood smoke. Warmth stole around her heart when she remembered how he'd said he wanted them to be a team to take care of Bertie. Her mouth curved upwards, and it felt as though it was the first time she had smiled properly since losing Gemma. 'I'd love to see your ideas.'

'Good.' Rafa's smile made Ivy's heart leap, and she could not explain the feeling she had that she had come home after a long journey.

Rafa had intended to base himself in Rome during the week and return to the castle at weekends to maintain the pretence of his engagement to Ivy. But as one week slipped into the next he found himself opting to work from his study at the castle most days and went to Vieri Azioni's headquarters only when it was absolutely necessary.

His conscience pricked that he could not ignore Bertie when there was a strong possibility that the baby was his flesh and blood. More of a concern was his fierce awareness of Ivy. He'd assumed that he would barely notice her presence in the vast castle, but he had been wrong.

She joined him for breakfast every morning, and he

could not hide behind his newspaper while she chatted to him about a book that she was currently reading, or a film they had watched together the previous evening. She was always cheerful and charming to his staff, and somehow the castle seemed a brighter place since Ivy had arrived.

For the past four days and nights, Rafa had stayed in Rome to negotiate a business deal. He was frustrated that Ivy had been on his mind a lot. Now his heart rate accelerated in anticipation of seeing her again. The helicopter dipped low over the trees and moments later the castle came into view. The building looked less fortress-like in the afternoon sunshine, although it was still an unconventional home, Rafa conceded. He did not understand why the Castello Dei Sogni was the only place that felt like *his* home. Perhaps it was because the ruined castle had needed rescuing and so had he. They had found each other.

The legend of why the castle had been built reminded him of why he would not risk his heart again. A wife, a child, a family of his own—he had thought he'd had everything until his life had come crashing down. Tiffany had made a fool of him and being separated from Lola had nearly destroyed him. He had missed being a father, but he'd decided never to have a child, reasoning that he could not miss what he did not have. It followed that, if he never fell in love, he could never be hurt.

When the helicopter landed, he gathered up his briefcase and a file of wallpaper samples he planned to show Ivy. She was enthusiastic about his plans for the refurbishment of the library, and most evenings over dinner they discussed ideas for the library and the various other rooms in the castle that were yet to be renovated. Rafa could employ an interior designer, but he was reluctant to allow a stranger to be involved in his private bolthole. The thought struck him that he did not think of Ivy as a stranger, even though he had known her for less than a month.

He strode into the castle and almost stepped in a dish of milk that had been left on the floor in the entrance hall. The dish tipped over and milk ran across the flagstones. *What the blazes?*

The butler came out of the kitchen, whistling a tune that Rafa vaguely recognised was a song from a popular stage musical. *Seriously!* Arturo could best be described as impassive, and he was certainly not prone to spontaneous whistling. He stopped mid-way through the chorus when he saw Rafa.

'*Signor*, I was not expecting you until the evening.'

'Evidently. Arturo, why is there a dish of milk in the hall?'

'It is for the cat, *signor*.'

'Cat?' Rafa decided that he must have landed in a parallel universe when he followed the butler's gaze and saw a fat ginger cat jump down from the window seat and stalk past him into the sitting room.

'Signorina Ivy rescued the cat after she found it abandoned outside the gates of the castle,' Arturo explained. 'The vet thinks that the kittens will be born in the next day or two.'

Kittens! Rafa cursed beneath his breath. It was bad enough that the solitude in his fortress had been disturbed by a gorgeous woman who tempted him, and a cute baby who tugged on his emotions, without the addition of a pregnant stray cat. 'Where is Signorina Ivy?'

'I believe she is in the ballroom.'

The strains of the tune Arturo had been whistling were audible when Rafa neared the ballroom. He opened the door and halted. Ivy was dancing and did not notice him. He leaned against the door frame and could not take his eyes off her as she twirled, leapt and kicked her legs high in the air.

She was wearing tiny, sparkly shorts and a crop top that revealed her taut midriff. Her long legs looked stunning in black stockings with wide bands of lace around the tops of her thighs. Rafa had arranged for Ivy's flat in Southampton to be cleared and her belongings sent to the castle.

Heat unfurled in his groin. Ivy's body was supple and sexy, and he was mesmerised as he watched her. He guessed the routine was one that she had performed when she'd been a show dancer on a cruise ship. The music pumping out of the speakers quickened in tempo, echoing the drumbeat of desire pounding in his veins.

Ivy spun round and saw him, but she did not stop dancing and beckoned to him. 'Come over here, I need you.'

Rafa was uncomfortably aware of his arousal straining against his trouser zip as he walked across the ballroom.

'Stop there,' Ivy told him when he was close to her. 'I need you to be my dance partner and catch me when I jump into your arms.' She spun round faster and faster, keeping time with the music that was building to a finale. 'Ready?' She made a graceful leap, and Rafa quickly thrust out his arms and caught her against his chest. 'Ta da!' She giggled at his stunned expression.

Her brown eyes made him think of molten chocolate, and her laughter was infectious. 'You are crazy,' he told her. A little of the ice around his heart melted and he laughed out loud. He couldn't remember the last time he had really laughed. It felt…good.

'The dance is meant to be a duet. I need a dance partner—I could teach you the steps. I heard that you were pretty quick around the basketball courts.'

'Playing basketball and dancing are hardly the same. It's true that I was the fastest player in the American professional basketball league.' Rafa did not try to disguise his pride. He'd been the best in the game and had been called a legend by the California Colts' legions of fans.

'Do you miss playing basketball?'

He nodded. 'I miss my team mates and the excitement before an important game.'

Ivy was the first person to show an interest in his sporting career since Rafa has moved back to Italy. He had dominated the basketball courts in the US and around the world for nearly a decade, but his father had thought that playing sport was not a serious job, and had put emotional pressure on Rafa to commit his future to Vieri Azioni.

He acknowledged that since he'd joined the company he'd enjoyed the challenges of corporate business. But basketball had been his independence and where he had found himself, instead of being a replica of his father. That was until Tiffany had made him question everything Rafa had thought he knew about himself.

'I guess you miss being a show dancer,' he said, running his eyes over Ivy's sexy costume.

Her smile became wistful. 'It feels like another life when I worked on cruise ships. When my sister died, and I became responsible for her baby, my life changed for ever. But I don't regret being Bertie's guardian. He is my only chance to be a mother after my brush with cancer.'

Rafa stared down at Ivy's pretty face. Her cheeks were pink and she was breathless from dancing. He wished he could carry her up to his bedroom and make love to her. His body tightened as he imagined her naked body flushed with sensual heat.

'I've never met anyone like you,' he said roughly. She was so full of energy, and she had brought light and laughter into the castle and into his life. He did not only want to take Ivy to bed. He liked talking to her, and being with Bertie and her. Rafa knew he was on dangerous ground. The embittered man he had become after his divorce warned him to keep his distance, but he was drawn to Ivy's shining light like a moth to a flame.

Abruptly he set her down on her feet and silently cursed his rampant libido when his gaze was drawn to the outline of her nipples beneath her top. 'We seem to have acquired a cat,' he muttered.

'Oh, have you met her? Isn't she sweet? I've named her Jasmine.' Ivy's big brown eyes filled with tears. 'The poor little thing had been abandoned and she is about to have kittens. Arturo has promised to feed Jasmine and her family when I'm not here.'

'Why won't you be at the castle?'

She seemed surprised by the question. 'I assume I'll

move out when we end our engagement. I didn't tell Arturo that our engagement is fake,' she said quickly when Rafa frowned. 'I mentioned that I will take Bertie to visit my family. I spoke to my mum a few days ago, and she invited me and Bertie to stay with her in Cyprus in early September. That will be about the right time for us to break up, don't you think?'

Rafa did not know what to think. He was surprised by how much he disliked the prospect of Ivy and Bertie leaving the castle. But the baby scandal story in the media would soon be yesterday's news and there would be no reason to continue their fake engagement.

CHAPTER EIGHT

'I MUST GO,' Ivy said as she glanced at her phone. 'Anna has messaged that Bertie has woken from his nap.'

They walked back to the main hall and saw Arturo emerge from the study. 'A file has just been delivered by a courier,' the butler told Rafa. 'I left it on your desk.'

Rafa assumed the file contained work documents and wondered why his PA had not given them to him before he'd left the office. He opened the study door and frowned when the ginger cat wove around his ankles and preceded him into the room.

'Jasmine has been showing signs that she will give birth to her kittens soon, and she seems to like your study,' Ivy murmured. 'I hope you don't mind.'

'What makes you think I'd mind my study being used as a labour ward?' he muttered, but his sarcasm was lost on Ivy.

'Thank you!' Her bright smile had a peculiar effect on Rafa's heart rate.

The cat was curled up on an arm chair in the study and gave Rafa a disgusted look when he walked in. The file on the desk was marked confidential and, when he opened it, he was startled to find several documents and a handwritten note to him from his father's personal assistant. Beatriz had worked for his father for twenty years and had retired soon after his death. She had been devoted to Rafael. The note explained that she had hidden the enclosed documents when Rafael had died, to protect his privacy.

With a sense of foreboding, Rafa read the first document—a letter that had been sent to Rafael Vieri from Gemma Bennett, informing Rafael that she had given birth to his son.

The second document was a letter that Rafa's father had written to Gemma Bennett. Rafael had accepted that Bertie was his son, resulting from an affair he'd had with Gemma while they had been on the cruise ship.

Dio! Bertie *was* his father's child. Rafa was stunned by the revelation even though he had realised it might be true. Reading his father's confession that Rafael had been unfaithful to his mother was painful. He had respected his father and looked up to him, but now he had evidence that Rafael had been fallible and imperfect.

Rafa's jaw clenched as he read what his father had written to the young woman who had been the mother of his illegitimate son. Rafael explained that his wife had been diagnosed with a terminal illness and he must take care of her. He was unable to have a role in his baby son's life, but he would arrange for a generous financial settlement to be paid to Gemma.

Rafa frowned. Ivy had not said that her sister had received money from his father. The date on the letter caught his attention and he realised that it was the date of his father's death. His father must have written to Gemma literally just before he'd died. The letter had not been sent, which was why it was included with the documents Beatriz had kept.

When Gemma had been killed in a tragic accident and Ivy had become Bertie's legal guardian, she had mistakenly believed that Rafa was the Rafael Vieri with whom her sister had had an affair.

Rafa pinched the bridge of his nose. His priority must be to protect his mother from ever discovering the truth, and for that reason he had allowed everyone to think that he was Bertie's father.

It *must* have been Ivy who had told the story to the news reporter. Other people in the boardroom had heard her accuse him, and it was true that some of the directors had doubted his suitability to be his father's successor. But he could not believe any of them would have risked the company's reputation by involving the press in the scandal. Carlo Landini, the only other person who had been present that day, despised the paparazzi.

Rafa did not know what Ivy had hoped to gain by telling the reporter that she was the baby's mother instead of her sister. He could not trust her. There was a risk that when he ended their fake engagement she might tell the press the true identity of Bertie's father. He would have to keep a close eye on her, but he doubted she would agree to remain at the castle indefinitely.

He stood up and paced around the study. A shocking idea had come into his mind. If he made their engagement real and actually married Ivy, the media would be convinced that Bertie was his child, and his mother would not discover the truth. After his disastrous marriage to Tiffany, he had vowed never to marry again. But he was desperate to protect his mother from learning about his father's betrayal. Rafa grimaced. He had never been able to make his mother happy, but now it was in his power to prevent her from being heartbroken.

And then there was Bertie, who Rafa now had proof was his half-brother. He had a responsibility to the baby, who was an innocent child and an heir to the Vieri fortune. Rafa felt protective of him. Every child deserved to be loved and Bertie was not responsible for the circumstances of his conception.

What the hell was he going to do? He needed a drink and took a bottle of single malt from the cabinet, pouring a generous amount into a glass. Disillusionment had left a bitter taste in his mouth. He was disappointed with his father. Once again, his faith in someone who he'd trusted had been shattered. It reinforced his belief that trust was a fool's game, Rafa thought grimly.

The cat jumped down from the chair and padded over to him. Rafa bent down and held out his hand to the animal, cursing when he felt sharp claws rake across his skin. A hissing noise similar to the sound of a kettle coming to the boil came from the cat before it shot under the desk.

'Very wise. Never trust anyone,' Rafa muttered.

Rafa had returned to the castle in time for dinner. Ivy had spent the last twenty minutes deciding what to wear. She'd settled on a pale blue dress which left one shoulder bare and showed off her slim waist. The hem of the chiffon skirt floated around her ankles when she walked, giving a glimpse of her strappy silver sandals.

Was the dress too obvious? Her reflection in the mirror revealed a hectic flush on her cheeks and a sparkle of excitement in her eyes. She felt like a teenager on a first date, and in truth she had barely any more experience of men than she'd had at seventeen when she'd become ill. But she had recognised desire blazing in Rafa's eyes when he had caught her in his arms in the ballroom.

She knew he had wanted to kiss her. Perhaps he was waiting for her to give him a sign that she wanted him to take her to bed. He had backed off after she'd told him she was a virgin, but sometimes she caught him looking at her with a gleam in his eyes, which had restored the self-confidence that cancer had stolen along with her hair and her first boyfriend when she had been a teenager.

Her seductive dress sent a signal that he would have to be blind not to see, Ivy thought as she gave a final twirl in front of the mirror and the side-split in the skirt opened to reveal her lace stocking top.

The sound of crying from the baby monitor alerted her that Bertie was awake, and when she hurried into the nursery he was red-faced and tears glistened on his dark eyelashes. Usually he went to sleep after his last feed, but he had been unsettled, and Ivy was worried that he was unwell.

'What's the matter, Bobo?' she crooned to the baby as she lifted him out of the cot. Anxiety made her tense, and she winced when her shoulder gave a twinge. It had felt much better since she'd had a few sessions with the physiotherapist Rafa had arranged for her to see, but she must have strained a muscle while she'd been dancing earlier.

She turned her head when the nursery door opened and Rafa walked in. He was still wearing his business suit, but his tie was missing, and he'd undone the top few buttons on his shirt. It looked as if he'd been running his fingers through his hair, and his jaw was tense, but nothing detracted from his devastating good looks.

'It's unusual for Bertie to be awake at this time,' he commented.

'I don't know what's wrong with him. Anna would probably have an idea, but she has driven to L'Aquila to have dinner with friends and will be back later tonight. I've changed Bertie's nappy, he doesn't seem to have colic, and his temperature is normal. He is crying like he does when he's hungry, but he had a bottle of formula an hour ago.'

'He might be hungry. Babies often have a growth spurt at around four or five months old. I read a lot of parenting books when Lola was a baby,' Rafa said in a gruff voice.

Ivy felt guilty that she had stirred up painful memories for him. 'I don't have any experience of looking after a baby and I feel so useless,' she admitted.

'You shouldn't, you are brilliant with him. Is your shoulder hurting? Here, let me take Bertie. Make up another bottle of formula and hopefully it will settle him.' Rafa cradled the baby in his arms and a curious expression flickered on his face. 'I know for certain that Bertie is my half-brother.'

Ivy tipped the contents of a carton of ready-made formula milk into a bottle. She gave Rafa a startled look. 'Have you had the result of the extended paternity test?'

'I received confirmation in an email from the clinic an hour ago, just after I had seen a letter which my father had written to your sister, accepting that Bertie was his child.'

'Gemma told me before she died that she hadn't heard from Bertie's father.' Ivy handed Rafa the bottle of milk and watched him feed the baby. 'I don't think she was surprised. A few years ago, her ex-boyfriend had swindled her out of her savings that she'd hoped to use for a deposit to buy a house. That's why we were living in a rented flat. Your father abandoned her. It's what men do,' she muttered.

'I have evidence that my father had arranged for a financial settlement to be paid to Gemma, but he would not have known that she had been killed by the time he wrote to her. He never sent the letter because he suffered a fatal heart attack. His personal assistant had kept the letters, but Beatriz decided that I should have them.' Rafa sighed. 'A cruel twist of fate meant that Bertie was an orphan when he two months old.'

Ivy still suffered flashbacks of the terrible night when Gemma had died. Memories of kissing her sister for the last time before she'd been rushed to the operating theatre, and her disbelief when the surgeon had explained that Gemma's life couldn't be saved, would always haunt her.

She gave a low cry and ran out of the nursery. Her feet took her downstairs to the small, informal dining room where Arturo planned to serve dinner. The French doors were open, and Ivy stepped outside onto the terrace. Dusk had fallen and stars pinpricked the purple sky.

A short while later, Rafa joined her. 'Bertie drank

all the milk and he is asleep now. Arturo asked if we are ready to eat.'

'I'm not hungry.' Ivy's voice cracked. 'I miss Gemma so much. When I started chemo and my hair fell out, Gem shaved all her hair off. She said we would beat my cancer together. She was the best sister, and I am determined to look after her son the best I can. But I didn't know why he was crying, and I'm worried about managing on my own. It's heart-breaking that Bertie will grow up without his parents.'

'You are not on your own. Bertie is my responsibility too, and we will be his parents,' Rafa told her.

'How can we be his parents?'

'I think we should both adopt Bertie.'

'I don't see how us adopting him will help,' she said wearily. 'For a start, I live in England and you live in Italy. Are you suggesting that we pass him between us like a parcel?'

Rafa's silence for some reason made the hairs on the back of Ivy's neck prickle. 'I am suggesting that we make our engagement real—and get married.'

'You can't be serious.' Ivy was dismayed by the way her heart had leapt at Rafa's proposal. The little girl inside her who had believed in fairy tales until she'd been ten, when her father had left and she'd realised she would have to fight off the big bad wolf by herself, had briefly hoped that Rafa was the prince of her childhood daydreams. Achievable goals, she reminded herself firmly. 'Neither of us wants to get married,' she reminded him.

'In ordinary circumstances, I would not choose to marry again,' he agreed. 'But the situation is far from ordinary. Bertie deserves to grow up with two parents who will love and care for him.'

'We can't lie to him. He has a right to know who his mother and father were.'

'When he is old enough we'll tell him about his real parents. But it will be some years before he can understand. By then, my mother will no longer be here. At least she'll have been spared knowing that her husband had betrayed her.'

Rafa raked his hand through his hair. 'My father was a decent man, and his behaviour was out of character. I believe he would have wanted me to protect my mother's feelings. It sounds as though your sister was a special person.'

'She was.' Ivy brushed a tear off her cheek.

'When the time is right, we will tell Bertie about them. We are his family now. Our marriage will be a sensible arrangement to allow us to be Bertie's parents, and I believe it will work, because we do not have any expectations of each other.'

'We don't have to be married in order to adopt him.'

'True, but I'm not planning to have children of my own and I want to make Bertie my heir. That can only happen if he is legitimate. Under the rules created by my great-grandfather, it is allowed for the heir to the Vieri fortune and the company to be adopted. Would you deny Bertie his birth right?' Rafa challenged her. 'If we marry, he will be my successor as the head of Vieri Azioni with the wealth, privilege and prestige that goes with the position. Just as importantly, we will give him a stable and secure childhood.'

'It's a crazy idea,' Ivy muttered. She must be crazy

to contemplate agreeing to marry Rafa even for a second. But her conscience had pricked when he'd asked if she would deny Bertie his birth right. Her sister's baby was related to the powerful Vieri family and his destiny was in her hands.

'How can you be sure you won't want a child of your own in the future?' She could not bear for Bertie to feel abandoned by Rafa, the way she'd felt when her father had left home and started a new family.

He scowled. 'It damn near destroyed me when I learned that Lola was not my daughter. I'd married Tiffany in good faith and believed she was pregnant with my baby. When I discovered how she'd lied to me, I vowed never to trust another woman enough to have a child.'

Ivy moved away from Rafa and stared over the dark garden. It was impossible to think when her senses were assailed by the spicy scent of his aftershave. Rafa knew because she had told him that she was unable to have children. Had he factored her infertility into his decision to ask her to marry him? He had been adamant that he did not want a child of his own.

But what about her? She couldn't deny that over the past weeks, when they had been living at the castle and she'd spent time with Rafa, her awareness of him had increased. But what she felt was more than sexual attraction.

She liked being with him and discussing his plans for the renovation of the castle. She had seen how gentle he was with Bertie, and she lived for one of his unguarded smiles that made her think she had broken through his barriers. She could easily fall for him, but he had insisted that their marriage would be a sensible arrangement. If she accepted his proposal, it would be like jumping into the abyss. Was she brave enough, or foolish enough?

'Marriage is a huge step. I need to think about it,' she told him.

'You need to think about marrying a billionaire?' The cynicism in his voice chilled her.

Ivy spun round to face him. 'I don't care about your money. All I care about is doing the right thing for Bertie, and I'm not going to rush into making a decision that will affect him for the rest of his life.' She closed her eyes to block out Rafa's arrogantly handsome face. 'I think I'll go to bed. It's been a long day.'

'It's only eight o'clock. Why don't you relax in the hot tub for a while? The jets might help your shoulder.' When she nodded, Rafa took out his phone. 'I've asked the staff to prepare the pool house and spa,' he said seconds later. 'I'm going to my study to catch up on some work.'

The pool house was at the side of the castle in what must once have been the orangery. At night, the glass roof revealed the canopy of stars in the inky sky. Potted ferns and other plants gave the room a tropical feel. The groundsman was leaving when Ivy arrived. He had switched on the jets in the hot tub and the water foamed and bubbled, creating a cloud of steam.

Ivy expected to find her swimsuit hanging on the hook, but it was missing, and she remembered that she had been wearing it when she'd walked back to the castle after her swim the previous day. There was no one around and, after hesitating briefly, she shimmied out of her dress and panties and stepped into the sunken spa.

The warm water was heavenly when she slid lower into the bubbles and positioned herself so that a jet was directed at her aching shoulder. She closed her eyes and tried to block out the debate in her head as to whether or not she should marry Rafa for Bertie's sake.

She had no idea how long she had been in the tub when a shaft of cool air stirred the fronds of the giant fern, and her heart missed a beat when she looked over at the door as Rafa strolled into the pool house.

'The maid thought you might need fresh towels,' he said, dropping the pile of towels he was carrying onto a lounger. 'She must have forgotten she'd brought some earlier.' He looked unabashed when Ivy glanced at the stack of clean towels on the counter.

'I'm sorry you interrupted your work unnecessarily.'

He came closer to the hot tub and started to undo his shirt buttons. 'I didn't feel like working. Too many other things on my mind.'

He slipped off his shirt and Ivy's mouth ran dry when she moved her eyes over his broad, bronzed chest overlaid with crisp black hairs that arrowed down his flat stomach. He put his hands on his belt buckle and she remembered that she was naked.

'You can't come in the tub,' she said breathlessly. 'I forgot my swimsuit.'

'I promise not to look.' His sexy grin sent a coil of heat through her, and she felt as if she might self-combust when he stepped out of his trousers to reveal black swim briefs that he must have put on before he'd come to the pool house. So much for his excuse of delivering towels!

His body was a work of art from his wide shoulders, tapered torso and flat abdomen. His hips were lean, and his long legs were powerfully muscular from his years of playing sport at a professional level. Ivy noted that his dark body hairs disappeared into his swim briefs that contained the distinct bulge of his manhood. He stepped into the spa, and she inched along the seat to put as much distance as possible between them.

'Mmm, this feels good,' he murmured, stretching his arms along the sides of the tub and dropping his head back against the tiles. He reminded her of an indolent sultan, and she would not have been surprised if half-naked concubines had appeared to fan him with palm leaves. 'Is your shoulder any easier?'

'A bit. You were right, the jets are helping.'

The water sloshed when he suddenly moved across the tub and somehow manoeuvred them both so that he was sitting behind her. She caught her breath when he settled his hands on her shoulders and pressed his thumbs into her muscles.

'I can feel a knot in your trapezius.' He pressed harder on her left shoulder and she yelped, but after a few seconds the pressure of his thumb started to ease the tension in her muscle. 'The trapezius is a big muscle that starts here.' His warm breath stirred the tendrils of hair at the base of her neck. 'It goes across your shoulders and down to the middle of your back.' The brush of his fingers on her sensitised skin was as light as gossamer, yet Ivy gave a shiver of reaction.

Rafa continued to massage her shoulders and she

gradually relaxed beneath his magician's touch. Steam from the hot tub drifted up to the glass roof and the low thrum of the jets made her feel as though they were cocooned in their own world, far from reality.

'What exactly do you mean by marriage?' Her voice was husky as she asked the question that had thudded inside her since his proposal. 'Would you want…?'

Words failed her. The knowledge that she was naked, and he very nearly so, increased her intense awareness of him, especially when he continued to massage her injured shoulder with one hand and slid his other hand around her rib cage to cup her breast. He splayed his fingers over the small mound and found her nipple, making her gasp as pleasure spread like molten liquid down to her feminine core.

'Oh, yes, I would want, *cara mia,*' he said thickly, before he lowered his head and pressed his mouth to her collarbone. 'I want to have sex with you.' Bold and to the point. The images his words evoked in Ivy's imagination were shockingly explicit. 'Tell me what you want, Ivy.'

He dropped his hand from her shoulder and drew her closer so that her back was up against his chest. Now both his arms were around her, and he played with her breasts, rolling her dusky pink nipples between his fingers. Ivy could not fight the waves of languorous delight that swept through her as Rafa caressed her. He lifted her onto his lap and she pressed back against him, catching her breath when the hard ridge of his arousal nudged the cleft of her bottom.

'Do you want me to do this?' Despite the hot water in the spa, his gravelly voice brought her skin out in goose bumps. She held her breath when he skimmed one hand over her stomach, and lower, to the cluster of curls at the junction of her thighs.

'Yes.' She was intrigued and could not deny her longing for him to touch her intimately. She felt boneless and her thighs splayed open to allow him to slip his hand between them. He moved her so that she was sitting sideways across his thighs and bent his head to claim her mouth in a searing kiss that added a new dimension to his sensual foreplay.

This time when he pushed her legs apart there was a new urgency in his touch as he unerringly found her slick opening. He parted her and eased a finger inside her, stretching her a little wider when one finger became two. She loved the feeling of fullness, and her internal muscles were already tightening, quivering as he moved his hand with a steady rhythm.

Ivy clutched his shoulders and moaned as her excitement built. Rafa captured her delighted cries with his mouth and thrust his tongue between her lips, mimicking the action of his fingers inside her. It belatedly occurred to her that she should offer him the same pleasure he was giving her but, when she moved her hand down to his briefs and stroked her fingers along his powerful arousal, he lifted his lips from hers and growled. 'Not this time, *belleza.* This is for you to enjoy.'

And then it was too late for her to think of anything but the wondrous sensations he was creating when he gave a twist of his fingers deep inside her and simultaneously rubbed his thumb across her clitoris. She bucked against his hand as her orgasm hit like a tidal wave, crashing over her, and it kept on coming in ripple after ripple of intense pleasure until she was spent and sagged against him.

Water streamed down Rafa's limbs as he stood with her in his arms and carried her out of the spa. Ivy twined her arms around his neck and pressed her body against his when he set her on her feet. What had happened in the tub had been a prelude and, although it had been amazing, she sensed there was more. She wanted Rafa to teach her everything, and her confusion must have shown on her face when he stepped away from her and shoved his arms into a bath robe before he draped another robe around her.

'I thought…' Her voice was thick with mortification. She had assumed he wanted to have sex with her, and his rejection opened the Pandora's Box of her insecurities.

Rafa slid his hand beneath her chin and tilted her face up to meet his glittering gaze. 'I want to make love to you for the first time on our wedding night, *cara mia*.'

'And if I don't accept your proposal? Her eyes widened. 'Are you using sex to blackmail me to marry you?'

Unforgivably, his lips twitched. 'Not blackmail. I prefer *persuasion*.' His expression became serious. 'You know it is the right thing to do—marry me so that Bertie can claim his birth right as the Vieri heir.'

Ivy bit her lip. Rafa was so forceful and resisting him was impossible—in every way, she thought ruefully. Her body became alive to his caresses, but she was aware that, while she had experienced ecstasy in his arms, he had always remained in control. He must have had dozens of mistresses who were more experienced than her, perhaps hundreds. She did not want to think of the glamourous women he had enjoyed before her. Worse was the idea that there might be others when his desire for her faded.

'Honesty is important to you, and it is to me too.' She held his gaze. 'I want a promise of fidelity so that Bertie doesn't grow up in an atmosphere of suspicion.' She remembered the arguments between her parents when her mum had suspected her dad of having an affair.

Rafa gave a harsh laugh. 'My wife cheated and led me to believe that I was a father. I will be totally committed to our marriage and always tell you the truth. Make no mistake, *cara*—if you marry me, I will demand equal commitment and honesty from you.' His eyes glittered. 'What is your answer?'

Ivy took a deep breath and prepared to jump. 'My answer is yes. I will be your wife.'

CHAPTER NINE

'HAVE YOU FLOWN in a helicopter before?' Rafa watched Ivy grip the arm rests on her seat as the chopper took off and felt guilty that it hadn't occurred to him she might be nervous.

'Only once.' She smiled. 'It was so exciting. The cruise ship had stopped in Hawaii, and I took a helicopter sightseeing flight over the island. The scenery was so beautiful. I'd planned to visit Hawaii again…but things changed,' she said with a soft sigh.

Ivy's life had been blown apart by her sister's tragic death, when she'd become Bertie's guardian. But her love and devotion for the baby were genuine, Rafa brooded. He believed her when she'd insisted that she did not care about his wealth and that her only reason for agreeing to marry him was to secure Bertie's rightful place in the Vieri family.

That was one of the motives behind his decision to make her his wife, he reminded himself. The other was his determination to protect his mother from discovering the truth about Bertie's paternity. The reporter from a national newspaper was still digging for a scandal, but Rafa was certain that, once he had married Ivy and claimed the child everyone believed was his, public interest would fade.

But he could not forget that Ivy had been responsible for the story which had been published in the newspaper. Every time he dropped his guard with her, he remembered that she had lied when she'd said she hadn't spoken to the journalist.

His third motive for proposing to Ivy was less altruistic. He wanted her in his bed—beneath him, on top of him, every which way he could have her. It should bother him that he was so desperate for her. It *did* bother him, but he told himself he was in control, although how he'd held back from possessing her fully in the pool house three nights ago he did not know.

She had been so delightfully responsive, and her soft cries of pleasure when she'd come against his hand had sharpened his hunger. But instinctively he felt it was right to wait so that he could make love to her on their wedding night, and he only needed to be patient for a few more hours.

The helicopter was taking them to their wedding destination. Following the civil ceremony, they would return to the Castello Dei Sogni for an evening reception for two hundred guests. The reception was due to finish before midnight and then, finally, he could claim his virgin bride.

'I don't know anything about San Alinara except that it is an independent microstate, famous for its nickname "Island of Love",' Ivy said.

'The island off the east coast of Italy is an ancient principality that has been ruled by the Pellegrini family for centuries. It has become a popular wedding destination because its laws allow couples to marry easily. But so many people choose to hold their wedding on San Alinara that there is a long waiting list.'

'How did you arrange for us to marry with only three days' notice?'

'The current ruler, Prince Stefano, is an old school friend of mine.'

'Of course he is.' Ivy gnawed her bottom lip with her teeth, making Rafa long to press his mouth to hers and kiss her until she stopped frowning and melted against him. 'I don't belong in your world,' she said in a low voice. 'I grew up on a rough housing estate, and I certainly didn't meet royalty at the local secondary school. I'm not glamorous and sophisticated.'

He shrugged. 'It doesn't matter where you went to school. We are marrying so that Bertie will grow up in my world, as you call it.' He studied her pale grey dress and matching jacket and wondered why he was disappointed that she had chosen a distinctly un-bridal outfit for their wedding.

A limousine with the royal standard flying from the bonnet met them at the airport to drive them to the registry office in San Alinara. 'Unfortunately I will be away on state business on your wedding day,' Prince Stefano had told Rafa when they had spoken on the phone two days ago. 'I hope I will meet your new wife and baby son soon.'

The curiosity in his friend's voice had almost tempted Rafa to explain the reason for his hasty marriage. He hated the web of deceit, but he would not risk the truth being exposed that would shatter his mother. He knew how that felt. He remembered the taste of bile in his throat when Tiffany had told him she'd been sleeping with another man. Maybe it had hurt his pride more than his heart, he acknowledged. Love, if it had ever existed between them, had left the building by then. But his ex-wife's betrayal over Lola had broken him, and when he'd put himself back together trust was a missing component in the colder, harder man he'd become.

The registry office was part of a grand old building that provided a charming backdrop for wedding photographs. Inside they were greeted by an official and, once the paperwork had been checked, they were shown to a private suite where they could relax before the civil ceremony. Ivy disappeared into the bathroom with the travel bag she'd carried off the helicopter.

Rafa fiddled with his tie and tried to ignore the inexplicable jangle of his nerves. He checked his watch for the fifth time and wondered when Ivy was going to reappear—or if. It occurred to him that she might have changed her mind. As he was digesting that unwelcome thought, the bathroom door opened and she stepped into the room.

His jaw dropped and his blood heated to boiling point and surged south to his groin. 'You look…' He was lost for words. Beautiful didn't come close.

Ivy was wearing a pure white column dress, utterly simple, yet the flowing lines could only have been created by an expert couturier. The shimmering silk moulded her slender figure, and the halter-neck top exposed her back, shoulders and elegant neck. Her feathery blonde hair framed her delicate face, and subtle make-up enhanced her big brown eyes, flecked with gold.

She looked ethereal and innocent but, when she

moved, the dress clung to her sweet curves and hinted at her sensuality that Rafa longed to explore. She was quite simply his every erotic fantasy in one exquisite package. The erratic thud of his heart warned him that the situation was spinning out of his control. He was not meant to feel like this. He did not want to feel anything. But the anxious expression in her Bambi eyes, the need for his approval in her hopeful smile, unfroze a little of the ice inside him.

He returned her smile, letting her see the genuine admiration in his eyes. 'You are perfect,' he assured her. And that could be a problem if he did not remain on his guard.

'These are for you.' Rafa presented Ivy with an exquisite bouquet of pink roses and delicate white gypsophila, commonly known as baby's breath. 'I remembered that pink is your favourite colour. I'm not likely to forget your pink hair when we first met,' he said drily.

Ivy did not want to think about how furious he had been when she'd turned up at Vieri Azioni's offices with Bertie and accused him of being the baby's father. 'Thank you. They're beautiful.' Lowering her face to the flowers to breathe in their scent gave her a few minutes to try to steady her racing pulse caused by the stark hunger in Rafa's eyes when he'd seen her in her dress.

She had been worried he might be annoyed by her decision to wear a bridal gown. But she was only ever going to have one wedding and, even though their marriage was a sensible arrangement, she wanted to look like a proper bride.

With hardly any time to prepare for the wedding after

Rafa's shock announcement that they would marry in three days, Ivy had called the personal stylist in Rome. Sophia had duly arrived at the castle with a selection of dresses, and Ivy had fallen in love with the simplicity of the white silk gown.

As long as the dress was the only thing she fell in love with, she warned herself. Rafa offered her his arm, and her heart missed a beat when she studied his grey three-piece suit that had been expertly tailored to mould his athletic build. The trimmed stubble on his jaw gave him an edgy sexiness that was reflected in his glittering eyes, and the sensual curve of his mouth promised heaven.

When they entered the room where the wedding was to take place, they were greeted by the registrar, who explained that the civil ceremony was legal and binding. The vows they were about to make were a formal and public pledge of their love and a promise of a lifelong commitment to each other.

Ivy felt Rafa stiffen, and fear clutched her heart. She had agreed to the marriage for Bertie's sake, but was she doing the right thing? If only she had some guidance, but the person she would have confided in and sought advice from had gone for ever.

Through a blur of tears, she noticed something fluttering around the room. A butterfly with vivid orange wings must have flown in through the open window, and now it landed on the bouquet of roses Ivy was holding. At Gemma's funeral an orange butterfly had fluttered around the church yard, even though it had been a bitterly cold winter's day.

A sense of peace came over Ivy. She had loved her

sister, and Rafa had loved his father and was desperate to protect his mother. They might not love each other, but their marriage was founded on their shared love for Bertie.

She turned her head and met Rafa's enigmatic grey gaze. 'Are you ready to proceed?' he murmured. The butterfly opened its delicate wings and rose into the air. Ivy watched it flutter across the room and out of the window.

'I am ready,' she said steadily.

In the early-evening sunshine, the Castello Dei Sogni was almost pretty. The helicopter landed in the grounds, and Rafa clasped Ivy's hand in his as they walked towards the castle where the wedding guests had assembled for the reception. Huge urns filled with colourful flowers stood on either side of the front door. Inside, the great hall had been transformed into a romantic idyll with arrangements of pink roses and silver cloths on the tables that had been set out for the wedding dinner.

Ivy did not know most of the guests, who were Rafa's business associates, but she had met some of his friends and their wives who lived in the nearby town of L'Aquila. The stylist, Sophia, had become a good friend, and Anna brought Bertie down from the nursery. Ivy hugged his little body and love flooded her heart. Soon he would be Rafa's and her son, and a Vieri, once the adoption was finalised.

Rafa had arranged for a photographer from a popular magazine to take exclusive pictures of the event. The proceeds from the edition carrying the wedding photos would be donated to a children's charity. It was a clever move, for it meant that he controlled the media coverage.

Ivy duly posed beside Rafa while he held Bertie. She knew he hoped the pictures of them as a happy family would put an end to the speculation about their relationship. He'd told her that the board members and Vieri Azioni's shareholders were pleased their chairman and CEO had given up his playboy lifestyle. As a damage limitation exercise, the marriage was a stroke of genius.

The wedding dinner was sublime, and a champagne toast was made to the happy couple, although the bride drank sparkling water. After the meal, the guests mingled on the terrace and were entertained with music played by a fifteen-piece orchestra.

'Rafa is a lucky man to have such a charming bride.' The voice was vaguely familiar, and Ivy turned to see the elderly man called Carlo who had spoken to her at the engagement party. It had been less than a month ago, but it felt like a lifetime since she had arrived in Rome hoping to meet Bertie's father.

Now she was married to Rafa and tonight she would be his wife in every way. When he had bent his head to kiss her at the end of the marriage ceremony, she'd expected him to brush his lips lightly over hers. But, at the first touch of his mouth, passion had exploded between them that had shocked her with its intensity and she'd sensed it had stunned him too.

The memory of his hungry desire had pulsed hot and needy between her thighs for the rest of the day, and she felt a mixture of anticipation and slight nervousness as the clock ticked towards midnight and the end of the reception.

Ivy pulled her mind back to the present and smiled at Carlo. 'You own a bank.' She remembered that he had been in the boardroom when she'd accused Rafa of being Bertie's father. The scandal had led Carlo to cancel an important business deal with Vieri Azioni.

'I used to own Landini Bank,' he told her. 'But earlier this evening I joined Rafa in his study and signed the documents to complete the sale of the bank to Vieri Azioni. I won't apologise for withdrawing from the deal when I doubted Rafa's integrity. If a man becomes a father out of wedlock, it is my firm belief that he has a duty to honour the mother by giving her his name in marriage and legitimising his child. I told Rafa I would not sell my bank to him until he had proved he was worthy to own it.'

Carlo laughed. 'The timing was tight. I am flying to Canada tomorrow to spend six months with my daughter. Rafa pulled off the wedding just in time.'

So that was why Rafa had disappeared during the reception. Ivy told herself it was silly to feel hurt by the discovery that their rushed wedding had been so he could secure a business deal. He hadn't explained why he'd organised the wedding at short notice, except to repeat that, once they were married, the news reporters would lose interest in them.

Rafa had such a forceful personality and he was used to having his own way. Was this how their marriage would be—him giving commands that he expected her to obey? Ivy's chin came up. Her new husband was in for a surprise if he believed she would be a biddable wife.

By the time the reception had finished and the guests

had departed, she felt brittle with tension and perilously close to tears. She escaped to her bedroom and found that her clothes had been moved by the staff into the rooms that she would share with Rafa from now on. The master suite comprised a sitting room and his and hers dressing rooms and bathrooms. The adjoining bedroom was dominated by a huge four-poster bed.

Thankfully, Rafa wasn't there. She could not face him when her emotions were on a tightrope. Ivy dashed into her dressing room and searched through the chest of drawers for her pyjamas, thinking she would make up the bed in her old room and sleep there tonight.

'Finally I've got you to myself.' Rafa had entered the suite without Ivy hearing him, and he stood in the doorway of the dressing room. His voice was as deep as an ocean, and he did not try to hide his satisfaction that they were alone. He had dispensed with his jacket, waistcoat and tie, and his shirt was unbuttoned to halfway down his chest. In one hand he held a tumbler of whisky and his other hand rested on the door frame. He seemed to be relaxed, but his eyes were as sharp as rapiers when he studied her.

'Don't come any closer.' She held out her hand as if to ward him off.

'It's understandable that you might feel nervous about making love for the first time, *piccola*,' he murmured.

'It's not… I don't.' She knew from the Italian lessons she'd been having from Anna that *piccola* meant 'little one'. Damn Rafa for sounding as if he cared when all the evidence showed that he didn't. Tears brimmed. She hated that she was a cry-baby. She hated that he was so big, strong and diabolically gorgeous.

'Is something the matter? I didn't imagine that you were sending me bad vibes for the latter part of the evening,' he said drily.

Ivy took a deep breath. 'I know our marriage is a sensible arrangement. But I hoped there would be honesty and respect between us.' Rafa's brows lifted, but he said nothing, and she continued. 'You should have told me that you had arranged our wedding so quickly because you wanted to do a deal to buy Landini Bank before Carlo Landini went abroad for six months. He told me you'd pulled the wedding off just in time. It would have been nice if you had informed me, that's—that's all I'm saying,' she faltered when Rafa pushed off the door frame and came towards her.

He reminded her of a big cat, but if she was his prey she wasn't going to wait around to be eaten. With the advantage of surprise, she darted past him, back into the bedroom. Belatedly she remembered that, as a professional basketball player, he'd been famous for his speed around the court. He overtook her before she was halfway across the room and spun her round so that her back was up against a post on the bed.

'I did not arrange to make the deal with Landini at the wedding. I'd forgotten about buying the bank, to be honest.' His eyes glittered. 'I had other things on my mind. Carlo asked if he could come to the wedding reception, and I invited him, because despite our differences in the past I like and respect the guy. It was a total surprise when he took me aside this evening and asked if we could finalise the deal. He was keen to hand over responsibility of the bank before his trip to visit his daughter.'

He slid his hand beneath Ivy's chin and tilted her face up to his. 'I do respect you and I will always be honest with you. I expect you to do the same.'

The air simmered with sexual tension. Apart from his fingers gently stroking her jaw, he wasn't touching her, but Ivy was so aware of him it *hurt*. She could feel the heat of his body and see the whorls of chest hairs where his shirt was open. He smelled divinely of his spicy aftershave and something earthier and intrinsically male.

'Do you want to know why I organised the wedding in as short a time as possible?' Beneath the bite of his anger was something raw that made Ivy tremble with excitement. 'This is the reason, *gattina*.' He angled his mouth over hers and kissed her with a fierce hunger that seared her down to her soul.

'I couldn't wait another day or endure another sleepless night while I fantasied about making you mine. I wanted the fantasy to be real, and if I could have married you even sooner you would not now be a wide-eyed virgin looking at me fearfully.'

He brought his mouth down on hers again and kissed her with a desperation that lifted Ivy's heart. His breathing was ragged, and she could feel the thunder of his heart when she pushed the edges of his shirt aside and laid her hands on his bare chest. The evidence of Rafa's desire gave her confidence in her strength as a woman and his skill as a lover. Her first and only lover, for she had not made her marriage vows lightly.

'I'm not afraid of you,' she told him huskily when he

moved his lips over her cheek and kissed his way up to her ear to gently bite the lobe.

'Good.' His chest expanded. 'If you're not ready to sleep with me, say so. I would never try to force you. I respect your right to choose what to do with your body, *cara.*'

The last vestiges of her tension drained away. 'I'll be twenty-five in a week. If I'm not ready now, when will I be?' She turned her face to his and kissed his stubbly jaw. The slight abrasion against her lips sent a quiver through her and each of her nerve endings tingled. 'My body chooses you,' she whispered.

He muttered something in Italian and captured both of her hands, lifting them so that her arms were above her head. He curled her fingers around the bed post behind her. 'Hold on tight,' he bade her.

Ivy's heart missed a beat when he held her gaze and she recognised the sensual promise in his eyes. His fingers brushed against the back of her neck as he unfastened the halter top of her dress. The shimmering silk fell away from her breasts and he cradled the pale mounds in his hands, brushing his thumbs across the dusky pink nipples until they stood proud and taut.

'Don't let go,' he commanded softly, and she obeyed the deep timbre of his voice, for he was a magician and she was enchanted by him. She tightened her grip on the bed post and gasped when he bent his head and drew her nipple into his mouth.

The sensation of him sucking the tender peak was so intense that she pinched her thighs together, sure he must notice the musky scent of her arousal. He moved across to her other breast to mete out the same exquisite torture until she was utterly molten down below and her legs felt too weak to hold her upright.

With a tug, Rafa pulled her dress down, and it made a pool of white silk at her feet. '*Bellissima.*' His breath tickled her stomach as he knelt in front of her and kissed his way down to the tiny scrap of white lace between her legs.

Ivy's inhibitions disappeared and were replaced by a longing for him to touch her there. Her arms ached but she gripped the bed post tighter when Rafa pressed his mouth against the damp panel of her panties. It was not enough, she wanted to feel him…

'Oh!' The sheer delight of his mouth on her sensitive flesh when he eased her panties aside drew a moan from her. With a flick of his wrist, he pulled her knickers down and spread her legs apart so that he could bury his face between them. His tongue lapped her slick opening and then dipped inside her in a shockingly intimate caress that took her to the edge. She was powerless to stop the shudders that racked her body as he brought her closer, closer…

She climaxed hard against his mouth and the intensity of pleasure was beyond anything she'd ever experienced. How could she have done when this was all new to her? Only Rafa had ever used his mouth on her this way and, as the pulses of her orgasm faded, Ivy was ready for even greater pleasure.

But she was eager to give as well as receive. When he stood and uncurled her fingers from the post, she twined her arms around his neck and pressed her body against him. He lifted her up so that her pelvis was flush to his and she circled her hips over the hard ridge that strained beneath his trousers.

'Witch!' He growled. 'I want the first time to be good for you, *cara*, but if you keep doing that I'm going to disappoint you and disgrace myself.'

She loved the rough tenderness in his voice. Her heart gave a jolt. Where had the L word come from? She quickly banished it and focused on what he could give her, instead of something that was never going to happen. Sex was going to happen, and she was aware of a little flutter of apprehension when Rafa laid her on the bed before he stripped off his clothes. His trousers hit the floor, followed by his boxers, and the awesome length of his erection made her catch her breath.

How was she here with this powerful, arrogant man who she knew did not trust her but nevertheless made her yearn for his possession with his mind-blowing passion? Perhaps he sensed her faint hesitation. He lay down beside her and drew her into his arms, one hand smoothing tendrils of hair off her face.

His kisses were unhurried and beguiling as he explored every dip and curve of her body with hands that were strong yet gentle. He made no demands, and she relaxed again and slipped into a world of sensory pleasure while heat unfurled inside her and licked through her veins, hotter, more intense, as his fingers parted her and prepared her.

When he took a condom from the bedside drawer, Ivy gave him a shy smile. 'It's okay if you'd rather not wear one. There won't be any repercussions.' She had come to terms with being infertile. But now she was a mother to her sister's baby, and Bertie was very precious.

Her thoughts scattered when Rafa hesitated before he returned the condom to the drawer. There was a steely purpose in his eyes when he lifted himself over her and braced his weight on his elbows while he used one thigh to nudge hers apart. He was so beautiful and so big… Her eyes widened when she realised that it was actually going to happen, and she would have to take his hard shaft inside her.

He eased forward and she felt the tip of him press against her opening. Slowly, carefully, he pushed his solid length inside her, pausing every few seconds to allow her to adjust to the sensation of him possessing her.

There was mild discomfort rather than pain. She was aware of a feeling of fullness, of being stretched. She slid her hands along his shoulders and felt the strength in his bunched muscles. His clenched jaw told her of the restraint he was imposing on himself, and his consideration and gentleness brought tears to her eyes.

'*Cara,* I'll stop if I'm hurting you.' His voice was gruff with remorse. He began to withdraw, but she wrapped her legs around his hips.

'It's fine, just…new.'

'*Dio*, I knew you would kill me.' He claimed her mouth in a tender kiss that quickly became intensely erotic as he began to move, pushing deeper into her, easing back and pushing again, a little further, a little harder, until the fire inside her burst into flame. They were in perfect accord. Her body arched to meet his powerful thrusts and his lips sought hers again and again, taking and giving, demanding and appeasing.

He filled her senses and there was only Rafa, her

husband who did not love her but who made love to her so sublimely that her heart trembled with the beauty of it. He took her higher and her entire body trembled as she strove for some unknown place that she sensed was there but was frustratingly beyond her reach.

'Relax and it will happen,' he murmured. She wondered how he knew when she did not know herself what her body was desperately seeking. He increased his pace, and there was a new urgency in the way he drove into her. Deep in her feminine core, something was happening, little tremors that became more intense with each devastating thrust of his shaft into her molten heat.

He slipped his hand between their joined bodies and gave a twist of his fingers that sent her tumbling over the edge and into ecstasy. She cried out as her climax cascaded through her, pulsing waves that, when they finally started to ebb, left her limp, boneless and replete.

Rafa had waited while Ivy rode out her orgasm, but now he moved again in hard, rhythmic strokes that prolonged her pleasure as his built to a crescendo. He lifted his mouth from her breast and she felt the tension of the muscles in his back as he remained poised above her for timeless seconds before he gave one final thrust and groaned as he spilled inside her.

She wrapped her arms around his big shoulders and held him while the storm passed. It moved her deeply that this powerful man had come apart and she had been the cause of his downfall. Tenderness filled her and she pressed her lips against his throat and tasted his sweat. In the languorous afterglow of their spent desire, she never wanted to let him go.

But she remembered the speculative look in his eyes

when he'd joined their bodies and, although her experience was limited, she sensed that he had always been in control. He would not want her to cling, and for her self-preservation she must hide the effect he had on her emotions.

That shouldn't have happened. Sure, the sex should have happened, but not the way his control had shattered when he'd been thrown into a mind-blowing orgasm. Rafa was amazed that he'd kept his hands off Ivy for as long as he had. But he hadn't expected it to be so spectacularly good, especially as she had been a virgin. Part of him, the cold and bitter part, had not entirely believed her until, with a gut-wrenching sense of shock, he'd discovered that she had told him the truth.

Rafa rolled onto his back and stared up at the canopy above the bed. His heart was still thundering in his chest, yet incredibly his shaft was already semi-aroused. He wasn't done with Ivy. Not nearly. Something inside him warned he would never have enough of her.

Possessiveness was an unfamiliar emotion for him. Before he'd met her, he had enjoyed a healthy sex life and had had countless lovers. Frankly, he had preferred women who were experienced and willing to accept his no-strings rule.

But when Ivy had tensed beneath him, and he'd realised how innocent she was, he'd felt a knife blade slice through his insides at the idea he might have hurt her. She was his. It should not make him feel like a king. He wondered why she had chosen to have her first sexual experience with him. His conscience pricked that he might not like her answer if he asked her. Those Bambi eyes of hers were so expressive. When he'd slipped the wedding ring onto her finger, he had read defencelessness and, more worryingly, hope in their velvet-brown depths.

He would provide Bertie and her with a comfortable life and every privilege that his fortune could easily afford to buy, Rafa assured himself. Ivy would want for nothing—except for his love, taunted a voice inside him. He couldn't give her his heart for the good reason that he kept it behind an impenetrable wall.

He turned his head on the pillow and watched her long eyelashes flutter against her cheeks. She was so tiny and perfect, like a delicate porcelain figurine. Her fragility made something tighten inside him, knowing that she had survived a life-threatening illness. The world would have been a greyer place without Ivy's golden laughter and the way she found joy in simple things.

He ran the back of his hand lightly down her peach-soft cheek. But, when he tried to draw her into his arms, she rolled away from him to the other side of the mattress. Rafa told himself he was relieved that she wasn't all over him, wanting to be cuddled and petted, but her rejection stung.

CHAPTER TEN

'THIS IS THE most amazing birthday present,' Ivy told Rafa happily. She stretched luxuriously on the sun lounger and stared up at the cobalt blue sky through the fronds of the palm trees.

She'd fallen in love with Hawaii on her brief visit a few years ago, and had been stunned when Rafa had told her he had booked a holiday on the tropical island to celebrate her birthday and their honeymoon. She had been persuaded to leave Bertie with Anna at the castle, as the trip was only for four days.

'You deserve some time to yourself.' Rafa was lying next to her on the double lounger. He propped himself up on his elbow and leaned over her to brush a few strands of hair off her face. 'And I selfishly wanted you all to myself, Signora Vieri.'

He lowered his head and claimed her mouth in a slow kiss that made Ivy's heart race. She had not expected being married to Rafa to feel so real. He was charming and attentive, and since their wedding they had barely been apart. They had been on some wonderful sightseeing trips around Hawaii and had walked hand in hand along the white, sandy beaches beside the glistening Pacific Ocean.

He broke the kiss when a waiter arrived to serve them exotic fruit cocktail drinks decorated with slices of watermelon and a little paper parasol. Rafa disappeared briefly and returned with a garland of vibrant pink flowers, known in Hawaiian culture as a *lei*, which he draped around Ivy's neck. She breathed in the exquisite fragrance of the exotic flowers and gave him a dazzling smile.

The fizzing sensation inside her was happiness, she realised. She had believed she would never be happy again after her sister's death, but the past few days which she had spent exclusively with Rafa had been wonderful. Ivy ignored the voice in her head that reminded her she did not believe in fairy-tale happy endings.

She touched the flowers. 'Thank you for these, and for bringing me to Hawaii. It has been memorable.'

Something indefinable moved in his grey eyes. 'I have enjoyed our trip too, *cara*. What would you like to do on our last night here? We could try the fine dining experience or watch a show in the nightclub.'

'Mmm…or we could swim in our private pool and order room service before we have an early night.'

'How early?' Rafa growled, and Ivy giggled when he scooped her into his arms and carried her across the manicured lawn to their luxury suite.

'It's only afternoon,' she reminded him. He gave her a wicked smile as he laid her on the bed and pulled off his swim shorts. The sight of his burgeoning arousal evoked a flood of warmth between her legs, and she shivered in anticipation when he tugged the strings of her bikini. 'You are insatiable, Signor Vieri.'

'That makes two of us.' He groaned as he bared her breasts and closed his mouth around one nipple, sucking on the tender peak until Ivy moaned with pleasure, and he transferred his mouth to her other breast. 'Do you have any idea how much you turn me on?' His voice was rough with desire.

'Some idea,' Ivy whispered as she curled her fingers around his erection. She loved this teasing side to Rafa. She loved his fierce passion and his hunger for her that made her feel as beautiful as he always told her she was.

She was falling in love with him. The thought crept into her head, and she realised that it had already put down roots in her heart. Sometimes she thought that Rafa was as surprised as she was by the intensity of their relationship. It wasn't meant to be like this, and she did not know how she was going to survive when his passion for her waned, as it surely would. She was just ordinary Ivy Bennett, not a glamourous socialite. What did she have that would captivate a billionaire tycoon?

She pushed her doubts to the back of her mind and twined her arms around his neck to pull his mouth down onto hers. He made a muffled sound in his throat when she initiated a kiss that was wild and fierce. Ivy had a desperate need to know that this at least was real, this urgent passion that held them both in its grip.

'Cara?' He lifted his head and stared into her eyes, frowning when he saw the shimmer of her tears.

'I want you to make love to me now,' she told him. 'Please, Rafa.'

'Oh, I will please you, *cara*.' To Ivy's surprise, he

stood up and held out his hand. When she got to her feet he turned her so that she was facing the bed and he bent her forward with her hands resting on the mattress.

His mouth was hot on the back of her neck as he feathered kisses down her spine, and at the same time he curved his hands over her bottom and spread her so that he could enter her with a smooth thrust that drove the breath from her body.

She was glad of his almost savage possession. The terrifying truth was beginning to dawn on her that he was the only man she would ever love. But love had no place in their sensible marriage. She could never tell Rafa that she was emotionally invested in their relationship. Instead she sobbed her surrender, urging him to take her harder, faster.

He held her hips and drove deep, filling her and completing her, driving them both towards the stars. It couldn't last, the crazy ride of their lives. Rafa groaned her name as he plunged into her, and the planets collided in a white-hot explosion that ripped through them and made them reborn.

Afterwards he stretched out beside her on the bed and pulled her into his arms. Ivy rested her head on his chest and listened to the gradual slowing of his heart rate.

Rafa brushed his lips over her hair. 'Happy birthday, *piccola*.' And then in a rougher tone, 'What are you doing to me?'

Rafa was surprised at how easily he slipped into married life when he and Ivy returned to the castle after their honeymoon. One morning a few weeks after the wedding he jogged through the forest until the trees thinned and he emerged into sunlight as he neared the summit of the hill. Behind him were the high peaks of the Apennine mountains, and from his elevated position he looked down on the Castello Dei Sogni.

He frowned as he remembered the legend of the man who had hidden away in the fortress so that love could not find him. In the summer sunshine, the castle's grey walls looked less forbidding. Perhaps even the strongest barricades had weak points and vulnerable areas where a slender girl with golden hair and Bambi eyes could enter stealthily and steal the heart of the castle's foolish owner.

He shook his head, amused by his fanciful ideas. He was not a fool, and his heart was safe, Rafa reassured himself. Admittedly, his marriage to Ivy was better than he could have envisaged. The sex was spectacular, and he couldn't get enough of her. But the truth was that what he felt for her was more than a physical response to their extraordinary chemistry.

What he felt for her. He was in dangerous territory, he brooded. But, the more time he spent with Ivy, the more he liked her. She confounded him daily. Her kindness and compassion were evident in everything she did, which was why his study was currently a feline nursery after the stray cat Ivy had rescued had given birth to her kittens beneath his desk.

Rafa grimaced. Jasmine, the cat from hell, clearly had a personal vendetta against him and dug her claws into his ankles every time he stretched his legs out under his desk. But Ivy adored the cat and her six kittens, so he did not complain when he threw away another pair of ripped socks.

He raked his hand through his hair as he remembered more of Ivy's delightful traits. She was funny, and he had laughed more in the past month during which she had been his wife than he'd done in a lifetime. His childhood hadn't been the happiest of times, Rafa conceded. His mother had always been distracted by her grief, and his father had put work above family. The occasional hiking trips to the mountains had been the times he'd felt closest to his father.

Now there was another Vieri heir. He'd never wanted to have a child of his own, but it was impossible not to love Bertie. Sometimes Rafa woke in the night with the thought that, if Ivy had disappeared back to England with the baby, he would never have known about his half-brother. But Ivy must have spoken to the journalist, who had then reported the facts of the story incorrectly. Rafa had married her to prevent the media and his mother from discovering the true identity of Bertie's father.

He always came back to Ivy's involvement in the newspaper story, and it was the reason he could not trust her. But did it matter? Rafa asked himself as he jogged back to the castle. Ivy was unaware that he had some doubts about her, and his misgivings reminded him as to why he should not be tempted to lower his barricades and allow her close.

He headed straight into the shower and then to his dressing room, to prepare for a dinner party they were hosting for some of his friends and their wives, who had quickly become Ivy's friends. It seemed everyone was drawn to her warmth and sparkle.

When Rafa walked into the bedroom, his breath left his lungs in a rush as Ivy did a twirl in front of him.

'You look stunning,' he said huskily. He heard the hunger in his voice, the rough note of need. *Dio*, when had he started to need Ivy? When hadn't he needed her? questioned a voice inside him.

Her gown was navy-blue silk overlaid with chiffon and embellished with tiny crystals that also adorned the narrow shoulder straps. The low-cut bodice did not allow her to wear a bra, and Rafa wished he could slide the straps down her arms and slowly bare her breasts with their rosy nipples that he loved to feast on.

He took a velvet box from his jacket pocket. 'This will be perfect to wear with your dress,' he said, opening the lid to reveal a delicate necklace of white diamonds, and a larger yellow diamond that matched the one on her engagement ring.

'Oh, Rafa, it's beautiful. But you shouldn't keep buying me things.'

'Why not?' He liked spoiling her and seeing her face light up when he gave her gifts. She had been as appreciative of the bunch of flowers he'd bought for her from a market stall in L'Aquila, on one of their regular visits to the historic town, as she was of an expensive necklace. Her guilelessness was genuine, which increasingly made him wonder if he *could* trust her.

He fastened the necklace around her throat and traced his finger over the yellow diamond nestling between her breasts. 'I'm glad you like it. I had it designed especially for you.'

'I love it.' Her smile was brighter than the most dazzling diamond. 'I wish I had something to give you.'

Rafa pressed his lips to the side of her neck so that she did not see his expression in the mirror. He was stunned to realise that Ivy's sweetness, and her laughter that filled the castle and filled him, were the only gifts he wanted. 'I will look forward to making love to you tonight when you are wearing only the diamond necklace,' he murmured, fascinated by the soft pink stain that spread over her cheeks.

It amazed him that she could still blush after he had kissed every centimetre of her delectable body. But the pink stain on her cheeks quickly faded, and during the dinner party he noticed that Ivy was paler than usual. The party was a great success with excellent food, fine wine and the company of good friends. When the last guests had departed, and Arturo had locked the castle doors, Rafa found Ivy had fallen asleep on the sofa in the snug.

'Perhaps I'm coming down with a virus,' she said, yawning as he lifted her into his arms and carried her upstairs. 'I'm so tired.' Her lashes lifted and the gold flecks in her brown eyes were as bright as flames. 'But not *too* tired,' she said suggestively. 'I've never had sex while adorned with diamonds.'

'You have never had sex with any other man but me.' Possessiveness swept through him. She was his. Ivy's blonde head drooped onto his shoulder, and she did not stir when Rafa carried her into the bedroom, undressed her and returned the necklace to its box.

He pulled the bed covers over her and was struck by how fragile she looked. She had been pale and unusually tired for a few days, and Anna had confided to him that Ivy had experienced dizzy spells recently. It was probably nothing to worry about, he told himself, trying to shrug off a sense of foreboding. Ivy had overcome cancer as a teenager and there would be no harm in persuading her to have a check-up with a doctor.

Ivy opened her eyes and focused blearily on the clock on the bedside table. It must be wrong. It couldn't be ten a.m. But her watch showed that she had slept until late. She sat up carefully and was relieved that she didn't feel nauseous, as she had the past few mornings.

She had tried to convince herself that feeling tired was to be expected when Rafa made love to her at least once every night. But her symptoms reminded her of how she'd felt as a teenager when she had been diagnosed with blood cancer. Of course it wasn't that—she was being over imaginative—but experience had taught her that life was unpredictable and happiness was precarious.

She hurried to the nursery, feeling guilty that she'd left Anna to take care of Bertie. Rafa must have left the castle hours ago. He had told her that he had an early-morning meeting at his office in Rome.

Bertie grinned when he saw her, showing off his first tooth. 'I hope he wasn't too restless during the night,' she said when she took him from the nanny.

'I think you should worry less about Bertie and more about yourself.' Anna gave her a concerned look. 'You have felt unwell for a few days.'

'I'm fine.' But she wasn't fine. Ivy gasped and handed Bertie to Anna before she ran into the bathroom just in time to be violently sick. Eventually it passed and she sat shivering on the edge of the bath. Fear gripped her. Suppose the leukaemia had come back? She blinked back tears as she imagined Bertie growing up without her.

At least he would have one parent in Rafa. Her heart cracked. If she had to have chemo and lost her hair again, would Rafa find her unattractive, as her first boyfriend had done? She could no longer deny to herself that her teenage feelings for Luke had been nothing compared to the overwhelming love she felt for Rafa.

'Nausea and tiredness can be symptoms of early pregnancy,' Anna remarked when Ivy returned to the nursery.

'I'm definitely not pregnant. It's impossible.'

'Babies come when they come. I understand that Bertie was a surprise pregnancy,' Anna said tactfully.

Of course the nanny, like everyone else, believed that Bertie was Rafa's and her child. Ivy hated lying and wished she could confide in Anna, who had become a good friend. But she had given her word that she would not tell a soul the identity of Bertie's father while Rafa's mother could be devastated by the truth.

'You can discuss your symptoms with the doctor,' Anna said. 'Your husband has been concerned about you and he arranged for the doctor to visit the castle.

Doctor Coretti duly arrived for a consultation with Ivy. She had to rely on his discretion when she explained that Bertie had been adopted, that she was infertile and could not be pregnant.

'It is best to rule out the possibility of pregnancy,' he murmured, handing her a test.

With a shrug, Ivy went into the bathroom, knowing that doing the test was a pointless exercise. A few minutes later she stared at the two blue lines in the test window and frantically re-read the instructions.

Two blue lines meant positive. Her heart stopped beating. She had been told that it would be virtually impossible for her to conceive naturally. She couldn't be pregnant.

The doctor spoke to cancer specialists in Italy and the hospital in Southampton, where Ivy had received some of her treatment. Apparently it was rare for fertility to return after the high doses of chemotherapy she'd received as a teenager. But sometimes miracles happened, Doctor Coretti said cheerfully.

Ivy could not absorb the mind-blowing news that she was expecting a baby. She had been so grateful to be alive after she'd recovered from cancer that she had accepted that being infertile from the chemotherapy was a small price to pay.

Her miracle baby. She placed her hand on her flat stomach and wondered if she dared believe there was a new life developing inside her. Rafa's baby. She dared not imagine what his reaction would be when she told him. He was bound to be as shocked as she was. She remembered how adamant he had been that he did not want a child of his own—it was why he had made Bertie his heir. But surely, once he got over his surprise, he would realise that their baby was a million-to-one miracle.

One thing was certain. She could not wait until the

evening, when he was due to return to the castle, to tell him about the baby, nor would it be fair to break the news to him in a phone call. Rafa had driven himself to Rome in his new sports car, which meant that the helicopter was available.

Ivy usually enjoyed travelling in the helicopter, but she felt horribly sick for the entire flight, and was glad to climb out of the cabin after the pilot landed on the helipad on the top of the Vieri Azioni office building. The views across Rome from the roof were incredible, but Ivy did not linger. Her nerves were jangling at the prospect of breaking her shocking news to Rafa.

A flight of stairs took her down to the floor where his office and the boardroom were, and she was met by his PA, who explained that Rafa's meeting had finished but he was still in the boardroom. 'I'll tell him you are here,' Giulia offered.

'No, I'll surprise him.' It would not be the first time, Ivy thought ruefully, remembering how she had slipped past Rafa's personal assistant and burst into the boardroom to confront him with Bertie. This time she knocked and took a deep breath to steady her nerves before she walked in.

'Ivy.' Rafa broke off his conversation with another man when he saw her. 'This is a delightful surprise, *cara*.' He must have noticed her tension and his smile faded. 'Did you meet the doctor?' The concern in his voice warmed Ivy's heart.

'That's why I'm here…' She broke off, puzzled when she recognised the man standing beside Rafa.

'Sandro, I'd like to speak to my wife in private,' Rafa murmured.

'It *is* you.' Ivy could not hide her shock as she stared at the older man. 'You're Gelato Man. Don't you remember me? We met outside the office building and you took me to a café and bought me an ice-cream.'

'I'm afraid I don't…' the man murmured.

'It was definitely you.' Her heart was racing. 'I remember you said that you had heard me accuse Rafa of being Bertie's father and suggested I could sell the story to the press. You even gave me a reporter's business card and contact details.'

The man called Sandro looked at Rafa. 'I think your wife must be confusing me with someone else. I'm sure there is a simple explanation.' He gave Ivy a patronising smile. 'Memory can play tricks on us,' he said before he walked out of the boardroom.

'I know he was the man I met,' Ivy insisted to Rafa.

'*Cara*, Sandro Florenzi has worked for the company for forty years. Isn't it possible that you are mistaken?' Rafa said quietly.

'You don't believe me?'

'I have known Sandro all my life. He was a good friend of my father's.' Rafa frowned. 'I admit that Sandro had hoped to become chairman and CEO and he was disappointed when I succeeded my father. But I am sure he would not do anything to harm Vieri Azioni. I trust him.'

'But you don't trust me, even though I am your wife.'

Rafa did not reply, and his silence felt like a knife in Ivy's heart. He raked a hand through his hair. 'I will talk to Sandro and try to get to the bottom of the mystery. Why don't I take you to lunch, hmm?' He ran his finger lightly down her cheek. 'And this afternoon we'll go shopping.'

Ivy wondered if Rafa could hear her heart shatter. He would buy her anything she wanted, but she did not want material things. *You want him to trust you and love you,* whispered a voice inside her. But he would never do either and the fairy tale she had started to believe might come true turned to dust.

'Rafa…' She prayed for a second miracle. 'I… I'm pregnant.'

'Repeat what you just said,' Rafa demanded. He must have misunderstood. Ivy could not really have said she was pregnant. But her stricken expression told him what he definitely did not want to hear. He swore. This was the second time that Ivy had burst into the boardroom and detonated a bomb that would blow his life apart.

'You assured me that you were unable to have a child.' His phone rang, and with a curse he pulled it out of his pocket and switched the device off.

'I believed I was infertile,' she said huskily. 'When I had cancer, my monthly cycle stopped as a result of the chemo. After a few years I started to have sporadic periods, but I was advised that I would almost certainly never fall pregnant naturally.'

'So how did it happen?' He felt sick. It was as though he was revisiting the nightmare when Tiffany had told him she was expecting his baby, and he had been a gullible fool for two years when he'd believed Lola was his daughter. The difference now was that Ivy had insisted it was safe for them to have unprotected sex because she was unable to have children and he had believed her.

Dio, would he never learn that all women were liars? Rafa thought savagely. A few minutes ago Ivy had accused the deputy CEO of treachery when she'd said that Sandro had urged her to tell the news reporter the story that Rafa Vieri had fathered an illegitimate child. Rafa had been tempted to believe her, despite Sandro's denial. Recently he had begun to doubt her involvement in the news story. But she must have lied about being infertile, and it stood to reason that she could have lied about Sandro Florenzi.

Rage burned like acid in Rafa's gut. He had been a fool to have fallen for Ivy's sweet smile that disguised her damning lies. 'I'll want proof,' he said curtly.

Ivy's head jerked back as if he had slapped her. 'Proof of what? That I'm pregnant or that it's your baby? I've shared your bed every night since we married six weeks ago. When would I have had a chance to play away, even if I'd wanted to? You know I've only ever had sex with you.'

Tears sparkled on her lashes like tiny diamonds. Ivy cried easily, but she was quicker to laugh, and she was the most responsive lover he'd ever known. She held nothing back when they made love, and she was open in her adoration and devotion to Bertie. Rafa did not doubt she would love this baby with the same fierce intensity. *His baby*. Ivy's unguarded emotions had led him to lower his guard and even to start to trust her, which was something he had vowed he would never do again.

His jaw clenched when she came to stand in front of him and he breathed in the floral scent of her perfume, delicate yet subtly sensual, like Ivy herself. 'Maybe you don't believe that I had cancer and I pretended that the treatment had left me infertile.' Her voice shook, but her wounded gaze did not waiver from his.

'I don't…' he began roughly.

'Do you think I made it up that my hair fell out?' She touched the feathery blonde layers that framed her face. 'When my hair grew back after I'd finished chemo, it was a lighter colour, and it breaks easily, so that I can't grow it long. My hair wasn't the only thing that having cancer changed. It made me doubt my body, and it taught me that life is fragile. When I started feeling nauseous and tired recently, I was scared…'

The crack in her voice dealt another blow to the fortress that Rafa had built around his heart. 'I thought the cancer had come back and I might not be around to see Bertie grow up.' She wiped away her tears and more fell. 'Perhaps you think it would be better if I was ill instead of pregnant?'

'*Dio!* Of course I don't.' He pinched the bridge of his nose. His tension was off the scale. 'It's a shock.'

Ivy nodded. 'I was worried about your reaction when I told you. But I didn't expect you to accuse me of lying. I know what your ex-wife did, but you can't keep punishing me for her crimes. And I can't stay married to you if you will never trust me. It hurts too much.' She swallowed. 'I deserve better. Our baby deserves better than to grow up with parents who hate each other.'

'I don't hate you.'

'You will resent me and our baby if you believe that I deliberately tried to fall pregnant.' Tears streamed down her face. 'You don't love me.' It was an anguished cry. 'I could bear it if I knew you would love our baby. But you won't, will you? You're good with Bertie, but I've noticed how you hold back from loving him. You are determined to barricade yourself in your fortress so that love can't find you.'

And make a fool of me, Rafa thought darkly. 'You are being melodramatic. When you've calmed down, we'll discuss—'

'There's nothing to discuss. I'm keeping my miracle baby—at least, I hope I will.' Her mouth trembled. 'I'm only a few weeks into my pregnancy. Experience has taught me that life doesn't have "happiness guaranteed" stamped on the box.'

CHAPTER ELEVEN

IVY TIED RAFA in knots, and her vulnerability made him want to hold her in his arms and promise her that the baby would be fine. But he did not know what the future held. One reason why he had been adamantly opposed to fatherhood was because he had suffered the agony of losing a child when his ex-wife had taken Lola away.

He glared at his PA, who appeared in the doorway. 'I'm sorry to interrupt, Rafa, but your mother called your mobile, and when you didn't answer she came through on the office line. She sounded upset and said she needs to see you urgently.'

What else could go wrong? Rafa wondered. He turned to Ivy. 'We need to talk rationally, but right now I don't feel rational,' he said grimly. 'Go to the penthouse and I'll meet you there as soon as I've visited my mother.'

She walked out of the boardroom without saying another word. Rafa called the pilot. It would be much quicker to travel across the city by helicopter, and he wanted to get back to Ivy as soon as possible.

At the hospital, he hurried to his mother's private room and felt a pang to see her looking so gaunt. He leaned down to kiss her cheek and was surprised when she clung to him for a moment.

'What is wrong, *Mamma*?'

'Your father's assistant came to see me.' Fabiana's voice shook. 'Beatriz gave me a letter that Rafael had written just before he died. His death was so sudden. When Beatriz found some of his personal documents and realised they would cause a scandal if they fell into the wrong hands, she hid them to protect his reputation. But she was sure your father had meant me to see the letter. Here it is.'

Rafa read the letter his mother handed him. His father had been completely truthful about the brief affair he'd had while he'd been on a cruise that had resulted in the young woman giving birth to his baby. Rafael had explained how desperately sorry he was for the pain and upset he had caused everyone involved but that Fabiana, his beloved wife, had a right to know the truth.

'I don't know what to say,' Rafa admitted as he returned the letter to his mother. '*Papa* made a terrible mistake in what he did, but he was right to be honest with you.'

Fabiana nodded. 'There were never secrets between us. Rafael loved me, and my love for him has not diminished. He was a good husband. And you, Rafa, are a wonderful and loyal son. Bertie is Rafael's son, isn't he?

'I have been lying here thinking about it,' she said softly when Rafa froze. 'It was too much of a coincidence that Bertie is the exact age that the child from your father's affair would be. But I don't believe that Ivy is Bertie's mother. She is not good at lying, and she knew very little about pregnancy symptoms.'

Dio! Rafa thought of the astounding news Ivy had just told him, that she was pregnant with his baby. His reaction had been diabolical. Remorse shredded his insides as he acknowledged that Ivy was an unconvincing liar because she was innately honest. But she had agreed to be his fiancée and then his wife to protect his mother's feelings. In the end, the pretence had been unnecessary because his father had admitted what he had done.

'Ivy's sister Gemma was Bertie's mother,' he explained. 'But she died, and Ivy became his legal guardian.'

'I suppose Ivy came to Italy to ask you for help to bring up your half-brother. But you instantly fell in love with her and decided to marry her.'

Rafa stared at his mother. He had been about to deny that he'd fallen in love with Ivy, but with a jolt he realised that he was the biggest fool of all time.

You don't love me, Ivy had sobbed, and he'd frozen. Love hadn't been part of the deal. They had agreed that their marriage would be a sensible arrangement. Ivy had admitted that she wore her heart on her sleeve, and he'd sensed that she hoped for more than he could give her. He had made it clear that he couldn't give her love. He'd been honest.

Had he, though? Rafa forced himself to look inside his heart. He had never told Ivy that he loved seeing her face on the pillow beside him every morning. He'd never told her that his once gloomy castle was filled with light and laughter now that she lived there with him. He certainly hadn't told her that he was scared the way she made him feel weakened in some way.

What had he done? Rafa closed his eyes and saw

Ivy's tear-stained face. He knew in his gut that Sandro must somehow have been responsible for the news story. And he did not doubt that Ivy had believed she was unable to have children after her cancer ordeal as a teenager. She had called their baby a miracle and that was exactly what her pregnancy was. An even greater miracle would be if she gave him a second chance to put things right between them.

'*Mamma*, I have behaved appallingly to Ivy,' he said raggedly.

His mother squeezed his hand. 'She will forgive you because she loves you. Go to her, *mio caro figlio*.'

Rafa called Ivy as he tore out of the hospital. 'Are you still at the penthouse, *cara*? I'll be with you in a few minutes.'

'I didn't go to the penthouse. I'm on my way back to the castle in a taxi because earlier I felt sick in the helicopter. I'm going to take Bertie to England and make a home for him and the new baby.' She swallowed audibly and Rafa pictured her big brown eyes brimming with tears. 'My phone battery is about to die, but there is nothing for us to say to each other. I want more than you can give me. I need to know that you trust me and… and care for me a little.'

'I do…' Rafa swore when the line went dead.

The journey to the castle in the helicopter took much less time than by car, and he arrived before Ivy. The castle felt empty without her. He wandered through the rooms, noticing how she had made the once gloomy fortress into a happy family home with potted plants everywhere, framed photos of Bertie and pictures from their honeymoon in Hawaii. He had taken the little signs of her presence for granted, but the idea that she might leave and take Bertie with her made his gut clench.

He wanted to persuade her to stay, but there was still a part of him that was reluctant to open up about his feelings for her and make himself vulnerable. Ivy's pregnancy was an excuse to push her into agreeing to continue with their marriage and would give him time to come to terms with the terrifying reality that the walls of his fortress were crumbling.

An hour passed, and then another. Ivy should have arrived by now. Rafa stood next to the window, watching impatiently for the taxi to turn into the courtyard. He replayed the awful things he had said to her over in his mind. He felt even more guilty after he discovered from a source who worked in the media that the reporter Luigi Cappello had confirmed Sandro Florenzi had given him the story alleging that Bertie was Rafa's illegitimate son.

He had misjudged the resentment Sandro had felt at missing out on becoming the CEO of Vieri Azioni. The baby scandal had caused the other board members and shareholders to withdraw their support from Rafa, as Sandro had intended.

He turned away from his vigil by the window when the nanny entered the study. 'Bertie is having his afternoon nap.' Anna's usual cheerful smile was missing. 'Have you seen the news report of the traffic accident on the *autostrada*? At least six cars were involved, and apparently there have been fatalities.' She looked close to tears. 'Ivy called me from a taxi when she left Rome, but I've been unable to get hold of her since then.'

'She said her phone battery had been about to die.' Rafa scrolled to a news site on his phone and read the report of the accident. Photographs showed a tangled mass of metal and wrecked vehicles, and emergency medics were treating the injured at the roadside. Dread felt like a lead weight in the pit of his stomach.

'The road has been closed since the accident happened,' Anna said. 'Apparently the traffic congestion is taking a long time to clear. Ivy is probably stuck in a tailback and will be home soon.'

'Yes.' He looked away from the nanny's sympathetic expression and returned to stare out of the window. 'Please, *piccola*,' he said beneath his breath. 'Please come home. I need you.' He thought of Bertie in the nursery, waiting for his beloved *mamma*, and whispered hoarsely, 'We both need you.'

Ivy shivered when she saw the blue flashing lights in the distance. The traffic on the *autostrada* was at a standstill and several emergency services vehicles had shot past on the hard shoulder. The wail of their sirens brought back memories of the road accident that had claimed her sister's life.

'Do you know what has happened?' she asked the taxi driver.

He did not speak much English, but he must have understood, and the meaning of his reply was clear. *'Incidente.'*

She hoped the people involved in the accident were not seriously hurt, or worse. Lives could be lost or changed irrevocably in an instant. Since she'd lost Gemma, Ivy had tried to live her life as fully and honestly as possible. That was why it had hurt so much when Rafa had accused her of lying about being infertile.

She had expected him to be shocked. After all, she still couldn't quite believe that she was going to have a baby. She held her hands over her stomach where the precious new life was developing. The baby would be a brother or sister for Bertie, for she would always treasure her sister's child as dearly as her own. But, instead of being in a family, she would be a single mother. Rafa had made it clear that he did not want their baby.

Ivy had no more tears left, and she felt angry with Rafa for his refusal to trust her, even though she hadn't given him any reason to think she had lied to him. She had always been honest with him. Although, that wasn't quite true, her conscience prodded her. She hadn't been honest about her feelings for him. She had hidden her love for him because she'd been afraid of his rejection.

Rafa had told her what his ex-wife had done, how Tiffany had tricked him into believing he had a daughter, whom he'd loved. It was not surprising that he had built a fortress around his emotions. Perhaps, if she'd found the courage to offer him her heart, he might have started to trust her, Ivy thought miserably. It was too late now. He had pulled up the drawbridge and love could not reach him.

The traffic was gridlocked and time passed slowly. An hour, two hours. She stared, frustrated, at her phone's black screen. She had told Anna she was on her way back to the castle, and she imagined how concerned the nanny would be when she failed to return.

It was likely that the traffic accident had been reported in the news.

Ivy wondered if Rafa was worried about her. Another half an hour ticked by and her anger turned to despair. She wished she had told him how she felt about him. The road accident that had resulted in the traffic jam emphasised that life and love could not be taken for granted. Rafa had been badly hurt in the past, and he deserved to know that she loved him, and that she would love his baby who was part of him. She was desperate to reach the castle and cuddle Bertie. She needed to start making plans for the future. A future without the only man she would ever love.

Rafa rested his forehead on the window pane. His eyes ached from staring into the distance for a glimpse of the taxi and it must be why his lashes were wet. Big boys were not meant to cry. But a stupid, foolish man who hadn't appreciated the treasure he had been gifted until he faced the gut-wrenching possibility that he might have lost his golden girl—he cried. Silent tears leaked from his eyes and burned in his chest.

He should have told Ivy that he wanted their baby, their miracle. A choked sound of agony was ripped from his throat. If Ivy had been injured, would the baby survive? He wanted to protect her from hurt and pain, and he'd wanted to protect himself, he admitted. Who wanted love when it risked tearing your emotions to shreds? He'd thought he was safe in his fortress, but love had found a way in when he hadn't expected it and had captured his heart.

Lights appeared in the darkness outside, car headlamps that turned through the castle gates. Rafa heard his pulse thundering in his ears as he shot out of the room and took the stairs two at a time. He halted, and his gut clenched as he realised that in the dark he hadn't seen if the car was a taxi…or a police car bringing devastating news that Ivy had been hurt in the traffic accident. He wouldn't allow himself to think she might be dead. He could not bear to lose her.

Before Rafa reached the door, it opened and Ivy walked in. He was amazed that his legs kept him upright. She looked confused to see him.

'Why are you here?' she said in a defeated voice. 'I thought you would be at the penthouse.'

Ivy wished Rafa would say something instead of staring at her as if she were a ghost. The expression on his face made her heart thump, but he always had that effect on her, she thought wearily. Somehow she would have to get over him, in a hundred years or so. She wondered if he would try and prevent her from taking Bertie away. They would have to come to an arrangement over visiting rights. Maybe he would want custody. She felt sick as she added that new worry to the long list in her head. She could not bear to be parted from Bertie.

But she couldn't stay married to Rafa and have his baby when she would never have his love. It was destroying her, destroying the self-confidence she had found since she'd married him. Worst of all, it was destroying the sense of hope that had carried her through her cancer treatment and losing her beloved sister—the hope that she would one day find a man who loved her. She had reached the end of the fairy tale and discovered that happy-ever-after was a foolish dream after all, just as her mum had found with each of her failed marriages.

Rafa strode towards her and Ivy caught her breath at the wildness in his eyes. His skin was pulled tight over his cheekbones and his jaw was clenched. She had a sense that it was taking his immense willpower to hold himself together.

'Where else would I be but where you are, *tesoro*?' His voice was strained, as if it hurt to speak.

'Don't,' she whispered. She was fooling herself to think he sounded as if he cared about her when she knew he didn't. 'I don't want to be married to you any more, Rafa.'

She heard his sharply indrawn breath. 'I know I have given you every reason to despise me, *piccola.* But if you would give me a chance to show you…to tell you…'

'Tell me what?' She did not understand why he sounded so—broken, as if the idea of her not being his wife hurt him deeply.

'I…' His throat worked as he swallowed hard. 'I know it was Sandro who spoke to the journalist.' For some reason, Ivy had had an idea that he'd been about to say something else. 'I should have believed you, and I will spend the rest of my life trying to win your forgiveness.'

'It doesn't matter now.' She'd forgotten about Gelato Man. 'Why should you have believed me? I know your first wife deceived you.'

'You are nothing like Tiffany.' Rafa's eyes blazed. 'You wear your honesty like a badge, but I was too blinded by my prejudices and bitterness to see the beauty of your heart.'

'Please don't.' Ivy could not take much more, and tears brimmed in her eyes. 'There was an accident and people died.'

'I was terrified that I'd lost you.' Rafa's voice broke and, if Ivy's heart hadn't already been in a million pieces, it would have shattered then. He touched her jaw, and she was startled to see his hand was unsteady. The sheen in his eyes turned them from grey to silver and she did not dare attempt to define the emotion blazing from beneath his thick lashes.

Ivy remembered the promise she had made to herself in the taxi that she would be honest about how she felt about Rafa. Everything was telling her that he felt something for her. Maybe what he felt wasn't love, but it was no reason to withhold her love from him.

'I thought I could marry you and not fall in love with you,' she confessed. 'But I was wrong. I was already in love with you on our wedding day, and I have loved you more with every day since I became your wife.' She put up her hand to hold him off when he moved towards her. 'I love you, but I can't stay in this marriage.'

'Because I don't want the baby,' Rafa said tautly.

Hearing him say it destroyed what was left of her composure and she dropped her face into her hands as sobs tore through her.

'*Tesoro*. Ivy, *amore mio*.' Rafa groaned, pulling her into his arms. 'I want our baby more than almost anything in the world. The only thing I want more is for you to love me as much as I love you.'

She opened her mouth but no words came out. 'You said you would never fall in love. I understand, I do. Your first wife hurt you with her lies…' Her voice tailed off and her heart stopped when she saw that Rafa's eyelashes were wet.

'I love you.' He rested his forehead against her brow. Ivy put her hands on his chest and felt the thunder of his heart beneath her fingertips. 'I tried to deny how you made me feel, and I thought I could be happy with the friendship that grew stronger between us every day. But the truth is that you stole my heart from the beginning, and I never want it back. It's yours, *piccola*, and I know you will take care of it because I trust you beyond words.'

'Rafa…' She was afraid to believe him.

'I want our baby and I will love him or her,' he said intently. 'I already do because the baby is part of you. One day we will tell our eldest child that he is special because we chose to be his parents, and we'll tell our second child how lucky we are to have been given a miracle.'

He captured her tears with his thumbs and gently wiped them from her cheeks. 'Every day I will tell you how much I love you, and if I am luckier than I deserve to be then perhaps one day you'll believe me.'

Rafa's hands shook when he framed her face, and the tenderness in his kiss healed Ivy and made her whole, made her believe in a love so strong it would last a lifetime.

'I love you. I can't remember a time when I didn't,' she admitted softly. She smiled against his mouth when he kissed her and told her that she was his world, the love of his life. His wife. Their passion had always been electrifying, and it blazed when Rafa drew her closer and ran his hands over her body as if he was scared she might disappear.

'I don't deserve you,' he murmured as he swept her up into his arms and carried her upstairs to their bedroom. 'I am going to spend the rest of my life showing you how much I love you.'

'Will you start now?' she asked when he tumbled them down on the bed and they undressed each other with trembling hands.

Rafa drew her into his arms and kissed her with tender passion that quickly became urgent as desire and love combined, and each caress felt new and wondrous.

'I will, my love,' he promised.

EPILOGUE

NICOLO VIERI ARRIVED with minimum fuss—although a good deal of stress for Rafa, who would willingly have endured Ivy's labour pains—on a sunny spring morning. The baby was born in the castle and, once he had been thoroughly inspected by his *mamma*, who pronounced him perfect, he was introduced to his big brother. Bertie had grown into a lively toddler who was adored by his parents, and baby Nico was a treasured addition to the family.

When Anna took Bertie off to play in the garden, Ivy carried her newborn son over to the window to give him his first glimpse of the world, but he remained steadfastly asleep. 'He's so beautiful,' she whispered, entranced by Nico's long eyelashes curling on his cheeks. 'I never imagined I could be this happy.'

Rafa came to stand behind her and wrapped his arms around her waist. 'Do you have any idea how much I love you, *curore mio*? You and our children are my world.'

Outside the window an orange butterfly settled on the ivy that grew over the castle's walls. It remained there, opening and closing its delicate wings, before it took off again. Ivy watched it fly up into the blue sky and smiled.

* * * * *

STRANDED WITH MY FORBIDDEN BILLIONAIRE

LUCY KING

MILLS & BOON

CHAPTER ONE

If someone had told me six weeks ago that, come November, I'd be aboard a speedboat jetting towards Nick Morgan's private island in the Indian Ocean, five thousand miles from my flat share in London, with the intention of requesting his help, I'd have stared at them in astonishment and asked what they were on.

For the sake of my older brother, Seb, with whom he'd been friends for years, Nick and I were just about civil to each other whenever our paths crossed, but we didn't get along.

We'd met when he'd started at our exclusive boarding school in the same year as my brother. They were both thirteen and I was eleven. Seb and I were the children of a multimillionaire financier who had single-handedly funded the school's new business studies centre. Nick was the clever son of a single mother, who had grown up in poverty and been awarded a free place. He found me impossibly spoilt and shallow, I knew, while I considered him absurdly aloof and uptight.

Since then, our fortunes had dramatically reversed but things between us were still as frosty as ever and, under normal circumstances, hell would have to freeze over before I'd ever seek him out.

But then I won one hundred and eight million pounds on the national lottery—give or take a penny or two—and was very nearly scammed out of half of it, and that changed everything.

'You need proper professional help, Millie,' Seb told me when I rang him in a panic, my heart pounding and my palms sweating as the delayed shock of the win, the near miss I'd had with the fraudsters and the realisation of how suddenly vulnerable I was on so many fronts finally hit home. 'Get in touch with Nick. He does this sort of thing for a living and he's extremely good at it.'

Seb was right. Over the last decade, Nick had made a fortune from dishing out top-level financial advice and the sales of products he'd developed off the back of it. He'd started his career as an advocate of the high risk, high reward way of making money on someone else's payroll before switching to a slower, steadier approach to wealth management when he set up on his own. He'd developed an unshakeable reputation for both ability and trustworthiness and, grudgingly, I had to admit that if anyone was the man for the job, it was probably him.

There was just one teeny tiny problem.

'Nick hates me,' I said, recalling with a shiver the hard set of his jaw and the chill that appeared in his slate-grey gaze whenever he laid eyes on me these days.

'He doesn't.'

'He does.'

'Either way,' said Seb, clearly reluctant to venture down that rabbit hole yet again, 'how is that relevant?'

'It might make him less inclined to help.'

'I very much doubt that. The fees he'd earn would be astronomical. He won't be able to resist.'

'But he already has billions,' I said, all too easily able to envisage a scenario where he coolly heard me out and then baldly refused, as if trying to make some kind of a point, to mete out an unnecessary lesson in humility, perhaps. 'Is he that driven by money?'

'He's *only* driven by money,' came the dry reply down the line from San Francisco. 'But seriously, Mills, he'll take care of you. He's the man you need. Believe me.'

I didn't need any man, least of all one who loathed me, nor did I want to be taken care of. When our father lost everything virtually overnight eight years ago, a month before my twenty-first birthday, I'd crash-landed in the real world. Among other things, I'd learned the importance of self-reliance and the value of independence, and now fiercely guarded both. And while men were fine for the rare occasion I fancied a spot of company on a cold night, the only proper boyfriend I'd ever had had unceremoniously dumped me the minute I became penniless. The experience had been crushing and I wasn't keen to repeat it.

But one hundred and eight million pounds was a mammoth responsibility. I knew nothing of investments other than that as well as up, they could go down, down and down some more, and my brush with the scammers suggested I might possibly have inherited my father's rash decision-making when it came to handling a fortune. I did need help, I had to admit. And, with Seb's suggestion flashing like a beacon in my head and the unsolicited offers of advice from people I'd never heard of still coming in thick and fast, I'd eventually thought, *better the devil you know.*

So I'd emailed Nick, who informed me that if I wanted to see him I'd have to hop on a plane, and now here I was twenty-four hours later, halfway around the world, part furious that I was so desperate for his help I'd had to acquiesce to his summons, part relieved he hadn't simply told me to get lost.

As the boat I'd picked up in Dar es Salaam sped across the sparkling sapphire water with James, the driver that came with it, at the helm, the small land mass shimmering on the horizon grew and solidified. I shaded my eyes against the bright sun that blazed in a cloudless sky and, in an attempt to distract myself from the nerves that were twisting my stomach because I had no idea of the reception I was going to get, focused on the scenery.

The glorious stretch of curving white sand beach fringed with palm trees that hove into view was like something out of a glossy brochure. It was perfect, alluring, and so mesmerising I barely noticed the water turning to a light jade in colour as it shallowed, or the boat gradually slowing. It was only when we bumped against something solid, jolting me out of my trance, that I whipped my head round to find out what was going on and realised with a quick skip of my pulse that we'd arrived and I had a welcome party.

Of one.

Nick.

Who was standing on the gently bobbing pontoon with his arms folded across his broad chest and looking at me with his habitual inscrutability.

His face was set, his eyes were dark and his jaw was rigid, but that was where the familiarity ended, I noticed, my mouth drying and my skin prickling in a most peculiar way as I took in the rest of his appearance. His usually immaculate hair was longer than normal, and ruffled. Instead of his customary tailor-made suit, he had on a pair of turquoise board shorts, patterned, no less, with a multicoloured tropical plant print. In place of the inevitable pristine white shirt that he always wore with the two top buttons undone was, of all astonishing things, a lemon-yellow polo shirt.

What was going on? I wondered, baffled and not a little unsettled by the unexpected sight of some toned tanned biceps and a pair of long, surprisingly muscled legs. So much colour. Such informality. Could he be ill? And where, in all that was holy, were his *shoes*?

'Nick, hi,' I said, parking these bewildering questions for later analysis and plastering on a bright smile while deciding to attribute the jitters bouncing around inside me to the long overnight flight.

'A pleasure to see you as always, Amelia,' he replied as he deftly caught the rope that James cast in his direction, and pulled it taut.

Despite the distracting flurry of activity and the impressive flexing of muscles, I tensed minutely and inwardly winced at the lie. At any lie, in fact. The closest, most important relationship of my youth—the one I'd had with my father—had turned out to be the biggest lie of all and these days I valued honesty, no matter how brutal.

So I didn't reply with a socially conventional but meaningless 'likewise'. But nor did I react to Nick's use of my full name with my usual roll of the eyes, because at thirty thousand feet above Egypt I'd come up with a simple yet mature strategy for this meeting.

One, ignore the past and focus on the present.

Two, keep things professional at all times.

And finally, perhaps most importantly, stay calm and resist the temptation to respond to Nick's dislike of me by instinctively exhibiting the silliness and superficiality he expected, in a sort of sticking two fingers up at him kind of a way.

Instead, I breathed in through my mouth and out through my nose, deeply and slowly and repeatedly, until the sulky teen in me had flounced off and I was channelling Zen-like serenity.

'Thank you,' I said smoothly, accepting the hand he held out and stepping off the boat and onto the pontoon.

He let me go abruptly and frowned down at the huge suitcase James was struggling to lift up and out. 'How long are you planning on staying?'

'Not long,' I said, surreptitiously rubbing my hand against my skirt in an attempt to dispel the strange tingling sensation that lingered while Nick relieved James of his burden as if it weighed no more than a feather.

'It feels like you've packed for weeks.'

'Just a fortnight.'

He shot me a look, a flicker of alarm breaking through the ice-cool reserve, which meant he had to be seriously rattled by the idea. 'A fortnight?'

'Don't worry,' I assured him as he tossed the rope back to James. 'I don't intend to spend it here.'

Perish the thought. I knew when I wasn't wanted. And it was fine. I was well used to being on my own, and actually, I preferred things like that. Experience had taught me relationships weren't to be trusted. I'd learnt the hard way how fickle other people could be, when those I'd considered my friends, including my then boyfriend, had ghosted me at a time I'd needed them most.

I couldn't even rely on family, I'd eventually come to realise. My father, whom I'd adored, had emotionally distanced himself the minute he'd discovered my mother was having an affair with her personal trainer and had decided to redirect all his efforts into winning her back. Thanks to my role in the breakdown of their marriage in the first place, my mother and I had a tricky relationship at the best of times, and my brother, the only person I might have been able to count on, lived five thousand miles and eight time zones away so was therefore more often out of reach than he was in it.

But none of that was anything new. I'd accepted it and adapted to it years ago. And if the self-reliance and the tough outer shell I'd developed meant that I allowed no one to get close, that I had no one to talk to about my hopes and fears, or anyone with whom to share my tumultuous and conflicted feelings about my lottery win, well, the occasional pang of loneliness was a small price to pay for self-preservation. True friendship, love of the romantic kind, marriage in particular, required a level of trust I simply couldn't see myself ever embracing. Emotional involvement in anything only led to confusion, pain and heartbreak. It was far easier, far *safer*, for me and for others, if I steered well clear of all of it.

'I wasn't aware I'd invited you to,' said Nick, his tersely made point snapping me out of my ruminations and obliterating the twinges of regret I nevertheless felt at the way things had turned out.

No, well, quite, I thought, determinedly pulling myself together. And thank goodness for it. Days of stilted conversation and keeping out of each other's way? The tension and awkwardness would be unbearable and very much *not* my idea of a good time. 'I've booked myself a room at a hotel on Zanzibar.'

At the *best* hotel on Zanzibar, in actual fact. Where, according to its website, Scandi minimalism met hints of the Middle East amidst twenty hectares of lush tropical gardens. Where, for my first holiday abroad in eight years, two weeks of pampering and indulgence awaited me, along with a waterfall bar, two infinity pools and a villa that came with a dedicated butler. Instead of schlepping to and from the office where I worked as a manager in the dark November mizzle, I'd be sliding on my sunglasses and trotting to my sun lounger with a book. There'd be long, blissful naps and lazy, luxurious massages. Yoga for breakfast and lobster for dinner, and, with any luck, a tan.

Just like old times.

Well, not *quite* like old times, perhaps. Old times would have also involved diving with my dad, the two of us gliding among the fish and the coral in the silky silence thirty feet beneath the surface of warm turquoise water, the connection and trust between us stronger than steel. Or so I'd always imagined, until amidst the wreckage of our misfortune I'd discovered that he wasn't the hero I'd believed him to be, that the unique bond I'd thought we shared was nothing more than an illusion, that I didn't actually know him at all…

But still.

I could hardly wait.

'The helicopter's coming to pick me up in an hour,' I told Nick, shaking off the conflicting emotions of grief and loss, pain and betrayal that could still blindside me, even now, seven years, six months and twenty-one days after my father's fatal heart attack, and dragging myself back to the present.

'Good,' he said flatly. 'The quicker we sort out what you want from me and you go on your way, the better.'

He turned to stride back up the pontoon, my suitcase in his hand, while I stood there waving James off, his words ringing in my ears, suddenly feeling a little dazed, a little winded, and thinking that perhaps, on reflection, brutal honesty wasn't quite all it was cracked up to be.

CHAPTER TWO

IT WAS A five-minute walk along a sandy path that cut through dense verdant vegetation to reach Nick's house, which gave me ample opportunity to reflect upon my bizarre response to the feel of his hand around mine and the quick tightening of my chest at his parting shot.

The former was easy enough to explain. Despite having known each other for eighteen years, Nick and I had never actually touched. Not once. Which was odd when I'd always been the touchy-feely sort. But as a surly teenager, he'd radiated back-off vibes, and in the years following my sixteenth birthday pool party at which I'd irretrievably shattered all possibility of a friendly sort of relationship, any contact would have resulted in frostbite.

These days, whenever we met—mostly on the occasions my brother was over from the States and arranged a get-together—we tended to give each other a cool sort of nod and a very wide berth. So it was little wonder that actual frostbite-free physical contact, however fleeting, would come as a shock so intense I could still feel it zinging through me.

The sense of being thumped in the solar plexus at the

implication that he couldn't wait for me to leave was harder to fathom. It suggested that I cared about what he thought of me, but that wasn't the case. I truly didn't. His continued brooding yet unspoken disapproval of my superficiality—once undoubtedly justified—was unwarranted these days, and if he couldn't move on and accept that I was no longer an over-indulged, self-absorbed teenager then that was his problem, not mine.

Maybe it stung because up until that moment he'd never openly expressed his dislike of me, and to have it confirmed somehow made it unequivocally real. Or maybe, with the stress I'd been under recently and the lack of a support network, which I'd been feeling more acutely than usual, I was simply more sensitive to a barb that otherwise might have bounced right off, and overreacting. Who knew? And what did it matter? Ultimately, all that was important was securing Nick's help in managing the fortune that had dropped into my lap and already caused so much trouble.

The shrubbery thinned and the path came to an end, along with my ruminations, which were flattened by the impact of the sight that met my eyes. Built from wood painted a blinding white and possessing innumerable windows and glass doors off which the sun glinted, the two-storey villa was vast and stunning. Tall pillars on the ground floor supported a veranda that wrapped around the first, providing the long wide terrace below with dappled shade. The enormous raised rectangular pool had clear sides so the water within looked like a thick solid slab of cobalt. A vast swathe of emerald-green grass edged the beach, beyond which lay the sparkling sea. Palm trees swished in the breeze and brightly coloured flowers stood in planters dotted around the grounds. As tropical paradises went this one was unbeatable, and I'd seen a few.

'This is a lovely house,' I said with what had to be the understatement of the century as I hauled my jaw off the floor and followed him up the wide timber steps to the deck.

'I like it.'

'I can see why you choose to spend the winters here.'

'I'm not a fan of the cold.'

'Oh, I don't know,' I said, acutely aware that sweat was about to start trickling unattractively down my temples, although why the attractiveness of anything should matter I had no idea. 'Hot chocolate, roaring fires and cashmere. What's not to like?'

'Winter isn't hot chocolate, roaring fires and cashmere for everyone,' he said in a tone that shrivelled my stomach and sent a flush to my cheeks that had nothing to do with the heat.

No. Right. Stupid of me. Nick had grown up with very little. I remembered my brother telling me once years ago when I must have been about thirteen that his mother had frequently had to make the choice between eating and heating. Unable to comprehend such a situation and, in all honesty, not particularly interested in my brother's lanky taciturn friend anyway, I'd shrugged and put it from my mind, one of the many moments of which I'm not proud.

'I guess not,' I said, berating myself for yet again speaking without thinking, which unfortunately happened all too often in his vicinity, and pushing aside the shame of the past to focus on the present. 'I've heard cashmere attracts moths anyway.'

With one quick disbelieving glance in my direction, Nick strode through a pair of open French doors into a bright, airy kitchen that was the size of the poky flat in zone four I shared with two others, dumped my suitcase and then headed for a run of glossy wood units that stretched across the width of the far end of the room.

'Would you like a drink?'

God, yes, I thought wistfully as I set my handbag down on the enormous bleached-wood-topped island and perched on a stool. A large rosemary-garnished gin and tonic—something to settle the jitters and quench my thirst—would be heavenly. But it wasn't even midday and I didn't need another black mark against me, especially when I so badly needed his help. 'A coffee would be great, thanks.'

He turned to a machine that was all buttons and spouts and looked as though it could orbit the earth, and while it hissed and burbled, I took the opportunity to study him.

No doubt this casual look of his was such a surprise because whenever we did meet these days he clearly came straight from work and it was hard to imagine him in anything other than a suit. And equally obviously, it was because we were always in the company of others, my attention diverted, that I'd never before noticed the breadth of his shoulders beneath the fine wool or the corded muscles of his forearms that appeared when, having taken off his jacket, he inevitably rolled up the sleeves of his shirt.

I'd certainly never seen him doing anything as pedestrian as stirring a spoonful of sugar into a macchiato, I mused, my gaze narrowing in on the action. It was strange how fascinating his economy of movement was, how mesmerising his hands were. If the touch of his palm against mine could send a sizzle of electricity shooting up my arm, what effect might it have on other parts of my body? Such as my waist…my thighs…my breasts…?

A shocking image of him abandoning the machine and spinning round to haul me into a crushing embrace slammed into my head then and I instantly went hot. My mouth dried. My lungs froze. My pulse gave a great kick and then started racing.

What was going on? I wondered, frantically scrubbing the all too vivid vision from my mind and struggling for control. Why was I even *thinking* of his hands on me? I hadn't before. A clinch of any kind, crushing or otherwise, had never crossed my mind. Well, not for years, at least. So why now?

Objectively, I could see he was exceptionally good-looking. He'd grown out of his lankiness years ago, and at well over six foot, with a broad, lean physique and a harshly beautiful face composed of strong, masculine features, he was the epitome of tall, dark and handsome. And judging by the way he had a different woman on his arm in every photo I'd ever seen him in, I wasn't the only one to know that.

But this was *Nick*. Impossibly and eternally uptight, judgemental and disapproving, and therefore very much *not* my type any more.

'Here you go,' he said, and I jumped, rattled by the lurid waywardness of my thoughts. He slid the cup of hot strong deliciousness in my direction, and frowned. 'Are you all right?'

No. I wasn't all right at all. I'd clearly lost my mind. But I had to get a grip, because he was as sharp as a knife and if he somehow managed to figure out what was going on in my head… It didn't bear thinking about.

'I'm fine,' I said, somehow managing to drum up a breezy smile while inwardly pulling myself together and outwardly fanning my face. 'I'm just not used to this heat. And it's been a hectic twenty-four hours.'

'You must be desperate to have flown all this way so quickly.'

He had no idea. For a moment I wondered if he took pleasure from having me dangling from his strings, but, quite frankly, I doubted he took pleasure in anything. I'd certainly never heard or seen any evidence of it. Naturally I hadn't paid those photos all that much attention, but even when in the company of a stunning blonde he seemed to exude cool indifference.

'I am,' I said, taking the cup and belatedly thinking I should have asked for my coffee to be iced since yet more heat sliding through my body could well lead to combustion. 'I got your email and caught the next available flight.'

'I'm flattered.'

'You didn't leave me much choice.'

Not that it had been that much of a hardship, once I'd got over my indignation at being summonsed so high-handedly. I'd decided to fly first class, which had been as comfortable as I remembered. The lounge. The personal service. The comfort, the quiet and the champagne you didn't have to pay extra for. Everything I'd once taken for granted, I'd realised on the occasion I'd flown to Scotland with a no-frills airline, although, actually, none of it got you to your destination any faster.

Of course, the experience had cost a lot—even more once I'd guiltily paid extra to offset the increased carbon footprint flying first class generated—but I didn't need to worry about that now. Financially, I didn't need to worry about anything ever again, as long as I stayed away from scoundrels out to fleece me. And no doubt once that properly sank in, I'd be thrilled and excited and over the moon with happiness instead of anxious and nauseous and, at times, downright petrified.

'But thank you for agreeing to see me,' I added, recalling my intention to remain professional and in control and, above all, mature. 'You're bound to be busy and I realise that my coming here must be very inconvenient.'

'Perhaps you should tell me what you want from me,' he said, leaning back against the counter and folding his arms across his formidable chest in a move that for a second made my mouth dry and my heartbeat flutter. 'Before your helicopter gets here.' He glanced at his watch. 'Time is marching.'

Yes. Good plan. Enough of this pulse-skipping nonsense and bizarre disappointment that he hadn't contradicted my allegations of his busyness and my inconvenience. I was here for one thing, and one thing only.

'Six weeks ago, I won one hundred and eight million pounds on the lottery,' I said, reminding myself sternly of what that one thing was, which was absolutely *not* a steamy embrace from a man who'd always despised me.

Nick's only response to my news was a minute arch of an eyebrow, but then presumably, unlike me these days, he was used to such vast sums. To him, the amount could quite possibly be small change. I, on the other hand, had nearly passed out when I'd learnt how much I'd won.

'That would buy a lot of handbags.'

I instinctively bristled at the barb, but heroically rose above it. 'Well, that would depend on the handbag,' I said coolly. 'But I have other plans for it.'

'Which are?'

'Currently a bit overwhelming. That's why I'm here. I need your help.'

He was silent for a moment, then tilted his head and said dryly, '*Now* you need my help?'

Ah, yes.

That.

It had occurred to me he might bring it up. It was one of the reasons I hadn't contacted him for advice the minute I'd got over the shock of winning—apparently there was no statute of limitations on shame.

Shortly after the freezing of my father's assets, which had meant the repossession of my London penthouse, the abrupt mid-course end to my university studies in Zurich and the cutting off of my five-figure monthly allowance, Nick, sprinting his way up the ladder of the financial institution he'd joined on leaving Cambridge, had offered me a loan. A large one. Distraught, humiliated and an emotional wreck after everything that had happened, I'd flippantly flung his money back in his face, convinced that he was rubbing my nose into his success and my misfortune. He'd taken it badly, judging by the way he hadn't allowed me to apologise for the manner in which I'd refused him, hence the continued frostiness.

'I'm not unaware of the irony,' I said, shifting awkwardly on the stool while my cheeks warmed.

'What took you so long?'

'I thought I could manage,' I admitted with a frown. 'But the sharks started circling and I came to think otherwise.'

'What happened?'

'I nearly bought a tropical island that didn't exist.'

'I'm not surprised.'

Ooh, ouch. 'I know,' I said, ignoring the sting I felt pierce my chest like the pointiest of darts. I'd been a fool, and it annoyed me beyond belief because I thought I'd shed the innocence and naïveté of my youth years ago. 'Silly me, right?'

'Lottery winners are exceptionally vulnerable to fraud, in my experience. The shock tends to destroy logic.'

'You can say that again,' I muttered. 'I haven't been thinking straight in weeks.'

'Didn't anyone from the organisation tell you that you should do nothing until you've had some advice?'

'Yes,' I said with a sigh, unable to summon up much despair at the censure I could hear in his voice since it was wholly justified. 'They did. And I got advice. Just the wrong kind. I'd requested anonymity—and told nobody outside the organisation apart from my mother and my brother—but I was nevertheless bombarded with offers of help. It didn't occur to me that the news must have got out anyway and that some of those offers would be less than genuine. I know it should have.'

'What stopped you going through with it?'

'Seb,' I said, my mind reeling back to the moment I realised that I might be being taken for a fool and tens of millions of dollars. The plummeting of my stomach. The nausea rising up my throat. The cataclysmic shock and the blind panic. 'He said if it sounded too good to be true it probably was. I sent him the details and he did the digging I should have done and discovered it was a sham.'

'You're lucky to have him.'

'I am,' I said with a nod. 'He was the one who suggested I contact you. I should have done it weeks ago. I know you're the best at what you do.'

'So why didn't you?'

'I guess I just didn't think you'd be prepared to help.'

'Why not?'

I stared at him for a second, momentarily lost for words. Did he really not know? Surely he couldn't be oblivious to the tension that throbbed between us, the strange sort of antagonism that developed whenever we came within six feet of each other, or the turbulent history we shared. Surely it couldn't all be a figment of my imagination? 'Well, we're not exactly friends, are we?'

His brow creased, a tiny frown that was gone in a flash that suggested I could have put it a little less bluntly. 'That's irrelevant.'

'How so?'

'I never let the personal get in the way of the professional.'

'Then you'll help?' I said, thinking it was a relief to know we were on the same page when it came to that, at least, and mentally crossing my fingers.

He gave a short nod. 'I'll help.'

CHAPTER THREE

So Seb had been right, I thought, noting the determined set of Nick's jaw and the glint of resolve—and possibly pound signs—in his eyes. He *was* willing to put profit above clearly uncomfortable personal feelings and petty point scoring. Or maybe he felt he owed my family something. Payback for the weekends and holidays he'd once spent with us, perhaps. Whatever his motives, he was prepared to help, and thank God for it because up until this very moment I'd had no idea how truly stressed and overwhelmed I'd been by everything.

Recently, my hard-won self-reliance hadn't felt like a strength. A noose round my neck would be a better description. Since the win, many had been the night I'd stared up at the ceiling riddled with anxiety, wishing I found it easier to trust in others and regretting that I couldn't let people get close. One hundred and eight million pounds was an inconceivable, terrifying amount, and I'd had no one nearby to even talk to about it.

Until now.

Now I had the most unlikely of knights in shining armour, I realised, my defences fracturing at the knowledge I wasn't in this alone any more. Nick would take care of my fortune. He wouldn't rip me off. He had more than enough money of his own. On this, at least, I could trust him, I was sure, and the relief that then flooded my system was so profound, so immense it was almost palpable. The tightness in my muscles vanished. The tight knots in my stomach dissolved, and the tumultuous emotions I'd been keeping such a tight lid on lately—shock, worry, excitement, fear, to name but a few—burst free, buffeting me on all sides with a ferocity that whipped the breath from my lungs and blitzed my mind.

Beneath the onslaught, my heart pounded, my mouth dried and my limbs turned to water. The hand I pressed weakly to my chest trembled. My self-control was fast becoming history. I was seconds away from disintegrating into a sobbing grateful heap in front of a man who already thought me a superficial naïve fool, and alarmingly, distressingly, there seemed to be nothing I could do about it.

Until Nick's voice cut through the fog and the madness.

'Are you about to start crying?'

The horror I heard in his tone stopped the whirling of my thoughts and the emotional battering of my nerves in their tracks. Reeling back from the brink of collapse, I blinked rapidly and swallowed down the painful lump lodged in my throat. I took a deep breath and as my head cleared of the dizziness I straightened my spine and got a grip of both my teeming emotions and my still warm cup.

'No, no,' I said, taking a quick sip of coffee to disguise my distress and somehow managing to sound more or less normal. 'Of course not.'

'Are you sure?'

'Absolutely.'

It had been a close call but, thanks to Nick very much not being the sort of man to offer me a shoulder to weep on, danger had been averted at the last minute. If ever there was a time for a brutal lack of sympathy, a second ago had been it, and for that I was grateful.

'Good.' He gave a brisk nod, all business now, which my still fragile composure appreciated. 'So what *do* you want to do with your money?'

This was better. Plans. Logistics. I could handle practicalities far more than I could deal with emotion right now, and I'd been considering the options for weeks.

'First, I'd like to buy a house,' I said, calling to mind the list I'd made with its many question marks, all caps and crossings out.

'You could buy a dozen houses.'

'I don't need a dozen,' I said. 'Just the one will do.'

'A three-storey mansion in Chelsea with a garage for a fleet of cars?'

A replica of the home in which I'd grown up? Was that a dig? I tilted my head and regarded him thoughtfully for a moment, but it was hard to tell. He was giving nothing away. And yet I didn't think I'd imagined the sardonic tinge to his words.

'I'm not sure a man who owns an island paradise in the Indian Ocean as well as penthouse apartments in half a dozen capital cities across the globe is in much of a position to judge,' I said, bristling a little.

'Who's judging?'

'You are. As usual.'

He frowned. 'As usual?'

'Yes.'

'I'll rephrase the question.'

'I'll save you the bother,' I replied, really not needing to be on the receiving end of another potentially barbed comment. 'I haven't decided what I'd like to buy or where I'd like to live yet,' I said, only knowing that I didn't want to look back and recreate what I'd once had and lost, since it held few reliably happy memories and had all been built on sand anyway. 'But it will have space, a garden and no flatmates.'

'What else?'

'I'd like my mother to be provided for for the rest of her life.'

Nick's response to that was a sharp lift of his eyebrows and it triggered another stab of irritation. 'There you go again.'

'You're overreacting.'

'Next you'll be calling me hysterical.'

A glimmer of what looked like weary exasperation flickered across his face. 'I'm merely surprised.'

Yes, well, while his exasperation was rude and outrageous, his surprise I could understand. My mother and I had barely spoken since the funeral. Things between us were complicated and feelings ran deep. By monopolising my father's attention as a child, I'd inadvertently come between them. The jealousy and resentment she'd felt had led to her affair. Ultimately, I'd driven my parents apart and wrecked their marriage, so even though my mother had proved remarkably resilient in the face of adversity, dealing stoically with the aftermath of my father's fall from grace and then demise, ensuring her financial security was the least I could do. Would it assuage the guilt that still tormented me day in day out? I could only hope.

'We might not get along,' I said, having no intention of sharing anything so deeply personal with the annoyingly supercilious man before me, 'but she's still my mother.'

'I can draw up a few ideas.'

'That would be helpful.'

'What about Seb?'

'He's adamant he doesn't want any of it for himself,' I said, recalling the phone call in which I'd offered to transfer a lump sum to him and been turned down, which had unexpectedly hurt. 'But I know he's looking to expand his company. I thought I could maybe somehow help with that. Invest in it or something.'

On leaving university, Seb had moved to San Francisco to take up a job in Silicon Valley. A couple of years later he'd left to set up his own software business. The timing of the move could not have been worse. When they'd caught wind of our father's financial troubles, Seb's potential investors had jumped like rats off a sinking ship. If it hadn't been for Nick stepping in to provide the capital, he too might have wound up bankrupt.

'That could be an option,' said Nick with a short nod. 'What else?'

'What else would you advise?'

'A portfolio of short-, medium-and long-term investments.'

'All right,' I said, just about convincing myself that

that would be wise. Who cared if it felt a bit dull? Dull was sensible and I was all about the sensible these days. 'I'm open to ideas. But nothing reckless.'

On the skids and veering further and further off the rails, my father had taken increasingly high risks in the hope of clawing back his mounting losses. The fallout had been catastrophic and a direct hit wasn't something I ever wanted to experience for myself.

'Nothing I do, either professionally or personally, is reckless.'

No, he was the most coolly controlled person I'd ever met. Sometimes it made me want to provoke and prod him just to see what might happen if he was pushed to his limits. That I'd always managed to resist was something of a miracle. 'I'm delighted to hear it.'

'Have you considered charitable donations?'

'I have a very long list. I'll email it to you.'

'Do you still have your job?'

'Yes.'

'Do you intend to keep it?'

'For the time being. If I can. Managing the office of a stationery company isn't exactly setting the world on fire, but it gave me purpose and structure at a time when I had none and I feel a certain degree of loyalty towards it. I get on well with my colleagues and right now it's the only thing in my life that's stable.'

'Were you serious about the island?'

Ah, yes, the island. A dream I'd had for God knew how many years, a dream that had been formed when diving with my father, that had inspired my degree in marine biology, and been dashed when overnight I'd had to leave university early and get a job that would slowly but surely pay off the six-figure debt on my credit card.

Once upon a time, I'd pored over maps and trawled through data. I'd compiled lists and calculated costings. There'd been nothing I hadn't known about endangered marine species and ecosystems. I'd filled a dozen archive boxes with my research and I'd hung onto them for months before eventually, reluctantly, heartbrokenly throwing them away.

'Very much so,' I said, thinking of the new folder I'd recently created on my laptop into which I was pouring ideas for everything I longed to achieve and was now within the realms of possibility if I didn't screw it up, which unfortunately was entirely possible. 'I'm hoping to set up some sort of marine conservation sanctuary. Bring in experts to build coral reefs and implement breeding programmes. That sort of thing. But I don't have the faintest idea how to go about it.'

I half expected Nick to laugh at me, to tell me it was way too ambitious a project for someone with absolutely no experience—which was why I'd kept my plans deliberately vague—but, 'I'll look into it,' was all he said.

'Thank you,' I said with genuine gratitude, the weight that had been crushing my chest for weeks lifting so suddenly I felt as if I were floating. 'Don't forget to send me a contract.'

He frowned. 'A contract?'

'Your terms and conditions. Your fees.'

His jaw tightened in a curious way, as if I'd offended him or something, which was bizarre. 'Sure,' he said with a strange twist of his mouth. 'Give me a week or so to put together a proposal. I'll be in touch then. In the meantime,' he added, pushing himself off the counter and striding past me, pausing only to grab my suitcase as the whoop-whoop sound of an approaching helicopter filled the space around us, 'here's your ride.'

Seven days later, I was sitting at a table that overlooked the sparkling sea, replete after a platter of lobster followed by a fresh mango and papaya fruit salad. I took a sip of my postprandial limoncello, then settled back to watch the jet skis criss-crossing the bay and the yachts drifting along the horizon against a backdrop of an azure sky dotted with fluffy white clouds.

As warm dreamy languor spread through me, I reflected that the best hotel on Zanzibar was exactly the experience I'd hoped for. It was everything the website had promised, and more. The food—local, seasonal and mouth-wateringly spiced—was exquisite. My villa was the ultimate in luxurious comfort and I'd spent hours in the soothing tranquillity of the spa being pampered to within an inch of my life. I'd been diving each day and my tan was coming along nicely. With every minute that ticked lazily by, the stress and anxiety of the last couple of months faded that little bit more.

Of course, it might have been more fun to have a friend here to share it all with, and dining on my own meal after meal had begun to pall a little, but at least I could do what I wanted when I wanted and didn't have to worry about whether that friend was interested in me or my money. I knew well that possessing a fortune didn't come without its problems—especially with regards to other people's take on it—and everything was so much simpler without the whole poor little rich girl dynamic.

If I found the luxury and extravagance of my surroundings ever so slightly overwhelming, the bling of the well-heeled clientele over the top and not a little obscene, that was just because I wasn't used to them any more. Diving, with the conflicting feelings about my father that it triggered, would get easier with practice, I had no doubt, and soon I'd stop thinking about how much this was all costing and what else that money could buy, how much good it could do. I had more than enough to go round, and, now that Nick was on board, it was in safe hands.

Yesterday he'd sent me an email with his ten-page report. Over dinner, I'd scrolled through the tables, the figures and the recommendations with the intention of reading it more thoroughly this week, but it had struck me then that if I wanted to I could wash my hands of the details and know that my fortune would be well looked after. I didn't much like Nick's attitude towards me, but I'd always known where I stood with him. He'd never made any secret of the fact he found me lacking. He didn't mince his words or adopt a facade around me. I found his consistency on this, the absence of pretence, unexpectedly reassuring and I was certain that with my money, at least, I could trust him.

The buzz of my phone, which I'd silenced for lunch, jolted me out of my reverie. I put down my glass and picked it up. It was my brand-new financial advisor, no doubt calling to discuss his report. As a kick of adrenalin struck me in the stomach and a frisson of anticipation rippled down my spine I hit the green button and lifted the device to my ear. 'Hello?'

'Amelia,' said Nick, sounding even terser than usual. 'Are you all right?'

'I'm fine,' I said, slightly perplexed by the way his voice seemed to grate over my nerve-endings until I realised we'd never spoken on the phone before, which was undoubtedly why it felt so odd. 'Why wouldn't I be?'

'Have you been in touch with your family?'

'No. I haven't been in touch with anyone for days. What's wrong?'

'So you haven't seen the headlines?'

'What headlines?'

'Forget it,' he said, and cut the call.

For a moment I sat there staring at the phone in astonishment. What on earth had that been about? I'd never heard him so agitated. He'd sounded almost unhinged. But if he thought I was forgetting about anything after that, he could think again.

With my heart hammering like a steam train, I stared at the home screen, a powerful sense of misgiving sweeping through me. Was someone I loved hurt? What headlines could he be referring to? And why did I have seventy-eight unread emails in my inbox when an hour ago there'd been none?

Fifteen minutes later I had the answers to all the questions rocketing around my head, and a dozen more. Somehow, news of my lottery win had hit the papers. Under ordinary circumstances it might have merited a paragraph on perhaps page twelve, but the events of eight years earlier had elevated it to page one with links to opinion pieces and analysis.

It was all there. Everywhere. Rehashed photos of my hedonistic teenage years. Blistering commentary about privilege and responsibility and the frailty of human nature. Sycophantic messages from people I hadn't spoken to in years. Brutal reminders of a painful time.

And now, as if it had happened yesterday, memories slammed into my head one after the other like a thundering cascade. The shock I'd felt at the loss of money and status. Worse, the crucifying plunge of my father from the pedestal I'd put him on. The reassessment of everything in my life I'd believed to be true. The cruel mockery of strangers and the bewildering abandonment by so-called friends. The guilt, the humiliation, the fallout that had lasted far longer than the headlines.

This time round, in addition to raking over the past, there were also opinions on the unfairness of luck. Photos of the building where I lived now lay alongside the Chelsea mansion in which I'd grown up, with suitably catty captions. They'd even tracked down my work colleagues, who'd known nothing of my win, who wouldn't understand why I hadn't told them, who might well be hurt by the omission. None of them had commented yet, nor had either of my flatmates, but it was only a matter of time.

Just as it could only be a matter of time before the press found out where I was. How long did I have? If past experience was anything to go by it would be hours rather than days.

At the thought of what might be to come—the ridicule, the spite, the relentless pressure—the limoncello turned to battery acid in my stomach and the lobster and fruit revolted. Despite the warm breeze rustling through the palm trees, I couldn't breathe. My hands shook. Nausea rolled through me. Paradise had become poisonous.

Sweating, with panic tightening my throat and my heart beating too fast, I headed back to my room and rang first Seb and then, out of a weird kind of desperation, my mother, but both calls went to voicemail. I hung up, feeling achingly alone, hatefully pathetic, vulnerable and weak.

What was I going to do?

I couldn't stay here. It was doubtful I'd be recognised by any of the guests, but I was a sitting duck for a pap with a boat and a long-lensed camera. Yet if I left, where would I go? I couldn't go home. I'd be mobbed. And there was no one there for me anyway. Seb was on the other side of the world and why I'd called my estranged mother was beyond me.

I needed time to regroup and restore my defences. Somewhere safe. Secure. Where I'd be accommodated and protected, if not welcomed. Where at least if I was judged, I'd be expecting it.

I wasn't as alone as I felt, I reminded myself, a glimmer of light flickering in the darkness as I recalled the resolve with which Nick had told me he'd help with the management of my fortune. Could Seb have been right yet again? Was Nick indeed the man I needed right now?

He had to be. There was no one else.

'Do you want me to come and get you?' he said curtly, answering on the first ring.

I swallowed hard, hating the tightness of my throat

and the crushing pressure on my chest, hating my despair and dependency, especially on him. 'If it's not too much trouble.'

'I'll be there in an hour.'

CHAPTER FOUR

THE CLOUDS HAD thickened quite a bit by the time we arrived back on Suza, Nick's island, but that was about as much of the journey as I registered. Stunned and distraught, I'd barely been aware of even moving as I'd packed up my things and settled my bill, let alone taken note of my surroundings or the man who'd so swiftly come to my rescue. I'd lost the capacity for speech. Thoughts had spun through my head like the whirring engine of the boat carrying me and my suitcase to relative safety. Even the jarring bounciness of the waves couldn't distract me from the chaos roiling around inside me.

How could it be happening all over again? Where would I find the strength and resilience to get through it? Could I even begin to hope that in this clickbait-y world today's headlines would be tomorrow's fish and chips wrapping?

Every cell of my body was on the brink of splintering, I realised as Nick showed me to an elegant guest suite and set my suitcase beside the enormous bed. Tears of frustration and helplessness had been stinging my eyes since I'd read the headlines and my nerves were stretched to snapping point. But I refused to break down in front of him. He'd run a mile, no doubt with a sigh of yet more exasperation at my drama, and then I'd have another thing to feel awkward about.

'I'll leave you to settle in,' he said, his jaw set, his expression stony, the irritation I could feel vibrating off him completely understandable when my being here had to be disruptive, inconvenient and the very last thing he needed.

I swallowed hard and accepted the guilt as just one more emotion piling in on top of the rest. 'I'm so sorry about all this.'

He shot me a dark, frustrated look. 'How is it your fault?'

'Isn't everything?'

'No.'

'It certainly feels as though it is,' I said, my voice thick, my throat tight. 'I'm the one who lived a shallow and frivolous life back then and was regularly photographed stumbling out of taxis before falling from grace. I'm the one with the winning lottery ticket now. But thank you for coming to my rescue. I had no one else to call.'

Something flickered in the depths of his eyes, but it had vanished before I could even begin to decipher it. 'Not a problem,' he said, turning on his heel and heading for the door. 'If you need anything, let me know.'

I felt marginally stronger after a weep fest and a shower, but I had no doubt it would take a lot more than that to unravel the tangle of emotions churning through me. On top of everything else that had happened recently, processing this latest development was simply too much for my poor battered and bruised brain to handle.

As if in solidarity, the puffiness of my eyes and the redness of my nose were proving an insurmountable challenge for my make-up, and as I stared at myself in the mirror, flinching at my reflection, I was sorely tempted to hole up in my room until I'd made sense of everything going on. Only when I'd constructed a rock-solid facade of cool indifference would I be ready to face my reluctant host.

But that could take days and I couldn't stand the idea of being alone with my tumultuous thoughts for a moment longer. They were too huge, too complicated, too overwhelming and I was teetering on the brink of total collapse. Nick had said to let him know if I needed anything, and right now I needed a distraction. I'd already texted Seb to let him know where I was, and reading the hundreds of emails that were still flooding in appealed about as much as morbidly scouring the headlines. But there was always the financial planning report Nick had sent. *That* required attention. So, having shoved on a pair of sunglasses to achieve the result that make-up had failed to do, I lifted my chin, pulled my shoulders back and headed downstairs.

Following the faint sounds of his voice, I found him in a room that had to be his study, facing the window and staring out to sea with his big broad back to me. He was raking one hand through his hair in what looked like a gesture of frustration and holding his phone to his ear with the other.

'I want them gone,' he was saying with a cutting coldness that sent a shiver down my spine despite the heavy warmth of the air breezing in through the window and fluttering the papers on the enormous mahogany desk. 'The pictures. The articles. The photographers. I don't care what it costs. Just get it done. Now.'

He hung up and turned slightly to stash the phone in the back pocket of his jeans and went still when he caught sight of me. He looked me up and down in a way that made me strangely aware of what I was wearing—a short yellow dress with spaghetti straps that suddenly felt a lot skimpier than when I'd put it on—and for the briefest, most bizarre of moments I forgot how to breathe. My lungs seized. My breasts tightened and tingled, and my temperature shot so high I felt as if I were about to spontaneously combust.

But before I could work out what on earth was going on, his dark, unexpectedly stormy gaze landed on my face and his brows snapped together, which instantly refocused my attention and loosened my chest enough for me to breathe and my brain enough to engage.

'Who was that?' I said, making a pre-emptive strike designed to deflect both a remark on the evidence of my earlier distress, and—an even greater threat to what little self-possession I was clinging onto—an albeit unlikely enquiry into how I might be feeling.

'My head of PR.'

'Were you discussing me and the situation I find myself in?'

'Yes.'

Of course he was. I wasn't surprised. Despite his earlier 'not a problem', I knew I was exactly that. 'I completely understand your wish to rectify things.'

'Do you?' he said with a slight rise of his eyebrows. 'I doubt it.'

'It's obvious. The sooner the furore dies down, the sooner I can go home and leave you in peace.'

Something undefinable flitted across his face. 'Peace would be good,' he muttered darkly. 'In fact, peace would be excellent.'

'Can you really make it all go away with a phone call?' I asked, ignoring the odd tightening of my chest at the confirmation that he *really* didn't want me here and wondering instead if he could possibly be that powerful.

'A couple of phone calls,' he corrected. 'And yes. I can.'

Right. Obviously he was that powerful. Which was strange when I could still remember him as the gawky guarded teenager who'd first come to stay. But he now had billions and money talked.

'I can't help wondering how the press got hold of the news in the first place,' I said, stepping into the room and catching up some papers that had blown off the desk and were fluttering to the floor. 'And who put two and two together and came up with the conclusion that former wild-child socialite Amelia Huntington-Smith and plain old office manager Millie Smith were one and the same.'

'You sound as though you suspect me.'

What? I straightened abruptly and stared at him. 'That's absurd. You'd have zero to gain, and, despite the fact that we are very much not friends, I really can't see you engaging in anything quite so underhand.'

'It's a relief to know you trust me,' he said dryly.

'I do with my money. And that's all that matters. But nevertheless, *someone* leaked it.'

'And I have *someone* looking into it.'

'Who?'

'An investigator I use to dig into the backgrounds of all potential clients before I take them on.'

'Did you dig into me?'

'No need.'

I bristled at the bold certainty of his tone. 'You don't know *everything* about me, Nick,' I said. In fact, he hardly knew anything. He just thought he did.

'I know you're not a money launderer.'

True, but conceding a point to him had never appealed and it didn't now, so instead I dialled back to the fact he'd put an investigator on the case. 'What will you do if you get a name?'

'*When* I get a name,' he said, 'I will ensure they never work again.'

'Wow,' I said, impressed despite myself. He'd do that for me? For my family? Surely he didn't owe us that much? Then again, he was my brother's best friend and true friends helped each other out. Or so I'd heard. 'Thank you. I think.'

'You're welcome.'

'What did Seb say when you spoke to him?' I asked, trying not to feel hurt that my brother hadn't rung me back before asking Nick to rescue me yet again.

A trace of bafflement flickered across his face. 'I haven't spoken to him for weeks.'

Oh. 'Then you're not acting on his behalf?'

'No.'

Right. On reflection, though, I didn't know why that

came as a surprise. Nick had always had bags of initiative. He didn't sit around waiting for life to happen to him. How else would he have made so much money before hitting thirty? 'I imagine your innate sense of justice would override any iffy personal feelings you might bear a person.'

His eyebrows lifted. 'My innate sense of justice?'

'It's not as if you're acting out of any particular concern for my welfare, is it?'

'Why wouldn't I be?'

'Because you can't be any more concerned with my welfare than I am with yours.'

He looked a bit taken aback by that and I regretted being quite so honest, but it was nothing but the truth and I couldn't quite bring myself to apologise.

'Was there something you wanted, Amelia?'

I shook off the twinge of something that felt oddly like disappointment—ridiculous when I didn't even *want* him to be concerned about me or vice versa—and reminded myself of why I'd sought him out. 'I thought we might take this opportunity to go through your report.'

'Now?'

'If you're not busy with something else.'

His response, when it came, was lukewarm. 'I suppose it has to be done at some point.'

'Great.'

In response to Nick's muttered, 'Have a seat,' I sat down while he fiddled around on his computer. As the printer began spewing out pages, I thought about the icy tone with which he'd issued his instructions to his head of PR and the strangely fierce expression he'd adopted when he'd clearly noted I'd been upset.

For the briefest of moments he'd looked as if he'd wanted to rip things apart with his bare hands and I couldn't help wondering as I watched him gather up the sheets and staple them together what it would be like to have someone who offered that level of unwavering support on your side, who instinctively fought your corner. A person might be able to achieve anything they wanted with that kind of backing. They could try everything, secure in the knowledge they'd have the best of safety nets if it all went wrong, and figure out at leisure who they really were and where they fitted in the world.

Not that I'd ever experience anything like that. Until I overcame my trust, self-esteem and guilt issues—which were so deep-rooted they were now an integral part of me and therefore pretty damn insurmountable—it simply wouldn't happen. And that was fine. Self-reliance was *my* safety net. My only one, sure, but an excellent one nonetheless. So there was no point wishing things were different or envying those for whom relationships were easy. I just had to get on with things and focus on a future that would take up all my time and require all my energy anyway.

Nick handed me a copy of his report and then folded his large frame into the seat on his side of the desk. 'Have you read it?'

'Briefly.'

'Shall I summarise?'

'Please do.'

Flicking back and forth between the pages with one hand while spinning a pen around his fingers of his other, he started by reiterating my wishes and then moved on to his suggestions for facilitating them. From there, he segued into a complicated and detailed description of suitable investment options and products and the deployment of fiendishly clever fiscal vehicles and mechanisms, which I followed for a while until my fascination with his mouth took over and zoned me out.

Mesmerised by the way it moved, I could hardly take my eyes off it. His lips came together, then parted to reveal the flash of white teeth and a tantalising glimpse of his tongue, and did it all on repeat. How had I never noticed its sensuality before? Because it generally took the form of a grim flat line whenever he turned in my direction? Or on occasion, curled into a faint twist of disapproval? And why did I suddenly long to know how it would feel—hard and passionate on mine or light and teasing as it travelled over my skin?

'Amelia.'

At the terse delivery of my name, I blinked and came to, snapping my gaze up to his and battling the violent blush I could feel sweeping right through me. 'Yes?'

'I asked if you had any questions.'

Questions? About what? I hadn't taken in a word. But he didn't need to know that. Nor, thank God, since I was still wearing my sunglasses, could he have any idea I'd been transfixed by his mouth.

Sternly reminding myself to focus on the reason I was sitting opposite him, I took a deep breath, banished the feverish heat from my body and pulled myself together. 'No,' I said with a brief nod and a cool smile. 'No questions. That all seems very comprehensive. Very thorough. I'd expect nothing less from the best. Although given your competence in this area, I am somewhat surprised you haven't yet found me an island.'

'It's been a week,' he said bluntly. 'I work fast, but not that fast.'

'My fake advisors found me one within three days.'

He arched one dark eyebrow. 'And you didn't find that unlikely?'

'Funnily enough, the private island real estate market isn't something I'm an expert on.'

'Which was why you were such an easy target.'

Ouch. 'Thank you for pointing that out.'

He sat back, rested his elbows on the arms of his chair, still rolling the pen around his long tanned fingers. 'On the subject of islands, though, it would be useful for planning purposes to know what you intend for yours.'

'I can email you the folder,' I said, determinedly keeping my eyes off his hands, off his mouth, off everything but his eyes and thinking instead of my research. My report was ten times the length of his. He wasn't the only thorough one. Mine had pictures. Maps. Links. Even a glossary, which, come to think of it, his could have done with.

'An outline will do.'

Would it? I wasn't so sure. I hadn't told anyone the full extent of my dreams. Not even Seb. They were so personal, so fragile. On the other hand, how could Nick help with the implementation of my plans if I didn't share the details with him? Might he have some advice? He did own an island himself, after all.

'Promise you won't laugh?'

'Why would I do that?'

'You may well think I'm overreaching and question my sanity. Even I swing between convincing myself it's the best idea on the planet to wondering what on earth I think I'm doing when I'm anything but an expert.'

'I promise I won't laugh.'

'All right,' I said, mentally crossing my fingers and hoping for the best, which was basically Nick listening and absorbing and not responding with disbelieving scorn. 'So, as I mentioned when I was here last, one of the areas I'm interested in exploring is the revival of coral reefs. Quite apart from being an important ecosystem for underwater life, they protect shorelines from the effects of hurricanes. They provide millions of people with a crucial source of income. Did you know that the tiny animals that build them offer the potential to develop new drugs to treat disease?'

'I did not.'

I scoured his expression for signs of disdain, but could see none, so judged it safe to continue. 'No, well, it's a little-known fact,' I said. 'Anyway, because of overfishing, pollution, oceanic acidification, not to mention general man-made destruction, the reefs could disappear within thirty years. But it doesn't have to be terminal. Marine protected areas—sort of giant national parks in the ocean—can help make reefs healthier and more resilient. And genetics are important too. One day, scientists might be able to develop coral that can cope with the marine conditions and restore the reefs.'

'Really?'

'Yes,' I said, warming to my theme. 'But mainly, though, my interest lies in the hawksbill turtle. I saw one once in the Great Barrier Reef and it was love at first sight. They're magnificent creatures. Their shells are exquisite. I've made a study of them. They help maintain the health of the reef. They use their pointy beaks to feed on the sponges that feed off the reef's surface. They've been around for the last hundred million years, but over the last century their population has declined by four fifths. There are only eight thousand left. This is not good, I think you'll agree, and I'd like to set up a breeding programme to increase their numbers. Ideally, I'd buy a landmass that came with a reef and the potential to achieve all this as well as recruit the necessary personnel. So there you have it. Those are my plans, in a nutshell.'

I stopped and waited for a response, but Nick didn't seem to be paying attention. He was staring at my mouth in much the same way I'd been staring at his earlier. His eyes were dark and a faint frown creased his brow. He couldn't possibly have been distracted by my impassioned speech as I had when he'd been talking about financial products, could he? No. The idea of it was absurd. Whatever he was doing, he was *not* entertaining thoughts of kissing me. I probably had something stuck in my teeth—yet another cause for disapproval, no doubt.

'Nick.'

He blinked and gave his head a quick shake. 'What?'

'Are you even listening?'

He shifted in his seat, as if trying to ease some kind of discomfort and, with a faint wince, pulled his seat forward and rested his elbows on the desk. 'Of course I'm listening,' he said, his voice a little gruff. 'Coral reefs and hawksbill turtles. Marine protection areas and breeding programmes. Quite a departure from stationery.'

'Stationery has never been my passion. It's hard to get excited about paper-clip orders and A3 supply issues. Tropical waters, and what lives in them, on the other hand, have been something of an obsession of mine ever since I learned how to dive with my father. I even studied marine biology once upon a time.'

'I remember.'

'The fact that I didn't get to finish my degree is something I'd like to rectify,' I said. 'If I can get back on a course, that is. It's been a long time. My studying skills are rusty and it's entirely possible I wouldn't be intellectually up to it. But I'm willing to give it a shot.'

'You'd be more than intellectually up to it.'

I sat back, momentarily stunned. 'Is that a compliment?'

'No. It's a fact,' he countered. 'And here's another. You didn't have to quit in the first place.'

In response to that, my eyebrows shot up and my jaw dropped. What on earth was he talking about? At the time, Nick had been off forging his own future but he'd known full well what was going on in the Huntington-Smith world. Thanks to the tabloids, everyone had.

'Of course I did,' I said flatly. 'I had no means of funding the course and a six-figure credit-card debt to pay off.'

'You could have accepted my money.'

'Well, yes, in theory I could have, I suppose,' I conceded, although back then, with my entire life crumbled to dust, I'd been in no fit state to do anything. 'But I would still have had to pay it back. You or the bank.

It made no difference. I would have had to get a job to pay the bills either way.'

'You wouldn't have had to pay it back.'

I stared at him. 'What?'

'What I offered you wasn't a loan,' he said. 'It was a gift.'

A gift? I frowned. 'Are you sure?'

'I'm hardly likely to forget.'

No. I wasn't likely to forget that particular encounter either. It had not been pleasant. 'I didn't know that.'

'You didn't give me a chance to explain.'

That was true. I'd rejected it out of hand barely before he'd finished what he was saying. He'd unexpectedly turned up at my flat one evening shortly after my father's death, immaculate in a five-thousand-pound suit, not a hair out of place. Flustered, wretched, and acutely aware of how shabby I and my environs looked in comparison to him, I'd just wanted him gone. 'But why would you offer me a gift?'

'Because I could.'

'Any opportunity to rub my nose in our reversal of fortune, right?' I said a touch bitterly, remembering all too clearly how humiliated I'd felt, how much I'd hated him in that moment for reminding me how far I'd fallen and how much I'd lost.

A thundering silence followed my words. Nick visibly recoiled and paled beneath his tan, a tiny muscle pounding in his jaw. 'Is that what you think I was doing?'

'I don't blame you,' I said, the memories that were descending thick and fast accelerating my pulse and tightening my chest. 'I deserved it.'

'You didn't deserve any of it.'

I did. After all, I'd once rubbed his nose in the material differences between us, hadn't I? Furthermore, I'd destroyed my family, and, however unintentional, there was no absolution for that.

'And you could not be more wrong about my reason for offering you the money.'

'Then what *were* you doing?'

'You'd suffered enough.'

I stared at him, my stomach beginning to churn. 'So it was pity?'

'No.'

'Charity?'

'No.'

But it had to have been at least one of those two things because if it wasn't revenge what else was there? It had never occurred to me that Nick had felt sorry for me. The thought of it, the realisation that he might continue to do so, made me feel physically sick. Disapproval and disdain I could just about handle. Pity, with the hateful weakness and helplessness it invoked, I could not.

'Well, whether it was a gift or a loan,' I said, suddenly desperate to redress the balance, to try and claw back some modicum of dignity, 'I'm glad I didn't take your money. It's impossible to overstate how much I would have hated being beholden to you. I'm not all that thrilled about it now, to be honest. I loathe the fact that I need your help. I can't stand it that I had to ask you to come and pick me up from Zanzibar. I didn't want your charity or your pity or any special favours then, and I certainly don't want them now. And before you claim again that you weren't motivated by either, you tell me why a man driven solely by money would still not have sent me a contract or details of his fees.'

I stopped, my heart pounding and my head spinning, the silence thundering. Nick's expression revealed a split second of shock before it became utterly blank, and his voice, when he spoke, was cold and clipped. 'I'll get onto it right away.'

CHAPTER FIVE

BECAUSE I WAS desperate to flee the suddenly horribly tense atmosphere in the study and needed to sort through everything that was swirling around in my head with increasingly hammering persistence, I took a walk outside.

All Nick had said when I'd abruptly announced my intention to get some air and surged to my feet was a curt, 'Stick to the paths.' He could have been shocked, he could have been furious, he could have been relieved. The ice-cold impassivity that had descended over him made it impossible to tell.

I followed his undoubtedly prudent advice and set off down a wide sandy track that wound through vegetation that grew denser and lusher the further I progressed into it. The rustling palms and heavily laden fruit trees were alive with caws and squawks. Brightly coloured butterflies of all hues and sizes fluttered around bushes from which came chirrups and squeaks. I could feel and smell the heat and humidity as if they were tangible.

At the westernmost point of the island, as far from the villa as it was possible to get, I came across a second jetty, next to which was a boathouse that contained several surfboards, a kayak and sails of various shapes and sizes.

In one of the white sandy coves I wandered down to, I found, among the driftwood that had washed up on the shore, a metre-long coconut crab and two green sea turtles. I sat on a rock and spent a good ten minutes watching a fish eagle hovering twenty metres above the surface of the sea and then swooping down majestically to capture its prey.

But Nick's island wasn't quite the tropical paradise now it had seemed the day I'd originally turned up. Unlike then, this evening's sun kept disappearing behind ever billowing clouds. The air was growing increasingly thick and heavy and the swell of the sea seemed to be rising. There was a sense of turbulence and disruption rippling through my surroundings, and it matched exactly the uneasy churning of my thoughts.

When I recalled the way in which the conversation Nick and I had had earlier had ended, I was swamped with remorse and mortification. I didn't think I'd ever forget the glimpse of stark shock I'd caught before he'd retreated behind a wall of stone. For a split second, he'd looked as if I'd struck him, somehow wounded, but then why wouldn't he? For all his imperviousness towards me, he had to have *some* sort of feelings and my words had been harsh.

That I'd been thrown off balance by shameful memories and the discovery that he'd pitied me was no excuse. Once again backed into a corner and on the attack, I'd let my emotions get the better of me and lashed out. I'd laid waste to the veneer of civility we'd always maintained and been unpardonably rude, while he—with the exception of the odd pointed comment or two—had been nothing but supportive. He hadn't had to agree to help me with my fortune. He hadn't had to rescue me from Zanzibar. And yet I'd told him I resented it all.

What on earth had I been thinking? I wondered as I took a breather and stood on a promontory from which I could see for miles. Had I completely lost my mind? Until a contract was signed, Nick could withdraw from the deal at any moment, leaving me in as vulnerable and exposed a position as before. What if he sent me packing and to hell with the press attention back home? I'd only have myself to blame. But more importantly, I wasn't that person any more. I wasn't reckless and rash and I didn't speak without thinking.

Burning up with shame and the need to put things right—and not just because I did, in fact, need his help—I returned to the villa with far less regard for the scenery than I'd had when I set out.

By following the mouth-watering scents of ginger and garlic, I found Nick this time in the kitchen. He was standing at the hob that was embedded in the island, agitating a frying pan. His hair was wet and he'd changed clothes, which suggested he'd taken a shower, but judging by the tension radiating off him and the rigidity of his jaw it hadn't been a relaxing one.

Bracing myself for a hostile reception—inevitable, given the chill with which he'd sent me off on my walk, and totally deserved given my inability to get a grip on my emotional volatility—I took a deep breath and tried not to think about the unpleasant way my dress was sticking to my skin.

'Something smells good,' I said, nerves nevertheless tangling in my stomach as I advanced towards him.

He glanced up at me, his eyes shuttered, his expression unfathomable. 'How was your walk?'

'Breezy.'

'You were gone a long time.'

'It's a beautiful island.'

'It is.'

'I came across a boathouse.'

'Did you?'

'Are all the boards and boats and other things in it yours?'

'Yes.'

'Do you use them?'

'When I'm not working.'

All too easily I could see him kayaking around the island and kite-surfing across the sea—no wonder he had muscles and a tan—and it was with quite some effort that I hauled my thoughts into line. I was on a mission and I would not be derailed.

'I'm sorry for what I said earlier,' I said, hopping onto a stool and battling back a fresh wave of remorse at the memory of it. 'All those things about charity and favours and about hating the fact that you're having to help me. I haven't had to rely on anyone for eight years and it's taking some getting used to. And then there's the stress I've been under lately, what with everything that's been going on. Nevertheless, none of that is any excuse. I overreacted. I was rude. I apologise.'

Not a muscle flickered in response to my words, which was disappointing but not entirely unexpected when he'd never made it easy for me to apologise. 'I've emailed you a contract,' he said, abandoning the pan and wiping his hands with a cloth. 'And details of my fees.'

'Thank you. I'll take a look later.'

'Drink?' He tossed the cloth into the sink then nodded in the direction of the tall glass in front of me that looked to be a gin and tonic, judging by the cubes of ice and the sprig of rosemary.

'You must have read my mind.' I half expected a flash of alarm to skitter across his face, but he remained as taciturn as ever. 'However, I'm glad you can't,' I added, reaching for the glass as if it were a lifeline. 'My mind is a mess.' I took a fortifying sip of my drink and sighed in appreciation as the fragrant scent of rosemary wafted into my head and the alcohol hit my blood. 'This, on the other hand,' I said, putting the glass back down, 'is perfect. My favourite combination.'

'I'm not solely driven by money, Amelia.'

In surprise, I jerked my gaze to his and found him looking at me with an intriguing intensity. Had I hit a nerve? Was that a hint of vulnerability I could hear? How interesting. 'It would be understandable if you were.'

'Because of where I come from?'

'It's nothing to be ashamed of.'

'I'm not. The circumstances in which I grew up were wholly beyond my control. Shame stems from things that have been done badly and could have been done differently. Things over which you *do* have control.'

Yes, well, I knew all about that, and I had the feeling that he knew I knew. 'Believe me,' I said, shifting on the stool to ease my sudden discomfort, 'if I could go back and do my time again, there are many things I'd do differently.'

'Like what?'

'How long do you have?'

'However long it takes.'

If that were true, he'd be waiting a long time because it was never going to happen. Apologising for my bad manners was one thing, baring my soul to a man who had such a low opinion of me was quite another. And why was he so interested in my shortcomings anyway? So he could gather together yet more ammunition to use against me?

'I'll bear that in mind,' I said, having no intention of giving him a reason to think even less of me than he already did. 'So what else *does* drive you, apart from money?'

'Prudent planning. Tax efficiency. Taking the best care I can of the assets my clients have and solving their problems.'

Such as mine? 'Talking of problematic clients,' I said, sternly reminding myself that the only assets I wanted him taking care of were financial ones, 'is there any news on the press frenzy back home?'

'Not yet.'

Oh, dear. That didn't bode well. How long was it going to be until the fuss had died down back home and it was safe for me to leave? How much more of this awkwardness, this stalking each other like caged tigers, were we going to have to tolerate?

Maybe time would pass more quickly with conversation. Maybe I could implement the strategy I'd developed on the plane over to rise above such small-mindedness with maturity and serenity by doubling down on the small talk. It was worth a try.

'What's for supper?'

'Red snapper.'

'Delicious,' I said, my stomach giving a faint rumble. 'My diet over the last eight or so years has consisted mainly of soup and pasta. This last week I've been making up for lost time by ordering seafood whenever I can, and it's been heavenly. How can I help?'

'You can lay the table,' he said, selecting a long knife from a rack and beginning to sharpen it on a steel with the expertise of a professional chef not unlike the one who'd come to teach me and ten of my friends how to prepare sushi for my twelfth birthday. 'Plates and cutlery are in the cupboard in front of you. There's a salad in the fridge.'

I busied myself with setting the table, pleased to have something to focus on other than all that efficient competence, which was oddly mesmerising and unaccountably compelling, as well as the memories of the once golden, now tainted times I'd had as a child. 'I didn't realise you cooked.'

'How else am I going to feed myself?'

'I don't know,' I said, straightening a fork. I'd never given it any thought. Why would I? I'd only mentioned it to fill the prickly silence. 'Order in?'

'Where from?'

It had been a joke—not one of my best, admittedly—but as I glanced out into the dark starless night, it occurred to me that Nick made an unsettling point. We weren't in London, where food delivery was one click of an app away. We were out here on a small island off the east coast of Africa, surrounded by the Indian Ocean, all alone, just the two of us. Rustling up a simple supper in a low-lit kitchen to the sounds of a seething sea and the warm humid breeze swishing through the leaves of his palm trees outside.

Which, come to think of it, felt unexpectedly intimate, I reflected uneasily as I headed to the fridge. We'd never been alone together before. At least, not like this. There'd been that one time when he'd picked me up from a party in London I hadn't been finding all that much fun and driven me home in stony silence, but that had been different. I'd been seventeen and on a mission to get over my crush on him. He'd been nineteen and with one of his interchangeable leggy blondes, who he'd ousted from the passenger side of his second-hand two-seater convertible with a smouldering smile filled with sensual promise that had filled me with envy.

But while I'd been so achingly aware of him sitting close beside me, and I could still recall every moment of it all these years later, my skin hadn't prickled on that occasion as it was suddenly prickling now. I hadn't experienced then quite the fire that was currently rushing along my veins. There'd been far less of a buzz, far fewer butterflies, and any burning up inside had been down to helpless, sullen jealousy.

'So where do you get supplies?' I asked, determinedly focusing on the pedestrian and reminding myself that not only was it stiflingly warm this evening—hence the fire and the prickling, obviously—but also that Nick and I were anything but intimate. We were tolerating each other's company under duress.

There was nothing romantic about any of this, and why was I even *thinking* of romance?

'I have a delivery from the mainland once a week,' he said, sliding the snapper from the pan onto a board and proceeding to de-bone it with the newly sharpened knife. 'And I fish.'

I set the salad on the table and stared at him, unable to contain my amazement. 'You fish?'

He paused mid slice and glanced up at me. 'Why the surprise?'

'I don't know,' I said, flustered by the sardonic tinge to his words and the lingering concerns about intimacy. 'I guess it just doesn't fit with the image I've always had of you. The sharp suit… The pristine shirt… The polished shoes…'

'I'm not always in a suit.'

No. He wasn't. This evening he was wearing faded jeans and a pink—pink!—shirt that was, of all astonishing things, untucked. He might have had a shower, but he hadn't shaved, and a faint five o'clock shadow adorned his jaw. With his thick dark hair touching his collar instead of being closely cropped as usual he looked…untamed. Almost piratical. Which, I had to admit, was an exceptionally good look on him.

I could hardly believe that I'd met him eighteen years ago and had thought I had him all worked out. Clearly I knew nothing. Not that I needed to know anything, of course. He was my financial advisor, that was it. Whether his rigidly controlled guard ever came down was no more my business than what might lie behind it. Which version of himself he preferred—immaculately suited or casually beachified—was of no interest to me whatsoever. Continuing the conversation, however, to keep my mind from frustratingly wandering down inappropriate avenues, *was* important, even if it did feel like wading through treacle.

'Did you catch this?' I asked as he placed a fillet on each plate and brought them to the glass-topped driftwood dining table that easily sat twelve.

'Yes. This morning.'

An unnecessary and unwelcome vision of him at the helm of a brilliant white yacht, shirtless, muscles flexing as he threw out a line, shot into my head before I despairingly shoved it right out again.

'I'm impressed,' I said, sitting down and flapping out a napkin.

'So easily?'

Why I'd imagined him semi-naked might be incomprehensible but at least I could understand his icy scepticism. Once upon a time, in my circle of so-called friends, disdain, feigned or genuine, had been cool, which was obviously anything but cool. 'People change.'

'Do they?' He took the seat opposite me and seemed to fill my vision despite the width of the table.

'Well, some do,' I said, inordinately grateful for the intricate wooden structure that supported the glass slab and would prevent any accidental bumping of knees. 'You haven't. You're more consistent than anyone else I know.'

'In what way?'

Ah. So that had been a silly thing to say because now I had to come up with examples. And since I had no intention of embarking on a lengthy explanation of exactly how I knew what his opinion of me had been for the last decade or so—which might suggest I cared when I absolutely didn't—I had to rack my brains for something more prosaic.

'Well, obviously the evidence is limited,' I said, faintly surprised to discover that I didn't have to rack them for long. 'But whenever I see you, you always have the top two buttons of your shirt undone. You have a habit of spinning things around your fingers. Toothpick, beer mat, coin, pen. Whatever's to hand. You walk into the bar, the room, or wherever it is we happen to find ourselves unavoidably in the same vicinity and you look first right, then left and then you frown, as if you're searching for something or someone and you're annoyed you can't find them. You're perpetually displeased to see me and your girlfriends are, without fail, tall and blonde and never last longer than a month.'

At that, a flicker of alarm did dart across his face. 'I had no idea you were so perceptive.'

Neither did I, come to think of it.

'There are lots of things you don't know about me,' I said coolly, picking up my knife and fork and assuring myself that the flutter of my stomach was down to hunger, not unease. 'The main one being that, unlike you, I *have* changed.'

'Have you?'

'I had no choice. I was appalling.'

'You were spoilt.'

'I was,' I agreed. 'I was an obnoxious brat. As you once so eloquently pointed out. At my sixteenth birthday party, if I recall correctly.'

'You wanted me to be your plaything.'

Another moment I wasn't particularly proud of, I

thought with a wince that I didn't even try to hide. Mid-way through an afternoon of hanging out by the pool, egged on by my so-called friends at the time, I'd sauntered up to him and demanded he come and entertain us. When he'd icily refused, I'd muttered something about chips and shoulders, told him he wasn't good enough for us anyway and sashayed away.

In my defence—not that I deserved one—I'd been all shaken up inside. Nick had been the topic of conversation and it had confused the hell out of me. Up until then he'd barely been on my radar. He'd simply been a friend of Seb's, who, since his mother lived four hundred miles north of the school and worked all hours, and his father wasn't in the picture, often came to stay at weekends and during the holidays, but ultimately had been as unworthy of interest as my brother.

However, that afternoon, I'd seen him for the first time through my friends' eyes—an eighteen-year-old hunk with a tall athletic frame and a brooding way about him that had suddenly sent shivers down my spine and my hormones into overdrive. In response to the chaos caused by the buzz of attraction that had weakened my limbs and accelerated my pulse and the sting of his rejection that had hurt more than I could possibly have imagined, I'd behaved cruelly and clumsily and I could absolutely understand why from that day forward he'd treated me with such contempt.

'I didn't really,' I muttered, feeling my cheeks turning beetroot as I cut off a bite-sized chunk of fish. 'I was impressionable and had lousy friends. They bet me to get you to hang out with us. I should have said no and left you alone. I should never have insulted you the way I did. I'm so sorry. It was unforgivable. I didn't even mean it. I realise the apology comes thirteen years too late, but you have it nonetheless.'

For a moment he just looked at me, his eyes dark and locked onto mine, while my heart thumped so loudly I could hear it in my ears. Then he said, 'I neither want or need it,' and it was like a slap across the face.

My breath caught. My flush deepened. No. Well. That was fair enough. I'd always known I'd burned virtually every one of the few bridges we'd shared. It had never bothered me before. Somehow, it did now. My throat was tight with shame. Regret was stabbing me in the chest. And for the life of me I couldn't work out why. It wasn't as if I wanted to play with him now. 'I understand.'

'You couldn't even *begin* to understand,' he said with equal bluntness, but this time I didn't flinch. I didn't react at all. Because it was becoming pretty bloody clear I understood absolutely nothing.

The end of the meal couldn't come fast enough. Despite my best efforts to keep up the small talk, conversation became increasingly stilted. My barrel-scraping questions and observations about island wildlife, water sports and the welfare of his mother met with ever more monosyllabic responses and an ever-deepening frown.

'What's the one thing you want but you don't have?' I asked, doggedly determined to keep going in an effort to avoid long, uncomfortable silences.

'Peace and quiet.'

'Where do you see yourself in five years' time?'

'Working. Making more money to give away.'

'Give away?'

'I fund bursaries. Scholarships. Charities that support those kids that want to do better but are held back by where they've come from.'

That was admirable. But then presumably there were only so many penthouses and islands one man could buy. 'What are you afraid of?'

'That your questions will never come to an end.'

They did after that. I was all out of small talk. Which was a shame because without that to focus on, to my intense frustration, I found it almost impossible not to keep staring at him. He was so big, so close, and right in my line of vision. My gaze kept snagging on his hands and his mouth as he sliced up the fish and ate. Bizarrely, a vision of him surging to his feet, pulling me into his arms and spreading me across the table to do with me what he wanted took shape in my mind, and, once there, wouldn't shift.

My inability to keep a clear head around him was becoming increasingly intolerable. I loathed the way my self-control seemed to disappear in his vicinity and the jitters that took up residence inside me like a swarm of bees. I hated the fact that no matter how often I instructed myself to think of him in a purely professional context, I couldn't.

The second I got to my room I'd be calling James and arranging to be picked up just as soon as was humanly possible, I vowed as I put my knife and fork down and polished off what was left of my drink. Who cared about a raking-up of the past and a few crappy headlines? I was older and stronger this time around and I would *not* be a victim. Emails could easily be deleted. Spurious requests to connect on social media could easily be ignored. Of course I'd be able to recognise an ulterior motive. And after I'd explained, my colleagues would surely understand why I'd told them nothing of my win.

Once home, I need never speak to Nick again. We could communicate by email and revert to nods and a very wide berth on the unfortunate occasion our paths did have to cross in the future. Upon reflection, the status quo wasn't *that* bad.

'Right, well, thank you for supper,' I said, once the kitchen was clear of the most excruciating meal I'd had in years. 'And despite what I said earlier in your study, thank you for all your help too. I realise it didn't sound like it at the time, but I *am* grateful. I know how I'm lucky to have you. I mean your services, obviously,' I hastened to clarify, but it didn't sound much better, so I added, 'Or rather, your financial services,' which, to my despair, only made it worse.

Nick merely stood watching as I flushed and floundered and dug myself into an ever bigger hole and I felt like banging my head against the wall in frustration. Would I *ever* be able to speak to this man without my words producing an unintended consequence? Or was I a completely lost cause?

'Anyway, you'll no doubt be delighted to hear that I'll be out of your hair tomorrow,' I said, prepared to move heaven and earth to facilitate such a move if I had to. 'I'm aiming to be on a plane first thing.'

'That's not going to happen.'

My heart skipped a beat. What? No. Why? 'Do you

have doubts about your influence over the press back home?'

'Not at all,' he said, with an ominous glance in the direction of the open French doors and the night beyond. 'I do, however, have doubts about the weather.'

CHAPTER SIX

It was with a mixture of consternation and relief that I made my escape and fled to my room. But while the consternation over the weather and the implications of its deterioration lingered, the relief didn't last nearly as long.

I barely noticed the luxurious comfort of the space I occupied. I didn't have the wherewithal to appreciate the cool white walls, the honey-coloured wood floor and the soothingly neutral soft furnishings and I gave the gleaming en-suite only the most cursory of glances as I set the water temperature to cold and stepped into the enormous walk-in shower. I was too preoccupied with ruminating on the conversation Nick and I had had at supper, trying to unravel the myriad thoughts and questions swirling around my head and keeping my roiling emotions in check.

Why could I not stop thinking about him in inappropriate contexts? was the question uppermost in my mind as I brushed my teeth and climbed into bed. Such as a state of nakedness. Or a steamy embrace in which we kissed as if the world were about to end. Was the stress I'd been under finally taking its toll and breaking me down? Was it the shock of seeing him out of his usual environment? Spending time with him alone? What?

Surely I couldn't be attracted to him, I thought with a shiver of apprehension, lying there in the thick, heavy dark, a hot and achy pulse throbbing in the pit of my stomach. The crush I'd perversely developed on him in the aftermath of the pool party hadn't been *that* bad, even if once his many physical attributes had been pointed out, it had been annoyingly impossible to ignore them.

Although it had taken three years of determined effort—burning the candle at both ends by studying for my school exams during the term and partying hard in the holidays and my year off—I'd eventually got him out of my system. There was zero point in continuing to want him, I'd realised, gazing longingly at him one evening while subtly shooting daggers at the back of the girl he was with. He was never going to suddenly turn round and want me back. He went for tall willowy blondes, and, even without the complication of how little he thought of me, I was an average height curvy brunette.

I'd come to the decision that it was time to grow up and move on, and I genuinely assumed I had. I'd hung up my dancing shoes and accepted a university place in Zurich. I'd put my embarrassing youth behind me and knuckled down to study, my dream of working in marine conservation driving me to achieve top marks and become the best, until my family lost everything and my life imploded and I had to scrabble around in the rubble for some kind of future.

But what if I *hadn't* moved on? What if I'd merely

buried the attraction beneath the weight of my studies and then the brutal upheaval of my existence, aided and abetted by Nick's continued disapproval of me? Could it have lain inside me all these years, dormant, like a volcano waiting to erupt?

No, I decided firmly as I tossed and turned, trying to find a cool spot in the bed. There was no volcano, dormant or otherwise. The fundamentals hadn't changed. He still dated blondes and he still loathed me. I'd be on a hiding to nothing, and I wasn't that much of an idiot.

My crazy response to him a week ago had to have been a result of the stress of the situation I'd found myself in messing with my reason. And now, most likely, it was the weather. No doubt the electricity that sizzled through me was down to the dark gathering clouds. The plummeting air pressure had to be responsible for the churning of my stomach, and it was the soaring heat and humidity of the air that had caused my core temperature to rise. It simply couldn't be anything else.

Nevertheless, despite these assurances, despite the thousand-thread-count sheets and the rhythmic rush of the sea, sleep was a long time coming.

I woke at six in the morning to an almighty clap of thunder and winds that sounded as though they were battering the palm trees and whipping up the sea. The hot air was suffocatingly thick and, within seconds, the faint patter of rain peppering the roof had turned into a deluge so loud I could barely hear myself think.

I groggily sat up and tried the switch of the bedside lamp to no avail, and my stomach plummeted. Nick had been right—I wasn't going anywhere today. Heaven and earth were indeed moving but instead of facilitating my escape, they were prohibiting it.

I got up to close the window I'd left open last night to alleviate the stifling heat and made my way across the dim, shadowy room, every muscle I possessed aching in protest. After such a fitful night, my eyes were gritty and sore. I felt as though I'd aged a hundred years and then been run over by a truck.

Everything was chaos, both inside and out, but there was no need to panic, I assured myself, breathing deeply and steadily as I stared out at the oppressive gunmetal sky through which not a single speck of blue peeked and the grey malevolently churning sea. I might have been on the back foot ever since the moment I'd contacted Nick requesting an appointment, but that didn't mean I had to remain there. All I had to do was locate my gumption and remind myself of my resolve to stay cool, collected and professional.

To that end, I would stop thinking about him naked. I would not entertain any more images of us kissing. I would get through the next day or two or however long the storm lasted by resolutely rising above such trivialities. By occupying the higher ground, as it were.

Of course there was no *literal* higher ground in the immediate vicinity but the house seemed sturdily built. Despite the gale that was howling outside, the window I'd just closed wasn't even rattling. I had nothing to worry about. Really. The tops of the palm trees might be being blown every which way but it wasn't as if debris were flying around. Presumably, Nick would have storm-proofed the house. A financial-planning guru would mitigate the risks and protect his assets, wouldn't he?

A sudden thump on my door made me jump back and shriek, and I had an instant vision of the roof nevertheless ripping off and all the furniture on the landing being swept up into the maelstrom.

'Amelia?'

Phew.

Not the roof.

Nick. My reluctant host, my sternest critic and very definitely not a man I was foolish enough to still be attracted to.

In an effort to calm my thundering pulse and quell my anxiety over both the weather and the havoc he played on my equilibrium, I pulled my shoulders back and set my jaw, then padded across the floor and opened the door. Storm lantern in hand, he stood on the landing looking dark and severe, tousled and stubbled and rumpled in a way that would have made me wonder if he'd just rolled out of bed had I been remotely interested in thinking of him along those lines, which I absolutely wasn't.

'Yes?'

'Put some clothes on and come downstairs,' he said tersely, having briefly raked his gaze over the white camisole and shorts set I was wearing, which was climate suitable but unfortunately left little to the imagination. 'Be quick. Take this.' He handed me a heavy torch from which shone a bright sweeping beam. 'And stay away from the windows.'

Five minutes later, I was sitting at one end of the cosy sofa that stood in the windowless inner hall of Nick's palatial villa, dressed in leggings and a sweatshirt, a combination that I trusted would meet with more approval than my nightwear. Under any other circumstances I might have bristled at the high-handed way he'd bossed me about, but under these, I had to admit I was rather glad he seemed to know what he was doing.

In addition to the lamp he'd been carrying earlier, a further three illuminated the space, two on the floor and one on each side table. Half a dozen torches were lined up on the console table that stood against the opposite wall, along with several bottles of water and a selection of snacks.

'So what exactly is this weather system we're currently experiencing?' I asked, eyeing the preparations warily, Nick's competence in this area not doing quite enough to completely erase my apprehension about the storm raging outside. 'A hurricane?'

He checked his phone, frowned, then tossed it aside and began to pace. 'A hurricane is known as a cyclone in these parts,' he muttered, clearly as frustrated as I was by the annoying turn of events that had screwed up both our plans. 'But no. It's a tropical depression.'

'What does that mean?'

'Light unorganised winds and minimal damage.'

There was a sudden crackle of lightning and a booming rumble of thunder that rent the air, both loud enough to make me want to cover my ears, and I didn't dare think about what stronger winds and less than minimal damage might mean.

'Is it likely to get worse?' I said, once the echoes had stopped reverberating off the walls and the flash of illumination had faded.

'Not according to the forecast,' he said. 'But that may change. Not that we'll know about it. The satellite dish is down and the electricity's cut out. For some reason the back-up generator hasn't kicked in.'

My stomach sank. Oh, dear. None of that sounded good. 'Can you fix it?'

'Probably. But voluntarily venturing outside right now would be lunacy. I secured the outdoor furniture last night just in case, but there's always the risk of a loose roof tile or the strike of an unexpectedly large wave.'

A vision of him lying bleeding on the terrace and then being swept out to sea slammed into my head, and my heart gave a great lurch. My head swam and my stomach turned and for a moment I thought I might actually throw up.

'Could the island flood?' I asked, swallowing down the panic and assuring myself that since Nick, by his own admission, wasn't the reckless sort, that scenario was highly unlikely.

'It hasn't before.'

Before? 'How often does a storm like this hit?'

'Only once in the five years since I had the house built. That time it blew in the windows, but it was stronger.'

Hence his brusque instruction to steer clear of them. 'The hotel made no mention of anything.'

'It developed without warning,' he said. 'It happens.'

Much like his recent effect on me, I thought darkly, watching him shove his hands through his hair as he continued to glare at the floor and pace, about as removed from cool, in control and immaculate as it was possible to be. It had been years since he'd aroused anything other than frustrated irritation in me, yet from the moment I'd stepped foot on this island, I'd experienced virtually every emotion there was.

'How long do they last?' I asked, deciding it would be wise to focus on the practicalities instead of my intensely confusing and unwelcome response to him.

'If we're lucky, it'll be over in a matter of hours. If we aren't, it could be days.'

Days?

God.

'So what do we do in the meantime?'

He paused mid-step and shot me a look that was as dark and stormy as the sky. Something in it ignited a fire in the pit of my stomach and sent heat streaking along my veins. 'Sit it out.'

Sit it out? That wasn't what he'd been thinking. If it was, my heart wouldn't suddenly be thumping like a steam train and my mouth wouldn't be bone dry. But if it wasn't, then what *had* he been thinking? Why the flames? Why the burn? I had no idea. But did it matter? No. It did not.

What was important was remaining calm and in control. All I had to do was adapt to the situation. I was good at that. I'd had plenty of experience. Giving up a top university place to get a nine-to-five job. Swapping the beautiful Chelsea mansion for the grotty flat share in Hanwell. Getting round by sketchy public transport instead of a shiny chauffeur-driven Rolls. Budgeting, bargaining and the marked-down aisle at the supermarket. Vouchers, energy deals and a knackering weekend job in a bar. I'd got used to it all in the end.

So however long we were trapped here it would be fine. As I'd told myself repeatedly over the years, it was simply a question of mind over matter. The lanterns with their softly flickering light weren't romantic. They symbolised a potential catastrophic natural disaster. The confined space we occupied wasn't cosy. It was claustrophobic. Especially with Nick taking up so much room and stirring up the air with his incessant pacing. The tension radiating off him was making me feel as if I were sitting on knives. My nerves were buzzing and every time my supposedly loose top brushed against my body, shivers ran up and down my spine.

'Look, why don't you come and sit down?' I said, pushing up my sleeves and shifting to alleviate the prickling sensation, but only succeeding in tightening the fabric around my chest and making matters worse.

'I'm fine where I am,' he muttered, his gaze briefly flickering in my direction.

'You're making me nervous with all the pacing and glowering.'

'Too bad.'

'Did you not sleep well or something?'

'No,' he said, coming to an abrupt halt at the console table and grabbing a bottle of water. 'I did not sleep well.'

'Neither did I,' I replied. 'The heat was unbearable. I feel rough as anything.'

'It wasn't the heat,' he said, cracking open the lid and throwing me a pointed look that had me bristling.

'Are you saying it was me who kept you up?'

His expression darkened and something flared in the

depths of his eyes that sent a hot shiver down my spine. 'That's exactly what I'm saying.'

His words were brusque, his voice was tight, and inwardly, I reeled. He didn't pull his punches. I knew my presence was a problem for him but, perhaps naïvely given last night's grumpiness, I hadn't expected quite this level of hostility. 'I'll be off as soon as I can.'

'It won't be soon enough.'

Well, to hell with chilly politeness. The gloves were now off. 'I realise the situation isn't ideal,' I said tartly, 'but—'

'Not ideal?' he cut in, the incredulity in his tone slicing through me like a knife. 'This situation is about as far from ideal as it's possible to get.'

Surely it wasn't *that* bad. We were safe. For now. Assuming the weather didn't worsen. 'Aren't you being a little overdramatic?'

'You're Seb's sister.'

I blinked in surprise at this non sequitur. 'What does that have to do with anything?'

'Apparently, not nearly enough.'

'No. Well. I can understand your concern. Naturally, you wouldn't want anything to happen to me on your watch. I mean, what would you tell Seb? But ultimately, I'm no one's responsibility but my own. And you didn't *have* to come and fetch me from Zanzibar, you know.'

He frowned. 'What?'

'You could have left me at the hotel.'

For a moment he just stared at me as if I'd grown two heads. Then he said, 'Could I?'

'Yes,' I said with a firm nod, not liking his condescending, knowing tone one little bit. 'I'd have been fine.'

'You called me wanting my help. You sounded far from fine. You sounded distraught. Do you seriously think I'd have ignored that?'

No, I had to acknowledge grudgingly, noting the tight set of his jaw and the resolve in his expression before he lifted the bottle to his mouth and poured half the contents down his throat. He wouldn't. Because, despite his many flaws, not all of his traits were unfortunate. Annoyingly, he had a decent streak a mile wide. He'd paid his mother back a hundred times over for her determination to see him succeed and the sacrifices she'd made to achieve that. He'd helped my brother out of a tight spot with his start-up and funded my mother's counselling course.

The instance he'd picked me up from that party wasn't the only time he'd fished me out of trouble. Once, when I was twelve, he'd sent packing the bunch of girls cornering me in the school dining room for reasons long since forgotten. On another occasion, he'd bodily removed a guy who'd been getting a little too handsy at the club in which we'd celebrated Seb's twenty-first birthday.

'OK, fine, you're right,' I said exasperatedly. 'I was distraught and I didn't give you a choice. But you were wrong about one thing.'

His brows snapped together. 'What?'

'This,' I said, waving a hand first at myself, next at his scowl and finally around the space, 'clearly *is* all my fault.'

He rolled his eyes.

He actually rolled his eyes.

And quite suddenly I'd had enough. Of his disapproval and his arrogance. Of the constant scepticism and the capacity he had to make me wither and squirm. Of my inability to simply brush it all off. It had been going on for years and I was sick of it.

With an urgency that came out of the blue to hit me square in the gut, I needed to know exactly what Nick thought of me and why. I wanted him to explain, so I could fix it. Because deep down I loathed the tension and the animosity that existed between us. The skirmishes that characterised our simmering battle of attrition were more wounding than I'd allowed myself to acknowledge. I couldn't stand seeing him when my brother was over from the States, or running into him as I occasionally did, and tensing right up, on edge and confused, unable to fully understand what was really behind the rock-bottom opinion he had of me.

Why did he refuse to see that I'd changed? I didn't make it *that* easy for him. I wasn't *always* deliberately flippant and silly. And why wouldn't he let me apologise for the mistakes I'd made over the years? Why wouldn't he grant me the forgiveness I badly wanted?

Despite my intention to simply rise above it all, I couldn't. If I was being brutally honest, frustrated irritation hadn't been the only emotion he'd roused in me over the last ten years or so. His attitude hurt. A lot. Here, now, was the opportunity to rectify any misapprehensions and get some answers. As soon as the weather improved I'd be off, and that would be that. Unaddressed, things between us would go back to the way they'd been before. And although I couldn't work out why, I truly didn't think I could bear it any more.

'What exactly is your problem with me, Nick?'

He went very still, the slight narrowing of his eyes his only movement. 'What on earth are you talking about? I have no problem with you.'

'Come off it,' I said, years of bottling it up unbottling as I leapt to my feet and took a step towards him. 'Every time our paths cross you can't help but look at me with disapproval. You practically quiver with it. You're dismissive and disdainful. I've been subjected to your stony glare and rigid jaw ever since that afternoon by the pool. Over a decade ago. And I get it. I was horrible back then. Selfish and arrogant and pampered. And I know I didn't behave any better when you offered me that loan, gift, whatever, five years later,' I continued hotly, on a roll now. 'But in mitigation, I was a wreck. My entire life had turned upside down. I'd just lost my home, my university place, my family, my sense of self, such as it was. I wasn't thinking straight. I was hurting. Humiliated. I didn't know what was what. My father had just died. My mother was no help and my brother was in the States. I didn't know where to turn. My boyfriend had dumped me and all my friends had vanished practically overnight.'

'*I* didn't.'

'*You* weren't a friend.'

His jaw tightened and his frown deepened. 'So you keep saying.'

'You never give me a chance to apologise for the things I've said or the way I've said them,' I said, ignoring the strange twist of my chest at whatever it was that flitted across his expression. 'Or explain. Every time I try, you just walk away or brush it off. You've been aloof and distant for years, and I want to know why. I'm not the person I used to be. I've learned to be better. Nicer. And I am. So why do you still hate me so much?'

'I don't hate you,' he said, a muscle hammering in his jaw and a dark flush tingeing his cheekbones. 'And I don't disapprove of you. I don't disapprove of you at all.'

I gave him a *yeah, right* look, but wasn't about to get into a 'yes, you did, no, I didn't' kind of a back and forth. 'Well, you make a damn good show of it,' I said, the evidence piling up in my head demanding a voice. 'Every time we meet and I try and say hello, you blank me. Whenever I say something—anything—you get this bored look on your face. You came to my rescue yesterday, yes, but it was clearly under duress, and at supper, you dismissed yet another attempt on my part to apologise for the things I've said and done. What else am I supposed to think other than that you loathe me?'

'That's never been my intention.'

'Then what *was* your intention?'

'Why do you care?'

That stopped me in my tracks, both literally and figuratively. I froze a foot away from him, my breath catching in my throat and my head spinning.

I didn't care.

Or did I?

If I didn't, his attitude towards me wouldn't have the power to hurt me. His rejection of my frequent attempts to apologise wouldn't have stung so badly. I wouldn't have felt the need to apologise in the first place. If I did, it would explain why I inevitably went home after encountering him feeling bruised and bewildered. Why the digs and the slights and the judgements had stuck to me like burrs.

I *did* care, I realised, feeling weak and a little light-headed. I wanted him to think better of me. I hated that he was still so wrong about me. As for the *why*, though, I hadn't a clue. 'I have no idea.'

'Well, when you find out, let me know,' he said. 'In the meantime, I think I *will* go and check on the generator, after all.'

CHAPTER SEVEN

For a second or two, all I could do was stand rooted to the spot, staring blankly at Nick's broad back, narrow hips and long legs as he stalked off in the direction of the French doors that led from relative safety into wild wet mayhem. I was too busy reeling with astonishment to even think about formulating a response. And by the time it did occur to me to race after him and demand to know if he'd completely lost his mind, he'd flung open the doors as if the hounds of hell were at his heels and disappeared into the storm.

What on earth was going on? I wondered dazedly, my heart thundering as the doors slammed closed behind him. Was battling the horrendous weather really more appealing than answering my questions? Was his opinion of me genuinely that bad? And as for wanting to know why I cared what he thought of me, well, perhaps if and when he figured it out, he could let *me* know.

I got that my tirade had come out of the blue. It had taken even me by surprise—although all pressure cookers needed release at some point—so maybe it shouldn't have been that much of a shock. But why the sudden need to check out the generator? He'd only just declared such an act lunacy.

I couldn't unravel any of it. Everything was such a muddle. But really, only one thing mattered right now, and that was the fact that Nick had just taken leave of his senses and was now out there at the mercy of a savage mother nature.

What if something happened to him?

A dozen images slammed into my head then, tightening my chest and challenging my ability to breathe, but I ruthlessly shoved them away. I refused to contemplate a world without him in it. For better or worse—mostly worse, admittedly—he'd been part of my life for eighteen years, and things were just beginning to get interesting. But what could I do? I could hardly go after him. I had no choice but to trust that he knew what he was doing even though he'd looked and sounded as if he'd become unhinged.

The minutes dragged by like hours. I drank some water and ate a croissant. Outside, something creaked alarmingly. Somewhere inside the house, a door slammed. I discovered there was something to be said for pacing, and that the wringing of hands was actually a thing.

All I could think about was what might be happening outside and Nick's safe return from it. We hadn't cleared the air. There were things I needed to know and avenues I wanted to explore—the details of which were still unclear—but apart from all that, if something *did* happen to him, how would I tell his mother?

She'd made such sacrifices for him, her only son. She'd worked three jobs. And yes, he'd more than paid her back, buying her a house, and supporting her to retrain as a teacher, but she'd fought so hard, so tirelessly to give him a better future, and to have him perish so senselessly—

I didn't get to finish that thought. With a thunderous bang, the doors through which Nick had exited flew open. I leapt nearly a foot in the air and whirled around to find him striding back in. He was drenched from head to toe, the rain sluicing off him as he battled to close the doors behind him. His shirt was plastered to his body. His jeans had darkened to navy. A puddle was forming at his feet, but he was alive and looked to be in one piece, and the relief was so immense it nearly took out my knees before swiftly morphing into a tsunami of red-hot anger.

'Are you mad?' I yelled as I stalked towards him on legs that were shaking so hard they were barely keeping me upright. 'What the hell were you *thinking*? How could you be so bloody irresponsible?'

'I needed some air,' he said, shoving a hand through his hair and dashing the water from his eyes.

Air? *Air?* Had he taken a blow to the head? Mine was about to explode. 'You said you weren't reckless but you could have been *killed*.'

'You care,' he said, stalking towards the downstairs bathroom, leaving a wet sandy trail in his wake. 'I'm touched.'

As I followed him, every cell of my body in turmoil, I didn't know whether I wanted to hug him or strangle him. Probably both. Because I cared more than I wanted to admit, which made no sense at all.

'You're definitely touched,' I said grimly, watching him grab a towel and rub it over his head. 'And to think I'm trusting you with my fortune. *I* must be mad.'

'We need power.'

'And do we have it?' I demanded. 'Because as far as I can tell the lights are still out.'

He tossed the towel onto the towel rail and strode past me. 'No. We don't. It would appear the problem with the generator isn't an easy fix.'

'So you risked your life for *nothing*.'

'Not for nothing,' he said flatly, heading for the staircase. 'For my sanity.'

'Your sanity? You must be joking.'

'I can't think of anything I find less amusing.'

'Am I honestly that bad? Were my questions really that difficult to answer?'

'You have no idea.'

'What does that mean?'

'Who knows? I sure as hell don't.'

'You're not making sense.'

'You're driving me insane.'

Ah, but he didn't know how worried I'd been. Even *I* had had no idea how worried I'd been. It was all very well for him to scowl and growl like this. He wasn't the one left behind to imagine the worst. 'If I am overreacting, it's because I was scared out of my wits.'

He stopped at the bottom of the stairs and turned to me, pinning me to the spot and stealing my breath with a look that was unsettlingly deep and searching, although marginally less fierce than before. 'Were you really worried about me?'

'Yes.'

'Why?'

There it was again. Another probing yet unanswerable question that sent me into a spin of confusion. I shifted my weight from one foot to the other, the sudden awkwardness awakening the jitters in my stomach and making me offer up the most superficial of explanations. 'Because if something had happened to you, what would have become of my money? Of me?'

His expression cleared and his mouth twisted. 'You've survived worse.'

Had I? Probably. Yet the dread that had mangled my guts was something I'd never experienced before and hoped never to experience again.

'And you'd soon find another financial advisor.'

'I don't want another financial advisor,' I said, recoiling at the thought of it. 'I want you.'

He gave a bitter laugh, which made no sense when he ought to be flattered that out of everyone on planet finance I'd chosen him, even if he was the best, but we were getting off track.

'At least you're back now,' I said, the panic and anger receding a little and some self-control returning as my racing pulse slowed. 'And by the looks of things, unharmed.'

'Sure.'

But as he put his hand on the handrail and turned to head on up, it struck me that something wasn't quite right. Despite the staircase rising up from the centre of the room, bannisters on both sides, he was using his left hand to hold on. In fact, come to think of it, he'd been using only his left hand since he'd stormed in from outside. And now he had his back to me, I could make out a rip in his shirt at his right shoulder and a darker stain against the wet grey cotton.

'You're not unharmed, are you?' I said with a lurch of my heart and a clench of my stomach.

He stilled on the first step. 'I'm fine.'

'What happened?'

'A loose roof tile. As I predicted. It's nothing. Just a scratch.'

It wasn't just a scratch. Not if blood was seeping through his shirt. But whatever it was, an inch or two to the left and it could have been a whole lot worse. 'You're incredibly lucky it missed your head.'

'I don't know about that,' he muttered. 'It might have knocked some sense into me.'

'Let me take a look.'

He turned an inch in my direction, his jaw tight and a deep frown creasing his forehead. 'I said it's fine.'

'It's not fine,' I countered. 'You're bleeding profusely.'

'Profusely is exaggerating it somewhat.'

'How do you know? You can't see it.'

'It'll stop soon enough.'

'There's no need to be stoical.'

'There's no need to make a fuss.'

A fuss? A *fuss*? 'You're being absurd.'

'I don't want you touching me.'

He made it sound like a fate worse than death and I flinched, each word piercing my chest. Whatever he'd claimed just before storming out, he really did find me horrible.

'I don't particularly want to touch you either,' I said, determinedly stamping out the tiny stabs of pain and lifting my chin and setting my jaw, because I was not letting this go. 'But the last thing either of us needs is for you to get an infection.'

For one long moment, I thought he was going to continue to resist. I could practically see the war against common sense raging inside him, but then he turned more fully towards me, the glare in his eyes abating a fraction, and, judging by the slight slackening of his muscles and the harsh exhale of his breath, appeared to relent. 'Fine.'

'Do you have a first-aid kit?'

'In the kitchen. In a cupboard, top left.'

'I'll go and get it. You sit down.'

Beyond relieved to have won *that* battle at least, I went to see what I could unearth. When I returned to the inner hall we'd been occupying earlier I found Nick sitting on one of the side tables, which he'd cleared of the lantern and pulled away from the wall. Pain was etched into his expression and I reckoned that had the lighting been better I would have seen that beneath his tan he'd gone a little pale.

I set the first-aid kit down on the console table and moved to stand behind him. 'Take off your shirt.'

He tensed. I swallowed hard. Despite the chaos rampaging outside, everything seemed very quiet and still in here. Apart from my pulse. That was racing. And pounding in my ears. I'd never stood this close to him before. I'd never been so achingly aware of the parts of my own body that were responding to the proximity and heat of his.

It ought to have been a blessing that I couldn't see his face or watch him undoing his buttons, his long fingers deftly working the fastenings, inch upon inch of skin and muscle presumably being slowly revealed as he freed one and moved to the next. But it wasn't. Because my imagination was conjuring up the visual anyway.

Then he peeled back the sodden shirt, slowly, carefully stripping it from his right side first and then the left, and I didn't have to imagine. Right there in front of me was an expanse of smooth tanned skin that covered defined muscles I'd never have thought he could ever have possessed. The last time I'd seen his naked torso he'd been eighteen and lanky and storming off after I'd derisively told him he was beneath me. In the thirteen years since then he'd filled out. And *how* he'd filled out.

He leaned forwards, resting his elbows on his wet denim-clad thighs, and for a moment I just stared at the view, mesmerised by the way the flickering light of the lanterns cast dancing shadows over him and marvelling at the strength and power of his upper body. Until my gaze zoned in on the cut, which to my relief didn't look as bad as I'd feared, and I snapped out of my stupor.

I had to stop ogling. My hands were no use curled into fists, even if that way there was absolutely no danger I might reach out and stroke him. If I leaned in any closer—all the better to capture his mouth-watering scent—I ran the risk of toppling right on top of him and he hardly needed further injury.

Inhaling deeply for one last heady hit of salty sweat, tropical rain and pure masculinity, I pulled myself together. Nick was effectively my patient. It was my role to patch him up. I needed to concentrate.

'Be gentle with me.'

'I'll try,' I said, opening the box and extracting a

bottle of alcohol, some of which I dabbed onto a wad of gauze. 'But this is going to sting regardless.'

I touched the gauze to the edge of the cut and he flinched. 'Sorry.'

'It's fine.'

'I'll be as quick as I can. At least it's stopped bleeding.'

'I told you "profusely" was an exaggeration.'

I resisted the urge to roll my eyes and focused instead on what I was doing. 'Once it's all cleaned up, I'll apply some antiseptic cream and then an adhesive dressing.'

'Look at you, Florence Nightingale.'

'I do have some uses.'

'Not just a pretty face.'

I froze. My pulse skipped a beat and then began to gallop. 'Sorry?'

'What?'

'Did you just call me pretty?'

'No. Ignore me,' he muttered. 'Come to think of it, I may well have suffered a bang to the head. I could have concussion.'

Ignore him? Like that was going to be possible. Whether he'd meant to or not, he'd paid me a compliment. Not a fact. An actual compliment. By his account, for the first time ever. It was dizzying stuff and bewildering as hell, and I wished I could see his expression and look into his eyes, no matter how unfathomable they might be, because what was going on?

'Keep still.'

'I'm not moving.'

Then maybe it was the room. Or me. My hands seemed to be trembling a little. My foundations were rocking. I couldn't quite believe that Nick Morgan, of all people, considered me pretty or understand why he'd chosen this moment to say it. *Was* he concussed?

Taking a deep steadying breath, I squeezed some antiseptic cream onto the wound and tried not to think about the fact that I was touching him, rubbing his lovely smooth skin in small slow hypnotic circles. About how easy it would be to stop rubbing and start caressing him with the whole of my hand, in larger circles that spread across the entire width of his shoulders and lower. About the hot heavy beat that was beginning to drum between my legs and how warm I was growing.

What would he think if I actually did it? I wondered, struggling to contain the urge to act on the impulses rising up inside me. What would he do? Would he leap away in horror or would he let me carry on? And if he didn't recoil in disgust, how far would he allow me to go? Could I run my fingers through his hair? Slide my hands around to his chest and press a kiss to the side of his neck?

Through the sluggish fog clouding my brain I heard him release a ragged breath, sensed something in his body give, as if a wave of defeat had washed over him, and saw him drop his head, chin to chest. 'Enough.'

'What?'

'I've had enough. I can't take this any more.'

'OK.' The fog pulverised, I whipped my hands off him, appalled by the suspicion that he thought I'd been groping him against his will. 'Sorry.'

'No. I don't mean the rubbing. You can carry on with that.'

My heart thudded. 'Then what do you mean?'

For the longest of moments he didn't reply. He sighed deeply again and shuddered, and then he said, 'Do you really want to know why I've kept my distance from you all these years?'

His voice was low. Gravelly. It skated over my nerve-endings and sent shivers down my spine, but at least it pulled me out of fantasy land and back to reality. The part of me that feared the shame of what he might reveal wanted to yell, 'No!' and retreat, but I located and clung onto the braver part of me, which was done with the antagonism and longed to correct whatever was wrong.

'I really do.'

'Do you remember what you were wearing the afternoon of your party by the pool?'

I picked up a cloth and frowned, the heat and the chaos swirling around inside me dissipating a little. What did that have to do with anything? 'No.'

'A pink bikini with tiny red strawberries all over it,' he said gruffly. 'A sheer white sarong tied at the waist. Your hair was held off your face with a pair of sunglasses and you were wearing a gold chain around your right ankle.'

My heart knocked against my ribs. 'That's a lot of detail.'

'I can recall all of it.'

'I'm not surprised.' The events of the afternoon had turned a relationship that hadn't even been a relationship into over a decade of icy hostility. I could recall quite a bit of it too. 'It was a memorable afternoon. Although not really in a good way.'

'I hadn't seen you for a while,' he said, the words slightly muffled by his chest. 'You'd grown up, and suddenly you were the sexiest thing I'd ever seen. I was dazzled. Instantly bowled over with lust. It knocked me for six, and I was still floundering when you sidled up to me and demanded I entertain you and your friends as if you owned me. Then you cut me down and it should have killed the attraction stone dead, but unfortunately it didn't. And that made me far more angry than your insult. How could I so badly want someone who thought so little of me? It made no sense. I had to stay away from you. For my own peace of mind. And since the attraction didn't fade, as I'd hoped, and you clearly didn't feel it too, I had to keep on staying away.'

He stopped and the silence that followed his words was immense and deafening. I was stunned. Speechless. Still wiping my fingers on the cloth even though the remnants of cream had to have been long since removed. I didn't know which bit to process first. The length of his speech? The fact that he'd once lusted after me and the implication that maybe he continued to do so? Or his misguided belief that I'd never found him attractive?

The shock of what he'd just said was too much to comprehend. Too huge. Only one of those clamouring questions could I even begin to address. However he'd felt about me before, he couldn't be attracted to me now. It was impossible. All evidence suggested the opposite.

And yet…

A montage of recent images and memories—from the afternoon I'd shown up here, then yesterday evening and this morning—broke through the dam of denial and flooded my head, suddenly pelting me with doubt.

What if the abruptness with which he'd dropped my

hand after he'd helped me off the boat the day I arrived suggested the contact had had the same electrifying impact on him as it had on me? What if he'd frequently run his darkening gaze over me not to find something of which to disapprove but because he'd been unable to resist the temptation to check me out? Could the deterioration of his mood at supper last night have been a result of the battle he claimed to wage on the attraction he felt for me? And when he'd said half an hour ago we'd get through the storm by 'sitting it out', was the reason I'd got the impression he was envisaging something else entirely because he had been? And was that something the two of us in here whipping up a storm of our own?

Could I have been so blinded by my own hang-ups that I'd misread the evidence? It was entirely possible, I realised dazedly. To all those questions and suppositions, the answer could well be yes.

'Yesterday afternoon,' I said, suddenly desperate for confirmation one way or another. 'When I was talking about marine conservation, you were looking at my mouth.'

'I wanted it on mine,' he said hoarsely. 'I wanted it on me everywhere. I thought taking a cold shower while you were out on your walk would fix it, but it didn't. I thought thinking of you as a sister would help. But that didn't work either. I've never felt frustration like it. And the worst of it is, you are and have always been utterly oblivious.'

'But you go for leggy blondes,' I somehow managed, dizzy with shock and lust and who knew what else.

'Only to try and cure myself of an absurd fixation with a pint-sized brunette.'

'Five foot five isn't that short.'

'Every inch of you is perfect.'

My heart pounded. Who was this man? 'The day I arrived here you implied you couldn't wait to get rid of me.'

'I didn't trust myself to be alone with you. I was irritated for not having anticipated it and putting us in that position.'

'It was rude.'

'It was instinctive. It felt necessary. Self-preservation if you like.'

I knew all about that. 'You haven't exactly been friendly since.'

'As you keep pointing out—as if I need reminding—we aren't friends. But even if we were, it must be pretty bloody obvious by now that friendly is not how I feel about you.'

I swallowed hard. 'Why did you never say anything?'

'I'm not that much of a masochist.'

'So why are you telling me now?'

'Because I need it to stop,' he muttered darkly. 'It's been going on for far too long. I need to move on. I need you to laugh at me the way you did by the pool and tell me I never had a chance in hell and never will. And if not now, when we're stuck here with nowhere to go, then when?'

I could do that, I thought, my head spinning. I could easily do that. One quick scathing remark and that would be the end to this.

But I didn't want to.

And besides, it would be a lie.

I could no longer kid myself that the electricity and tension gripping my entire body were simply as a result of stress or meteorology playing havoc with my senses. Everything I'd thought incomprehensible, as transparent as mud, had become crystal clear.

The pieces of the puzzle had all fallen into place and I could now see that *this* was what the last thirteen years had been about. Despite my best efforts, I hadn't crushed the crush in the slightest. All along, behind the aloofness on his side and the hurt and frustration on mine, beneath the thick layer of icy hostility and forced civility, had been the simmering mutual attraction that had flared into life that afternoon by the pool and never gone away.

That had to be why I sometimes filled with the overwhelming urge to provoke a reaction from him. Why I'd never attempted to greet him with a kiss and had taken such care not to touch him all these years. Subconsciously I must have known it would all have lit a fire inside me that would have been impossible to extinguish.

So what was the point of pretending I didn't want Nick when it was blindingly obvious I did? Especially when, against all the odds, the feeling appeared to be reciprocated. I longed for his touch. I dreamed of his mouth. I'd become so practised at denying myself the good things in life—I'd had no choice—but I didn't have to deny this. I could have both his touch *and* his mouth. All I had to do was admit it, which wasn't a challenge at all.

'I can't do that,' I said, beyond desperate to find out what might happen next and willing to do anything to facilitate it.

He tensed. 'Why not? Does the thought of continuing to screw with my head amuse you that much?'

'God, no.'

'Then what are you saying?'

'I may not remember what *I* was wearing that afternoon by the pool,' I said, miraculously having the presence of mind to quit the cloth and rummage around in the kit for a dressing. 'But I remember what *you* were. A pair of black board shorts. That was it. You'd never really crossed my radar before. But my friends were talking about you and suddenly you did. You were all I could see. You sent me and my teenage hormones into a complete spin. I didn't take your rejection well and in my immaturity I lashed out. I spent the next three years partying hard in an attempt to eradicate the shame and shake my attraction to you.'

Silence. And then, a rough, 'Did you succeed?'

'I thought I had.'

'Thought?'

'I've recently had cause to revise my opinion.'

'What cause?'

My heart thudded. 'You want me to spell it out?'

'I want no more misunderstandings.'

Neither did I. 'I am far from oblivious of you, Nick,' I said as I applied the dressing with inconveniently shaking hands. 'When I look at you now, I get dizzy. When you look at me, I get hot. I keep having visions of kissing you. I keep seeing you naked. You have no idea of the things I've imagined this last week. Touching you like this is not enough. I want to touch you everywhere. But that would be inappropriate seeing as how you're all patched up and we're done.'

'It would not be inappropriate at all,' he said, his voice so low, so ragged it sent shivers down my spine. 'And you know something else?'

'What?'

'We are far from done.'

CHAPTER EIGHT

NICK WAS UP and on his feet before I'd had time to catch my breath, and for a moment, as he spun round to face me, all I could think was that his chest—broad, tanned, muscled, lightly dusted with hair—was far more magnificent than anything I'd been able to envisage.

'You want me,' he practically growled, his entire frame radiating heat and tension as he took a slow deliberate step towards me.

I lifted my gaze to his and stood my ground, my heart thundering, every cell of my body alive and quivering with anticipation. 'And you want me,' I replied since denial at this juncture seemed thoroughly pointless.

'So what are we going to do about it?'

It wasn't a question that required an answer, and I knew that he knew that I knew that. The next move was obvious and I ached for it so badly it bordered on agony, but he'd just been injured and it gave me pause for thought. 'I ought to say, nothing.'

His blazing eyes narrowed minutely and his jaw clenched. 'Nothing?'

'You're hurt.'

'You've patched me up.'

'You asked me to be gentle with you.'

'I've changed my mind.'

The intensity with which he was looking at me rocked the floor beneath my feet and obliterated my reservation. The fire in his eyes…it was like standing in a blast furnace. I'd wondered what I'd find if he ever lowered his guard, and now I knew. Focus. Intent. Desire, hotter and wilder than I could ever have imagined. All, unbelievably, aimed squarely at me.

'So what do *you* think we should do about it?' I asked, my nerves fizzing, my voice so throaty it was almost unrecognisable.

'What we should have done a decade ago.'

'And that is?'

His dark glittering gaze dropped to my mouth and my breath caught while my pulse raced. 'This.'

He took one final step towards me, reached out to pull me into his arms and slammed his mouth down on mine.

The kiss detonated a bundle of need inside me that then rushed through my body like fire. I whipped one arm up to his uninjured shoulder and around his neck and the other around his waist, finally touching him as I'd longed to, and it was electrifying.

Every inch of me was pressed up against every inch of him. He was strength and silk, power and heat, and I was drowning in sensation, in a kiss that was blowing my mind.

He tangled his fingers in my hair and angled my head, deepening the kiss with a skill and intent that made me moan. Heat poured through me as I kissed him back with equal hunger. He surrounded me. Enveloped me. He was all I could see and feel. My senses were swimming. The thick length of his erection, which pressed hard into my abdomen, triggered a persistent throbbing ache deep inside me.

I groaned as he wrenched his mouth from mine and set it to my neck. I instinctively dropped my head back to give him better access, a move he immediately took advantage of by taking his time to explore every inch of it before lingering on my pulse.

He slipped that hand that wasn't in my hair beneath the hem of my top, planting it at the base of my spine and pulling me tighter against him and I felt it like a brand. I ran my hands over his back, his chest, tracing rock-hard muscles with trembling fingers, thrills rippling through me, and all I could think, with my one remaining functional brain cell, was that this was Nick. *Nick.* Who I'd known for a total of eighteen years yet hadn't known at all.

How I'd once thought him cold and aloof was beyond comprehension. We were generating enough heat to fire a power station, more electricity than the national grid. This man wasn't staid and disapproving. This man was a volcano of heat and desire and for some unfathomable reason he wanted *me*.

In the midst of the storm raging inside me, I dimly heard a crack of lightning followed by a rumble of thunder and he broke away. With flattering urgency he backed me up against the console table and swept aside the snacks, the water bottles and the torches as if he didn't have a wounded shoulder or a thought in his head other than this.

Breathing so hard my lungs actually hurt, I pushed my leggings and pants down and off. Nick grappled with his belt and sodden jeans while I yanked my sweat-shirt over my head, and then his mouth was on mine again and his hands were on the backs of my thighs. He lifted me up as if I weighed nothing and set me on the table. I parted my knees and he was instantly there, right where I was hot and aching and needed him desperately.

His hand cupped my heavy swollen breast and he rubbed a thumb over my nipple, which sent a sizzling shower of sparks shooting through me, but we'd had over a decade of foreplay. We had the rest of the storm to 'sit out' and take our time. Right now there was a mountain of pent-up lust to assuage, and I was going to explode if I didn't have him in the next thirty seconds.

'I need you inside me now,' I whimpered against his mouth, beginning to shake uncontrollably as desire continued to rip through me in ever stronger waves.

'I have no problem with that.'

He held my hips and tugged me forwards, while I spread my legs wide and wrapped my arms around his neck, and with one hard thrust he was buried inside me, so deeply, so fully, I actually saw stars.

For one staggering, heart-stopping moment neither of us moved. Neither of us even breathed. We just stared at each other, and I knew that the shock and disbelief that this was actually happening I could see in the swirling depths of his blazing eyes were reflected in mine.

Time seemed to stand still. All I could hear was my blood roaring in my ears. And as the seconds ticked by, my heart began to swell until it felt too big for my ribcage. My throat became so tight I couldn't speak.

To my horror, my eyes started to sting. So I pulled his head down and slanted my mouth over his and, as I'd hoped, a wave of blistering heat swept away the strange surge of emotion.

Nick swore softly against my lips and held me in place and then, with a great shudder, began to move. Focusing entirely on the physical way he was making me feel, I wrapped my legs around his hips and, taking care not to dislodge the dressing I'd applied to his shoulder, clung onto him for dear life.

With every confident, powerful thrust, my senses shattered that little bit more. He was hitting a spot deep inside me with laser-like accuracy. He didn't need to be told. He didn't need reassurance. It was as if he knew me—or rather, my body—better than I knew it myself. All I had to do was go along for the roller coaster of a ride, hurtling through the sky-scraping ups and the stomach-disappearing downs.

When he sped things up, my head spun. When he slowed things right down, it spun even harder. My breasts rubbed against his chest, the friction charging me with a thousand volts, so I pressed closer and lost my mind. The disintegration of his breathing and the increasing wildness of his movements sent thrills shooting through me. My own breathing was harsh and desperate, my lungs capable of nothing more than short sharp pants.

Beneath my palms the muscles of his shoulders and back bunched and flexed, the tension tightening them mirroring the unbearable tautening of mine. I felt feverish, fierce, desperate for something that was just out of reach. I wanted to bite him and taste him and do all sorts of wickedly wonderful things to him, but there was no time because, as if able to read my mind, he moved his hand from my hip to where we were joined, his fingers expertly finding my core, and within seconds I was coming so hard and fast I nearly blacked out.

The violent explosion that went off deep inside me flooded my whole body with wave upon wave of white-hot pleasure, racking me with shudders so intense I shook in his embrace. I wrenched my mouth from his, gasping for breath, while he pressed his face into my neck and surged into me one last time, hard and deep, letting out a rough groan as he found his own pulsating release.

His heart pounded against mine. His ragged breath burned my neck and his shoulders quaked. My limbs were weak. I felt boneless, as though I'd simply slither to the floor if he let me go. My mind was blitzed. I couldn't get over the fact that I'd just had the best sex of my life with a man I'd always thought I detested.

We stayed plastered up against each other for a moment, recovering from the cataclysmic encounter, but as our heart rates slowed and the sweat on my skin cooled, reality slunk in. The remnants of the heat and passion that had rocked my world a moment ago fled my body and awkwardness rushed in to take its place.

We were locked tightly together. I was naked. Nick's jeans were still open around his thighs. Supplies and my clothes were scattered across the floor. Where on earth did we go from here? Did we retreat to our corners to regroup and fortify our shattered defences or tumble onto the sofa for round two? What was there to say? He seemed to have no words and I was suddenly keen to fill the space.

'So that was unexpected,' I murmured, my voice raspy, my brain still trying to come to terms with the situation as I released my death grip on his shoulders and reluctantly removed my hands from his body.

He lifted his face from my neck, straightened a fraction, and stared at me, his eyes dazed, a dark flush streaking along his cheekbones. 'Was it?'

'Did you imagine it would be like that?'

'No,' he said with a slight shake of his head. 'I had no idea.'

'You sound awestruck.'

'I am. It surpassed my wildest dreams, and they've been pretty wild. You're astonishing.'

My chest gave an odd little squeeze, an aftershock of such mind-blowing pleasure, no doubt. 'You're the opposite of everything I thought you were. You're not cold. You're not aloof. You don't dislike me.'

'No.'

'I'd never have guessed.'

'That was the idea. Imagine the fun you'd have had mocking me. My ego wouldn't have been able to take the rejection.'

'I wouldn't have mocked. I'd have probably hurled myself into your arms. But I can see how you might think that. Sorry.'

'No,' he said with a quick shake of his head. 'If anyone needs to apologise, it's me. I went too far.'

A hot, apologetic Nick with the glimmer of sincerity and warmth in his eye was too much of a turnaround for me to process and I filled with an urgent need to get back onto more practical ground. 'How's your injury?'

'What injury?'

'Very funny.'

With the ghost of a smile, Nick rolled his shoulder and didn't even wince. 'It's fine.'

'Well, I'm not,' I murmured. 'I'm seizing up.'

He gently eased out of me and inched away and I missed his hardness and his heat immediately. I wanted to reach out and pull him back and forget myself, forget everything in more of his devastating kisses.

But he froze and frowned, and I shivered, an arrow of apprehension darting through me. 'What's wrong?'

'No condom.'

His words hit my brain like bullets, shattering the hazy afterglow with a brutal dose of reality. The implication of his realisation tilted the world on its access. My heart crashed against my ribs. My blood chilled. Protection hadn't even crossed my mind. We'd been so caught up in the rush. So frantic, so needy.

So careless.

'I can't believe I didn't think of it,' I said, a leap of alarm taking flight inside me even though there was zero point in panicking when it was far too late for regret and nothing could be done about it right now anyway. 'I *never* forget.'

Nick took a step back, then tugged his jeans up and refastened them, all traces of wildness and desire and humour gone. 'It's not your fault,' he said grimly. 'For the first time ever, I didn't think of it either. I was unable to think of anything, let alone get you upstairs to my room where there's a box. Are you on the pill?'

'No.' I slid off the console table and reached for my clothes with shaking fingers.

'Anything else?'

'No.'

He shoved his hands through his hair and then rubbed them over his face. 'Right.'

I slipped my top over my head and pulled on my pants and leggings, my stomach clenching and my heart pounding as I worked out the timeline. 'Date-wise, we could have a problem.'

'We won't have a problem.'

'What do you mean?' Could he somehow magic up some emergency contraception? Did he think that crossing fingers and hoping for the best actually worked? Or was he talking about abortion?

'If what we just did does turn out to have consequences,' he said, picking up his still damp shirt and frowning at it as if repelled by the thought of putting it back on, 'I'll take care of you.'

What?

It came as no surprise that Nick would want to do the supposedly right thing, and that was all well and good, but I hadn't spent years building up my self-reliance only to give it all up at the first hurdle. If, in nine months, a mini combined version of the two of us came along, I'd cope the way I'd learned to—by putting one foot in front of the other with my chin up and my jaw set, determined to look on the bright side. There was no guarantee he'd stick around—nobody ever did—and I wasn't about to put my faith in someone only to have them let me down by vanishing either physically or emotionally, or, quite possibly, both.

'There's no need for that,' I said, instinctively recoiling at the very idea of it. 'I have resources.' One hundred and eight million of them, in fact. 'I'll deal with it.'

'*We'll* deal with it.'

'At least it's not the nineteenth century, thank God. At least you don't have to marry me or anything if things do take a turn for the unexpected. Heaven forbid.'

He glanced up at me, his gaze dark and oddly unsettling. 'Do you have something against marriage?'

'You could say that.'

'What?'

I frowned. How was it important? Why did he want to know? And weren't we supposed to be focusing on the fact that we'd just had unprotected sex? 'We're drifting off topic,' I said, rather regretting the slip of the tongue.

'That horse has bolted,' he said and tossed the shirt onto the sofa. 'There's nothing we can do about it right now. Humour me.'

Yes, well, he might have a point about the bolting horse, but humour him? *That* wasn't going to happen. There was nothing remotely funny about the disintegration of my parents' marriage and the role I'd played in it, or its effect. My issues with trust and my insecurities over who I was and whether anyone would ever value me for me rather than what I did or didn't have weren't a source of amusement either. Besides, I never talked about my innermost hopes and fears. I had no one close enough to confide in and I wouldn't know how even if I wanted to, which I didn't, especially not now, when I was feeling so off kilter.

The sight of Nick's still bare chest and the memory

of how it had felt plastered to mine mere moments ago were messing with my reason. I couldn't rid my head of an image of the hypothetical consequence of our moment of madness—a little boy with Nick's dark hair and my blue eyes, perhaps, or a little girl with my brunette waves and his cool grey gaze.

My initial panic at the thought of an accidental pregnancy had been instinctive, the result of social conditioning and ultra-stern lessons at school, but deep down I longed for a family and a place to belong. I dreamed of unconditional love and honesty, a future in which I could make up for the lack of both in my past. Deep down, I hated and regretted that I couldn't get over all the obstacles that prevented it.

The events of the last half an hour and the thoughts streaming uncontrollably through my head now were making me feel confused and vulnerable in a way that I loathed when I'd fought so hard to be strong, and the need to protect myself by restoring my defences and keeping him at bay surged through me like a tidal wave.

'We had sex, Nick,' I said, ruthlessly burying the thoughts, the emotions and the images in order to regain control of myself. 'Long-overdue sex that's hopefully expunged the craziness from our systems, and great sex, I grant you, but that's all it was. It doesn't mean you can ask me personal questions. It certainly doesn't give you the right to dig around in my psyche. So back off.'

But if I'd hoped he'd take offence and storm off in much the same way he had earlier, the sharp shake of his head suggested I was to be disappointed.

'When we're finally getting somewhere?' he said,

fixing me with a dark look that burned right through my skin and into my soul. 'Not a chance.'

In response to the glint in his eye and the determined set of his jaw, a tremor of alarm ran down my spine, followed hot on its heels by the need to set him straight. 'We're not getting anywhere.'

'What do you mean?'

'This—' I waved a hand between him and me and the console table around which the torches, bottles of water and snacks lay scattered '—was a one-off.'

'Are you sure about that?'

Of course I was. The part of my brain that was still drugged by the lingering memories of extraordinary pleasure and in need of another fix could forget it. Nick wasn't a random guy I met in a bar and took home for the night. He'd been part of my life for over half of it. We had history. He was way too disturbing to fool around with further. He had the potential to threaten the armour-plated sense of self-preservation I'd worked hard to achieve.

'One hundred per cent,' I said with a decisiveness designed to eradicate the sliver of regret that nevertheless shot through me. 'It was a brief, necessary release of tension. Nothing more.'

'What if I want more?'

What? My heart gave a slight lurch. 'Do you?'

'Yes,' he said, lifting his arms to fold them across his formidable chest.

'How much more? A day? A week? What?'

'More than you, by the sounds of things.'

'Well, *more* is never going to happen.'

His gaze sharpened. 'Never?'

OK, so that was a bit revealing. It was hard to stay focused when he was standing there in the dimly flickering lamplight naked from the waist up, like some sort of gorgeous demonic Greek god. But I had to get a grip before I told him everything. 'I mean, not at the moment and definitely not with you.'

He frowned. 'Why not?'

'Because my life is too complicated and you're my brother's best friend.'

'So?'

'Imagine the awkwardness when things eventually fizzled out.'

'It would be no more awkward than the last thirteen years have been, and what makes you think it would fizzle out?'

'Neither of us has any experience of a proper long-term relationship,' I said, thinking of the way I never allowed anyone close enough to attach myself to them for anything longer than a week or two and his revolving blondes. 'My only one was a disaster and yours last no longer than a month. And then there's the fact that you're you and I'm me.'

'Which means what?'

'You're successful and brilliant. You know exactly who you are, where you belong and where you're going. I'm a failure and not brilliant at all. I don't have a clue who I am or where I belong or where I'm going. I grew up with everything, then had nothing and am now potentially on the way back to where I started. It's incredibly confusing. You're supremely sorted. I'm a basket case, riddled with hang-ups and issues. Quite apart from anything else, the differences between us are chasm-like.'

'That's ridiculous.'

Now it was my turn to fold my arms across my chest and arch an eyebrow. 'In what possible way?'

'You're not a failure. You've made the best of the hand you've been dealt and no doubt will continue to do so. Your intentions for your money are sensible. Your marine conservation plans are exciting and well thought through. You're gritty and determined. Resilient and hard-working. The way you adapt to your circumstances is impressive, your relentless optimism is enviable and even though I didn't much appreciate the way you turned down my financial assistance all those years ago, I always admired your pride.'

I stared at him, my jaw practically on the floor. He'd rendered me speechless. I couldn't even begin to formulate a response but that didn't matter because he hadn't finished.

'Furthermore,' he continued before I could even think about swooning at his…what was that? Praise? 'I might know where I'm going and who I am, but sure as hell don't know where I belong.'

At that, my head spun even harder. He had to be joking. He was so self-assured. His confidence bordered on arrogance. I'd never met anyone more comfortable in their environment, whether having come from the office or out here in paradise. 'Seriously?'

He nodded, the fading light from the diminishing lanterns as they ran out of gas making it harder to work out his expression. 'Materially, I grew up with nothing. You know that. My friends back then had nothing either. All we had to look forward to was a future of yet more nothing. Then I went to that school where everyone oozed polish and confidence, where everything was possible and the future was for the taking. Even the sun seemed to shine more brightly. I was a fish out of water. I spoke differently. I dressed differently. And after I'd been there a while, the same was true when I went back home. I didn't fit in in my old world. I certainly didn't fit in in my new one where it was impossible to forget I was very much a charity case.'

The trace of bitterness I could hear in his voice tightened my chest. A charity case? I'd had no idea he'd felt it so keenly.

'You were an all-round star,' I said, suddenly burning with an unfathomable urge to redress the balance. 'You won every prize going, whether in the classroom or on the sports fields. That wasn't because anyone felt sorry for you. It was a very competitive environment. You weren't *allowed* to win. You just did. All the time. You completely deserved your place there. Far more than I did. I mean, let's be honest, it's not a coincidence that my father built the business centre the year I showed up.'

His brows snapped together. 'Do you really think that?'

'The evidence speaks for itself.'

'That's utter rubbish,' he said. 'You're one of the brightest people I know. You aced your exams and the university you went to only takes the best.'

'Ah yes, but who's to say my dad didn't pay for me to get in?'

'How can you think so little of yourself?'

I hadn't always. I'd brimmed with confidence once upon a time. But the shattering of my beliefs had led to a reassessment of everything and as a result I was permanently riddled with doubt. 'It's hard not to when people have always just sort of abandoned you.'

'What people?'

'My friends. My boyfriend at the time. My parents. They all disappeared in one way or another when the going got tough. There was clearly nothing about me personally that was worth hanging onto then. It's hard to believe that there might be now. Even Seb lives half-way across the world. All those adjectives you used to describe me—they aren't innate. I simply had no choice if I wanted to survive.'

'You underestimate yourself.'

'I don't. I know what I am,' I said, realising from the set of Nick's jaw—clearly outlined despite the dying light—that I wasn't going to win that particular argument and deciding it would be more worthwhile to redirect the conversation back to him. 'And if anyone's underestimating themselves it's you. Look at what you've achieved. Yes, you were given opportunities by others, but you made the most of them. Not everyone who went to that school did. One of my classmates even ended up in jail. You obviously inherited your mother's work ethic. Your success is wholly your own. If you truly have everything you could possibly need, then you more than deserve it.'

His gaze was intent on mine. 'I don't have *everything* I could possibly need.'

'No, well, everyone needs a place to belong.' I thought of the way he'd once wolfed down his food and the patched and darned second-hand uniform that had made him an easy target for the entitled jerks at school, of which I'd been one albeit without the bullying streak. And then I thought of the sports car, the confidence and the success, the custom-made suits and the watches, the penthouse apartments and the private tropical island we were stuck on. 'Although I must admit you seem very comfortable in the world you currently inhabit.'

'I enjoy the trappings that come with success, but I saw what happened to your father's businesses and the consequences of that. I take nothing for granted. I'm under no illusion I couldn't lose everything—' he snapped his fingers '—just like that.'

'That doesn't seem likely.' Nick had billions and he wasn't desperate to win back a wife who'd gone astray. 'By your own admission you're not reckless—what happened earlier with the generator notwithstanding—and you never let the personal interfere with the professional. And that's another reason for drawing a line under what just happened. We're in business together.'

'You're not an ordinary client.'

'Nothing about any of this is ordinary.'

'Least of all you,' he said, the certainty of his voice sending a brief dart of doubt arrowing through me that I batted aside because I'd had years to ruminate on everything and I knew what was what. 'Your inferiority complex is unnecessary, Amelia. Our so-called chasm-like differences are non-existent. You're using your brother as an excuse. He wouldn't give a toss what we got up to. And to hell with the personal-professional conflict of interest. I'm too good at my job for that to be a concern.' He took a purposeful step towards me and my heart began to race. 'You should know that I want to do what we just did again. Over and over again. We have years of wasted time to make up for and there are things I've imagined doing to you that would have you screaming with pleasure and begging for mercy.'

The heat that was now blazing in his eyes ignited a fire in the pit of my stomach quite suddenly, my head emptied of everything but one single thought. 'What things?'

Wicked wasn't a word that I'd have ever associated with Nick, yet it was the only way to describe the gleam that appeared in his eye and the smile that played at his mouth. 'I guess you'll never know.'

CHAPTER NINE

BEFORE I COULD give in to the insane yet impossible desire to demand detailed, physical clarification on the matter of *the things* when they were neither here nor there, I swiped a torch from the floor, turned it on and announced I was off for a shower. That it would be cold as a result of the power cut and the generator breakdown, which Nick pointed out, was not a problem. I was hot and sticky and desperately needed to cool off. I could only hope that there was enough water left in the tank to do the job properly.

Once in the relative sanctuary of the bathroom, I checked the window and the storm that was raging beyond. After a swift assessment that resulted in the conclusion that the risk of harm was minimal, I set the torch down and stripped off my clothes. I switched the tap to cold, then braced myself and stepped in.

But the shower wasn't the cooling, cleansing experience I'd been anticipating.

The minute I ducked beneath the flow of water—which, this being the tropics, wasn't nearly icy enough—it struck me that Nick's scent and his mark on me were sluicing off my body and being washed straight down the drain, and it felt strangely like a loss.

As I lathered up, the memory of his hands on me and the way he'd held me tight while he took me to the edge of the world and then hurled me over it slammed into my head and wouldn't budge.

When I ran the loofah over my abdomen, the sensitive skin there tingling and twitching, I found myself wondering what—if anything—was going on inside and what action I'd take in the event I made it to a pharmacy in time.

And then, as I stood rinsing off the bubbles, hoping to feel the zesty freshness my shower gel promised but instead feeling hotter and more skittish than ever, remnants of our conversation began to rattle round my head like the most fiendish of riddles.

Did he really not consider me a failure? Had he actually meant all those astonishing things he'd said about me? Could we be more alike than I realised and was it at all possible we had hang-ups about similar things? And why, oh, why could I not stop thinking about the nature of the things he'd said he wanted to do to me?

To my despair, my resolve to move on from what had happened on the console table was no match for my imagination. Vivid, erotic snapshots of the two of us together on a bed fogged my vision and muddled my head. The memory of the dark intent in his eyes made me tremble and shiver in a way that I simply couldn't stop.

In the days and months to come, would I always look at him and wonder, what if? Would I regret my decision to keep him at arm's length or find relief in it? Despite my concerted efforts to convince myself otherwise, deep down, I suspected I knew the answers to both those questions. Denial was hard to cling onto when the desire flooding my system was so insistent and refused to stay at bay. I wanted to know exactly how wild his wildest dreams had been. I yearned to feel his weight on top of me, pressing me down as he took what he wanted and made me scream as he'd promised.

By the time I switched off the water and stepped out of the shower I'd come to the conclusion that I'd overreacted by declaring fifteen minutes of passion a one-off. There was nothing momentous about what we'd done. People had spectacular sex all the time. I'd simply overanalysed the situation and got a little spooked. It had been so sudden. So unexpected. So unbelievably good.

But that was no reason to panic, I assured myself, rubbing my still tingling skin dry and slipping on my dressing gown as my pulse began to race. Scorchingly hot sex didn't have to mean anything. The *more* Nick had suggested he might want would never refer to an actual relationship, so, contrary to what I'd told myself earlier, he posed no threat to my defences. However good *the things* he'd imagined doing to me were, I certainly wasn't going to wind up weak, vulnerable and exposed to a whole lot of heartache when our relationship inevitably went wrong because we would never get to the relationship stage.

I'd let the shocking revelation about how he'd always wanted me, the abrupt reversal of everything I thought I'd known and the implications of a missing condom get the better of me. Once again I'd felt cornered and gone on the attack. But 'sitting out' the storm with him wouldn't be dangerous. We had to pass the time somehow, and probing conversation of the kind Nick had already attempted on a number of occasions, which might become increasingly harder to deflect if he kept up the pressure, didn't appeal in the slightest. Discovering what he wanted to do to me, however, did. A lot.

I was barely aware of picking up the torch and heading out of my room. The thundering of my heart drowned out my reason and my body seemed to have taken over. I felt as if I were floating as I went downstairs and searched the rooms, sweeping the bright beam of light around the spaces. Order had been restored to the inner hall where we'd made such a mess, I noticed, but of Nick there was no sign, so I went back upstairs.

I can't have knocked on the door when I reached his room. I must have simply walked straight on in. I had no hesitation in following the sound of running water. No qualms about slamming to a halt at the door that was ajar and staring transfixed at the reflection I could see in the full-length mirror that was in my line of sight.

Nick was in the shower, water pouring over his broad shoulders and the strong planes of his back, which was marred only by the square patch of the clearly waterproof dressing. He stood, legs apart, facing the controls. One hand was planted on the tiles high above his head, the other was wrapped around himself, moving up and down with quick, hard strokes.

My pulse hammered. My breath caught. Heat poured through me, charging along my veins and electrifying my nerves before pooling between my legs and throbbing deep inside. I couldn't move. My feet were glued to the floor. Wild horses couldn't have dragged me away even though I was invading his privacy in the most intimate way possible. I wanted to push open the shower room door, ditch my dressing gown and join him. I wanted to bat aside his hand, sink to my knees in front of him and drive him to completion myself.

But it was too late. His movements were becoming more frantic, less controlled. His jaw was tight and his muscles were straining. His raised arm was trembling. The hand on the wall clenched into a tight fist and then he let out a tortured groan. Great shudders racked his powerful body. His chest heaved as he fought for breath and shook.

The wave of lust that hit me like a torrent nearly took out my knees. I gasped, or maybe moaned, and it must have been loud and harsh enough for him to hear above the flow of water and the raging storm outside or maybe he suddenly caught a reflected flash of the torch beam, for he froze. He lifted his head and snapped it round. His gaze collided with mine in the mirror and for one agonising second neither of us moved. I was incapable of it. I was transfixed by the wildness of his expression. His eyes were dark and glazed. He looked savagely untamed and I shivered.

He switched off the tap and reached for a towel to wrap around his hips and disappeared from sight. Outside, the wind still howled and rain continued to batter the house. Inside, here, within me, the need to flee his understandable wrath at having such a private moment invaded warred with the urge to stay and achieve what I'd come to achieve, and I dithered, but a second later the decision was taken out of my hands.

Nick opened the door and leaned his uninjured shoulder against the frame, his laser-like gaze pinning me to the spot so fixedly I couldn't have moved even if I'd wanted to. 'Does it turn you on to watch?'

His voice was very low and it skittered across my skin, raising goosebumps all over me. I was so aroused, I was wet and aching and my knees were shaking. Five minutes ago I'd have said I didn't know if voyeurism was my thing. Now I knew differently. 'It certainly turns me on to watch you.'

'What are you doing in my room?'

I could hardly remember. Even my own name was a struggle to recall. But my hands itched to touch him. My mouth tingled at the thought of being crushed to his, and what I wanted flooded back on a wave of heat. 'I've changed my mind about our console-table encounter being a one-off.'

He arched one dark eyebrow. 'What happened to never again?'

'I panicked. I was in shock. I overreacted. But I was wrong. I must have been mad to think that once was enough after the build-up of all these years. I want more. I'm keen to know your every intention towards me.'

'My *every* intention?'

I nodded. 'I want you beneath me, above me, in every possible position. I need to know what these things you have in mind for me are. I want you to know the things I have in mind for you. And I'd far rather regret something I have done than something I haven't.'

He tilted his head, the intensity of his focus flipping my stomach. 'You'd regret it?'

Oops. Probably. But admitting to it might put him off, and that was the last thing I wanted. 'Only if it turns out to be mediocre, but I can't see that happening.'

'You still want me to be your plaything.'

I didn't know what I wanted him to be, other than naked and all over me. 'You give as good as you get,' I said, my heart beating hard and fast. 'Your "I guess you'll never know" was a deliberate taunt. You knew my imagination would go into overdrive.'

'And did it?'

'Yes.'

'God, you're dangerous.'

'Would you care to elaborate?'

'Not right now.' Nick pushed himself off the door frame, the set of his jaw, the intent in his gaze the most blazing I'd ever seen. 'Do you have anything on beneath that dressing gown?'

'Why don't you find out?'

He took the torch from my fingers and with one quick tug at the belt, one slide of his hands beneath the slippery fabric, Nick stripped the entire garment from my body. I gasped in shock and shivered, but not from cold.

'As I believe I pointed out this morning,' he murmured, drinking me in so intently I started to burn, 'every inch of you is perfect.'

I didn't know about that. My body was pretty average really, unlike his. I thought of him in the shower, the strong back and the long lean legs, all those lovely powerful muscles. Every inch of him truly was perfect, approximately nine of them, mouth-wateringly so. 'Likewise.'

I stared at his mouth, desperate for his kiss, and lifted my chin while I leaned towards him but he jerked his head back. A tiny chill rippled through me and with a frown, I froze. 'Games?'

He gave his head a minute shake. 'Payback.'

Before I could work out what he meant he'd pulled me into the shower room and moved behind me. He set my torch next to his on a shelf, angled me so we both faced the mirror and, after a moment, murmured, 'Now that's a view.'

I stared at my reflection. My cheeks were flushed, my eyes had darkened to indigo and a pulse hammered at the base of my neck. My nipples were tight and hard. Nick was a head taller than me and far broader and if he put his arms around me I'd be cocooned in heat and strength, but he didn't. Instead, he put his large warm hands on my shoulders and began to slide them down my arms.

He took my right hand in his and pressed it to the triangle of curls between my legs. The left he placed on my breast, and my entire body shuddered. I knew what he wanted me to do and I knew he wanted to watch. Nerves fluttered in the pit of my stomach. I'd never done anything like this before. It would have been way too sophisticated for the one and only relationship I'd had back when I was twenty and it was far too intimate for the casual flings I favoured nowadays.

In all honesty, it felt too intimate now, with the shadows dancing over the walls and us while outside the storm continued, but I couldn't have stopped even if I'd wanted to. The heat in his gaze was mesmerising and I was hypnotised. A sudden, unfamiliar but mighty wave of invincibility and power swept through me, filling me with strength and resolve. I wanted him to lose control the way I knew I was going to. I wanted him to beg for mercy. I wanted him to want me as much as I wanted him and for us to generate enough steam to power an engine. But there'd be time for that later. In the meantime, there was torture.

He released my hands but I kept them where they were. Locking eyes with him, I caressed my heavy, swollen left breast and rubbed my nipple, and had to bite my lip to contain my moan at the sensations that sizzled through me.

Without stopping, I instinctively widened my legs and between them, I stroked my fingers through the curls and the soft slick flesh until I found my core. I rubbed the hard, aching nub in small circles that stoked the need powering along my veins and made me tremble even harder. I was feverish. Electricity was zapping through me. Every nerve-ending I possessed was throbbing madly.

Behind me, Nick's jaw was tight and his breathing was becoming increasingly harsh and fast. He tore his gaze from mine and lowered it to my body and my hands, which made the desire shooting through me strengthen almost unbearably. He pulled me back against him and secured me there, his fingers digging into my hip, and I could feel the hard length of him pressing into me at the base of my spine. He swept my still damp hair to one side and set his mouth to my neck, branding my skin with a trail of scorching kisses.

On a shuddery exhale, dazedly wondering exactly who was torturing whom, I released my breast and lifted my arm to clamp my hand to his head. He slid his hand down my side and resumed the caressing, only it was so much better when he did it, and I arched my back to press my breast harder into his palm.

The tension building inside me was exquisite. The rush of anticipation and excitement was thrilling. My head spun and my breath quickened. I was so hot and my fingers were moving faster and harder, increasingly out of my control. The pleasure was rolling in and I closed my eyes and dropped my head back against his shoulder, a guttural moan sounding low in my throat.

Nick increased the pressure of his mouth on my neck and his hand on my breast and with one tiny pinch of my nipple, I was coming hard and breathlessly, spinning off into a splintering world of ecstasy where nothing existed but him and me and this.

I was still shaking and panting when I felt him scoop me up into his arms. My head continued to spin and my heart to pound as he carried me to the bed and dropped me in the middle of it. But when he ditched the towel wrapped around his hips and came down on top of me, the warm heavy weight of his naked body as delicious as I'd hoped, a fresh wave of desire gripped me and in an instant I wanted him inside me with an urgency I could scarcely believe.

His head descended, his eyes as dark as the shadows all around, blocking out the flickering light of the lanterns that stood on the bedside tables, the room, everything but him, and I gave up thinking altogether and succumbed to the renewed sensations flowing through me.

His mouth fitted with mine so perfectly my chest ached. The kiss that followed was a hot languid exploration that went on for ever, not simply an entrée but a main event to be savoured.

I wound my arms around his neck and threaded my fingers through his hair and the growl that sounded low and rough in his throat vibrated against my lips and sent hot shivers down my spine. As the onslaught on my senses continued, the heat and need rising within, I writhed beneath him in a futile attempt to alleviate the growing pressure, but it only made things worse.

He pressed against me, now exactly where I wanted him. One tilt of the hips and he could be inside me, and I so badly needed that but he had other ideas. He took my wrists in his hands and pressed them to the mattress and set his mouth to the spot where my jaw met my neck. I dropped my head back and shivered at the sensations rippling through me.

He explored my throat with thorough and devastating care, and moved his mouth achingly slowly down my chest until he came to my breast. He captured my hot tight nipple between his lips and I would have jack-knifed off the bed if he hadn't been pressing me down. I moaned, and he applied more pressure, his tongue driving me wild, and turned his attention to the other breast.

Too soon, he shifted down, dropping kisses down over my ribcage and my abdomen, the skin there jumping and twitching in response to the sparks he was generating and then he was pushing my knees apart and his mouth was there, on me, where my fingers had been only moments ago.

I was so sensitive it almost hurt but he knew exactly what he was doing. He read my body like a book. He licked me lightly and carefully and then, when my breaths shallowed and my moans deepened, with increasing intensity. I whimpered and clawed at the sheets and panted, the tension building while the ache deepened.

'Enough,' I breathed, grabbing his head and pulling him up. 'Enough.'

He kissed me, which made my head fog even more, then rolled away and sat up to rummage around in the drawer of the bedside table. Over the thundering of my heart I heard the crinkle of foil. I turned my head to see his shoulders were shaking as he applied the condom and I couldn't wait a moment longer, which he must have sensed because a second later, he was back above me, parting my legs and moving between them. He pushed into me, hard and deep and sure, and I completely lost what was left of my mind.

By the time Nick and I finally collapsed in an exhausted heap amidst the wreckage of his bed however many hours later, the wind had dropped and, although still squally, the rain wasn't hammering down quite so hard. When I eventually woke up the following morning, however, I saw through the balcony doors that the sea was now millpond flat, the palm trees were battered but still and the sky was once again a deep cerulean blue dotted with the odd scudding cloud.

I blinked at the warm sunshine streaming in and bathing the room in soft golden light and, with a wince, stretched. Every muscle in my body ached. I had stubble rash in places I hadn't thought it possible to have stubble rash. Nick had been true to his word. He'd made me scream. He'd had me begging for mercy on more than one occasion, and I'd returned the favour. We'd done things I'd never tried before but would definitely be adding to my previously limited repertoire. We'd only stopped to eat and rehydrate and refuel the lanterns as it began to get dark.

'Good morning,' came a gruff voice from the door to the bathroom.

I stilled mid-stretch and glanced over to find Nick standing there leaning against the frame with nothing on but some close-fitting underwear that left nothing to the imagination, looking at me in a way that made me shiver and ache suddenly in a different way. 'It's a very good morning.'

'Regrets?'

'None in the slightest. How's the shoulder?'

'Fine. Like I said, it's just a scratch.'

I rolled my eyes and grinned, which elicited a smile from him in return before he slid his gaze from mine to the view beyond the four walls of the room. 'The storm's over.'

'So I see.'

'I took another look at the generator. The power's back on. You can charge your phone.'

'I'm not sure I want to,' I said with a faint shudder at the thought of how many emails and missed calls I might have. 'Can you let Seb know we're OK?'

'Sure.'

'And the headlines? The photographers?'

'Gone.'

'Thank you.'

'So there's nothing to stop you from leaving.'

As his observation hung in the space between us, I realised with a disconcerting and unpleasant jolt that, theoretically, he was right. Not only had the threat of the press been neutralised, I'd also electronically signed the contract he'd emailed me while despairing about my response to him and fretting over the weather, so in that respect I'd achieved what I'd set out to achieve. The tension between us was history and we'd made a good start on clearing up all those misunderstandings. I could get up right now, put a call in to James and pack my things. I could be home in less than twenty-four hours.

But I couldn't think of anything I wanted to do less. I wasn't done here. Not by a long shot. Why on earth would I willingly give up the best sex of my life when it was still so new and exciting? Besides, the new level of understanding we were beginning to reach was fragile and needed further strengthening. Basically, this whole thing felt like unfinished business.

'Do you want me to?' I asked, my breath catching and my heart skipping a beat since it was impossible to tell from the look on his face what his opinion on the subject might be.

He shook his head. 'No.'

My lungs relaxed and warmth flooded through me, the relief almost overwhelming. Thank goodness for that. I didn't need to stay long. I had a job and a life to get back to, a fortune to manage and a future to plan. So there'd be no danger of whatever was going on here turning into something more, of emotions becoming engaged or of me finding myself suddenly in too deep and unable to get out, as I'd feared only yesterday. There simply wouldn't be time.

'Well, I suppose I don't need to go just yet,' I said, my heart pounding wildly as, incredibly, desire began to drum through me all over again. 'As you pointed out, we have years to make up for. I can always get the morning-after pill flown over. And I do have a few days of leave left. It seems a shame to waste them, don't you think?'

'Good decision,' he practically growled as he slowly stalked towards me, weakening my muscles and melting my bones with his athletic grace and powerful intent. 'A truly excellent decision.'

CHAPTER TEN

It was a good couple of hours before we resurfaced. When my stomach gave a rumble that put a stop to proceedings, Nick declared it was time for brunch and headed downstairs. I returned to my room to freshen up and to tease the knots out of my very tangled hair, which took quite a while given the mess he'd made of it. At the entrance to the kitchen, I gave him a twirl with a jazz hand 'ta-da' and he glanced up from the chopping board to give me a smile that stole the breath from my lungs and the wits from my head.

'If I'd known we were dressing up,' he said, evidently appreciating the one formal dress I'd packed judging by the heat in his gaze as it roamed over me, 'I'd have put on my tux.'

He didn't need a tux. He looked just fine in the pair of loose jogging pants he wore low on his hips. Better than fine. He looked good enough to eat but my body couldn't take any more and I was ravenous in a different way. 'You're funny.'

'I can be. You're stunning.'

'In this old thing?' I said, brushing aside the squeeze of my chest in response to his compliment and instead sidling towards him with a wave of one hand at the strapless pale pink sequinned bodice that flared out to a knee-length tulle skirt of the same colour. 'It's the only clean item of clothing I have left to wear.'

His eyebrows rose and his eyes darkened. 'Nothing else?'

'Nothing else.' Let him make of that what he wished. 'It's very liberating. Nice and airy.'

'Your clothes have always given me trouble,' he said, turning to the fridge and extracting a bowl. 'The image of you in that bikini stuck to my brain like a limpet. It didn't matter what you wore after that. I inevitably imagined you naked. It was immensely frustrating.'

'Am I meant to apologise?'

'You're meant to eat. You need to keep your strength up.'

I ignored the sizzle of heat that wound through me at that and the wonderment that we, who had been simmering and glaring at each other for years, were now flirting like pros, and instead eyed the smorgasbord before me. A plate of fat prawns surrounding a small bowl of aioli. Thick slices of crusty bread sitting between a pile of round juicy olives. Slices of cheese, miniature cucumbers and a stack of fragrant chicken skewers.

I hopped onto a stool, my mouth watering and my stomach giving another loud rumble. 'This looks delicious.'

'It's what I like to eat.'

'Is there anything you don't?'

'Potatoes,' he said, pushing a plate in my direction. 'I ate a lot of those as a kid. They remind me of being so hungry I hallucinated. I try to avoid them where possible.'

I pulled the plate towards me. 'What was it like?'

'Hasn't Seb filled you in?'

'I never really asked.'

'It wasn't much fun,' he said with what had to be a massive understatement as he rummaged in a drawer for cutlery. 'The village we lived in was badly deprived. The school was dismal and there wasn't a lot else to do. My mother was permanently exhausted. She worked her fingers to the bone but there was never enough money and never enough to eat. And it was always freezing.'

My heart gave a tiny, totally natural squeeze. 'Is that why you spend so much time here?'

'Yes. I hate the cold.'

'I can't begin to imagine.'

'And a good thing, too.'

He shut the drawer and turned to grab a couple of napkins and as he moved I noticed on the counter behind him a bottle of chilled champagne standing next to two cups of steaming coffee.

'What are we celebrating?' I asked. 'Off-the-charts chemistry? A truce?'

'Progress.'

I frowned at that, a ribbon of unease winding through me that I didn't think I could attribute to hunger. Where did he think this was going? Surely the sex and the flirting weren't giving him the wrong idea?

'Not *that* much progress has been made.'

'I disagree,' he said, handing me a knife and fork and a napkin. 'Look at where we are now compared to where we were yesterday. Imagine where we could be tomorrow.'

'We'll be right here,' I said pointedly. 'Right where we are. This is just sex, Nick.'

'There's no "just" about it.'

'You know what I mean.'

'I do,' he said and brought the cups of coffee to the island. 'But I don't think you quite understand the significance of what we're doing.'

I bristled and thought about stabbing something other than a piece of cheese with my fork. 'Are you patronising me?'

'Not at all. I'm simply streaks ahead of you.'

'I don't even know what that means.'

'Eat.'

Too baffled and annoyed to do anything else, I picked up a spoon and ladled some olives onto my plate, then added a couple of chicken skewers, only to pause when he suddenly said, 'Tell me something.'

I glanced at him and frowned. He was always trying to get me to tell him things one way or another, yet what could I do? Respond with a blunt 'no'? That wouldn't stop him. 'What?'

'That guy you were seeing at the time your father lost everything. Is that really the only relationship you've ever had?'

'Pretty much.'

'How come?'

'I have issues.'

'I thought we'd dealt with those.'

If only it were that simple. 'Different ones.'

'Which are?'

I tilted my head and narrowed my eyes at the man who was looking like the picture of casual interest as he started piling food onto a plate of his own. He was pushing me into another of those corners and the urge to go on the attack by deflecting the conversation reared up inside me. But this time, despite my irritation with him, something was stopping me following through on it. I couldn't keep avoiding difficult conversation. Sooner or later, he would start to notice, perhaps to wonder why, and then push even more relentlessly for answers.

And perhaps it wouldn't be such a bad thing if I shared with him a thing or two. It might be uncharted territory but perhaps I ought to try and match his efforts to move on from the past and reach a plane on which we could peacefully coexist. I hardly needed to go into detail. There'd be no need for an in-depth emotional analysis of anything. He'd been an on and off member of the audience at the show that was my life since I was eleven. He knew many of the facts already.

'My parents, for one thing.'

'What about them?'

'You can't have failed to notice their marriage was strained, even before my father lost everything.'

'I do recall a number of occasions when things seemed off,' he replied as he sat beside me, unnecessarily close, in my opinion. 'There was that fortnight we spent on the Amalfi Coast when she flew home early. Meals during which she barely said anything. Sometimes, I seem to remember, she looked downright miserable.'

'Things *were* off and she *was* miserable,' I said, burying the flurry of memories of the days spent diving with my father as we explored the coastal waters of the Tyrrhenian Sea, which had felt so special until they hadn't. 'She had an affair. That was why my dad screwed up with the money. He was trying to win her back and it made him desperate and careless.'

He turned his head and levelled me a look that had me feeling distinctly on edge. 'Is that it?' he said, his eyebrows lifting. 'Their example was a bad one so you've sworn off relationships for good?'

His scepticism raised my hackles, but my defences were indestructible on this. However hard he tried, he wasn't going to wheedle anything more out of me. There was carefully revealing a few minor elements of inner angst for the benefit of our future interactions and then there was the inconceivable baring of the soul. 'Isn't that enough?'

'No. I don't think it is.'

'Too bad.'

'Have you never been in love?'

I started and nearly choked on an olive. Nick? Talking about love? What was going on? 'Why on earth would you want to know a thing like that?' I asked, once I'd recovered from my coughing fit.

'I'm curious.'

'Have *you*?'

'Yes.'

He had no problem answering the question and it was on the tip of my tongue to ask who with but I bit the words back. It was irrelevant. None of my business. Furthermore, I didn't need to know. 'Are you still in love with them?'

'Yes.'

Oh. OK. That whipped the wind from my sails. 'Yet you're sleeping with me.'

'Now who's being judgemental?'

I frowned. He had a point. I had no reason to care. It wasn't my moral dilemma. Nevertheless, it was just as well I didn't want him for anything more than temporary excellent sex because if I had, I'd have been riddled with jealousy. But I didn't, so I wasn't. The tightness in my chest was a lingering effect of nearly choking on the olive, that was all.

'So what's your excuse?' I said, nevertheless keen to move away from that particular subject.

'What do you mean?'

'You're thirty-one. Rich. Successful. Hotter than the sun and not that deficient on the personality front, as it turns out. There has to be a reason why you're still single. An aversion to commitment, perhaps?'

'You're assuming it's me.'

I was. 'Isn't it?'

'I don't have an aversion to commitment.'

'The brevity of your affairs would suggest otherwise.'

'It doesn't suggest anything of the sort.'

'Then why have you never aimed for something more?'

'Maybe I'm working on it.'

Right. So was that why he'd been so keen to address the issues between us? Was he trying to get the overwhelming and inconvenient attraction he felt for me out of his system so he could move on to the woman he was in love with? Quite possibly. And that was completely fine.

'Well, personally,' I said, picking up a skewer and using my fork to push off the tiny chunks of fragrant chicken with a fraction more force than was possibly required. 'I never allow anyone close enough to get to that point. Like I said yesterday, people let me down. They disappear when they get to know the real me. I don't need that kind of hassle in my life.'

'That sounds lonely.'

It was sometimes, but it was a sacrifice I was more than willing to make. 'At least I stay safe and avoid any unnecessary pain,' I said as I dipped a piece of chicken into the aioli. 'And anyway, I don't think you're one to lecture on loneliness, when you're always out here on your own.'

'I'm not always out here on my own.'

That was a surprise, although I didn't know why I was so taken aback. Just because I had issues with other people it didn't mean everyone did. And the friction that existed between us could well be unique. He got on well enough with Seb, after all. And other women, one in particular it would appear.

'I'd have thought the blondes would burn,' I said a bit waspishly. 'The sun's very strong.'

'I wouldn't know,' he countered as he peeled a prawn. 'I've never brought any of them here. I was talking about my mother and her husband. Friends.'

Right. Well, that was something of a relief to know. But… 'But you have condoms. In a box. In your room.' And I remembered this, why?

'I picked them up at your hotel on Zanzibar.'

'So even in the midst of my misfortune, you were thinking of sex?'

His eyes darkened and his gaze dipped to my mouth and lingered. 'When it comes to you, I'm always thinking of sex. Among other things. Plus, I'm an optimist.'

Yes, well, no amount of optimism would get me back into bed right now, when I was hungry and feeling suddenly so out of sorts. And besides, I was now curious about something else. 'What other things?'

'You don't want to know.'

'That bad?'

He thought for a moment, then eventually said, 'Over the years, you've meant chaos and disruption. Monumental upheaval and a constant battle for control. Stress and frustration and endless cold showers. I've resented you for having that effect on me. I've despised myself for not being able to conquer it.'

So it was that bad. I should never have asked. 'And now?'

'You still mean all those things.'

'No wonder you described me as dangerous,' I said lightly while feeling, of all unexpected things, a little upset.

'Don't forget gritty, hard-working and optimistic.'

'Not to mention resilient and determined.' Currently being demonstrated by my resolve to get over myself. 'And there was me thinking you'd always considered me impossibly silly and superficial.'

'Not for a long time.'

I leaned back and stared at him in surprise. 'Really?'

'You may have had your moments when you were younger,' he said, 'but underneath it all you were… kind.'

I blinked. Of all the adjectives he could have chosen

after describing my more destructive qualities, that was not one I'd ever have considered. 'Kind?'

'You were forever finding small injured animals and taking them in. Frogs. Squabs. Bumble bees. If it was missing a wing or had fallen out of a nest it had to be saved.'

'I'd forgotten that,' I said, slightly taken aback that he remembered. 'I didn't always succeed.'

'But you always tried. You fought for the weak. You championed the underdog. Do you recall coming to my defence once, when some kids at school were taunting me about where I was spending the holidays? I was handling things fine on my own, but that didn't stop you flying into the melee and telling everyone exactly what you thought of them. You were small but fierce. Like a mini Boadicea. I was impressed.'

I searched my memory, but it didn't take long. 'I do remember,' I said, thinking that was one moment involving him that I could be proud of at least. 'I was eleven to your thirteen. It was the end of your first term and I was with my parents, picking Seb up. You and I hadn't met at that point. I just saw injustice and reacted. But if I'd known how disruptive and unwelcome you were going to find me,' I added a touch tartly, 'I might not have bothered.'

'I'm glad you did.'

When had I lost that fearlessness? I wondered, mopping up the juices on my plate with some bread. When did I stop caring about those in need of help? When did I become more interested in clothes and make-up and a bunch of pretty rotten friends?

'Do you know what you also were?'

I snapped myself out of my turbulent thoughts and refocused. 'I'm not sure I want to.'

'You were influential.'

My eyebrows shot up. 'Influential?' That was an improvement on resented and chaotic, although it could hardly have been any worse.

'Firstly, if it wasn't for you and the conversation we once had about it, I'd still be messed up about having a father I've never met. I'd still be feeling guilty about spending so much time with your family instead of my mother. And secondly, without you I wouldn't be who I am today. Your comment about me being beneath you—' He broke off, a flare of heat lighting the depths of his eyes and I went hot, despite the lingering pique at the knowledge he'd found me so impossibly frustrating. 'It sparked my drive to succeed. To make money. To be and do better than everyone else. I admit there was the money element. I wanted to get my mother and myself as far away from where we came from as possible. I swore to myself that neither of us would ever be hungry or cold again and didn't stop until I achieved that. But I was initially driven by you and your disdain. That's why I've never needed or wanted your apology for that afternoon by the pool, Millie. If anything, I ought to thank you.'

Nick fell silent but the noise in my head was deafening. I was, in part, responsible for the man he'd become? My adolescent petulance had led to his stellar success? I didn't know whether to be ashamed of that or proud. I didn't know what to think any more. I went from hot to cold and back again. I was influential and chaotic, annoying and Boadicea, resented yet desired.

But suddenly none of that seemed to matter. It was all swept aside by the Millie. He hadn't called me Amelia. He'd called me Millie. For the first time ever. Which, for some bizarre reason, had my heart flipping about all over the place, an unstoppable smile curving my mouth, and all my outrage and pique, my objections and concerns melting clean away.

'You're welcome.'

After brunch, we ventured outside to inspect the storm damage. The ground was waterlogged. Leaves and branches lay scattered everywhere and the flowers in the planters were trashed. Much of the debris had ended up in the pool and I spent a good quarter of an hour watching and admiring as a shirtless Nick scooped it out, which eventually led to a scorching interlude on a sun lounger.

Later, once we'd cleared up the worst of mother nature's fury in the immediate vicinity of the villa, he grabbed my hand and led me down the path to the jetty, which remarkably remained intact. He dragged the boat from its shelter with an impressive display of muscles and fired it up, and ten minutes later we were motoring around the island to check on the rest of it.

The beach at the cove I'd explored yesterday lay beneath half a dozen felled palm trees, their freshly jagged trunks jutting out of the churned-up sand. The door to the boathouse at the top end of the island was hanging off its hinges and as Nick steered the boat into the shore I could see that the sails had been blown off the walls and the kayaks and boards had slipped from their supports.

The devastation that lay all around was a side to paradise that didn't appear in the brochures—and I didn't dare imagine what it would have been like had the storm been stronger and lasted longer—yet it occurred to me as Nick cut the engine and jumped off the boat into the once limpid but now murky shallows that, extraordinarily, out of it, in our tiny corner of it, at least, had come harmony.

Because of it, we'd been forced to confront our history. We'd cleared up the torturous past and paved the way for a smoother future. And while he'd frequently tied me in metaphorical knots, which had hampered clarity on certain subjects somewhat, there'd been honesty.

Best of all, it hadn't been as bad as I'd feared. I hadn't been forced to disclose anything particularly deep or shameful. I wasn't overexposed and emotionally vulnerable. In fact, if anyone had been revealing, it was Nick with the 'Millie' that perhaps proved he no longer considered me quite such a disturbing nuisance these days.

'You're very quiet,' said Nick, jolting me out of my reverie and drawing my attention to the fact that while I'd been wool-gathering he'd pulled the boat up onto the sand and unloaded bits of the kit he'd randomly accumulated earlier, just in case.

I stood up and smoothed my dress, only to have to do it again after he'd planted his hands on my waist, lifted me off the boat and let me slide down his body as he lowered me to the sand. 'I've been thinking it feels as if we're in some sort of parallel universe,' I said, a little breathless after the gallantry that hadn't been necessary but was deliciously thrilling all the same.

'In what way?'

'You and me working together and not glowering at each other, for one thing.'

He handed me a drill and an electric screwdriver then loaded himself up with rope, a couple of planks of wood and the toolbox. 'It does make a change.'

'I can't envisage you in a suit any more,' I said, running my gaze over his tousled hair, the reflective sunglasses that glinted in the sun and the shorts that this afternoon were electric blue with white stars. 'Or in an office. It's all very weird.'

'It's progress.'

Well, yes, I thought as I followed him up the beach to the boathouse and mulled it over. I supposed it was in a way, although, worthy of a champagne celebration? I wasn't so sure. 'Do you ever wonder what things could have been like between us if you'd done them differently?'

Nick dumped everything he was carrying on the deck, lifted his sunglasses to the top of his head and narrowed his eyes as he inspected the damage. 'Frequently.'

'If I'd swallowed my pride and accepted the money you offered me,' I said, adding the drill and the screwdriver to the pile, 'I would probably have finished my studies. I might have pursued a career in marine conservation and already have achieved everything I want to for the turtles.'

'You wouldn't have had to live in a flat share and survive on soup.'

'True,' I said with a tilt of the head. 'But I'd still have resented you for it, I suspect. And it's not been so bad really. I've lived the last eight years on my own terms and I know I can rely on myself and there's value in that.'

Nick picked up a plank and a hammer and handed me a box of nails. 'You can rely on me.'

Could I? Who knew? As the terms and conditions of our contract stated, past performance was no guarantee of future results. 'I prefer not to.'

'I know.' He lifted the plank into the space where one was missing and gestured to me to hold up one end of it. 'It's disappointing.'

I held out the box of nails and he extracted two. 'It's nothing personal.'

'It feels pretty personal.'

An incomprehensible surge of shame and regret swept through me then, but I pushed it back down because there was no reason to feel either. 'So what would you have done differently in this parallel universe I'm imagining?'

'I'd have let your comments that afternoon at your pool slide,' he said, banging in the nails and reaching out for more, which I duly furnished him with. 'We'd have ended up in bed a whole lot sooner than yesterday and wasted a lot less time.'

'But it would still have been just sex and it still wouldn't have lasted.'

'It would have lasted a damn sight longer than the couple of days you've set aside for it, trust me.'

'But you see, that's exactly the problem.'

Nick paused, hammer aloft, and looked at me quizzically. 'What is?'

'Trust.'

He frowned. 'You said you trusted me.'

I stared at him. 'When?'

'Yesterday. When I asked you if you thought it was me who leaked your news to the press.'

Ah. 'I said I trusted you with my money.'

His eyebrows lifted. 'And that's it?'

I nodded. 'That's it. I don't trust anyone. I want to, somehow, but I can't. It's simply too ingrained. An impossible habit to break, if you like.'

'Stemming from everyone abandoning you at a time you needed them most?'

'Quite.'

'That's understandable,' he said, and stood back to admire his handiwork. 'But I disagree about it being an impossible habit to break. Trust is a choice.'

'That's easy for you to say,' I said, annoyed at the way he was so casually brushing aside something that I felt so deeply. 'You haven't been let down by virtually everyone who's supposed to be on your side.'

'I'm on your side and I haven't let you down.'

'It would only be a matter of time.'

He turned to me, the intensity in his gaze nearly taking out my knees. 'Do you really believe that?'

'Yes. Why?'

'I assumed you thought more of me.'

'I don't think anything of you,' I said, stifling a sigh of exasperation. 'That isn't what this is about. I keep telling you that.'

'You keep telling yourself that.'

What did that mean? That he knew me better than I knew myself? That was a bit presumptuous. 'Anyway,' I said, moving on from irritating observations that were too cryptic to work out, 'don't you ever worry that your friends like you only for your money?'

'No.'

'Well, I do,' I said, as he turned his attention to the

door. 'After what happened before, I'm petrified I'll make bad choices again. I still can't quite bring myself to believe one hundred per cent in people's motivations. It's even more of a concern now that I have all this money.'

'So why play the lottery?'

'Because I wanted a little bit of what I once had,' I said a tad wistfully. 'I wanted to be able to spend money without worrying about it. And there are things I miss. Like fresh flowers and amazing food. Not even having to think about bills. I never really expected to win, certainly not the amount I did. I realise that my complaints are very much of the "my diamond shoes are too tight" variety but the responsibility is immense and, frankly, terrifying. When I think of how close I came to losing it my blood runs cold.'

'Don't blame yourself for being susceptible,' he said, retrieving a ladder from the boathouse and propping it up against the side of the building. 'It happens.'

'I bet it doesn't happen to you.'

'You'd be surprised.'

I watched him pick up the electric screwdriver and refix the door to the hinges with unexpectedly attractive competence and thought of his strength, his self-assurance, his drive to succeed and his single-minded focus. He might have issues about his place in the world but, presumably, one didn't rise from nothing to become a billionaire businessman without a little bit of ruthlessness and a whole lot of savvy. The idea of him being susceptible to anything in any conceivable way was laughable. 'I would indeed.'

CHAPTER ELEVEN

HAVING REPAIRED THE damaged building the best we could with the limited kit we had, Nick and I returned to the boat and loaded it back up. While he opened the throttle and steered in the direction of the longer western coast of the island, I closed my eyes, sat back and lifted my face to the breeze.

But it wasn't as relaxing an experience as I might have been forgiven for thinking it would be. The conversations we'd had today kept spinning round my head and with every passing minute the unsettling sense of foreboding winding through my body was strengthening. I was feeling increasingly on edge and jittery, untethered and at sea metaphorically as I was literally.

I didn't like the way he said things that I simply couldn't work out or that he constantly seemed to think he knew something I didn't. The fact that the only area in which we were on the same page was sex worried me but not as much as the realisation that, despite my concerted efforts to keep what was going on strictly physical, I wanted to cross the line into the personal.

I wanted to know everything about him. The big things and the small. His hopes, his fears, his dreams.

I wanted to know what his favourite colour was. His musical tastes. More about his background, which had to have been so formative, and where he really hoped he'd be in five years' time. I didn't want to leave Suza until I knew it all. I didn't much want to leave at all.

The trouble was, he was so much more complicated and layered than I could ever have imagined. So much more interesting and compelling and surprising.

Take the talking that had been going on. When I'd first met him, he'd been adolescently sullen. For years, we'd exchanged the most cursory of words. But not any longer. I'd learned more about him in the past week or so than I had in eighteen years and whereas, only ten days ago, he'd stared at me in horror at the mere hint of tears and I'd been convinced that his was not a shoulder to cry on, I now had the feeling that perhaps it was.

And none of this was good.

I didn't need to know any of the things I longed to know. My heartstrings shouldn't have been tugged by his brief revelations about his upbringing. I had no business wondering what it might be like to have him truly on my side, to be loved by him. The way he'd corrected my chronically low self-esteem in so many different ways shouldn't mean anything. I oughtn't to care about the fact that he'd seemed gutted by my revelation that I couldn't rely on him and would never trust him.

This wasn't some great sweeping romance where everyone sailed off into the sunset and lived happily ever after. This was simply an attempt to examine the past, work through misunderstandings and address the unacceptable and intolerable tension so we could move forward, while having some seriously fantastic sex. Yet I was in danger of losing sight of this.

I was normally so level-headed, so sensible, but around him I behaved completely irrationally. Since my return to Suza, I'd allowed him to push and challenge me. I'd talked to him, with barely a moment's hesitation, and while I'd just about managed to keep my deepest secrets to myself, I'd told him enough.

I was out of control and it had to stop. What we'd been doing didn't feel thrilling any more. It felt impossibly dangerous. If we continued with this even a day or two longer, I could see myself falling further under his spell, further into a deepening pit from which there'd be no escape. I might start craving conversation, seeking his opinion and wanting that shoulder to cry on. I might share with him the conflicting feelings I had about my father, the sorrow and regret I felt about being too afraid to let anyone close. And if I did, I'd be barrelling down a path that would only lead to more pain when he left, which everyone did, one way or another.

I should never have given into temptation and stayed. I should have paid attention to the warning signs, of which there'd been many. But it wasn't too late to rectify the situation. The clarity of my mind and the strength of my resolve were matched only by my desperate need for self-preservation.

After disembarking I strode up the jetty, aware that Nick was hot on my heels. He took my elbow and steered me towards a sofa upon which I knew he intended to take me to heaven and rob me of my wits. But that couldn't happen so I shook myself free and headed for the stairs instead.

'Where are you going?' he said, capturing my wrist and drawing me so close that for the briefest of seconds I wondered what on earth I was thinking by intending to give up this crazy hot desire.

But it was precisely because of the ease with which he made me lose my reason, my control, that I needed to stick to the plan. So I pulled away, smoothed my dress, and from a safe distance said, 'To my room.'

'Why?'

'I need to pack.'

He froze at that, a frown creasing his brow, bewilderment flickering across his face. '*Now* you want to leave?'

'Yes.'

'Why?'

'There's no reason not to,' I said, holding at bay all the arguments that countered this. 'Thanks to you, the press has retreated. We've expelled the lust from our system and sorted out our differences, which bodes well for future encounters. There are things back home I need to be getting on with and I have a job to return to, not to mention a pharmacy to visit.'

'What's going on?'

'I thought we were on the same page but we clearly aren't. So I need to go.'

'I'd like you to stay.'

Well, that was just tough, I thought with a firm shake of my head, as much to convince myself of my resolve as him. 'This fling of ours has been a lot of fun, Nick, but it's over.'

'It isn't a fling,' he said, the intensity in his gaze for

some reason triggering flutters in my stomach and accelerating my pulse. 'At least not for me.'

'What are you talking about?'

'I'm in love with you.'

In response to Nick's startling declaration, my heart gave a great lurch and then began to pound, the only sound in an otherwise dead silent room.

'What did you say?'

'You heard. I'm in love with you.'

I frowned, confusion lancing through me. What on earth was he talking about? Had the hot blazing sun yesterday gone to his head?

'That's ridiculous,' I said, even more at sea than I'd been fifteen minutes ago. 'Why would you say such a thing?'

'Because it's true.'

'After two days?'

'No, Millie. I've been in love with you for years. Probably in some shape or form ever since you flung your fists around in my defence as a fearless and feisty eleven-year-old.'

What? 'Years?' I echoed faintly. 'But you've been paving the way for someone else.'

'Someone else?'

'When we were talking about the brevity of your relationships and I asked you why, if you didn't have a problem with commitment, you didn't seek something more, you said you were working on it.'

'Yes. But not someone else. You. I've been working on you. Last night, you asked me what the one thing I wanted but didn't have was,' he said, the steadiness of his voice and his air of absolute calm a complete contrast to my bewildered thoughts. 'Well, it's you. The reason I've never committed to anyone is because the only person I want to commit to is you. I want to marry you, Millie. I want to have a family with you. I want everything with you. You asked me once where I saw myself in five years' time. I see myself with you. With a child that we may or may not have already created. Maybe two. What am I afraid of? That it'll never happen.'

He stopped, clearly waiting for some kind of response from me but I didn't have one. My mind had gone blank. I didn't know what to say. I could scarcely breathe. How on earth could he be in love with me? It made no sense at all. He had to be joking. But he didn't look as if he were joking. He was as serious as I'd ever seen him and as it hit me that he really believed what he as saying, deep inside I could feel the stirrings of panic.

'I think you're confusing love with lust,' I said, my stomach beginning to churn violently.

'Believe me, I am not. I know the difference. I've done things for you it wouldn't even occur to me to do for anyone else. I've pulled you out of bars when it was anything but convenient. I've looked out for you and not just because your brother asked me to when he left for the States. I offered you that money not out of pity or charity but because I couldn't stand the thought of you suffering any more than you already had. You pointed out that whenever I walk into a bar I look around as if in search of someone. That someone is you. Your welfare is all that's ever mattered to me. That's why I came to pick you up on Zanzibar. That's why I shut down the press. I did all of it for you. Only you.'

'But you find me chaotic and disruptive,' I said, every bone in my body, every stunned cell in my brain rejecting what he was saying.

'And beautiful and strong and brilliant. I always have. Even when you were telling me I was beneath you and throwing my money back at me. I've been trying to tell you how I feel about you, to show you, and I hoped I'd have more time, but if you're really going to leave then I'm done with subtlety. I'm done hiding. We've wasted too much time already and after the last twenty-four hours, I don't think I could stand a return to the way things were before. I know you have a problem trusting people. I know you're afraid of being let down. I know you doubt people's motivations, but you can trust mine and you can trust me. I will never let you down. Let me love you. Love me back.'

This was all too much. The pressure bearing down on me was crushing the breath from my lungs and draining the blood from my head. My defences were under such heavy assault they could buckle at any moment, but for now they were still intact, thank God, and I had to take strength from that. I had to use them to quash my weaknesses, to bury my vulnerabilities and above all to protect my heart.

'I can't,' I said, suddenly seeing things very calmly and very clearly.

'You can.'

'I thought you were the one person who had never lied to me, Nick, but you've been knowingly lying to me all along. You say you've loved me for years but for years you let me think the opposite. I understand your reasons for it, but you treated me horribly. With the impression you gave of disdain and disapproval you made me feel even more worthless than I already did. You hurt me.'

He flinched as if I'd slapped him and went white beneath his tan. 'I didn't know that.'

'For me, what we've been doing has always been a short-term thing. It's all it ever could be. I never asked you to fall in love with me. I never wanted it. I certainly don't deserve it.'

'You do. Everyone does.'

Not me. 'You couldn't possibly understand.'

'Then explain it to me.'

'I have nothing to offer and I can't be responsible for other people's happiness,' I said, my throat tight, my heart beating impossibly fast. 'The breakdown of my parents' marriage. The affair. Our misfortune. My father's heart attack. It was all because of me.'

'What the hell are you talking about?'

'My father and I were like two peas in a pod. Right from the start, we were close. Really close. On reflection, exclusively so, sometimes. Maybe it was because I looked so like him. I don't know. But Seb told me once that my mother had told him she felt invisible and neglected. She admitted to him that she was jealous of our bond. I'm the reason she had the affair. I'm the reason my dad tried to win her back and lost everything in the process. It's all my fault.'

'That's insane.'

'It's easy for you to say. You don't have to live with it. Regret doesn't constantly hover around the edges of your conscience. Guilt and shame don't niggle away at you day and night. You weren't there. I was. I know what happened.'

'You know what you think happened.'

I bristled. 'What does that mean?'

'I know your mother regrets your estrangement. I know she can't understand it.'

'How?'

'She and my mother talk from time to time. They discuss us.'

Us? There was no 'us'. I could never be part of an 'us'. And how on earth could my mother not understand the reason we barely spoke? I'd ruined their marriage. Wasn't it obvious? 'It's not her fault.'

'It's certainly not yours. If anyone it's your father's. It was his marriage to ruin and he was no saint.'

What did *that* mean? 'Yes, well, he's not around to ask, is he?'

'I think you're using it as an excuse,' said Nick, not quite so steady now, not quite so calm. 'I think you're scared.'

'Of course I'm scared. I'm terrified. Why do you think I haven't had a long-term relationship since my one pathetic boyfriend ghosted me the minute I became penniless? I've spent years building up my defences to protect myself against hurt and to become as invincible as I can possibly be. To let no one close enough to threaten that. I'm not going to throw it all away just because you claim to be in love with me.'

'It's more than a claim.'

'So you say.'

'You called *me* from Zanzibar.'

'Because there was no one else.'

The tension throbbed between us. Then Nick shoved his hands through his hair and rubbed them over his face.

'You know what?' he said, resigned, defeated, hollowed out. 'Fine. Have it your way. Be obstinate. Stick your head in the sand. I've waited for you for years, Millie. I've been tormented by you and wanted you and loved you for years. I had hoped that at some point you'd come to realise you feel the same way.'

'I don't.'

'I get it. Believe me, you've made yourself perfectly clear. So enough. We're done. Go ahead. Pack up your things. I'll take you to the airport myself.'

As I could have predicted, the boat ride to Dar es Salaam was horribly awkward and uncomfortable. Neither of us had anything to say, not even a comment about the stunning sunset. Nick stood at the helm, staring resolutely ahead, lost in thought, while I sat to his left, the wind whipping through my hair as I counted down the minutes to my departure.

I'd done absolutely the right thing in setting him straight on the situation, I assured myself repeatedly as the boat ate up the nautical miles. I had nothing to feel guilty about. It wasn't my fault he fancied himself in love with me. He'd soon come to realise he was mistaken and then he'd be amazed he'd ever thought it in the first place. The memories of my time here would fade eventually. By the time we next met, it would be as if none of this had happened.

'One thing before you go,' he said, once he'd offloaded my suitcase into the car that was waiting at the quayside.

'Yes?' I said, bracing myself for more revelations I didn't want and would never be ready for.

'I apologise for the way I've made you feel all this time. If I'd known… Well.' He shoved his hands through his hair then stuck them in the pockets of his jeans, swallowing with apparent difficulty. 'You said I haven't had to live with regret, guilt or shame but I will, for that. I'm sorry I hurt you, Millie. I'm sorry I made you feel worthless when you are anything but.'

He took a step back and gave a short nod. 'Have a good flight.'

CHAPTER TWELVE

IN CONTRAST TO the heat and bright colours of the Indian Ocean, London at the beginning of December was cold and grey, although the twinkling lights strung between lampposts and the Christmassy shop windows did give the illusion of festive bonhomie.

On my return I used up the rest of my leave methodically going through the hundreds of emails clogging up my inbox and the messages I'd received via social media, which wasn't as traumatic as I'd once thought, and engaging the services of a house finder.

It was with some trepidation that I eventually went back to work and I had apologies and explanations prepared, but I needn't have worried. To my amazement and relief, my colleagues understood. No one had talked to the press. Every single one of them was happy for me and it was such a relief I was even able to laugh at the odd joke about me being able to buy the company and give myself a raise.

I went to a couple of parties with my flatmates, who were equally sanguine about my win, and whether it was because I'd had time to brace myself or because I felt so invincible after resisting Nick's considerable charms, I found it surprisingly easy to spot the sycophants.

Naturally, I hadn't heard from him in the fortnight I'd been back and that was fine. I'd left my dress behind, having changed into a more flight-appropriate outfit that was more than a little damp having been through a quick wash, but I wasn't expecting to see it again. I didn't need to know how he was doing any more than I needed to feel any guilt for the way I'd handled things. He was the one who'd pushed for something I was incapable of giving. He'd said he got it but he didn't, not really. He couldn't possibly understand my dread of letting someone close enough to destroy me. Or the gut-wrenching deep-seated knowledge that there was simply nothing about me that was worth loving, despite what he'd said.

Over and over again I told myself I'd had a lucky escape, and so had he, but of one thing I wasn't quite so certain. However much I tried to stop myself, I kept revisiting the points he'd made about my mother.

Could I have had it wrong all this time? was the main question that kept ricocheting around my head. Could she truly regret our estrangement? But if she genuinely didn't blame me for what happened, if her affair and the subsequent breakdown of their marriage really weren't my fault, she'd have done something about it, surely? Something more than the occasional call and the odd email and text.

But perhaps that *was* my fault, I was beginning to feel. When I thought about it honestly, her calls were more than occasional, and I never returned them. I told myself that I was simply too busy but that wasn't true, and I had no excuse for deleting the emails and texts without reading them or shutting down the conversation every time Seb attempted to broach the subject.

Why did I do that? Because I didn't want to think even worse of my father? But the truth of it was, he'd been as flawed as anyone, as Nick had pointed out, so perhaps I should never have put him on that pedestal in the first place. After all, there was only ever going to be one way off it. And maybe I'd always needed to cling onto the belief that I was guilty as justification for protecting myself and my fragile, vulnerable heart.

The trouble was, if I allowed myself to believe that Nick was right about that then I had to consider the fact that he might have been right about everything else he'd said. About me and who I was. I'd have to accept that I really was gritty and determined, resilient and optimistic. I'd have to believe I was worth as much as anyone else. I'd have to trust him. I'd have to lower my guard and put myself in his hands. In the hands of a man who said he'd loved me for years.

Which could never happen.

Because once he got to know the real me he'd soon realise I was unlovable, wouldn't he?

And yet…

He *did* know the real me. He knew me warts and all. He knew how I took my coffee. What my favourite drink was. He'd seen me at my worst—whether stumbling out of a club or on the point of dissolving into a puddle of misery—and hopefully at my best. And, ultimately, he hadn't been put off by any of it. He'd wanted me regardless of my many flaws.

As the scales began to fall from my eyes, I realised

that he'd always been there for me. He'd defended me. At my father's funeral, even though I'd been too devastated to notice much, I'd noticed he'd stood close by. He'd looked out for me on numerous occasions and still was. Even at the height of our hostilities, he'd wanted to help me.

I'd wondered what it would be like to have someone like him on my side, who believed in me, and I'd had that without even realising it.

And when I'd suspected the truth about my feelings for him, I'd been so terrified about what they might mean, I'd deliberately pushed him away.

But what was so bad about any of it? He was everything I'd dreamed of but never thought I could have. He was generous and tenacious, sexy and thoughtful, and apparently in love with me. Because of him, I'd discovered who I really was. I'd regained my confidence in my abilities. Instead of being petrified of the money, I was now excited about the plans I had for it. With the exception of a couple of understandable blips, I wasn't rash and reckless. I made good decisions.

But I didn't always have to take them on my own. And I didn't have to always be on my own. The truth of it was that I missed him more than I'd ever thought possible. Now I'd had a glimpse of what it was like to have someone to talk to and share things with, my return to solitude meant I was lonelier than ever. Drinks with colleagues and the odd party courtesy of my flatmates did little to alleviate it for more than a couple of hours and I was only so strong.

Despite trying to convince myself otherwise, keeping thoughts of Nick and the memories of our relationship, the good and the bad, out of my head was far harder than I'd anticipated. I'd catch a glimpse of a tall dark-haired man in a suit and my heart would leap and then plummet because of course it wouldn't be him. He was on Suza in the sunshine and warmth, kite-surfing and sailing, having put me out of his head with a resolve that I'd surely facilitated.

How could I have done that? How could I ever have told him that what he was feeling wasn't real? My arrogance had been breathtaking, my cruelty staggering. When I recalled the look on his face when I'd basically told him he didn't know the difference between lust and love my heart twisted in agony and shame.

The regret I'd felt over various things in my past was nothing compared to the regret I felt now, because with all the realisations raining down on me, the hardest, the most painful, was that I loved him too.

That was why he had the ability to hurt me so badly. Because I cared so much. He was the only person I wanted to talk about things with. The only person I wanted to keep close. When he'd ventured out into that storm the dread I'd felt had had nothing to do with me and my money and everything to do with losing him.

And of course I trusted him. Why else would I have put on that show for him in the shower room, exposing myself both literally and metaphorically? Trust was a choice, and it was a choice that deep down I suspected I'd made days ago. He hadn't once let me down and I knew in my gut that he never would.

I'd been so blind, so stupid, so fixed on my issues and doggedly pursuing a course of action that I'd thought would keep me safe. But all I'd succeeded in doing was throwing away the best thing that had ever happened to me.

What on earth had I been thinking? What had I done? Would he ever forgive me? And was there anything I could do to fix the catastrophic mistake I'd made?

Twenty-four hours later, I was back on Suza, waving James off as he sped away in his boat, only this time I had no luggage and a pretty good idea of the reception I was going to get.

With every step I took up the jetty and along the wide sandy path that led to the villa, my heart pounded that little bit harder and my stomach tightened with ever increasing knots. I hadn't told Nick I was coming. I hadn't wanted him to take himself off and go into hiding, which he'd be perfectly justified in doing. But I knew he was here. I'd got my brother to check.

The hot midday sun beat down on me from a cloudless azure sky, though that wasn't the cause of the film of sweat that coated my skin. The gardens, the terrace and the beach bore no trace of the storm that had ravaged the island only a few weeks ago. The lawn and the flower pots were immaculate. The pool shimmered. The house, however, appeared to be closed up. The windows were shuttered. Everything was eerily quiet.

Nick could be out kite-surfing or sailing, of course, but what if he wasn't, in fact, here at all? I wondered suddenly as I glanced around for signs of activity and found none. What if Seb was wrong and my journey had been made in vain? How would I make amends for everything then?

Straightening my spine and lifting my chin, I fought

back the doubt and swallowed down the nerves. I had a speech prepared and I would do everything possible to see that it was delivered. If I had to wait, for however long, then so be it. If Nick truly wasn't around I would track him down until I found him.

I knocked on the front door and waited, my heart in my throat as the seconds ticked silently by, but there was no response. So I tried the handle, and, when it yielded, opened the door. I paused only for a second to consider whether or not I'd be invading his privacy if I headed on in. Of course I would. But did I care? No.

I walked through the cool airy space, batting away the memories that were cascading into my head in order to concentrate on the goal. There was the console table, I noticed, an intense rush of heat infusing my body despite my determination to focus. There was the spot where I'd told him he was mistaking lust for love. The sitting room looked as untouched as it had been before, but the kitchen was a mess. Papers were strewn across the dining table and chairs stood awry. Empty wine bottles lined up on the island and dirty plates lay next to the sink.

But of Nick there was no sign.

Feeling strange and off balance, as though I were having an out-of-body experience, I climbed the stairs, my limbs seeming to function without my direction. I checked the rooms, and eventually found him passed out on his back in the room that I'd once occupied, my pink dress screwed up in a ball beside him.

At the sight of him, unshaven, drawn, haggard but still so gorgeous my heart ached, the numbness disappeared and every emotion I'd managed to keep at bay—the sorrow, the regret, the remorse, the love I'd denied for so long—started battering me on all sides. How could I ever have given him up? Now I was here, could I actually put things right?

Desperately hoping I could, I leaned down and gave him a shake. 'Nick.'

He grunted and swatted at my hand, so I did it again. Harder. *'Nick.'*

That provoked more of a reaction. A split second after I'd said his name his eyes opened and he looked at me for about two seconds before he grabbed me and pulled me down on top of him. He clamped one hand to the back of my neck and planted the other on the small of my back and kissed me until I was hot and dizzy. With a muffled groan, he rolled me over and ran a hand over me, which made me moan and wrap myself around him since I'd missed him and this so much, at which point he froze and reared back, evidently fully awake now.

'You,' he growled, extricating himself from me and leaping off the bed as if he'd been burned.

I ran a trembling hand through my hair, my heart hammering like a steam train, my breathing so laboured I was going dizzy. 'Me.'

'What the hell are you doing here, Amelia?'

So I was back to Amelia. That was understandable. But those kisses of his had been something else and they strengthened my resolve as much as they weakened my knees.

'I didn't think you'd answer my calls,' I said, getting up and tugging my clothes into place with fingers that were trembling as a result of his passionate embrace.

'So you thought you'd break into my home instead.'

'The door was unlocked.'

'What do you want?'

'To talk.'

'I think we've said all there is to say, don't you?'

The bitterness in his voice chilled me to the bone, but what had I expected?

'No. I don't,' I said heatedly. 'There is more. So much more.'

The look he threw me was dark, his brows snapping together. 'Are you pregnant?'

What? 'No.'

'So you made it to a pharmacy.'

Not exactly. I'd put it off and off and then it had been too late. At the time I hadn't understood why I'd dithered but I'd realised later that I must have subconsciously wanted to be for ever linked to him all along. Nature, on the other hand, had had other ideas. 'There turned out to be no need.'

'You must be delighted.'

'Yet I'm not.'

'I'm not up to these riddles,' he said tightly. 'My head aches. Please go away.'

He stalked to the door and held it open, but I ignored it. 'I've come a long way to see you,' I said, planting my feet more firmly to the floor.

'That's not my problem.'

'I called my mother. You were right about her. She doesn't blame me for anything. She'd told Seb that she was jealous of me when she was at her lowest and regretted it ever since. It was all in my head. And you were also right about my father. He was no saint. He had affairs too. I was labouring under a number of misapprehensions and for years I let this dictate my life, but I can see now that none of it had anything to do with me.'

'I couldn't be less interested.'

'In fact, you were right about everything.'

'Not everything.'

I took a deep breath, overwhelmed by the need to get the words out that were piling up in my head. 'I'm so sorry for how I reacted when you said you loved me. I wasn't ready to hear it. My response was shocking. The things I said were appalling. I'm devastated I hurt you. I was scared. I still am. You hit that nail on the head too. Everyone I care about leaves me. But that was no excuse.'

'I would never have left you.'

'I know that now,' I said, my chest tightening with pain and regret. 'I was blinded by the hang-ups that I've had for far too long. I couldn't see what was right in front of me. You've never let me down and I know you never will. I do trust you. I love you. I really really do. I think I have for years. That's why your attitude towards me hurt so much. Deep down, I've always envied my brother for his relationship with you. I've been so jealous of the blondes. I mean, one night you rescued me from a party and I actually wanted to scratch the eyes out of the one you were with. I know your habits. Your fears. I know you. And you know me. We belong together, Nick.'

'No,' he said flatly. 'We don't. I offered you everything and in return you destroyed me. You're a reminder of my weaknesses and I don't need that.'

'I'm so sorry.'

'There is nothing for you here, so please, just go.'

'I don't want to go.'

'And I don't want you to stay.'

Right.

Right.

I blew out a breath and nodded slowly even though inside I was falling apart at the realisation there was nothing I could say or do to change his mind. I'd ruined everything. I'd killed whatever he'd once felt for me. I'd been such a fool and I had no one but myself to blame.

On legs that were shaking like a leaf, my heart breaking, I made it to the door and past him, even though I so badly wanted to stop there, beg him for his forgiveness and—

'Wait.'

My heart stopped and then began to thunder. Hope surged. I whirled around. 'Yes?'

'You forgot your dress.'

He thrust it at me and I took it numbly. 'Thank you.'

As I stumbled downstairs, my throat tightened painfully and hot tears started to prick at my eyes. What was I going to do? How was I going to get over this? Somehow I managed to pull out my phone and pull up James' number. He couldn't have got very far. I hadn't been here very long. I'd hoped for a better outcome.

And then, at the bottom of the stairs, as my finger hovered over the small green button, I paused, my heart crashing against my ribs.

No.

This was wrong. I couldn't just leave. Not yet. I hadn't turned over every stone. Not by a long shot.

What if Nick was just trying to protect himself the way he had done for years? Wasn't throwing up a shield of aloofness and detachment and keeping me at arm's length what he did? Could that be behind his stubborn resistance now?

I had to know the truth and, as the fearlessness that I'd lamented losing suddenly stormed back, I burned with a need that was fiery and unstoppable. So I dropped the phone back into my bag, spun on my heel and leapt back up the stairs, adrenalin powering along my veins while my heart thumped with hope and anticipation, only to come to an abrupt halt when he burst onto the landing and strode towards me.

'Just so as you know,' I said, needing to get the words out before he said or did something to prevent me, 'wherever you go, I will follow you. I will lay siege to you. I will not stop until you let me prove to you that I love you. I will fight for you ceaselessly and however long it takes, I will win.'

'Is that so?' he said, his eyes blazing with something that put a rocket beneath my pulse.

'It's a promise. I am gritty and determined, remember? You won't stand a chance. Your armour will be obliterated. Your weaponry will be demolished. You might as well give in now.'

'Too late,' he said, taking a step in my direction and scrambling my head with his proximity and his scent. 'I already have.'

I went still. My breath stuck in my lungs while my head spun. 'What?'

'I have no defences against you, Millie. Not any more. That feeble attempt at it upstairs proves it. I can't let you go again. I've been utterly miserable without you. I've been drinking too much in an attempt to forget you but it doesn't work. Nothing works. You're everywhere. In the house, in my head, in my heart. I've been so tormented I've taken to sleeping with your dress. My apology on the quayside was pathetically inadequate but the sentiment was right. You are not worthless. You mean everything to me. I will spend every day for the rest of my life proving it to you, if you'll let me.' He stopped and frowned. 'Are you about to start crying?'

'Yes,' I said with a sniff, my heart swelling with love and relief and joy. 'Sorry. I know how much you hate tears.'

He reached out and gently wiped my cheeks with his thumbs. 'This is the last time I make you cry, I promise. I love you.'

'And I love you.'

He drew me into his arms and kissed me then, long and slow and deep, and I knew in that moment, without the shadow of a doubt, that wherever in the world we might be, whatever we might be doing, together was where we belonged.

EPILOGUE

Five years later...

HAVING LEFT THE six research students in charge of the lab, I wandered down to the white sandy beach to where Nick was frolicking about in the warm turquoise water of the Indian Ocean.

He'd found me the island six months after we got married and it was everything I'd ever dreamed of. A coral cay of around six hectares, it was, amazingly and conveniently, only a hop, skip and a jump from Suza.

The lab had been built fifty years earlier and could accommodate up to thirty. When I'd taken over, it had been dilapidated, overwhelmed by vegetation, and unfit for human habitation at least, but in the intervening four years I'd made considerable progress. While working on my degree in marine biology, which I'd finished, I'd sought advice and recruited the best. The station was now on the list of all the major universities, Zurich included, the reef was bustling with life and the hawksbill turtle breeding programme was going from strength to strength.

Numerous charities had benefited from my lottery

money over the years, and even my mother and brother had eventually been persuaded to accept some of it. But no one was more grateful for everything that had happened than me. I'd won things that money could never buy. Happiness. Contentment. Confidence. The love of my life and the family we'd created.

'Remember I once asked you where you saw yourself in five years' time?' I said, smiling as Nick emerged from the shallows, our four-year-old daughter hanging from one leg and our two-year-old son clinging to the other while my heart turned over as it did a dozen times a day.

'I remember,' he said, depositing our offspring on the sand and striding over to take me loosely in his arms. 'I think I said that I saw myself with you and our one or two children.'

'What's the verdict?'

'That the reality surpasses my wildest dreams, and you know how wild those can be.'

'I do.' Even after five years, the passion burned hotter than ever, the wicked glint that I could see beginning to light the depths of his eyes never very far away. 'So. I was thinking…'

His gaze dipped to my mouth and his eyes darkened, his expression filling with the intent that without fail made my heart skip a beat. 'You must have read my mind.'

'Not that,' I said with a grin. 'The children…'

'What about them?'

I gave my abdomen a light pat, then wound my arms around his neck, lifted my mouth to his ear and murmured, 'How would you feel about a third?'

* * * * *

COMING SOON!

INNOCENT MAID FOR THE GREEK
Sharon Kendrick

His throat constricted. "Obviously, this changes everything," he said tightly. "I'm not having sex with a virgin," he snapped.

She was shaking her head, the glossy spill of copper curls tumbling down over her shoulders and he wondered if she had any idea how lovely she looked right then.

"I still don't understand," she whispered. "You want sex with me and I definitely want sex with you. A piece of paper says we're legally married – so what's the problem? Please explain it to me."

He chose his words carefully. "The fact that you haven't been intimate with anyone else is significant."

"How?

He shrugged. "It suggests you still care for me and will read too much into it," he continued repressively. "And I really don't want that to happen."

Mia stared back, her heart slamming hard against her ribcage as she took in what he'd just said. "Of all the arrogant things you've ever said to me, Theo Aeton – and there have been plenty of those," she breathed. "That one really tops the lots."

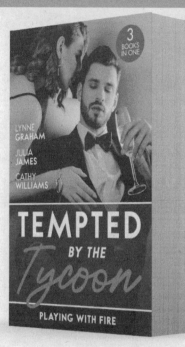